Rachel Dove is a writer and [...] West Yorkshire with her hu[sband...] and their animals. In July 2015 she won the *Prima* magazine and Mills & Boon 'Flirty Fiction' competition. She was also the winner of the Writers' Bureau Writer of the Year Award in 2016. She has had work published in the UK and overseas in various magazines and newspaper publications.

Deanne Anders was reading romance while her friends were still reading Nancy Drew, and she knew she'd hit the jackpot when she found a shelf of Harlequin Presents in her local library. Years later she discovered the fun of writing her own. Deanne lives in Florida, with her husband and their spoiled Pomeranian. During the day she works as a nursing supervisor. With her love of everything medical and romance, writing for Mills & Boon Medical Romance is a dream come true.

Also by Rachel Dove

Single Mum's Mistletoe Kiss
A Midwife, Her Best Friend, Their Family
How to Resist Your Rival
A Baby to Change Their Lives

Also by Deanne Anders

Nashville Midwives miniseries

Unbuttoning the Bachelor Doc
The Rebel Doctor's Secret Child

Flight Nurse's Florida Fairy Tale
A Surgeon's Christmas Baby

Discover more at millsandboon.co.uk.

FAKING IT WITH THE FIREFIGHTER

RACHEL DOVE

SINGLE DAD'S FAKE FIANCÉE

DEANNE ANDERS

MILLS & BOON

All rights reserved including the right of reproduction in whole or in part in any form. This edition is published by arrangement with Harlequin Enterprises ULC.

This is a work of fiction. Names, characters, places, locations and incidents are purely fictional and bear no relationship to any real life individuals, living or dead, or to any actual places, business establishments, locations, events or incidents. Any resemblance is entirely coincidental.

This book is sold subject to the condition that it shall not, by way of trade or otherwise, be lent, resold, hired out or otherwise circulated without the prior consent of the publisher in any form of binding or cover other than that in which it is published and without a similar condition including this condition being imposed on the subsequent purchaser.

® and TM are trademarks owned and used by the trademark owner and/or its licensee. Trademarks marked with ® are registered with the United Kingdom Patent Office and/or the Office for Harmonisation in the Internal Market and in other countries.

First published in Great Britain 2025
by Mills & Boon, an imprint of HarperCollins*Publishers* Ltd,
1 London Bridge Street, London, SE1 9GF

www.harpercollins.co.uk

HarperCollins*Publishers* Macken House, 39/40 Mayor Street Upper, Dublin 1, D01 C9W8, Ireland

Faking It with the Firefighter © 2025 Rachel Dove

Single Dad's Fake Fiancée © 2025 Denise Chavers

ISBN: 978-0-263-32507-2

05/25

MIX
Paper | Supporting responsible forestry
FSC™ C007454

This book contains FSC™ certified paper and other controlled sources to ensure responsible forest management.

For more information visit www.harpercollins.co.uk/green.

Printed and Bound in the UK using 100% Renewable Electricity at CPI Group (UK) Ltd, Croydon, CR0 4YY

FAKING IT WITH THE FIREFIGHTER

RACHEL DOVE

MILLS & BOON

To my editor, Annie Warren.
Thanks for being you.

CHAPTER ONE

'I KNOW, RIGHT? Winonah, I can't believe it. I really did it! Station 17 is the place I wanted to be! I mean, I know it's a bit of a drive from home, but the reputation is second to none. I'm going to be right where I want to be. In the thick of things.' She let out a heady sigh. 'Oh, man, I swear, if I was girly, I'd be screeching right now.'

'Ew. Who needs all that demure garbage when you're going to be one of Brooklyn's finest!' Win whooped down the line when she heard that, making a woman step away as she passed by her on the sidewalk. 'I'm so damn proud, Lexie. I knew you could do it! Have you told John yet?'

'Nope. I wanted you to be the first to know, of course. He's at his boys' night, I thought I'd surprise him at home. It felt too big to just tell him over the phone, especially when he's probably in some loud bar. This way I can make a thing of it. You know, sex it up a bit. Thanks again for the movie rain check.' She pulled her coat a little tighter as she rounded the block. The bite in the air was cutting even for November. 'We're probably going to be on different shifts for a while, you know, and I've been so busy passing the firefighter tests I owe him a bit of TLC. I need to spend some time with him before I start next week. I was thinking a lot of sex, some good cooking and some nice afternoon naps on the couch when he's off shifts.' She thought of the coming week, when she would officially start as a lead paramedic attached to a fricking Brooklyn firehouse. It felt like someone else's life. She'd been working towards it for so long she'd almost forgotten that it would actually be real one day. 'Win, I know it will be hard, but I seriously can't wait. Those twenty-four-hour shifts are going to be something to get used to though, I bet. I feel like I need the next few days if only to catch my breath.'

'Oh, hell, no,' Win laughed. 'You practically lived in that ambulance of yours when you were a humble paramedic, and you're going to be bunking in with hot firefighters! You do not get to play the pity card with me. Try working in a New York ER for six months, you'll soon realise that I win. Last shift, a homeless guy brought in for exposure vomited on me. Twice. Working with hot specimens literally fighting fires and saving lives is a definite job perk. I want photos too. I need to see some eye candy, for my worst shifts.'

'Win,' Lexie laughed. 'I am not sending you photos of my colleagues, no matter how many bad shifts you have. Tuck it back in, pervert, and buy one of those charity calendars like the rest of the horny population.'

'Huh. You're no fun.' Lexie could practically hear her best friend's pout at the other end.

'I doubt Hunter will approve either. He already thinks I'm the bad influence, and you're his perfect little princess.'

'Yeah, well.' Win's tone turned wistful. 'Hunter is still studying all hours for the bar. I doubt he'd notice if I send him a naked picture of myself unless I was covered in legalese. I swear, he bolted upright in bed last night and yelled "send the brief!" I almost had a heart attack. I need to live vicariously through you at the minute to get my rocks off. Let me live, woman!'

'Nope,' Lexie laughed. 'Not a chance. Hunter will make it up to you, the dude adores you. He's just making his own dreams come true. This is my dream job, at my dream house. I am not going to mess this up for anyone, even you. They're going to have to haul me out of there in a box.'

'Wow, you really are no fun since you decided that John was the exception to your "all relationships are pointless" rule. I swear, you're almost…trusting. Flying the flag for being in love was so not on my bingo card for you this year.'

'Yeah, well…a girl has to grow up sometime.'

Only Win can call me out on my relationship hang-ups like this and get away with it.

John was different though. He'd been so sure of them, and when she'd done her usual thing of pushing people away, he hadn't faltered. He hadn't pushed her for too much, and taking things at her own pace had really allowed her to open up to him. Eventually. She was still independent, but he seemed to love that about her. He'd pretty much pursued her since day one, when they'd crossed paths on a call-out. She hadn't given him the time of day, figuring he was just some jock firefighter who wanted a good time, but he'd never given up. She wasn't one of those women who automatically drooled when they saw a man in uniform.

In fact, the opposite was probably true. Often the hours and toll of public service jobs meant that people were too career-minded to bother with relationships, or wanted something short-term and no strings. Swiping left and right on the opposite sex quicker than a spectator turned their head at a tennis match.

Personally, she struggled with both, which was half the reason she still felt shocked sometimes when she remembered that she had been with John almost a whole year. But he lived his own life, and allowed her to have her own, which was so important. It helped to keep the suffocation at bay. The fact he was a firefighter wasn't really an issue anymore, because it was John. She trusted him, the exception to the many rules that had forged her opinions and ideals of life.

She'd seen where relationships could get you, and men who willingly jumped into infernos and were worshipped by the general public didn't exactly scream one-woman man to her. Heck, her dad had been a run-of-the-mill construction worker, and he could never seem to keep it in his pants. Still, it was coming up on a year now, and slowly but surely, she was realising that John was in this for the long haul, and she didn't exactly hate it. Win's sulky voice cut through her thoughts, making her smile.

'So, no juicy firefighter pictures, is that what you're telling me?'

'No juicy snaps, no.' The apartment she shared with John came into view. She was eager to get into the warmth, and her frozen feet sped up. The tip of her nose was starting to smart from the cold, her jaw feeling rubbery as she huffed out steams of breath. 'I'm home,' she told her friend, if only to get her off the subject of half-naked men. She didn't need that in her head when she turned up for her first shift. This was going to be the next few years of her life, and she wanted the men and women there to take her seriously. More seriously than John did sometimes. He hadn't been totally sold on the idea of her joining the service, even though she'd told him her plans from the start.

I guess he's just protective. It's a good thing, right?

But if she was okay with him being in dangerous situations, then he had to apply the same principle to her. She wasn't exactly leaving an office job to pursue her dream.

Being a paramedic in NY wasn't for the faint-hearted either, and she coped with that. Thrived on the job, actually. Something about the urgency in situations fuelled her resolve, sharpened her mind. Being part of a firehouse? It felt like the culmination of all her training, and she knew John would relax once he got used to the idea. She couldn't wait to see his face when she told him she'd not only passed all of her exams but had landed a coveted spot as lead paramedic at 17. He was over at 36, and it was a good house, but Brooklyn and 17 were where it's at. They had some of the most decorated officers in the whole of New York City, and she was going to be part of it.

Oh, if her parents could see her now.

She smiled to herself as Win chatted away in her ear. Well, they obviously wouldn't care, but she would like them to know that she'd done so well without their help. She lived with a firefighter, was trained to save lives and now she would work for the NYFD. Not bad for a kid dragged up by two people who should never have been allowed to have a child in the first place. Life was finally coming together.

I can't wait.

When Win finally rang off, Lexie paused on the street corner, looking up at the night sky. She loved this time of year, cold as it was right now. Fall through winter, she was at her happiest. She was one of those women who loved the changing of the leaves, the pumpkin spice lattes, Halloween decorations. She lived for evenings snuggled under the blankets on the couch on her time off, watching the weather outside while she lost herself in a good book. Relishing the quiet and calm she never had growing up. Back then, she was always on alert for the next argument, the next slam of the front door when one of them would inevitably storm out. Usually to make more bad choices. *Home* didn't quite have the same ring to it when it was a lying, cheating nest of vipers. True love was for romance novels read by well-adjusted people. She focused on the stars in the sky, grateful that she had inner peace now. That she could stand here and enjoy the night and the oasis of quiet peace in the noisy city. Even her hectic job didn't dampen her love for this time of year. Sure, the holiday season brought out the weirdos, the drunks, and the lonely, all doing things to put themselves and others in need of medical treatment, but to her, it meant the promise of something good after. The fresh page of a new diary. A hopeful spring.

Man, I'm sentimental tonight. Suck it up, Lex. Hearts and flowers you most certainly are not.

She was getting sappy these days. It felt weird to her, but she was going to go with it.

After they'd spent Thanksgiving apart working, her first Christmas with John was coming up, and that was something else to get excited about. After years alone, she was looking forward to the holiday. She could picture them now, decorating the tree together, waking up Christmas morning even, if their shift schedules allowed it. Either way, for the first time in her life, she had a chance at roots. A proper family. After years of being so independent, it was nice to have someone to share life with, the good and the bad.

'Wow,' she laughed to herself. 'If Win could hear me now, she'd never let me hear the end of it.'

She was about to step off the sidewalk when she heard it. A giggle, carefree and happy. Girlish, even, in its intensity.

See? she told the stars. *Everyone's happy here.*

She was smiling to herself at the sound when she heard another. A deeper timbre so familiar to her it felt like her own heartbeat. A male laugh. One that dropped the smile off her face like a boulder rolling down a hill. Tucking into the deli front across the street, she focused on the car down the block from the entrance to her apartment complex. The instinct to hide in the shadows strong as she waited for her brain to contradict what her ears and eyes were telling her. As soon as she saw the cab, the breath huffed out of her, swirling out into the cold night. Her worst fears came true as she stood there, watching. The woman, a petite thing with long platinum blond hair under a cute beanie hat, was laughing as she tried to pull a man back into the cab. They'd been drinking, she could hear it in their voices as she watched them. Their cute little conversation changing her world forever.

'Baby, come on. We've had such a nice night. Come back with me. She won't know, she's not even home yet.'

On another planet, in another universe, she might have felt different about this display, found it funny even. A telling testament to how she'd always felt about trusting someone other than herself. She'd have told Win, said 'I told you so' and thanked her lucky stars that she wasn't dumb enough to buy into the whole relationship charade. She'd done it a million times over the years. Hell, she'd even put Hunter through his paces when he first started dating Win, desperate to make sure he was worthy of her best friend. But the man currently subjected to the baby talk from the inebriated woman was…well, hers. John was drunk too. She could tell. She could always tell, from the way he placed his feet on the ground, how the tone of his voice changed, even the way he ran his fingers through his hair. She could spot that head of hair a mile away, she was always teasing him about it falling into his face, like some regency gentleman from the books she liked to read.

'I have to work tomorrow, babe, I can't. I'll call you though. Maybe I can stay over with you this weekend? One of the guys owes me a shift.'

'Really?' she simpered, reaching up and pulling his face down to her lips. 'You're on. I just wish it was tonight,' she purred. 'I miss you in my bed.'

He moaned, pulling away only to kiss her again. Lexie could see the way he was holding her, his hands running all over her body. She felt sick. Those hands held her the same way. He kissed her with those treacherous, two-timing lips. She wanted to get in the shower and scrub her skin till all traces of John Coxley were expunged from her skin.

'You drive me wild, angel. You know I want that too. I can't wait. This weekend, I promise. We never have to leave the bedroom.'

She couldn't watch this anymore, but her eyes were glued to the ugly scene in front of her, her fists clenched tight. She wanted nothing more than to run over there and rip every strand of his hair out by the root. In reality, she just stood there. Hiding while she watched her man pawing the woman he'd obviously been out with for the night.

Somewhere in the back of her mind, she wondered how many times he had done this. Getting another woman to drop him off outside the place he shared with his live-in girlfriend didn't seem like a rookie move, and it made her stomach lurch. It felt more like something a man getting cocky with his infidelity would pull. The longer she listened to them, the sicker she felt. Her safe, happy world from just a few minutes ago faded away into nothing, replaced by the default feeling: molten steel running through her veins, hardening her. It strengthened her against feelings of broken trust and anger like this. She was both thankful she had been a witness and wishing she was anywhere else, like at the movies with Win, eating popcorn, oblivious. It was obviously where John and this woman thought she was. Not lurking on the corner of the street where she lived, watching John finally let go of the woman long enough for her to leave in the taxi with a breathy goodbye.

'I'll call you,' he said. 'When I can, okay?'

'You'd better, lover boy. Looking forward to another sleepover, sexy.'

Another sleepover?

Her stomach lurched, and she almost retched right there on the street. Confirmation sucked. He was seeing this woman. Ongoing. Had slept over at her place. Lexi's perfect Christmas dissolved in her head, replaced by John rolling around in sheets that weren't theirs. Whispering another woman's name in the night as he pulled her to him. It was laughable that she'd been planning to make it up to him tonight for being so absent lately, too tired, too occupied with work. All the while he was getting his needs fulfilled elsewhere.

She observed him as he watched the taxi drive away into the night, a deep sigh huffing out of him as he glanced up at the dark windows of their home. He shook his head and his shoulders deflated.

Checking if I'm out, scumbag? Joke's on you, buddy.

When the taxi was out of sight, she stepped off the sidewalk. It took a full five steps before he heard her, his head whipping round to see who was walking towards him. The look on his face…it was like nothing she'd seen before. His expression transformed like a kaleidoscope before her:

surprise, shock, realisation. She even saw a hint of anger there, a sprinkling of bravado. She could positively see the cogs turning in his head. The gears whirring into some sort of action as he stared at her, open-mouthed. Running his eyes up and down her body, as though he could gauge how much she'd seen and heard from her stance. She wasn't one to play coy.

'Don't tell me.' She breathed, trying to keep her voice strong and flat. 'It's not what it looks like. She's just a friend, right? Some strange woman you were giving a lift home to after your boys' night. Am I warm?'

'You're supposed to be at the movies.'

Ding-ding-ding. And the award for the stupidest statement when caught cheating goes to John Coxley! John, come on down! You have won the rest of your life without Lexie Olsen!

'Yeah, well, change of plan.' Her hand gripped the handle of her bag so tight she could feel her nails stabbing into her skin. She clenched harder when tears welled, using the pain to keep them at bay. 'Sucks to be you, I guess. Betting Beanie Barbie will be happy though.'

'This is not as bad as you think. Let's get off the street, I'll explain.'

The laugh that burst out with her sounded maniacal, so out of place on the quiet road that she almost turned her head to see who was laughing in such an absurd way.

'That's what you say to me? That's what you've got to say? Seriously? You brought another woman to our place! The fact I'm not at the movies. Is hardly. The point. Is it.' Her sentences were short, choppy. Rising with her anger. She took slow steps across the road. Taking her time as she glared at him standing there. Shuffling on his lying, treacherous feet. 'Who was that, John? And more to the point, why were you out with her? How many times have you told me you were out with the boys, and doing her? How many damn *sleepovers* did you have? Where was I? Working, or sitting upstairs waiting for you to come home, eh? Is it just her? Or is there more? Tell me, John, just how much of a sucker have I been, and how much of a slimy pig are you!'

'She means nothing. I know it looks bad, Lex, but I slipped. I didn't know how to get out of it. You've been so busy lately and—'

'Don't you dare!' He reached for her as she went to sidestep him to go inside, but she slapped his hand away. 'Don't you dare try to turn this around on me, you've been caught red-handed. She practically had your pants down. You were mauling her in the taxi. I can't believe you've done this. I told you how I feel about cheating. I told you!'

'I know, I know. Please, Lexie, just come inside and let me explain. I love you!'

She was halfway to the front door, but those words stopped her dead. Turning on her heel, she couldn't miss the unmistakable look of hope and relief that struck his features. She wanted to slap him, just to knock that spark of triumph off his stupid, lying face. He was like a stranger to her now, standing there all wet eyes and pathetic, trembling bottom lip. She was replaying every moment of their relationship over and over in her head, realising that the pieces hadn't fit for a while. The boys' nights that had picked up, the fact that he was on his phone more often. The extra shifts. There were no extra shifts, he'd been telling her he was working and slinking off to *her*. Every little moment between them over the last few weeks was running through her head like the reel of a horror film. She'd been so busy, so focused on passing her exams. She'd either not taken enough notice or had just not wanted to see it. It was like another layer had been added to the map of their relationship. And now the question marks were all connected into one horrible answer. She'd felt so guilty, being so consumed with her career, and all the while, he was doing this. The rose-tinted glasses she'd been wearing just mere minutes ago fell away, shattering into tiny pieces on the ground around her. She was furious with herself for putting them on in the first place. She knew better. Had known the truth of things from an early age, and yet still found herself in this situation. A dumb statistic, just like everybody else who ever bothered to let someone in.

Pathetic, a voice chided her. *You knew it would end like this.*

How many times had her parents fought like this?
I'm sorry, I love you.
I'll stop drinking, I love you.
He meant nothing, I love you.
She's just a friend, I love you.

As if those three little words were a mantra to whitewash all the stench and dirt. She never wanted to hear those words again.

'You don't love me.' Her voice was flat when she uttered the statement, but nothing had sounded so true to her own ears. The laugh that followed rumbled from her chest. No, from the very bottom of her stomach. Entirely without humour, dark, mocking. 'God, I'm so stupid.'

'No, no, Lexie, you're not. It's me that's the stupid one. I hate myself for doing this.'

I wish I felt that way. I wish I could just despise you right now. Shut everything else off.

The image in her head of them decorating the tree haunted her. Another Christmas on her own. Great.

Back to reality for you, paramedic.

A Christmas of patching people up and eating takeout alone in some soulless apartment she'd call a base. That molten steel was doing its job. Coursing through her veins, burning away any kind of feelings she might be having.

You can only trust yourself, remember? You knew this, Lexie. Don't forget it again.

'You're right.' She levelled a bored stare at John. He didn't deserve emotion from her. 'You are stupid. And you should hate yourself, but I think we both know that the thing you hate most is that you were caught in the first place.' She hated herself for asking, but she had to. Now she knew she'd been in the dark, she had to poke at every corner to shed the light. A rubbernecker to her own car crash of a relationship. 'Who is she?'

Lexi didn't want to know, really. She never wanted to know. It wouldn't bring her any peace, she understood that, but it was like an itch she had to scratch, poke at till it bled. She just needed the details, and then she'd walk away. Telling herself she didn't want to see, think about or hear that woman ever again after tonight.

The woman in that taxi was the complete opposite of her. Should that hurt less, or more? Lexi didn't know, she had no point of reference. This was the first time that she had been publicly cheated on and humiliated.

Served her right for giving this whole relationship thing a go in the first place. She almost wished that she had gone to the movies with Win tonight, so she could be watching a film instead and not be dealing with this. Out with her best friend, oblivious and happy. Just like she had been moments ago. Dream job, good relationship, nice place, plans for the holidays.

Everything had just been smashed against the sidewalk she was standing on. She felt like the taxi had run her over and crushed all her dreams under its tyres. She was starting a new job next week and now she had this to navigate. She hated him with a passion, even with the pain of loving him, and he was just standing there, staring at her with such a look of hurt and pain in his eyes that she wanted to die on the spot just to not have to deal with any of it. 'Who is she, John?'

'No one,' he muttered. 'She means nothing, a mistake. Please believe me, Lex. I should never have done this to you. I'm so sorry. Please—' He took a step towards her. She took two back. His jaw flexed, and frustration was clear in his body language. He pointed towards the doors behind her. 'Let's just go upstairs, it's cold out here.' He looked her up and down, guilt clouding his features. 'We can warm up inside, sort this out. We can get through this. I know we can. I'll do anything to make it better.' When he took a step closer, she held out a palm to stop him. Her next words were feral, more growl then voice.

'No. There is no talking about this, John. You can't take it back. You did this, it can't be undone. I don't want you near me. You reek of her.'

She was shaking, from the cold, from the shock. She had no idea which, just knew she couldn't seem to stop it. Her bag was quivering in her tight grasp. She looked down at her hands, willing them to still under her gaze.

She thought about her next move. She could go upstairs, sure. She could walk right into the apartment they shared. Look at all the things they had together. Her possessions mingled with his. She could tell him about her new job.

He could tell her about the blonde that he'd just sent away, maybe they could even talk about what was going to happen next. She could do that. People did, she knew. People made mistakes; partners cheated. Her parents did it enough while she was growing up that some part of her even thought it was normal.

She was never one of those types of women who believed in the whole soulmates thing. 'Till death do us part' was not a given. Even for the good ones. In her line of work, she knew life was short. Things changed. People changed. They lived, they loved, they died. People fell out of love, remarried. Time moved on regardless of what people did to each other.

She could choose, to go inside, talk. Right? It could be just a blip on their radar, a part of their past. She needed to decide her next move and act on it. Time wouldn't freeze while she was standing on this street, but she sure would.

So, she made a choice. Right then and there she made a decision that would determine the rest of her life. As soon as the words came out of her mouth, she knew that they were the right ones. Knowing that, and the fact that Win would be there for her when she turned up at her and Hunter's place later tonight, were about the only things stopping her from falling apart right in front of him. One thing Lexie Olsen didn't do was show weakness.

'I'm leaving. I'll send someone for my stuff.'

'What?' John ran his hand through his hair, shaking his head rapidly from side to side. 'You don't need to do that. We can sort this out. I'm sorry. I love you.' His foot lifted from the ground as if he was going to try to close the distance between them, but a second later he put it back down when she spat a rebuttal.

'Don't' was all it took to still his motion. 'I never want you to touch me ever again.'

'That's it? You're just leaving? What about us?'

Lexi tried to ignore the hammering in her chest as her heart tried to break its way out of her ribcage to lunge to the floor. Perhaps it would be better that way. Oh, she knew from her medical training it was just an organ. It sustained life but love and emotion did not reside within its chambers. Perhaps if they did, people would elect to have those pieces cut away. Hell, if she had a scalpel to hand right now, she might have even considered it herself. Since open heart surgery in the damn street wasn't an option, she did what she usually did. She squashed everything down deep, and hardened herself until her heart and head were pure steel. Impenetrable and invulnerable. Next to her, Wolverine would look like a marshmallow.

'There is no us. You don't do what you did to someone you supposedly love. That's not the kind of love anyone wants. I was busy working, for my future. Which half an hour ago, included you too.' She turned on her heel and headed down the street. 'It's over, John. Done. Burned to the ground. I'll arrange for my stuff to be collected when I can, but I don't want to see you. Like, ever. Don't bother calling me either. I won't answer.'

He didn't follow her, but he didn't stop shouting her name, asking her to come back till she turned the corner, and his voice died on the bitter wind. Right along with every hope she'd had for a better life.

If her parents could see her now? What a cruel joke life was.

CHAPTER TWO

This is one of the worst ones.

Alex Morrison's heart was beating like a snare-drum in his heaving chest as he searched the house with his buddy. There was so much at stake. So much could happen to change the occupants' lives for ever. All in their hands as they strode through the thick smoke filling the second floor of the neat family home. He knew what it was like, the pain of losing loved ones. Saving another person from that pain fuelled his progress through the house. The alternative, unthinkable.

No one's getting lost on my watch.

Flames licked around the door-frame as the two firefighters burst into the room. 'First floor all clear.' Kavanagh's voice came through the radio. 'Morrison, Hodgens, you found her?' Her being Charlotte, the homeowner's nine-year-old daughter. The father had been working from home at the kitchen table when the fire had started upstairs. Unable to get to his child in her room, he was being held back by emergency responders outside.

Hodgens pulled open the wardrobe, the light on his helmet illuminating the small space filled with hung clothes and shoeboxes lining the bottom.

'Not yet, but it definitely started in the master bedroom,' he radioed back, just as Alex checked behind a door on the far right. 'I'm thinking electrical fire. We're on the last room.'

'You have one minute,' Chief Maddison chimed in, his voice deep and steady. 'The roof's too unstable, we need to pull out.'

'Copy,' Alex said as he opened the door to the en suite and was met by a set of terrified eyes. 'Got her. Hodgens, let's go!'

Striding across the room, he bent at the knee before the tub. Charlotte, a wispy little thing with huge brown eyes stared back. 'I want my dad!' she shouted over the noise of the roaring fire, the cracking of wood as her house burned down around them. The thick smoke made her cough, even through the wet towel she'd wrapped around herself.

'Clever girl, using the towel like that. Your dad sent me, Charlotte, I'll take you to him,' Alex said, holding out a hand. In a fire, even the people looming out of the chaos to save them could be a terrifying sight to a frightened child. He'd seen grown men freeze in these situations, fear locking up their muscles. 'Come with me, sweetie, we gotta go. Now.'

The girl reached out her hand and he scooped her up one-armed. Making sure the towel was wrapped around her hair and face, he kept low. Hodgens was already at the window, smashing the glass, and Alex could see the ladder from the truck readying for their exit. Their chief in his ear ordered them to hustle over the roar of the fire, the house creaking and snapping around them in the thick, all-encompassing heat. As Alex passed the girl over to his waiting colleague, he heard the stairs, engulfed in flames, break apart and hit the bottom floor. He could feel the movement in the floor beneath his feet. Charlotte screamed, coughing hard as the smoke plumed around them. Even through his mask, Alex could feel it. Taste it. Hodgens was on the ladder now, Charlotte clung to him. *Time to leave*, he told himself, relief flooding through him now that the kid was out of the inferno.

The second his gloved hands wrapped around the ladder rail; the floor shifted beneath him. The window fell away, hitting the ground with a deafening crunch and Charlotte screamed louder. Alex's shoulder sang as he clung on with one arm. Hodgens gripped the girl to him sitting across the rungs. 'Morrison!' Hodgens reached out his free hand, and Alex reached for it as he dangled off the end of the ladder.

Too far. Damn it.

He could hear a panicked voice shouting his name from below. 'Alex! Hold on!'

The pain in his upper arm screamed at him as he pulled himself up enough to grab the ladder with the other hand, leaving him dangling in the air. Every muscle in his upper body sang, and he was grateful he hit the gym so much. Working those weights was the difference between him and the ground.

His colleagues were racing to help him. His mind was on the little girl screaming while her father lost his mind down below. 'Hodgens, take her down!' Alex shouted. 'You can't help me with her in your arms.' Charlotte was terrified, he could hear it in her voice as he clung to the metal. If he fell from here, it would be bad—death, broken limbs. Not an option. No way would he let the little girl have that in her head for the rest of her life. Watching someone die was not something you forgot in a hurry.

'Get that mat under him!' The chief was commanding his team on the radio. 'We have to pull back from the house, now!'

While the house was disintegrating behind him, Alex could hear the tension in his station chief's deep voice. He had to get out of this. And fast. Swinging his legs, he swayed his body from side to side until his feet hooked onto the underside of the ladder. Catching his breath, he peered up through the mask just as Kavanagh reached the top of the ladder and grabbed him.

'Quit hanging around,' he deadpanned as Alex swung himself around and came to rest in front of him.

'Sorry—' Alex grinned as he pulled off his mask '—sometimes, making an exit is just as good as making an entrance. Got to have a little flair.'

Kavanagh, face filled with soot, smiled as he pulled his friend to him. 'Let's get out of here, okay?'

One of the ambulances in attendance was pulling away when they got back to the rig. Alex was halfway to the chief when he felt an arm wrap around his bicep.

'Uh-uh. This way, Captain America.'

'What? I'm fine.'

'Oh, is that right?' She kept walking fast, and he let her lead him over to the waiting ambulance. He knew better than to get in this woman's way.

'When did you get your medical degree? Before or after you were dangling off a ladder like a spider monkey? You need to get checked out, regulations.' She held up her light, ready to check his airway. 'Open up, come on.'

He opened his mouth to protest, but the deep frown on Lexie's face had him opening his mouth for her. Anything to take that look off her face.

'Fine, but only because you were so worried about me. I heard you calling for me. You sounded pretty scared.'

'Yeah,' she shot back, her cheeks a deep shade of pink.

He lived to make her blush that shade. 'I didn't fancy having to ask Taylor to scrape you off the grass. I swear, you're going to make me grey. Open wide.'

He huffed, sticking his tongue out as Lexie checked for signs of smoke inhalation. Nodding to herself, she pushed an oxygen mask onto his face, ignoring him when he tried to speak over it and sticking a monitor clip on his finger.

'Mmph-mmph...'

'What was that?' Her lips pursed as she first checked the monitor, then pulled the mask away. 'Thank you, Lexie, for being so amazing? Thank you for caring whether I live long enough to finish my blessed shift?'

'I called you a hard-ass.' Her deep green eyes narrowed, turning them almost emerald, before she let the mask snap back onto his face with a twang. 'Ouch.' She shot him a cheeky grin. 'Thank you. Am I good to go?'

'Yep, no smoke inhalation, sats are good. Oxygen levels are normal. I want to check out your shoulder though, looks like you wrenched it pretty good.' He rolled it in response and, sure, it felt bruised, sore, but nothing major. 'Want to take a trip to the hospital, or do it at the station?'

'Station,' they said together, and she quirked her brow at him in triumph.

'You know me,' he said with a shrug. 'I don't want a fuss, and don't lie and tell me you're not looking forward to getting me naked back at the house.'

She snorted in response, packing away her kit. 'Sure, Alex, you called it. I lie awake at night, wondering when I get to see the great fire eater Morrison's muscular chest again.'

'Muscular, eh?' He stepped out of the ambulance, noticing his colleagues were almost done securing the scene.

'Pretty boring description. *Chiselled*, maybe. *Sexy*, definitely.'

'Modest?' She giggled. 'Never. See you back at the house.'

Alex tipped his hat in her direction. 'Race you there.'

Hodgens was smirking when they got back into the truck. 'What?' Alex asked.

'Nothing,' Hodgens smirked. 'Just wondering when you're going to get your grump back on, Stella. You seem to be enjoying that groove.'

'Huh? What are you talking about?'

'Oh, you know, how you used to be before a certain lead paramedic walked into 17. I swear, we thought you were going to be the Grinch at Christmas, but I don't know. We noticed a thaw. Haven't you noticed a thaw, Kavanagh?'

'Don't involve me in this.'

'Shut up,' Alex muttered, leaning over to jab Hodgens in the side with his elbow from the front seat. 'I'm still grumpy.'

'Not so much. What do you say, Kav?'

Kavanagh turned, pretending to scrutinise them both as he drove, turning the wheel smoothly so the truck pulled onto the road to head back to the firehouse. 'Oh, no. I'm not saying a damn thing. Leave me out of it.'

Alex went to fist-bump him, but stopped when Kav added, 'But I will say this.' He kept his eyes on the road. 'You do seem a little… I dunno, happier.' He side-eyed Hodgens. 'I mean, I forgot the dude knew how to smile, I don't want to jinx it. Heck, I didn't think he still had any teeth!'

Hodgens guffawed at Alex's eye-roll. 'Amen, brother!'

'You both suck,' Alex grumbled. 'And it's just banter. She's a friend. I like her. That's all there is to it, and if you guys keep ragging like this, you're going to make things awkward. If she thinks you're talking to me like this, she might get weird about it. You know what she's like. She's still new here. I don't want her transferring out of her first gig because you lot made something out of this. Don't make me get the sexual harassment guidelines out again.'

Hodgens glanced at Kav, who nodded back at him. 'Geez, sorry.' He wiped a smudge of soot from his top lip. 'We don't want that. Lexie's like a little sister to us, we don't want her to leave.'

'Hell no,' Kavanagh cut in. 'We wouldn't do anything to upset her. You know we only tease you because she's good for you. We don't rib her about it.'

'You wouldn't dare,' Alex muttered, mostly to himself. Lexie Olsen was a tough cookie, and every single guy at 17 knew and respected it. 'And she's not like a sister, she's my friend.' Sister. Ew! It sounded so…wrong. 'Just don't make it awkward.'

If Kav heard him, he didn't let on. 'It's good, that's all we're saying, man. About time you got happy again, you know?'

Alex didn't answer them. He spent the rest of the trip back looking out of the side window. He knew what they were getting at. Since Lexie had rocked up to the firehouse, all snark and curves, things had been different at 17. And it wasn't just the ribbing he got from his squad when she wasn't around. He'd rather die than admit it to those chuckleheads, but he *was* in a better mood of late. She had a knack for bringing him out of his head. Which, according to them, was a good thing. If he was honest, before she arrived, he'd never realised how bad he'd been. The fact that they kept ragging on him about the mood change gave him a strong clue though. Something about Lexie just kind of…

woke him up. He lived for their flirty chats, the way she ribbed him. He was protective of her, even with the guys. Something about Lexie Olsen was just…right. It was good to have a friend like her, and he'd started to realise that he felt pretty wound up about anything changing that. It was easy with her; in her presence he was more like the Alex he'd been a long time ago. Hell, he liked himself more when she was around, had a spring in his step. He'd hummed to himself making breakfast this morning before work. He hadn't done anything like that in forever. Usually, he just used his place as somewhere to sleep and store his stuff. For the first time in three years, he was starting to live and not just exist. Life didn't just start and end with work and his firehouse family. And Lexie was a part of that family that he *never* wanted to lose.

The thing with working in a firehouse was, it wasn't just a job. It was a home too. You had your own bunk, things from home. Working together was only a part of it. You ate, slept and showered in close quarters. Got to know what your colleagues liked, what pissed them off. What made them tick. A new person coming in changed the dynamic, for better or worse. When Lexie became the lead paramedic, from the very first day, it was like she'd burst in and blew the cobwebs away. The woman was always upbeat. Hell, she woke up every morning with a damn smile on her face. It took about two shifts to wrap every guy in the place around her pinkie finger. Her first shift, she'd brought them homemade cupcakes with little sugared fire hoses on them, and they were just gone for her after that. Alex sure was. She was so pretty, standing there with that huge smile of hers. It had knocked him off his feet the first time she shone that easy grin on him. There was something about her, like she'd brought the sunshine in with her. All he wanted to do was bask in the glow. He'd found himself wanting to know more about her. He'd watched her that whole shift, so distracted he'd messed up on his paperwork and had to redo it.

Not that he'd tried to talk to her. When she'd come to introduce herself, he was pretty sure he ended up mumbling something incoherent while staring at his boots.

Idiot.

She'd told him after that he'd been scowling, but he didn't let on it was anything else. She seemed to thrive on coaxing him out of his quietness around her, and he'd enjoyed it too much to tell her the truth. Besides, they were friends. The fact his heart had done a little skip was something he kept firmly under his firefighter helmet. A woman like that was too good for a war-wounded, battle-scarred man anyway. Especially one whose heart was off the market for good.

Even Chief Maddison, who was the biggest stalwart ever to grace the fire service, treated her like the daughter he'd never had. She was like pure energy, cutting through the smoke that often clouded around them. They might be fire eaters, but she was a chaser of darkness too. Not that she was all cupcake baking and pretty smiles. She was also, for want of a better term, a badass.

That first week on the job, Alex had been ready to jump in when a drunk man had got in her face on a call they'd gotten. The guy had managed to set his couch on fire after a heavy night of watching basketball and wasn't too happy when she tried to treat his burned arm. The dude had woken up on fire, his cigarette having dropped to the rug and lit up the fallen bottle of whisky lying by his feet. The skin was charred, hanging off his arm, and he was still moaning about his damn TV. Drunken people weren't the smartest. Alex had heard the shouting, insults hurled at his friend that made his blood boil. He wasn't letting up, and as Alex got closer, he could hear Lexie patiently telling the patient to calm down. Alex was running to the ambulance, heart in his mouth, when he heard a roar and a scuffle breaking out. Then a thud, followed by a muffled grunt.

He'd gone for Lexie.

Fearing the worst, Alex rounded the corner on the tips of his toes and there she was, standing over a now unconscious patient. She had a cut on her lip, and a syringe in her hand. Breathing hard, they had both stood still for a moment, taking each other in. His eyes assessed her for injuries. Seeing the blood on her lip made him want to grab the man and wake his ass up by doing something unprofessional.

'Lexie, your lip! You okay?'

'Yep. No sweat. Our Knicks fan here just needed to take a little nap,' she said eventually, her green eyes flashing with adrenaline. That was the first time he'd belly-laughed in, well, forever. As the rest of the team came running, they were confronted by Alex doubled up, laughing his head off while Lexie and her colleague treated the patient. And that was the first time in too many to count that he'd realised Lexie Olsen was someone who he'd really needed in his life. Someone to make him see the funny side again. And she'd pretty much reinforced that every shift since. They were the same, she and Alex. Something within them seemed to recognise the other, gravitate towards it. His quiet strength called to hers. He'd heard people they met on the job call her aloof, standoffish. That wasn't her. They just didn't get her. She was guarded, just like him. He could see it sometimes, in vulnerable moments. The smile she fixed to her face when he knew she wasn't quite feeling as sunny as she made out. He knew, because he used to do it himself. Before he'd given up and turned plain grumpy. In those moments, he'd fallen into a default of making her laugh. Pulling the sexy banter out of his back pocket that made her come back into the moment, into herself. It was selfish too because the result was the warmth that spread across his chest when he knew he'd hit the mark. Hearing her laugh, seeing that toothy grin of hers…well, it was part of his daily routine now. A need bordering on a craving. Even now, he didn't care whether he won or lost their little 'race,' the reward would be there either way. When her ambulance pulled into its usual parking spot well before the truck, she flashed a loser sign at him, and he let his laugh fly free.

Chest, meet warmth.

'See,' he teased. 'Total pain.'

'You hear that sound?' She curled her hand around the shell of one ear. 'That's the noise a sore loser makes.'

Kavanagh laughed behind him. 'We've been telling him that for years, Olsen.'

'Yeah, but I don't think he listened till I got here. Shoulder check time, buddy.' She clicked her fingers as he headed her way. 'Man, I wish I'd bet a porterhouse and a bottle of the good stuff on our race. Next bet, I'm getting the meat!'

Alex was about to throw a teasing comment back, but he never got the words out. He was too busy watching that easy smile slide right off her face when a deep voice called her name.

'Lexie?'

It was so fast, so unexpected, it made his teeth clench. She went from carefree to coiled in the space of a single word being uttered. He'd never seen her like that. It was like every bit of light and ease drained out of her. Even the green of her eyes dulled as her lips tightened. She turned towards the voice as if it hurt her.

'Oh, damn,' Kavanagh muttered at Alex's side. 'Looks like it's all gonna hit the fan now, dude. Heads up.'

He slapped Alex on the back and went to the break room, but Alex stayed put.

What?

Something about the way Lexie turned to the man standing at the entrance to the firehouse set his nerves on edge.

Who was this guy?

He was tall, stocky. Jeans, a thick black parka jacket topped off with a baseball hat that covered most of his face. Something about him was familiar, but Alex's eyes stayed trained on the woman between them. Her whole stance was off, like she was braced for danger. Alarm bells rang in his head so loudly he shook his head to focus.

'Hey, babe.'

Babe? Man, something in his chest didn't like that. He felt it snap tight under his ribcage.

Alex knew he should probably go, he should leave and let them talk in private. It was none of his business. She could handle herself. Lexie had walked over to him, right? She'd looked spooked, but it could just be the surprise of seeing him there.

Maybe I'm reading too much into this.

She'd been pretty private about her life since she'd arrived at 17. He knew that she'd moved into her place the same time she started, but that was about all he knew. It wasn't like he was exactly forthcoming about his life outside the station. It was one of the things he liked about their friendship. They didn't ask each other questions about their past. They were just Alex and Lexie. Jokesters together. It was fine. She wasn't some damsel in distress, needing her friendly local firefighter to fight her battles. He should just go eat and catch up with her later. If she needed help, he'd be there. He didn't get two steps before he rethought that strategy. Her next words told him his first reaction was right on the money. Damsel or no, he wasn't going anywhere in case she needed backup.

'Don't *babe* me.' Her harsh tone was a world away from her usual happy trill. 'What are you doing here? I told you I didn't want to speak to you, and now you're bothering me at work? How did you even know I was here?'

'I checked the postings.'

Postings? Was he in the service?

'I wanted to know where you were. You just disappeared! I gave you some space over Christmas, but enough is enough, Lex. We have things to talk about. I couldn't get hold of you; Winonah wouldn't tell me anything.'

'You rang her? How dare you involve her in this. She is my friend, not yours. Why would you think she'd even talk to you? She hates your guts!'

'Oh, come on, Lex. You left me no choice! Your stuff was cleared out when I was at work, you changed your number. Your email. No one at the hospital would tell me anything. I was desperate to see you.'

'Yeah, well—I got sick of listening to your whiny voicemails, and no one I know would have gone around telling you my business. Win saw to that. I told you that night, it's done. I have nothing to say to you.' Alex locked eyes with her when she glanced behind her. Her blush made him feel a little sick, so he threw her a little smile before turning to the noticeboard, pretending to read as though the little adverts pinned to it were undiscovered Tolstoy. 'Listen, you need to go. I don't need this, especially not here.'

'Please, Lexie. I've been going out of my mind. It's not done, not for me. Not even a little bit. I've been doing everything I can to prove you're the one for me, Lex. You don't even know. You have to speak to me at some point, and now I'm here I—'

Wow. This guy wasn't going to take the hint. Time's up, stalker.

'Hey,' Alex cut in as he strode over to stand by Lexie's side. So close that his shoulder butted up against her. Letting her know he was right there. 'Can I help you, bud?'

'It's okay,' Lexie muttered. 'This is John, my ex. And he's just leaving.'

And that was the moment the man took off his baseball cap and looked Alex square in the face.

John Coxley. John Coxley is her ex? How did I not know this?

Kav's words slid back into his head. He must have known. Was that why he was so unwilling to rag like the others?

'Your ex.' His dumb question came out like a statement.

'Morrison,' Coxley said with a dismissive nod. His eyes were on where his and Lexie's bodies connected and Alex fought the urge to lift his arm and tuck her closer to him. 'Hey, man, can you give me a minute with my girl?'

Heat bloomed in Alex's chest like a punch.

My girl? Oh, hell, no.

Lexie took a step between them, and the urge to pull her back against him was visceral. This guy was a total douche. She'd dated this door-knob? He didn't suit her. Not that he'd given much thought about the type of guy that would get Lexie's heart to flutter.

'I'm at work. Please, John, just—'

The chief walked in. 'Ah, Lexie, I see you met our new addition!' John shot her a wide grin before sidestepping them and accepting the chief's handshake.

'Hi, sir, glad to be here. Sorry the paperwork took so long. HR was backed up, or I would have been here for the start of my shift.'

Chief Maddison waved him off. 'No bother, glad you're here. Since Jenkins left, we've been using the pool, it'll be nice to have a permanent guy on the team.' He turned to them then, doing a double take at whatever he saw on their faces. 'Problem?'

Alex didn't hesitate. 'Well, actually, Chief—'

'No, sir,' Lexie cut in, the smile she gave him not even trying to meet her eyes. 'I actually know John, when I was based at the hospital we would cross paths from time to time.'

The chief brightened. 'Ah, great! At least you'll have a friendly face here. Lexie's our lead paramedic, and Morrison is our lieutenant on truck. You'll be reporting to him. We work pretty closely as a team here at 17, I'm sure you'll have heard.'

'You have a great reputation, sir,' John said smoothly. A little too smoothly. The guy reminded Alex of a snake oil salesman without the charm. 'It seems everyone on the service wants to be here. I know I do.' Lexie flinched, and Alex felt it in his bones. 'If you don't mind, Chief, I'll stash my stuff. Meet the squad.'

Maddison followed him into the house, chatting away, leaving the two of them standing there by the truck. Lexie was looking out of the open front doors onto the street, as if she might just bolt through them.

'He's your ex? How come none of us knew?'

When she met his eye, Alex's heart sank into his boots. She looked so…angry. A shaky kind of anger, as if she didn't know whether to burst into tears or punch the wall.

'Kavanagh did. He'd seen us out together before, but I asked him not to say anything. I wanted to keep my private disaster of a love life separate from the job, for as long as I could, anyway.' She chuffed out a hollow laugh.

'Not that it matters now,' she went on. 'God, I can't believe he did this. I can't tell the chief, because there're not even any rules about paramedics and firefighters dating. I don't want to cause some scene when I've only recently started here. There's no conflict. I looked into it when we began dating, because I was studying for the advanced exams to be in a station.'

Her head shook from side to side. 'I knew it would come out. You firefighters gossip like housewives, but I didn't think this would happen.' She blew out her lips, her face stricken. She didn't look like the Lexie Alex had gotten to know.

'I was happy here, you know? Stupid. I should have known not to let my guard down. This always happens when I do.' She folded her arms, only to unhook them to swiftly wipe a tear away from her cheek.

She was visibly trying to hold it in, and Alex's arms tingled from the effect of not folding her into him. He knew that she wouldn't want that.

'I should have known life wasn't going to be easy for once. Why change the habit of a lifetime, right?' She laughed again, this one a little softer, and visibly pulled herself together. 'I'm going to head out for a bit, the rig needs some gas anyway. Can you ask Taylor to come out here?'

Taylor, her partner on the ambulance, would no doubt be stuffing his face instead. Even by twenty-five-year-old former football player standards, the guy could eat. If the game hadn't blown his knee out, he might never have found his love for medicine, and Ding Dongs. Alex knew he'd cheer her up. When the two of them were together, they were like big sister and little brother.

'Sure, I'll get him. He'll come just for the snacks.' She didn't laugh. 'What happened between you, if you don't mind me asking?'

She closed her eyes, head tilting to the ceiling. 'Well, it didn't end well, put it that way. We broke up about a week before I started here. It's why I'd just moved into a new place.'

'You lived together?' Something burned in his chest. 'Must have been serious.'

'I thought so, at the time.' She shrugged, pulling her keys out of her pocket. 'Things change. I haven't spoken to him since he…' She trailed off, and something occurred to Alex that made his fists clench at his sides. Pain radiated up his sore shoulder, but he leaned into the pain.

'Did he hurt you?' He'd moved towards her without thinking about it, her chin now clasped between his fingers. 'Lexie, if he put his hands on you, I'll—'

'No, he never touched me like that.' Her eyes were wide, and he felt her breath roll over his hand before he pulled it away. He hadn't meant to do that, it was just…instinct. The relief that Coxley hadn't touched this woman was tangible. 'He did hurt me, but not that way.'

'He cheated, didn't he?' He'd seen Coxley out at events before. Heard the way he spoke about women. He'd instantly taken a dislike to him. That kind of guy wasn't someone he associated with. Women were playthings to men like him.

The thought of Lexie *living* with him, giving him her warmth, her smiles? It did things to his insides he didn't want to identify. She nodded, just once, a red blush staining her pretty pink cheeks. 'Let me guess, a hose bunny?'

Hose bunnies were as much a part of the job as fire and water. Some women, and some men, wanted nothing more than to date a firefighter. The uniform, the danger. The kudos of telling people that they were dating a real-life firefighter. It was a huge turn-on to them. Every profession that involved sport or danger, or both, had them. Hockey players had puck bunnies, and every station had their hose bunnies. It didn't really matter to them whether the firefighter was attached or not. That wasn't their problem, and fired up after a call-out, fuelled by adrenaline, many a colleague had fallen foul of their charms. He'd seen it before. Families ruined. Reputations formed.

He'd never wanted any of that. He'd been taken for so long, and after, well…it was no secret he was celibate at this point. Another nod from her. 'Sorry, Lexie. You didn't deserve that.'

You deserve the whole world.

'Not your fault.' She shrugged, twirling the keys on her finger. 'I'm just glad I caught him with a woman, you know? I might still have been in…that, if not. It's better alone.'

He turned over the sentence in his head. He wanted to say something, but the words wouldn't come. Hadn't he told himself as much over the past few years? She touched the top of his arm, pulling her hand away as fast as she'd placed it there.

'Listen, Morrison. I know we have our fun. You know,

ribbing each other, but if you could just keep this to yourself. I mean, I don't think *he* will, but I want to keep it professional. Everyone knowing I was cheated on? It's not how I want people to see me. I knew our relationship would come out sooner or later because stations talk, but the details not so much. I've wanted to be here, in this job for so long. I don't want the drama. I'm not going to let him run me out of here.'

'He won't,' Alex said. He meant it to be reassuring, but the words came out as a growl. 'I won't say anything, neither will Kav. It's not something I find funny. I'll go get Taylor, but drive safe, okay? Maybe let him drive. You're pretty worked up. Keep your radio on.' She nodded, rewarding him with one of her Lexie smiles.

I wonder if she smiled at Coxley like that? How can a guy have that, and not do everything to keep it?

He pushed the thought away. His friend needed him, and he was going to do everything he could to make this right for her.

'Thanks, Morrison.' Her attempt at sliding back into their easy banter. He took it.

'Hey,' he winked. 'I still plan on making you stump up for a porterhouse, Olsen.'

'Dream on, loser,' she called after him. When he'd passed the message on to Taylor, he took a seat at the huge oak table they all sat around to eat their dinner. The trainees usually did a lot of the kitchen work, earning their stripes. The candidate, a young kid named Jimmy Donahue, hadn't done bad either. Homemade burgers, potato salad and garden salad, fries. Alex grabbed a plate and tucked in, only half listening to the guys who were all getting to know the new addition to the truck. Kav was sitting next to him, and he bumped elbows with Alex.

'She good?' He kept his voice low, unheard over the chatter around them.

Alex nodded, his jaw tight. 'She went to fill up the ambo with Taylor. Think she needed a minute. Why didn't you tell me?'

Kav shook his head. 'Not my story. I already knew you didn't like him. A few of the guys I hang with work out of his old house. I saw them together on a few nights out. When she came here, they were already done. Given what we heard down at the bar, I wasn't mad about it. People talk, so I knew he'd messed up. She asked me not to say anything about them, so I didn't.'

'And the other girl, is he still seeing her?'

Kav's brows rose. 'She told you.' Alex stared back.

'Yep, and I like him even less. So, is he?'

'Nope. She was just some hose bunny who fancied her chances of becoming a WAG. When Lexie found them together one night, she iced him out. He's been moping ever since, apparently. Couldn't find her for a minute. I ran interference best I could and told the guys to keep it tight, but you know how people talk.'

'So, he came here for her?'

Kav pulled a face. 'I don't think so. Be pretty brazen, right? His house had its budget cut, a few guys were moved around.' Kav's eyes slid to John, who was animatedly telling a story about a shout-out, hands gesturing wildly as the others listened and ate. 'Wouldn't put it past him to pull a string or two though to turn things in his favour. He's a career climber. I would watch your back if I were you. I know he wants to be a lieutenant.'

'Yeah,' Alex sneered. 'Well, that nozzle is not getting anything that's mine.'

Kav's low laugh filtered through the noise. 'I didn't think so. How's she going to play this?'

Alex thought of Lexie, standing there so shell-shocked, anger and frustration marring her normally carefree Lexie-ness. 'I don't know yet, but we've got her back, right?'

He held up a fork-holding fist, and Kav bumped it. 'Yep, 17 for ever, brother.'

'So, Alex, is it?' John took that moment to address him. *Big mistake.*

The metal in Alex's hand bent slightly, and he loosened his grip as he looked over at the interloper.

'Lieutenant Morrison to you, newbie,' he countered. A couple of the guys around the table pricked their ears up at this, and Kav covered his laugh with a cough. John, to his credit, didn't let his smile dim. The flash in his eyes though, Alex did clock that.

'Sorry, Lieutenant. I'm still learning the lay of the land around here. Anything I need to know about 17?'

Alex pretended to ponder the question. The first words that sprang to mind were along the lines of pink transfer forms, but he kept quiet for Lexie. For the most part.

'Well, we're the best of the best. We all pitch in.' He took a bite of fry, pausing while he swallowed. 'We honour the ranks, but first and foremost, we're a team. Family.' He narrowed his eyes. 'You got a family, Coxley?'

John didn't flinch.

Arrogant.

'My folks moved to Michigan a few years ago. My sister has kids, so they wanted to be closer, you know. Help raise their grandkids. I had a girl, but we broke up a few months ago.' He looked down at his plate. 'I'm trying to fix it. Biggest mistake of my life was letting her go. Working on it though. I think there's something worth saving.'

Wow, he was smooth. Hodgens even patted him on the back! *Man, if he knew.*

'Oh, yeah?' Kav chimed in. 'How's that going?'

The alarm sounded, and the conversation was lost as the guys all scrambled to answer the call.

'Road collision. Two passengers trapped. Junction of West Street. Officers on scene.'

'Come on, Coxley,' Alex called over his shoulder as they raced to the truck. 'Let's show you how we do it here at 17.'

CHAPTER THREE

'HOUSE FIRE. *Truck required. Franklin Street.*' It was repeated over the radio. '*Ambo en route. One civilian injured from jumping out of second-storey window. No other occupants in house.*'

Lexie was sitting cross-legged in the ambulance when Alex went to find her after the call. Since John had been there she had pretty much hidden out here every chance she got. He was keeping his distance for now, but Alex could see him watching her. Like he was biding his time for the right moment. As if his presence was enough to wear her down. It cheered Alex to realise that he obviously didn't know Lexie as well as he thought. Cowboys with spurs on their boots didn't dig their heels in as well as Olsen.

The house call had been straight forward, luckily. A grease fire in the kitchen. The husband had been home alone, preparing dinner for his wife and toddler while they were at the park. The kitchen was totalled. The wife came running up the street pushing the pram, and when she saw her husband on that gurney, Alex knew she didn't see the house. She didn't see the soot on her husband's face or the open femur fracture from his fall, she just saw him. The way he pulled his wife and child into his arms told Alex that they weren't even thinking about anything but being together.

It was a good call, all in all. Lexie had been amazing. She

had beaten them there. By the time they'd arrived the casualty was under control and the wife on her way. Lexie didn't even react when John strode past her into the house. Like she didn't know him. Professional to a fault, even though she must have been feeling his presence, the change in atmosphere.

It got him thinking about what she'd said. She'd been cheated on, moved house, and started at 17 all in the space of a week, and no one had had any inkling that she was even upset. That kind of strength made her all the fiercer in his eyes. He wondered how a woman like that would ever let anyone look after her. Whether she'd ever admit needing that from another person. And how, knowing that about her, was he going to make this better for her?

He should stay out of it, but everything in him wanted to be there. To be the one who brought back that easy demeanour she had. Seeing her all coiled like this brought his mood down.

Coxley needed to be put in his place somehow, without affecting their work or their jobs. They were in the business of saving lives, and that took concentration. Team effort. Trust. Anything jeopardising that had to be nipped in the bud. Station 17 needed Lexie as she was before the new arrival. *He* needed that.

He watched her for a moment. Cursing as she pulled a box out of one of the overhead lockers with a huff and a four-letter word that turned the air blue. He couldn't see her face, but he knew her well enough to know that her features would be all scrunched up. Her shoulders were so tight they were almost up around her ears. Her stress upset him, and he wished he could wipe it all away, or let it roll through him and tamp it down like the embers of a fire. He'd felt jittery the last couple of days, and it didn't seem like the feeling was going anywhere.

'Should I come back?'

She whirled around on the gurney. She looked pretty cute sitting there, legs crossed, clipboard in hand. Her hair tied up in that messy bun that he liked on her. She usually had it scraped back neat, not a hair out of place when she was on duty. She even slept in her bunk like that. Seeing her like this, her hair loose, her body tense: it wasn't like her. It did something to his chest if he thought about it too hard. Made him want to punch something.

'Sorry. Bad morning.' She plucked a dressing pack off the bed, waving it at him. 'I'm trying to do inventory, but I've counted these things three times now and they still don't add up.' Her brow knitted. 'Oh, and I broke a vial of Thorazine, so that's more paperwork. You know, just to top my fantastic day off.'

'Accidents happen,' he said with a shrug, sitting down at the back of the ambo. 'That family on the last call were pretty cute, huh?'

'I know. He's going to be fine too. I thought he might need a lot of pins, but I followed up with the hospital and Win said that they managed to reset it pretty easily in surgery. They were lucky.'

'Your luck will get better too.'

'Yeah, well it comes in threes, right?'

Threes?

'What does?' Alex frowned.

'Bad luck.' She pouted, crossing her eyes comically as she counted on her fingers. 'With the broken vial and the… new addition to the house the day before yesterday, that's definitely my three. Luck can move on to some other poor sucker.' She sighed hard, writing something on her clipboard and replacing the box only to pull out another. 'Why is he here, Morrison? I mean, he never said he wanted to move. If he knew I was here, then why transfer to the same house? It's infuriating, and if I'd not made a pact with myself never to speak to him again, I might have asked by now. I just wish he'd leave.'

'Kav said there were cuts to his house, a few got transferred out, if that makes you feel any better.'

'Fine,' she muttered. 'So he's not a total stalker, but still, he knew where I was. He said it himself, so why come here?' She faked a cry. 'I mean, seriously? I just got settled in, you know? I was finding my feet, making friends...'

'I'm a friend?' He ducked when a tubular bandage shot at his head. 'Hey!'

'You're not a friend, you're a pain,' she huffed, but he could see the small smile lifting the corners of her sulky mouth. 'It just sucks, that's all. Win is going to go nuts when I tell her. I've been putting it off, to be honest, but I suck at lying.'

'Win not a fan of his, huh?' He wanted to meet this woman. He already approved. Whenever Lexie spoke about her, it was obvious that they were close. A ride-or-die type of friendship.

Her smile was wicked. 'I'm pretty sure she wants to delete him from the planet. She told me the other day she was even contemplating becoming a flat-earther, in case the theory came true and she could drop-kick him off the edge.'

Alex's uncharacteristically loud burst of laughter surprised even him when it came. And he didn't miss the look of delighted shock that passed over Lexie's stressed-out expression, erasing it momentarily. 'Seriously, she had a plan to rent a boat and everything. She had a patient trying to convert her I think, must have stuck in her head.'

He nodded, thinking. He could only imagine the conversations Lexie and her friend had. They seemed to be more like sisters.

It's good that she has someone in her corner outside of work.

Everyone needed that. A buddy. Something else she'd said pushed another question out of his lips.

'You said threes, right? What was the third thing?'

She side-eyed him, puffing a tendril of dark hair out of her eyes. 'Oh. Nothing, really.'

He quirked a brow at her. 'Try me.'

She completed another line on her clipboard as her teeth nibbled the pink bottom lip caged between them. 'My apartment. The hot water tank's on the fritz. I couldn't wash the dishes this morning, and my shower keeps going from burning hot to arctic freezing. If it works at all. I emailed the landlord, but he's not the most responsive guy in the world.

'Plus, I only have a six-month lease, and I don't want to annoy him so close to my renewal. You wouldn't believe the rents around here, but I was in a rush and it's close to work. I guess I should have looked into the place a little closer before taking it on.'

She shrugged, as if she was shaking off a memory. 'Thank God for the showers here, right? Although, with the way John's been eyeballing me like a kicked puppy every time I see him, maybe a little BO would actually improve my lot.' She leaned in closer. 'Kav's been a bit weird too. I know he kept my secret, but I think he feels awkward about it now. And some of the guys have noticed John looking. It's only a matter of time before they know we were together, and I expected that, but...' She groaned, dropping her head to her chest.

'It's the way it ended. Being cheated on is... I don't know. Embarrassing. Humiliating. I'm already the only woman here, now everyone has to know that I was a trusting idiot too? I need to be seen as strong. Being some girlfriend who was screwed over? I hate people knowing that. I don't want it to be a thing, it's bad enough having an ex around. Ugh, it's just so clichéd. Being seen as weak, I can't stand it. I need a distraction or something. To stop people from focusing on it.'

'Weak?'

Alex didn't see it that way. She was one of the strongest people he knew.

She took down burly alcohol-fuelled men with a calm word and a quick needle. Jumped into situations right alongside the men. 'Lexie, no one will think that. If I was in your situation, I'd feel the s—'

'Lexie?'

John chose that moment to come and find her. She dipped down, as if she was contemplating hiding in the ambulance, but after a moment, she shot Alex a look that told him to stay put and she stepped out. Alex had to hold the gurney to stop himself from following her. Hidden by the doors, he listened intently.

How can I help with a distraction?

She was right to feel how she did. Having people knowing she was betrayed hurt, and he knew how proud she was of being at 17. She'd told him how hard she'd worked to get there. Coxley would keep acting like he was, and soon everyone would know. He didn't want to see her fears come true.

'You need medical attention?' Her tone was clipped so short she barely finished each syllable.

Nice one, Lex.

Alex's fingers let up their death grip a little.

'Er...no. I just wanted to speak to you, while it's quiet.'

'Well, it might be quiet, but I'm busy. So, if it's not about work, I have to get on.'

Alex could hear John's sigh. Feet moving closer. Lexie pulled the door of the ambulance closed a little further, shielding him from view.

'I won't stop trying to talk to you, Lexie. I don't care if you go to the chief. I'll take the risk. You owe me the chance to explain.'

'I don't owe you a—'

'I love you, Lexie, but you don't make it easy.'

'What?'

'You don't. When we were together, you didn't let me in. Let me do things for you. I know I messed up, but it was just that one girl. I just got swept up. You were working so hard, all the time. Passing out in bed early, or at your desk when you were home. I felt like we were drifting apart, and I made the biggest mistake.'

'So...wait. This is my fault? For being independent, for studying for my career? John, I never looked at another guy the whole time we were together.'

'Oh, come on, I know that, but people make mistakes, Lex. I messed up, but you never let me in. It took you long enough to give me a chance. You're not the type of person to cheat, I know that, but—'

'No, but you are.'

There was a long pause. 'I know. I'm so sorry, if I could take it back I would. I ruined things, but I know that we can get over this. I know we can. You can trust me again. I know you can. We'll take it slow. Date me. I'm not asking you to move back in or anything. Just, date me again.'

'John, no.'

'Why not? It's not like you don't still love me.'

'I don't.'

'You don't? Right... After four months you just moved on. Except you didn't. I didn't.'

'No, you moved on while we were together which is a whole other ball game.'

It took everything Alex had to hold in the laughter that bubbled up. She was holding her own, and that humour of hers was still intact. Still, thinking about it, he wondered how much of that was a defence mechanism. She said she didn't love him. Did she mean that? He wished he could see her face. He felt like he'd be able to tell if he could set eyes on her.

'Are you going to sling that back at me forever? It's over. It was over that night.'

'Because I caught you.'

'No, because I was ending it anyway. I was going to wait till after Christmas was done, when you had your posting, and then I was going to tell you everything. Beg you to forgive me.'

'But I caught you in the act.'

Her voice was softer.

Was she...wavering?

Alex held his breath. 'Honestly, none of that changes anything. I just want to leave that in the past and forget about it.'

'You do, really?'

'Not in the way you think. I can't tell you it's over anymore. I won't change my mind.'

'But you're not seeing anyone?'

'None of your business. I'm going back to work.'

'That means there's a chance. I know you, Lexie.'

You don't. You're not listening to her. Back off.

'You don't just fall into relationships. I had to earn you, and I will again. Till I know there's no chance for us.' Alex could hear footsteps, John's voice further away. 'I love you, baby, and I won't give up on us. I'm going to win you back. I'll see you later.'

Neither of them moved until the doors closed and silence descended. Lexie came back and sat in her seat, picking up her task where she left off.

'Are you okay? I didn't mean to listen to that, but it was pretty hard not to.'

She shrugged, her face pale. 'It's fine. Looks like I'm going to need a bigger distraction than I thought. I don't think he's going to let this drop. Maybe I should just go to the chief?'

'If you want, but then it might be on the record. The chief does things by the book, and he's got a bit of a soft spot for you. I doubt you'll be able to keep this quiet much longer, either way. The guys would be on your side, you know. If you told them. They could help.'

Her eye-roll made his lips pull up into a smirk. 'Yeah, like a load of annoying big brothers being all overprotective would make this any easier. What are they going to do? Put worms in his boots, boogers in his food?'

Hmm. A little ragging on the newbie might be fun to watch.

'Okay, maybe not.'

'I'll think of something. Maybe this is nothing.' Under her breath, she added, 'He usually was all talk and no action.' She sniffed at a strand of hair that had dropped loose. 'Ew! The shampoo here sucks. I need to remember to bring my own in tomorrow, or I'll start smelling like you lot. I've been so distracted lately. The guys are definitely going to notice if I don't get it together.'

A distraction.

He remembered their earlier conversation. She was right, he'd noticed the looks from some of the guys. It wouldn't take long before they all knew about this. The guys were great, but they were also like an episode of *Real Housewives* when they got going. Even if they were well-meaning and would want to look after her, she would hate every minute of it. This thing would follow her around the service.

It wasn't like people from other stations didn't come into contact with them. One night out and it would be common knowledge beyond 17. The thought of that, even with the guys here loving Lexie to bits, it didn't sit right. The sting of being cheated on by that idiot, and everyone knowing they were working together too, it might be enough to cause a transfer, or worse.

He knew John wouldn't be the one to do it. He'd had the gall to come to *her* house in the first place, thinking he could win her back. Implying that she hadn't moved on and was somehow still pining for him, it was just so arrogant.

Which was of course, the guy's MO. He was one thing with her, and a wholly different beast with everyone else. Coxley's act was pathetic, like he was the one left broken. And that was another aspect of this whole situation that stuck in Alex's craw. He didn't think she would relent and give her ex another chance, he knew her well enough to strike that outcome out of his head, but having to watch her avoid Coxley, while he had the house thinking he was some lovelorn suitor?

Hell, no.

It wasn't Coxley's business whether she had moved on or not. Four months wasn't a long time. Coxley might be able to bed-hop with all the ease of an Easter bunny, but he'd been right on the money about Lexie.

She didn't trust easily, didn't bend to a man's will. If she wanted something she went for it. When Coxley wasn't getting what he needed, that constant attention from Lexie, he'd strayed. Case closed, or it would be if he hadn't decided to force his way back into her life. The feeling he'd had in his gut since clapping eyes on John Coxley was increasing in strength. Overriding everything else.

She needed someone to be there, defending her. If he could just find a way that wouldn't have her thinking it was overstepping. Then a thought occurred to him. A way to be there for her without her resisting. One of their little games.

It may just work.

It was a little out there, sure. But once his brain had sparked the idea, it was too hard to keep it to himself. They could easily sell it at 17. He thought of the guys teasing him about her, how convinced they'd been that the flirting was more than it was.

I can pull it off.

It wasn't like they'd be doing anything real. No feelings, just friends. The perfect solution. It was out of his mouth before the thought fully formed in his head.

'You need a boyfriend.'

Her hands stilled, and she blinked at him. Rapidly. A few times. He had to school his face not to laugh at her stunned reaction. Or back out. The second his idea was out there in the world, he realised he didn't want to run for the hills or take it back.

If Coxley wanted to see signs that she'd moved on, then maybe he could be the one to help his friend with that. His closet was free of hose bunny skeletons, and his position in the house would make people think twice about spreading the cheating thing too. Lexie would be protected, and even better—out of Coxley's greasy reach. The minute he saw her demeanour change; his whole body had been on high alert. He didn't like Lexie looking so unsure of herself. It...did things to him. Made him feel helpless. It made him think of his past, when he'd felt helpless before and still bore the scars.

He suddenly realised that the flirting with his friend meant more to him than he'd thought. He cared about this woman. Thinking of her and Coxley together twisted something deep in his gut. He'd never considered dating again, but pretending to be with Lexie? It awoke something. He could be close without the risks, do something to help her. He was a man of action in everything but his heart these days, but it beat a little faster now as he watched for her reaction.

'Geez, Morrison. Way to kick a girl when she's down, eh? Why don't you come back on my birthday? You can sneeze on my candles and tell me I'm wrinkly. That will be fun, right?'

He swallowed his chuckle. She half looked like she wanted to slap him, so laughing would most likely make it worse.

'No, I'm serious. You need someone.'

She snorted, her eyes scanning his face for something she didn't find. 'You've fallen out of buildings one too many times. The last thing I need to do is date some other loser who will turn my life upside down.' She pushed her tongue into her cheek. 'Although, if he was a handyman willing to do a freebie favour or two, I might consider it for half a second.'

'I'm pretty good with my hands.'

Geez, Alex. Innuendo much?

'I...er...mean that I fix all my own stuff at my house. I did a lot of construction before I started in the service. I could help. With the John thing too.'

'Alex, I can't let you do that. I can afford a plum— Wait? What?'

Alex swallowed.

Did it get hot in here?

'I could...be your fake boyfriend. We could pretend we're together. He thinks you haven't moved on? We'll prove him wrong. Shut this thing down. The guys know I hate chatter about personal lives. If they think we're together, the cheating thing will be a non-starter. Old news. I can stop it, all of it. John would have to leave you alone, and it won't affect your job.

'There're no rules against lieutenants dating lead paramedics,' he rushed to explain. 'Aisha and Eric over at 30 have been married for years, and they had no issues with dating back in the early days. John thinks he can wear you down, being around you all the time? Well, dating me would prove otherwise pretty quickly. The gossip would die down—'

'Gossip? Who's gossiping?'

Alex winced. Kav had told him earlier that John had let it slip to a couple of the guys that his ex was Lexie. To their credit, none of the guys had mentioned it, and they were playing it off well, for the most part, that they didn't know. It explained the looks he'd noticed that she'd been getting. The guys would want to check on her. They all had wives, girlfriends, sisters. Alex was pretty sure that given they'd not talked to her about it, Kavanagh would have told them in no uncertain terms to keep it zipped.

No one argued with Kyle Kavanagh. He might be a total teddy bear, but he was built and sounded like a grizzly. He was Alex's right-hand man in more ways than one on this.

'I'm sure I don't have to tell you that John is a talker. I think the cat's out of the bag already, and if he keeps grabbing you for chats—it's just not going to get any easier. If we pretend to date, it would have to look real, a secret between us. If we work this right, you can just get on with being at 17. Doing your job.' She was looking at him like she wanted to run away from the whole thing, but he kept talking. The more he turned it over in his head, the more sense it made.

'Alex, I can't involve you in all that. I...' She bit her lip, her cute little nose scrunching up. 'I don't know. God, this is impossible.' She groaned, her head dropping back as if her neck had forgotten how to support it.

Alex's palm wrapped around her nape, gently pulling her back. The little intake of air from her made his groin stir, but he brushed it off. It had been a long time since he'd touched a woman, but he wasn't dead. His friend was beautiful.

'Hear me out. We pretend to be dating. We get along, it's not that far-fetched that it could happen, right?'

His hand on the nape of her neck felt like a brand on her skin. He never touched her, but since John had arrived, he'd kind of made it a point to make contact. A strong shoulder by her side, the odd pat of her hand as he passed her. His fingers tingled from the contact as he held her. Giving her the time she needed to consider this. If she didn't want his help, he'd still be there. As much as she'd allow, but the fake dating thing? It would put him firmly in her corner without taking away her independence.

'If you think they won't buy it—' he began.

Her whispered response cut him off. 'No, I think people would believe that. We do get on well, in our own way.'

His lips twitched, a slight smirk finding the edges. 'So, are you saying you want to do this?'

She worried her lip, but she didn't move away. 'Tell me how it would work.'

He drew in a breath.

Why is my heart hammering?

'We do it our way, and we don't make a big thing about it. We just kind of let it be known that we're dating. I can tell the chief if that bothers you. Hell, I can even fill him in on the plan, if you want to tell him the truth.'

She fixed her eyes on his face, studying him intently. 'But...why would you do this? You don't date.'

'Well, I would be okay fake dating you. I want to help, Lexie. You deserve backup. This is what we do for each other. You shouldn't have to date some random guy to prove you're over John.' She smiled softly at his words.

'Yes, but what do you get out of it?'

What do I get out of it? Since this idea popped out of my mouth, I can't stop thinking about how much this might be the answer.

He got to look after her in a way that she would allow, and he got to wipe that look off John's face. Ever since that night in the bar, Alex had kept his ears open when he was in the same space. Something in his DNA just despised guys like Coxley. Alex was a one-woman type of guy, and he believed in respecting and caring for the things that you were lucky enough to have in your life.

Coxley thinks he's going to wear her down. I can see it in the way he's getting the guys to feel sorry for him. He's spinning this whole thing to ingratiate himself right into her life. Not on my watch!

'I don't like him. Pure and simple. I hate cheaters.' He didn't mention the churning gut, the sudden irrational need he felt to protect her. To stand by her side. He didn't understand it himself; he wasn't about to voice it. It wasn't dating, not for real, but the thought of being together in the world like that…? Something about it strengthened the offer in his mind. He didn't want to pick at it, but just go with it. If she agreed, maybe the boulder in the pit of his stomach from the last couple of days would crumble. If she got her smile back, it would be worth running the gauntlet.

She's worth this risk.

'I don't like the way he treats my friend.'

'Oh, yeah. Who's your friend?' she teased, before going right back to the lip-biting. He wanted to reach up and pull her lip free with his fingertips. 'I don't know. It's a big ask, I mean…' Her nose wrinkled up, and Alex decided it was his new favourite thing about her.

'It would solve a lot of problems. And it would only be temporary. John will soon get bored. He doesn't want me. He just wants what he can't have. I ghosted him, and he can't stand that. I know him well enough to realise he would move on once he got his way. He just can't stand the fact that I left without a backward glance.'

'He wanted you to pine for him, huh?'

Lexie's face hardened. 'Yeah, well he picked the wrong woman. I came to the realisation that I don't need anyone a long time ago. I always said I wouldn't date a firefighter, which is the kicker in all this. He had to convince me to go on a date with him in the first place.' She brushed a long strand of hair behind her ear. 'God, I hate him so much for this. Seriously. A fake boyfriend?'

'Well, technically you wouldn't be breaking the firefighter rule. It would have to be convincing, and we can't tell the guys. I love them, but they are like Real Housewives when it comes to spilling the tea.'

'I still don't know. It's a lot to ask of you. You don't even date.'

'No, that's true, but I do remember what it's like to be in a relationship. I can pull it off. And I can fix your water too.' She went to object but he was faster. 'Er, that's something that comes under the non-negotiable boyfriend duty category.'

He leaned in, pretending to sniff her. It backfired when he inhaled a lungful of her scent: the body spray she used, mixed with a slightly spicy floral perfume she favoured. It took everything he had not to let his eyelids flutter. 'Besides, I don't date stinky broads.'

The laugh she emitted as she pushed him away was all Lexie. The old Lexie. 'Broads? Geez, you're such a caveman.'

'Woman, all mine,' he grunted in a low voice, making her giggle again. 'Fix water. Chase off other men. Eat porterhouse steak and drink beer.' They fell silent after a while.

'Do you still love him?' he murmured.

The shake of her head loosened something inside him. 'No. Which proves that we can't have been that strong in the first place. I was upset, sure. Really upset, and angry that he did that. He's the only guy I've ever lived with. Trusted.' She sighed. 'It's weird, but when I saw him standing there, you know what I felt?' Alex shook his head, not daring to speak. 'Nothing. I just felt mad that I had to see him again. There were no feelings there. It was pretty obvious that I never knew the real him anyway, so there's nothing left to love.' She cocked her head. 'But I'm no expert.'

Narrowing her eyes, she asked, 'You ever been in love, Morrison?'

'Once.' He didn't elaborate. 'I'm no expert either.' He was happy, once upon a time. Truly settled. It felt like a long time ago, and he didn't realise he'd shut himself off quite so much until Lexie arrived.

'Is that why you don't date?'

His shrug was a disappointing answer, but he couldn't bring himself to say anything else. He'd have to tell her, if they did this. But right now wasn't the time. 'The guys are all pretty open about their love lives,' she mused aloud. 'But no one talks about yours.'

She'd noticed that? Huh...

The guys all knew he didn't speak about his past. Most of them had been front and centre while he tried to put himself back together.

He rolled his lips. 'They know better. Besides, these days there's nothing to tell.'

'Bad break-up? I can relate.'

'No,' he said, wincing at his blunt tone. 'You really can't Lex. It's not the same.'

The alarm went off, and they scrambled to get ready.

Saved by the bell.

'Building site incident. Truck, ambo required. One civil-

ian impaled on rebar. Two needing urgent rescue. Downtown Brooklyn. Rhodes Construction site.'

'It's a big one,' Lexie told him, shoving the rest of her supplies back into the hold and stowing the clipboard. 'Taylor,' she yelled as she slammed the ambo doors shut behind them. 'We gotta go!'

'We doing this?' Alex called over his shoulder as he threw his gear on. It was all ready to go, right by the truck doors. 'I'm in if you are. Could be fun.'

Shutting Coxley up and keeping him away from her sure would be. The thought of it put fire in his veins.

'I'll think about it!' she yelled before they hauled out of there, racing to the scene.

'Stubborn,' he yelled back, smiling.

She flipped him off. 'I prefer independent!'

CHAPTER FOUR

RHODES CONSTRUCTION WAS building condos in the area, and they were usually stringent about their working practices. It was rare to get a call out to one of their sites. The second the truck pulled up, Taylor hot on their heels driving the ambulance, the scene was chaos. People were out on the street, camera phones out, one guy was even standing there eating a hot dog like he was at the damn movies.

God bless America.

'Hodgens, Candidate—you get these people back further.' The police on scene were already shepherding people behind blue barriers. 'Tell the officers we need another fifty feet. No looky-loos.' He turned to Kavanagh. 'Kav, you're with me. Sarachek, Coxley—you're on the rebar guy. Stabilise him before you even think about cutting him out. Olsen has the lead on when to move.'

The two men nodded, running towards the casualty as Kav shouted over. 'It's too high for the ladder man, we won't get to him, and we can't risk stuff coming down on the truck.'

At the bottom of the building site, on the ground, was a man dressed in hi-vis, bleeding heavily. Above him, dangling from a security rope, was another guy, screaming in terror.

'Hey man,' the dangling man shouted. 'Is my buddy dead?

Is he dead? Brent, can you hear me? Oh, God, I couldn't hold him any longer! The scaffolding just gave way, man, I tried. I really tried. He was clipped in but the bar fell, and he just…he just…'

'We're coming for you,' Alex shouted up as he donned his safety gear. 'Your buddy's in good hands, okay? Just hang on, we'll get you down.' He turned to Kav as Chief Maddison pulled in behind them in his battalion car. 'The scaffolding must have malfunctioned. The guy is only still up there 'cause of his security harness. If that breaks, or something else comes loose, he's coming down with it. We have to get him from the inside. Chief,' Alex said, nodding to him. He'd run up in time to catch their plan.

'I agree. Take Kav, but watch yourself. Get another harness around him, we should be able to pull him in from the window holes.' He barked into the radio. 'Olsen, status?'

Lexie's voice came over the radio.

'Patient is stable for now. The rebar missed the femoral, but he's been run through the right leg and his head injury is priority. Broken ribs on left-hand side from the impact, I can't get to his left arm to assess properly but we need to cut him out now. There's no blood flow to that area, I'm pretty sure it's broken in several places, cutting off the circulation. I can see his fingers, they're blue. Taylor, I need the backboard, limb supports, oxygen and the defibrillator. He might flatline when we get him free. Neck collar on.' The radio cut off, and Alex could see her moving back to let the guys in, covering his head as Sarachek fired up the saw.

'Copy, Olsen. Fast and finessed, people. Let's get these guys out of here in one piece.'

Kavanagh and Morrison were the dream team. Trained on truck and rescue, they were a double threat that many firehouses didn't have. They were into the building in seconds, racing to where they needed to be. Kav secured two lines to the stone pillars in the building, clipping himself in and handing the other to Morrison. He clipped himself in, and took the lead, Kav watching his back. 'Kyle,' he shouted as he made his descent. 'This whole rig is like Lincoln Logs. It's just waiting to fall.'

'Roger that,' Kav called, radioing down to the chief for everyone to step back. 'Is the patient clear?'

Coxley came over the air waves. 'Negative, almost free. Cutting through last piece now.'

'Hurry it along, will ya?' Alex instructed. 'This whole thing could come down any minute, and—'

As he made his way down to where the guy was dangling at the wrist by his rope, the man shifted, grabbing for a closer bar. 'No,' Alex called. 'Don't move!'

Too late. The scaffolding bar shuddered and fell like a damn steel straw. 'Heads up!' He managed to call into the radio as he hustled down further just in time to grip the man's hand. 'Grab on, now!' He yelled, and the man pulled himself up enough for Alex to clip him onto the rope he was on. A loud clang of metal echoed on the street below, people screaming.

'Olsen!' he yelled into the radio. 'Status!'

Nothing. Even as Kav hauled the pair of them up and into the building, all he could hear was the chief shouting for an update. 'Damn this dust,' he was yelling. 'Does anyone have eyes on? Coxley, Savachek, Taylor, Olsen, check in!'

The second he was out of the harness, he looked at Kav. 'You good to bring him down?'

The man was shaken, a few cuts to the hands and face, but nothing major. The side that had been smacking into the building would be one big bruise tomorrow, but he could stand, talk. The shock had rendered him mute.

'Go,' was all Kav uttered. Alex might as well have flown down to the ground floor, he didn't remember any of it. His harness was still on, the sweat dripping down his forehead, as he ran to the scene. The scaffolding had kicked up so much dust and plaster, it was hard to see a thing. The guys were all running towards where the rebar guy had been, and the first thing they all saw was Taylor. He was cut up, a large gash across his forehead, as he was pulled along by Coxley, who was shouting and spitting out the dust coating his mouth.

'I couldn't see them! Get in there!'

Alex shot past him, and almost smashed into Savachek. And then he saw her. Covered in dust, her hands were all cut up, blood dripping as she gripped the backboard with the patient strapped onto it. She didn't skip a beat, her voice strong and commanding in the noise.

'Vitals are stable, but we need to clear his airway! I had to clamp his femoral, the scaffolding caused the rebar to shift but I had to get him out.'

'Lexie!' Coxley shouted, coming to her side.

Where I want to be, but I can see she is more than holding her own.

The guys took hold of the backboard, running it towards the ambo, but Coxley tried to stop her when she ran after it. 'Are you okay? Baby? Stop, let me just—' He lunged for her arm, and Alex's vision went red.

'Get off, John! Let me do my job, I'm fine!'

She left him in the dust, running past Alex to get to her patient. 'I'm in,' she said, as he flew past. John was standing there, looking pissed, and as Alex's heart rate returned to normal, he smiled. One thing Lexie Olsen didn't want was someone fussing over her. His instincts about her abilities overrode his seemingly feral need to protect her. She was her own woman. But yet, she was going to be his fake girlfriend. The protective surge of pride he felt carried him through the next few hours.

Game on, Olsen. I've got you.

Lexi's fingers curled a little tighter around her front door, bringing with it a sharp stab of pain. The rubble from the construction accident had done a bit of a number on her. She felt like she'd been slashed up good.

The chief had wanted to sign her off work for the rest of the shift, but Taylor was still working. They had ruled out a concussion, though he might have a little scar to show off. Andrew Taylor wasn't even fazed. *Cool, the ladies love a good war wound*, he'd quipped. She'd pretended to barf, but she knew that they'd been lucky.

She also knew that John had overstepped the mark. Treating her like some weak link in the chain. She didn't need anyone checking up on her, least of all him. Sure, he'd been in it with them, but it was she and Sarachek who had saved the guy. The second that saw had gone through that last bit of metal, they had hauled the casualty onto the backboard as fast as safely possible and pulled him out just before the thing came down.

It wasn't close enough to hit them, but the rubble and dust cloud it had kicked up was pretty intense. The debris had gouged through her hands as she'd moved to pull him out of there and to safety.

She'd never worked so hard to keep a guy alive as Taylor blew through the Brooklyn streets to the hospital. The clamp on his femoral artery had held, and his pupils were reactive and responsive. The fact that his friend had managed to lower him closer to the ground before he'd fallen had saved his life.

She wasn't supposed to, but she had checked in on his status after shift. Had texted Alex to let him know that the guy was stable, and his head injury was nothing life-threatening. He'd have a long road ahead of him, but at least he was still here. Alex had messaged straight back, asking for her address. It had taken her a good five minutes to reply, but now here he was. In her space.

They hadn't stopped texting since, talking about how it would work. Alex wasn't to be swayed, so she'd given in eventually. He was a friend, right? Win helped her out from time to time. It shouldn't be that different with Alex. If she was going to do this, she'd have to lower those walls just a little bit. She trusted him. As long as they communicated and kept their friendship strong, they might just pull this off.

'Wow. This is weird.'

The brow he quirked in her direction compounded her desire to take her words back. 'Weird? That your boyfriend came round to fix your broken water heater?' He looked up and down the corridor. 'Should I go buy some coveralls or something, make up an invoice?'

'No,' she laughed, feeling stupid. 'No, of course not. Sorry, come in. And it's *fake* boyfriend, remember?'

He leaned down to scoop up a toolbox she'd never even noticed, coming in close. Jamming herself against the doorframe, she felt his lips brush her cheek on his way past.

'Fair enough, but I personally think it's better to drop the *fake* bit, you know. People could be listening.' She closed the door, and he was right there behind her, his lips tilting into a wry grin.

'Listening? We're not at work.' She motioned towards the kitchen. 'It's just through here.' Padding through her small hallway in her socked feet, she turned back around when she realised he wasn't following. 'Alex?'

He pointed to his booted feet, before shucking them off. 'Just taking my boots off. Manners.'

'Oh.' She smiled at the little courtesy. 'Well, I wouldn't bother. Honestly. The carpet needs replacing anyway, and the whole place needs a good paint.' She ran her finger along the bumpy wall. 'I swear, the plumbing's as old as Abraham Lincoln, and the bedroom ceiling has this stain on it that I swear is getting bigger every time I—'

'Olsen.'

'Yeah?' Her eyes flicked to him. And straight down to his feet, which were clad in bright red socks. Socks that had little flames on them. Wow. She didn't expect him to wear something like that. At the firehouse, he was Mr Regulation.

'Take a breath. I'm not here to inspect the building.' Her face exploded.

Why am I like this?

'And for the record, the blushing is cute, but we need to work on the awkward thing you're rocking. You flinched just now when I kissed your cheek. We're supposed to be together. Coxley's never going to believe us at the house if you turn into—' he flicked a finger up and down in her direction '—*this.*' He lifted the toolbox. 'Where?'

'Right,' she stammered, leading him through to the rather dull kitchen. The heater sat in a cupboard jutting out from the wall. Dull in every sense of the word, from the colour to the clunky old cabinets. 'It's just here. I shut the water off already.'

Alex got to work straightaway, leaving her to linger there awkwardly. After a while he stopped and his grey eyes found hers. 'You know, it's weird to stare. I'm not on a calendar.'

Given the fact that he'd taken off his T-shirt and was standing before her in jeans that hugged his thick thighs just a little too well, it was kind of hard not to imagine him like that. 'Sorry,' she grinned, feeling that blush on her cheeks appear yet again. Giving her away. At this rate, she wouldn't need the heating fixed. The heat she was feeling between them was seemingly keeping them both toasty warm.

She'd always known that Alex was hot. He was tall, strong, kind. The kind of man any woman would look twice at walking down the street. Their flirty teasing at work was fun, no strings, no expectations. But now she was pretending to date him? It blurred the lines. One thing Lexie hated.

'Sorry. It's just strange, having you here.' It wasn't a lie. No one but Win and Hunter had been here since she'd moved in. He was the first man she'd had in her personal space in months. And now she was thinking about him being here again, and what that meant.

'I think we need some boundaries.' She sighed, looking at her watch. It was after four in the afternoon now. She didn't always sleep well in her bunk at the firehouse, and she'd crashed for a few hours pretty much the second she'd walked in that morning. 'Listen, do you want a beer?'

'Depends.'

'On what?'

'Whether it's a girly light beer or not.'

She snorted. 'Me, girly? As if. I have some pretty good IPAs. I keep the light stuff for Win when she visits.'

'Sure, I'd love one, then. Thanks.'

Alex had gone back to looking at the heater, a deep frown denting his brows that she didn't often see. Come to think of it, she'd seen it a lot more over recent days. It had been omnipresent in the early days at the station. He'd been one of the more aloof guys at the house, until she'd cracked him with a few jokes. Some days, her side quest was to get the big guy to lose that frown. Like now, when he flashed her that cute grin while taking the beer bottle from her.

'I know you want to talk boundaries,' he said eventually, glaring at the heater as if its very presence offended him, before giving her his full attention. She covered her smirk by sipping from her own bottle.

He is such a bear of a man.

'But I think we need to talk about this old thing.' He thumbed behind him. 'Because it's not safe. In fact, we need to get it condemned.'

'What? The landlord said it would probably be a minor repair.'

'Yeah, well, he doesn't want to shell out for a new one. Seriously, Lex—you can't stay here. I can't get the water back on. Have you got anywhere to stay tonight?'

She checked the time. 'I could ring Win I guess, but I think she might be on shift. She's picking up extras at the minute, with Hunter taking the bar things are a bit tight.'

Alex shrugged, draining his beer and packing his tools away. 'Okay, pack your stuff. You can stay at mine.'

'What? Oh, no, I'll be fine. I can go shower at the gym or something in the morning, and we're back on shift the day after.'

He pulled on his T-shirt. 'What about going to the toilet?'

'Well, that still works. It's just the hot water. I can…heat up a pan for the dishes. No biggie.'

He rolled his eyes. 'Not a chance. I'm not leaving you to live like this. I have a spare room.'

'I know, but—'

'Listen, I'm hungry. We can go to mine, order pizza and discuss these boundaries. We need to be on the same page for our next shift, and you need a shower and a good night's sleep in a warm house.'

He had a point. It was pretty obvious that she couldn't sleep here. They were friends, right? She trusted him. One night wouldn't be the end of the world.

'Is that another reference to my personal hygiene, Morrison?'

The grin was wide when he let it fly. 'Go pack a bag, Olsen. For both nights. You'll have the place to yourself tomorrow anyway. I'm visiting my folks, won't be back till late. You can pick the pizza.'

'Both nights? No, Win will—'

'Move it, Olsen. Fake boyfriend here, getting hungrier by the minute.'

All too soon, Lexie found herself sitting in Alex's car outside the firehouse. They were due on shift in twenty minutes. Yesterday, she'd spent the day watching movies in his house, arguing with the landlord, who was still saying the heater wasn't that bad. She'd gone to bed before he returned from his parents' place, and now they were here. Back to work, and it was the first day of pretending they were a couple. Taking into account the fact she'd practically hidden from him in his own house, this was going to be awkward.

'I really wish I'd followed you in my car the other night.' He had offered to take her back to pick it up before he left for his parents', but she'd had no need of it. No errands to run, and she hadn't wanted to put him out any further. It was weird enough taking the help he'd already offered. She hadn't even thought about the drive to work though, and what people would make of it. She was spinning, but Alex was calm. Too calm for someone who was about to lie to everyone they knew. 'Are we really going to walk in there together?'

The first night, over a large pepperoni, they'd come up with the rules for their little ruse. It was simple. They'd pretend to date until John lost interest and things calmed down at the firehouse. She was hoping that he'd get bored enough to maybe move houses again, but she wouldn't hold her breath. They'd keep it light, still be them, but be seen out together when there were any events where the squad came together. They were both professionals. It wasn't like she was about to start wearing his letterman jacket and going with him to prom to prove their point.

'Best way to kick things off, babe.'

'Babe?'

He waggled his brows at her. 'Just figured we should have pet names for each other, you know. Couple stuff.'

'John called me that.'

Alex's little dent made a reappearance. 'That's definitely out, then. Wasn't a fan anyway. Honey? Sweetie?'

'Vomit?' she countered with a grimace, making him laugh.

'How about Pain-In-the-Ass?'

'Aww, darling—' she made a heart shape with her fingers '—you complete me.'

He rolled his eyes. 'You really are annoying, you know that? Like a damn bug.' His eyes widened. 'That's it. Bug.' He booped her on the nose with one finger. 'Lexie, my little Firebug.'

She didn't hate it. 'Fine. What about kissing?'

He didn't speak for a minute, but she saw his grey eyes drop to her lips. 'I…er…that's your call. I don't want you to do anything that makes you uncomfortable. That's the total opposite of our goal here. We could probably pull this off without it.'

'I'm good with that. If this was real, we wouldn't be kissing at work. Out of work, I guess we might need to show a bit of PDA. At the station, it's not something I would do anyway.'

'No making out in the bunk-room. Got it.' She met him smirk to smirk, and the butterflies she felt in her stomach reminded her of her next stipulation.

'And no feelings. I will never date a firefighter for real. Not again. I have worked too hard and gone through too much to go through that again. Not that you wanted that.' She realised that she'd made it sound like he was pining for her or something. 'This is just two friends helping each other out. If one of us wants out, then we end it. No blame, we can just say that we're better off as friends or something.' She tried thinking about this from his end, and what it would mean for his personal life. 'And if you want to start dating someone, we end it then too. Clean and clear.'

'I won't,' he cut in, so quickly it made her do a double take. 'Want to date anyone else, I mean.'

'Well, sure,' she said breezily, ignoring the gut clench she felt at the thought of him dating someone. Maybe she was warming to this boyfriend thing. It was kinda nice having someone so in your corner like this. No game playing or having to work out what he was thinking.

With Alex, he just said it. It was interesting. New.

Not for the first time, she reminded herself that this was fake. He was a good, loyal friend. That should be enough. It wasn't like she was naive enough to think that he wouldn't be snapped up one day. Grumpy demeanour and occupation aside, Alex Morrison was a good catch. 'Maybe you don't want to date now, but I'm sure that will change. Plus, I have a well-tested theory that attached firefighters are to woman like flames are to moths. We've all seen a few moths fall into that trap, and women are no different. You'll probably get a lot of attention from this.'

She saw his throat work as he swallowed. 'I'm not looking to date anytime soon, and when I did date, I was strictly a one-woman man.'

Damn. She'd gone and implied he was going to be some kind of cheater now. 'Oh, no, I don't mean that you'd fake cheat on me, I—'

'I would never cheat on you, fake or not.' His tone was growly, certain. 'John never knew what he had. I would never be that blind.'

That shut her up. It was so absurdly romantic; she didn't know what to do with it. So she tucked it away to think about later. Or never. Whatever.

'I never dated, because I didn't feel the need to. I didn't want to.' He rolled his lips. 'I told you I'd been in love once, and that was true. I had a wife. A few years ago. Holly.'

The air whooshed out of her. He didn't wear a ring. She'd seen no evidence of a woman in his place. In fact, it needed a little bit of love, if anything. It wasn't quite bachelor pad tragic, but she could tell it was like her place. Just somewhere to call a base when he wasn't working. She tried to think of Alex with a divorcee label, and it didn't feel right.

'I'm a widower, Lex. The guys here knew her. It's why they don't talk about my lack of a love life. They saw what I went through.'

Her mouth went dry. She figured something must have sworn him off dating. A man like that didn't stay alone for long. As she watched him pick over his words, she realised that this was why. Why the other firefighters didn't mention him in the proximity of other women. They knew and respected him enough to protect his past. Just like they'd given her space when Coxley arrived. He'd been in love, and it had broken him somehow.

It made her heart clench to see him like this. The easy, flirty Alex sombre. Made her want to help him, repair some of the pieces.

'I don't talk about it much, but my wife…she died. Suddenly. Right in front of me.'

So, no divorce. The woman who left him didn't have a choice. She didn't cheat on him, or treat him bad. She left him alone in the world, to face a new future without her.

And now he was offering to fake date her, to pretend to care for her, be there for her. She didn't know a better man. It made her like him even more, made her want to be there for him too. Whatever he needed. She'd been flirting with a widower all this time, and never known. It had made her feel good, their friendship. Helped her get through the last few months. Offering to be her 'boyfriend' was his way of showing her she'd helped him too. He didn't need to say it, she knew. Somehow, they'd given each other what they'd needed and now she wanted to be there for him more than ever.

This fake relationship might just be the solution for them both. A safe space. Together. Right now, she was grateful for it. It meant she could comfort him, and she needed that right now more than she needed to breathe. Around Alex, her walls quivered and crumbled.

'I… I'm so sorry, Alex. I didn't know.' Her hands reached for his, clasping his huge palm in hers. 'How did it happen?'

His head dropped to where their hands joined, and he brought the other hand to cover hers, rubbing his thumb along her wrist.

'It was unexpected. Quick. We were out shopping together, just a normal boring Saturday, you know. We were talking one minute about what we wanted to get for dinner, and then she just sort of turned to me, held her head. She tried to tell me something, but the words wouldn't come out. Her mouth wouldn't work properly. I rushed over to her, but she hit the ground before I got there. She died right there, in the middle of the damn aisle. That was three years ago.'

She could see it. Him there, in that aisle, holding a woman he loved. Her heart near broke in half for him. 'I'm sorry. Was it a stroke?' He met her eyes then, and she was relieved to see the light was back a little in those beautiful grey eyes.

'Yep. She had a slow brain bleed, didn't suffer.'

'It must have been horrible. I can't imagine losing someone like that.' She couldn't really imagine being so entwined with someone. Alex had had a whole marriage. A love lost. She'd barely had a relationship in comparison. It made her problems seem all the sillier in light of his admission. 'Thank you for trusting me with it.'

'It was a long time ago. I just wanted you to know, in case it comes up. The guys know, but they know it's not something to talk about. I don't like to dwell. Just wanted you to have the facts. Seems like something you would know about if we were dating for real, you know.'

'Won't they think it's odd, you dating me?'

He huffed out a laugh. 'I'll deal with them. I don't think it'll be too much of a sell. Some of their wives and girlfriends have been trying to set me up on dates for a while, and they've seen us at the station together. Besides, they know better than to gossip around me. Kav will no doubt field any questions.'

That made sense.

The guys here were all about the jokes, but the respect for Alex was obvious. It did put a bit more pressure on her though. They would all think she was the first woman to be with Alex after his wife. The fact that he was doing this for her meant something significant, real or not. One thing she promised herself was that when this ended, she wouldn't let Alex be the bad guy. She'd protect the man he was, the man they knew him to be. 'Thank you for telling me. I feel a bit of a fool for banging on about kissing now.'

He laughed then, and they were back to being them. The same but changed somehow. She felt like she understood him a lot better. The fact that the guys at the firehouse commented on how much happier he'd been since she'd arrived made her feel like she might have helped him. Just like he'd been helping her. It loosened something in her chest that she didn't even try to dissect.

'I'm not entirely averse to the kissing,' he said after a long moment. His thumb had resumed the slow strokes on the inside of her wrist.

'You're not?'

'Definitely not. We have to sell it, right? If you were my girl, I'd be kissing you in public.' His eyes dropped to his watch, sighing. She tried her best to ignore those butterflies that had started up again. 'We need to get in there. You ready for this, Bug?'

She squeezed his hand. She could do this. She might think a little too much about the whole kissing thing and his lack of aversion to it, but she could do this. Friends found each other attractive all the time, right?

'Sure thing, kitten. Lead the way.'

He pulled a face. 'Kitten?'

'No? Not the one?'

'No, Bug. Keep thinking on that one.'

'Copy that, Sugar Buns.'

His eye-roll had her laughing for a full minute.

CHAPTER FIVE

SOMETIMES FATE JUST looked at a woman and said, *Yeah—it's your turn, girl. Go rock it.* Today, that woman was Lexie. She felt like the prom queen walking into the firehouse with her king, because the second they walked in, John saw them. Holding hands because Alex, the suave gentleman he was, had reached for it the second they'd hit the sidewalk. After coming around and opening her car door as if it was as natural as breathing air. Pulling her close enough to him to wrap their hands behind her waist. He was a solid form at her side. She gave her friend total credit on the full fake boyfriend service. Gold star. Would recommend.

Oh...put a pin in that, Lexie.

The dirty thoughts that 'full service' conjured in her head were going to make her blush again. And this prom queen had never been hit with the whole flamed cheeks thing before this. Something about Morrison just dragged it out of her. If she didn't watch it, she was in real danger of turning swoony.

Win would have a field day, but she was dodging her calls for now. Sending her quick texts about being tired, or busy. She needed to get her own head around the events of the last few days before telling her best friend. Knowing Win, she would want to come to the firehouse and cart John out with her bare hands. Even for a New Yorker, she was fiery. Speaking of fire, John had plenty in his eyes right now.

'Morning,' Alex tossed at him easily, coming to a stop in front of the ambulance and blocking her view of her ex with his broad back. 'I'll see you later,' he murmured to her, his voice low, sexy. 'I'm looking forward to tomorrow,' he said a little louder, and with a lot more growl. She was smiling up at him, their hands still entwined when his lips pecked hers. It was just a fleeting touch, but damn if she didn't like it. That, and the triumphant little wink he flashed her before turning away. Their fingers stayed wrapped around each other till the last second as he strode right past John and headed inside. She went to follow him, but John blocked her path.

'What was that?' John was looking at her like she'd just stolen his favourite toy. 'Are you seeing him?'

'I don't think it's any of your business. Let me by.'

'What about all firefighters being players?'

How did he know I'd said that? Oh, right... Win.

'I meant it.'

'But you're seeing Morrison, right?'

'I don't know, John. You seem to have all the answers to my life. You talk about me enough. You tell me.'

His nostrils flared. 'Were you seeing him when you were with me?'

Her fist flexed.

Don't deck your colleagues, Lexie. Stand down.

'Don't you dare. I wasn't the one cheating and you know it. I didn't even know Alex then.' A couple of the guys came out to check the equipment then, and she lowered her voice. 'Listen, I don't want to talk to you. I've made myself clear, more than once. We can work together, and that's it. My life and what I do with anyone else has nothing to do with you.'

'I won't drop this,' John huffed. 'I want you back. I made a mistake. We were together for a year, we lived together for Christ's sake! You're not the kind to just leave that, Lexie. I know you still care about me. Can we just talk, once? You and him can't be anything special.'

'Coxley, it's time for shift. Let our lead paramedic get to work. I need you to check the oxygen tanks in storage. Take the candidate with you.'

Alex's voice was all business. She could tell by the way John's shoulders drooped that he knew he wasn't getting anywhere.

'It's done,' she murmured, forcing herself to keep eye contact. 'I don't want to talk, John. You're just a colleague now. Nothing else, and I want you to leave me alone. Understood?'

'Coxley, today!' Alex pushed, and with one final determined look, John strode away. While she was passing Alex on the way to the lockers, he brushed his fingers against hers. She squeezed them back, a silent thank you for having her back. She felt him tug her toward him.

'You okay?'

'I don't need a minder, Morrison,' she chided, last-naming him to prove her point, but there was no heat behind her instruction.

'Oh, I know that.' He smiled. 'Just checking on my girl.' The tingle she felt was hard to hide, and from the way his eyes flashed, he'd picked up on it. 'I'm cooking next night off by the way.'

'I'm going back to my place.'

He shook his head. 'I just heard from your landlord. Apparently, someone told him that the water system in your place was a hazard and needed to be condemned.'

'Someone, huh? Like a firefighter in charge, perhaps?'

He quirked a brow. 'Maybe. These things are confidential. Discussing it would be against regulation. Long and short of it is, your place is off-limits till it's been replaced. He doesn't want a fine or people poking around seeing what else isn't up to code.'

'Right,' she scoffed. 'Looks like his tenant will need a bed for a little while longer, then.'

He shrugged. 'Apparently her boyfriend is happy to help. Pasta okay with you?'

Pasta did sound good. Food cooked for her, with a warm bed and a hot shower? Even the most independent woman would be stupid to pass on that. After two long shifts, it would be like heaven to have that waiting, instead of her dingy place with no water.

'Well, in that case, I'm sure she'd be grateful enough to provide the beer.'

'Sounds like a plan,' he said, grinning.

The plan worked, until dinner time. It had been a quiet day, most of her call-outs had been the usual. Her past patient Betty Anne calling to complain about the pains in her legs, caused by lymphedema from her heart condition. Mostly, She and Taylor knew she called because she needed the company. Someone to tell her that she was healthy enough. She'd had a heart attack recently and Lexie had been the one to attend. She knew it had scared Betty Anne, so making a sandwich and watering her plants when they had the time wasn't a hardship. She'd been referred to community nursing, but they were overworked and didn't always set these things up as quickly as was needed.

Next had been a kid at the park. He'd flung himself off the jungle gym and bumped his head, knocking himself out. He was going to be fine, but Taylor had had to comfort the very upset grandmother who was beside herself and had sobbed on his shoulder. Lexie was still laughing on the way back to the firehouse.

'I think you scored there, Taylor. I would expect some banana bread in your future.'

'Funny,' he moaned, but he had a smile on his face. 'At least the kid is going to be okay. Madness, isn't it? A day at the park and he ends up with five stitches.'

'It's character building. Every child has a scrape or two. At least he wasn't in some darkened bedroom twiddling his joystick.' She pulled the ambulance into the bay, patting her stomach. 'Just in time for food. I'm starving.'

Taylor winced. 'I think I overdid the snacks.'

Heading straight into the main area, Lexie went to the sink to wash her hands. Jimmy, the candidate, was just finishing off the food. The air smelled spicy, and Lexie's stomach rumbled. 'Tacos, Jimmy? Nice!'

He shrugged, a little blush creeping across his cheeks. 'Can't get tacos wrong. I'm not the best cook, but apparently Chief Maddison loves Mexican food.'

'He does,' Alex agreed, coming to the counter to pick up bowls of salsa and guacamole. 'Just in time for dinner, Bug. Come sit next to me.'

She tried to keep her face straight as Jimmy raised a curious brow their way. Alex took his seat, patting the one next to him and flashing her a mischievous grin. *Game time*, he mouthed, and when she took her seat, he draped his arm over the back of it.

'Tacos! Score, Jimmy!' Hodgens crashed into his seat next to them as the rest of the food was laid out. Kav claimed the chair on the other side of Alex, nodding at Lexie in his usual friendly way. 'So…' Hodgens grinned when the last two of the crew, one being a furious-looking John, took their places. 'Anything new to report?' His gaze flicked to Lexie and Alex, and the arm that Alex didn't move.

In fact, he moved it a little closer. She felt his thumb brush along her back and resisted the shiver it elicited.

What in the name of soft touches was going on here?

'My wife wants to redecorate again,' Sarachek chipped in, piling spicy meat into a shell. 'I told her no more grey or beige. Does she listen? Of course not. And the cost? I will never be able to retire.'

Hodgens rolled his eyes. 'Okay. Anything else?'

Kavanagh tonged some salad onto his plate. 'The new regulators are arriving tomorrow. Chief finally got them approved.' A hum of acknowledgement rippled around the table. Hodgens made a frustrated noise in the back of his throat, reaching for the bowl of grated cheese with a huff. Lexie heard Kavanagh laugh, and when she risked sneaking a look at Alex, he looked like he was enjoying every minute.

'What about you, Olsen?' John cut in. 'Any news you want to share?' Every head turned to look at her.

Jasper Newlin, one of the older members of the squad even lowered his paper to listen. Lexie felt like she was going to lurch across the table at any minute, and throttle John for making it awkward. What the hell was his game? She glared at him, and it clicked.

He didn't believe it. Either he was a genius who'd figured

out their plan, which was unlikely, or he genuinely thought that she couldn't move on from him. That she and Alex were some kind of rebound. She didn't know which annoyed her more, but she was riled enough to crack any taco shell she reached for right now.

She slid her eyes across at Alex, who gave her the tiniest little nod. The okay to out them. She felt the brush of his thumb again, and she knew what he was trying to tell her. *I've got your back.* It was all she needed. Reaching for the shell platter, she shrugged. 'Not much. Betty Anne's fine. She sends her love to everyone. Taylor's last patient is probably going to bake enough thank-you gifts for a cake sale.' She placed two shells on her plate. Added a third when her stomach grumbled at her.

'Oh—' she put the platter back, and reached for Alex's hand on the table '—and I'm dating your lieutenant.'

John's shell cracked in his hand, spilling meat down onto the plate. The table froze for a full minute, and Alex squeezed her hand before letting it go and passing her the bowl of taco meat. She shot him an easy smile. 'Thanks, Pookie. I'm starving.'

The table erupted, and when she next glanced at John, his chair was empty.

She was just started to drift off in her bunk when she heard her name being whispered. Sitting up, she saw Alex standing there. He was still in his uniform of white shirt and regulation pants. Arms folded, he looked like a snack. The lighting, low behind him, made his muscular form stand out. His tight, corded forearms rippling as he came a little closer, kneeling by her bed.

'You need something, Lieutenant? Hot chocolate, sleeping pill?'

He shook his head, his gaze dropping to the neckline of her nightclothes. She slept in PJs at the firehouse, her uniform ready to go in seconds on the chair by the entrance to her cubicle. 'Nice pyjamas. Not seen those before.' She blushed, and she could swear his whole face lit up when he saw it. 'I came to say goodnight. I have some paperwork to do.'

'You're not sleeping?' She went to get up, but he pressed her leg, halting her.

'Stay in bed. It's pretty cold in here tonight. I don't really sleep much.'

Interesting. She'd not really noticed that, even living in his space. 'The guys took it well, I thought.'

Alex's lip quirked. 'I actually think they're rooting for us.' He lifted his head, looking around the bunks before sliding his grey eyes back to look at her. 'Told you it would work out.'

'The chief doesn't know yet. He might not be so impressed.'

Alex laughed, a low quiet rumble as he pulled his phone out of his pocket and typed something. A second later, the phone on the side of her bunk vibrated against the wood. She rolled her eyes, reading the screen.

He does know. I told him this morning. He's fine with it.

Her cheeks flushed, despite her efforts. Well, it was out now. She typed back.

Does he know about John?

Alex read it, that frown reappearing before he raised his head, shaking it from side to side once. 'I thought that was your story to tell, if you want to tell it.' His voice was a gentle whisper, full of care, and it made her heart lurch.

'I'll tell him if I need to.'

Alex nodded again, giving her one last lingering look before standing back up. Sending her a little wave, he left, heading in the direction of his office, where his bunk was. Lieutenants had their own quarters, closed off from the rest of the bunks but still adjacent. She settled back under the covers, and her phone buzzed in her hand once more.

You do look cute in your PJs, Bug. I like your hair all loose like that. Best girlfriend ever. Goodnight. Sleep tight.

This man could not be this cute, surely? She'd idly wondered why he was single, when he was such a catch. Learning about his wife had made the pieces fit together. He was so emotionally mature, grounded in his life and the way he lived. His big love had obviously changed him, and it added another layer to his often quiet demeanour. The way he treated her and his respect for her independence made perfect sense. He lived his own life too, shaped by the events in his past. It kinda made her want to be there for him too. To cherish his kind ways, and allow him to see more of her softer side too. She could trust him with all parts of her, without worry of rejection or judgement. She felt seen around him. Appreciated. It was…beautiful. Made *her* feel beautiful. The warm feeling she felt around him was intoxicating. She ran her hand through her messy bed-head hair. She usually slept with it tied up, but for some reason, she'd taken it out tonight. Her boyfriend seemed to approve. Her phone beeped again, and she snuggled down to read the latest message.

You asleep already?

No, Kitten.

So, the kitten is sticking, then?

I like it. Suits you.

Seriously? In what way?

She grinned in the dark, enjoying this. It was an extension of them at their best. Flirting, teasing. She thought for a moment.

Well, you're cute.

I'll take that. Anything else?

Playful.

Back at ya. That it? Kittens aren't sexy.

So you think you're sexy?

I think you think I am. Caught you checking me out more than once.

Guilty. She pressed her lips together to stop the little squeak she felt from bubbling out.

Bet that made you blush, Bug. I like it when you blush.

This was...getting a little spicy. No one knew they were texting. Did he mean this for real?
She typed back.

Boundaries.

Partly because she wanted to remind him that this was fake, and partly to see what his response was.

Sorry. Didn't mean to overstep.

Damn. She didn't like the bucket of reality she'd just poured over them both.

It's okay, Kitten.

Again with the kitten? Guess it's a good thing your pet name for me isn't sexy. Night.

She waited for him to text something else, but the three dots disappeared. She put her phone down on the side and lay back on her pillow. It had been fun, a turn-on. She'd enjoyed it, but then she'd put him in his place. He wasn't saying anything they hadn't said to each other in person since they'd started their friendship.

'Killjoy,' she muttered to herself. He'd been there for her, and she'd smacked him with the boundary stick. He'd made a point of telling her things he liked about her, to check she was okay. Warm even. All without asking for anything in return. His wife had been a lucky woman, to have that to call her own. Reaching for her phone, she sent him a message before she could take herself out of it, and then settled down to sleep.

I don't know. I'm pretty sure I could make you purr, Kitten. Thanks for being you. Don't stay up too late.

CHAPTER SIX

'Jesus, Bug. Are you trying to kill me?'

She jumped at the sound of his husky, deep voice. A shock in the dark of his kitchen. She sprang up from where she'd been leaning against the counter, looking for rentals on her laptop and spooning Marshmallow Fluff out of a jar.

'Alex! You scared the bejesus out of me! I'm going to get you a bell, Kitten.' The name had definitely stuck. And the texting. The full squad had been fully on board with their new relationship, John being a little quieter. Though she had caught him watching her in the TV area while she was busy texting Alex. Their little conversations verged on being downright horny. On both sides. The longer this went on, the more she was enjoying it. Every shift got a little easier. The fake side of things feeling less fake as time went on. Every time they clocked off, he led her to his car, his fingers linked in hers. They cooked together, watched movies on the couch. It was getting a little too cozy, and her place was becoming a lot less appealing every time she went back there to check on things and pick some clothes up.

'Sorry,' he smirked, not looking one bit like he was. 'Couldn't sleep. What are you looking at in the middle of the night?'

'Rentals.' She blushed, clocking the fact he was only dressed in boxer shorts a little too late. The dim light from the hallway behind him only served to highlight the sculpted muscles of his chest. She tried and failed not to look at the thin line of hair that ran from his navel to the hem of his shorts as he pushed off from the wall he'd been leaning against and peered over her shoulder at the screen. She dared not stand up straight, knowing she was only clad in her short T-shirt and skimpy sleep shorts. If she turned around, she'd barrel right into that chest, his hard body. There would be no hiding her reaction if she touched him skin to skin.

It was getting harder not to react at all around him these days. She tried to convince herself that it was just because she hadn't been laid in so long, but that would be a lie. The telltale flutter between her legs didn't happen for anyone. In fact, Alex 'Hot Abs' Morrison was probably the only man who'd turned her on by the mere sight of him in his underwear. Even the ping of a new message on her phone made her lady parts tingle.

The lines were not just blurry now, they were supercharged with lust. All the more reason to get a new place. She'd just have to eat into her savings, put back buying a house a little longer.

'Rentals? I thought you were saving to buy?'

'Well, yeah…' She looked over her shoulder at him. Immediately regretting it and whipping her head back to the screen so fast she was pretty sure she hit him in the face with her ponytail. 'Sorry.' He pretended to choke, and then she felt him reach for her tied-up hair.

She sensed the change in the air between them as her skin rose in goose bumps. She was frozen while his fingers gently pulled the hair loose from the small fabric tie. One of her favourites, cream with little pink and red hearts across the cotton. A present from Win. When her hair was free, he smoothed it with one hand, before draping it over the opposite shoulder to him.

'That's better,' he murmured, his fingers brushing against the back of her neck. 'I like it when it's down like this. Plus, it hurts less when you whip me with it.' He jabbed a finger towards the screen. 'You don't have to move somewhere new, you know. Look at the rent on those places, you'll burn through your savings a lot faster with the extra expense. I'm pretty sure that you could break your lease and still get your deposit back. Or wait it out. You'd have to pay rent anyway, and the water heater's still not been fixed, right? Even if the landlord does what he promised, the place is a shack. No offence.'

'None taken. I can't do that, I have a month left, he won't lose that money. He'd make me pay it anyway, and if I try to break early then my deposit will be lost for sure. Not exactly in a position to sue him, am I? Besides, I need time to find a place even close to that rent.' She pulled a face at his sceptical look. 'Yeah, I know. I'm dreaming a bit on that one, but there must be at least one decently cheap place that's not a rathole. It's Brooklyn, not the ends of the earth. At this point, I'd take anything half-decent that's close to work and has hot water from something this century.'

'Just seems a little pointless on the money front. Why don't you stay here till you buy a place?'

She whirled around to face him. They were close now, so near to each other she could see the tiny blue flecks of colour hidden in the grey.

'Alex, don't be ridiculous. I can't do that.'

'Why not? You're staying here now, right? Everyone already thinks we're together. You could save a ton of money.

Plenty of people have housemates these days. It would make sense.'

'No, it wouldn't! We've been together five minutes, and it's not real, remember? What would everyone at the firehouse say?'

'Who cares? We know the truth, and it makes sense. They've all seen us arrive and leave together. It's not that far-fetched that two people in a relationship would choose to live together.' He waved his arms around the huge kitchen space. 'This place is too big for me on my own really, and I don't want you spending another night in your place. We can carpool for work, split the groceries. We've been doing that anyway. You can save up for your own place a lot faster. I don't need any rent, this place is paid for.'

'It's paid for?'

His easy grin dimmed. 'Er, yeah. Insurance payout for…'

'Oh, right.' His wife. Damn. 'Sorry. It's none of my business anyway.'

He shook his head. 'It's fine. After she passed, I didn't want to stay in our old apartment. We were saving to buy a house, so with the sale of that and the rest of the money, I saw this place. Figured it would be big enough for whatever came along.'

Whatever came along?

She'd always wondered why he'd bought a house on his own. The typical bachelor type didn't tie themselves to a house large enough for a family. Especially one who didn't seem interested in all that. He'd never spoken about it before. She'd assumed before coming here and really seeing the place that he'd lived here with his wife.

'The point is,' he continued, 'I have the room, and I'd love it if you stayed here. To be honest, I don't like the thought of you going back home. It's been nice having you here, and that place is a death-trap. No offence, but I'll sleep a hell of a lot better with you under my roof.'

She repressed the little shiver she felt at his protective words. If any other man had said that to her, she'd have probably mocked them. Told them she didn't need a man to come to her rescue, but it was different with Alex. More like they were in this together. But she'd been here before. John had convinced her to move into his place, and she'd trusted him. If a boyfriend could do that and leave her in the situation where she needed to live in a dump in the first place, then it could happen again just as easily. Alex owed her even less than John did.

'I can't do that, but thanks for the offer. My water situation will be fixed soon, I'm sure. I should be out of your hair in a few days.'

'Not really the point though, it's not just the water that's wrong with that place. Are you really going to put up with that?'

'Yep,' she said, chin in the air. 'Now, can we change the subject please?' She was pretty sure that she'd won for now, but his knitted brows told her that he wasn't going to let it drop for long. So, she decided to put them back on a more familiar footing. Their flirty banter usually worked.

'You know,' she put a little sing-song into her voice, while reaching behind her for the jar of pink Fluff. 'When you get all worried—' she scooped a dollop onto her spoon '—you get this little worry groove, right…here.' And she flicked it, so it landed right between his brows, covering the deep furrow of skin.

He flinched, and she rolled her lips to stop herself from laughing as he raised a brow, causing half the marshmallow to drip down the bridge of his nose. It came to a stop at the tip.

'That's better,' she managed to squeak out before a giggle broke free.

He shook his head, tutting slowly. 'Are you trying to distract me, Olsen?'

'Maybe,' she smirked. 'The frown's gone, so it worked. You went from…' She coughed down a laugh, her whole body shaking from the effort of holding it in. 'Grumpy to fluffy!' She broke, cackling as her stomach started to hurt. 'Oh, wow, that's your new nickname now, that's hilari—'

Alex shut her up when he grabbed her and ran his nose along one cheek. She felt the marshmallow, sticky on her skin, could smell the sugar. It was his turn to laugh now, as he dipped his head to coat her other cheek.

'Fair's fair,' he rumbled, pulling back. She tried to glare at him but he looked so happy, a devilish grin on his face that warmed her heart. She'd never understood why people thought he was so closed off. Right now, he looked like a teenager, just fooling around and having fun. Without thinking, she leaned in close and licked a drop that was smeared across his jaw. She felt him freeze beneath her touch, and her heart thudded.

'Sorry,' she breathed. 'I was just—'

He kissed her. He swallowed whatever she was about to say with his lips on hers. Sweet. Sticky. Hot. Exploring. Soft. Hard. She'd pictured it a lot, thought about it when she lay awake in her bunk. In the bed in his spare room. Their texting had kicked things up by a billion degrees, but this was still the hottest thing she'd ever done. Whatever she'd imagined wasn't a patch on the real thing. He kissed like he'd been starved for eternity for her touch, and the heat pooling within her made her thighs clench together.

Wow, I'm a horny cliché.

'Just what?' he asked when he pulled back.

Cliché to heck. Kiss me again, Morrison.

'I forgot what I was going to say.' She licked the sweet stuff from her lips. 'We're kissing now?'

'We're kissing now.'

'Oh. No talking about the kissing?'

'I'd rather be doing the actual kissing, but we can talk if you'd prefer it. I could text you. Tell you how badly I've been wanting to do it.' His gaze dropped to her mouth. 'I know what this is, if that's what you're worried about. I know the deal. No feelings. No expectations.'

Easy to say, but she was feeling everything right now. At some point his arms had wrapped around her waist. Her entire body had expectations. Dirty ones.

'Bug.' Something in his voice was deep, throaty. 'Tell me to go to bed. If you don't want this, just say the word.'

'I don't *not* want it.'

His lips twitched. 'Well, that was about as clear as mud. Shall I go get my phone?'

'I just don't want this to get weird. We both have baggage. I think that we need to consider whether this is right, between us. It's messy mixing real actions with a fake relationship. You're a widower, Alex. That's huge, I mean. Have you dated since, like ever? Even a one-night thing?'

He licked at his lips, not meeting her eye. 'No. I never saw the point. After Holly, I guess I just kinda figured that that part of life was over for me.' He swallowed. 'Is that what you want from this, dating?'

'That's a loaded question, given that we're smushed together right now.' He looked a little rueful, pulling away from her body. She regretted saying anything. It was really nice, being in his hold. 'This is getting complicated, isn't it? Maybe I *should* head back to my place.'

'No, I don't want that. Geez, I really messed this up, didn't I? I didn't mean to cross the line. I didn't suggest this…arrangement to get anything out of this.'

'I know that, I trust you.'

The look of relief on his face was super cute. This guy had been celibate since his wife passed. He wanted her. It was hard not to get a little thrill about being the one who made Morrison lustful. 'Listen, if I was in the market, or dated firefighters, you would be right up there on my list. I don't regret that kiss.'

'You don't?'

The pleased expression on his face as he grinned made her laugh. 'No, Alex, it was hot. I am attracted to you; I think we both know we…appreciate each other that way.'

His expression turned wolfish. 'Lexie, I appreciate you hard in that way. To be honest, that kiss is something I've wanted to do for a long time. Before this whole arrangement. I just didn't think I'd get the chance to…you know… act on it.'

Something did a backflip in her stomach.

'So…' he wrapped her in his arms again '…if I wanted to kiss my fake girlfriend, would she appreciate that?' His eyes dropped to her lips. 'I get you don't want anything further, and I have been out of the game a long time. I never felt the need to be close to a person like this, but with you, it's different somehow. All I'm saying is that this thing between us, it doesn't have to be complicated. It could be… I don't know, easy. Fun.'

'Fun,' she mused. 'If we're doing this whole fake relationship, maybe a bit of practice would be good. You know, for authenticity.' They'd gotten used to the touching thing at work. That came naturally now. Little pecks on the lips when they went into work and left. 'No strings, no feelings. We're just friends, helping each other out.'

'So, just friends faking a relationship and being roommates? Gotcha. Now which is it, Bug? Kissing or no kissing?'

'I haven't said yes to the roommate thing yet.'

'I haven't finished talking you into it yet.' His cocky smile melted her argument to mush.

'I mean it, Alex. I know we joke around, but...' She hated herself for saying it, but being this close to him, it made things real. He was a man who'd loved a woman so much that after she'd died, a piece of him had too. She'd been hurt by a man who couldn't even keep it in his pants for twelve months.

She needed to concentrate on her career, like she should have been doing in the first place. She wasn't the woman for Alex Morrison, she knew that. She was too stubborn, too driven to be the other half of someone else again. She'd tried once, and that was enough.

The issue was, being in this man's orbit made her wish she was the type of woman that could be Alex's forever. She'd liked him the first moment she'd set eyes on him. He was brooding, effortlessly sexy. Commanding in his role, strong and fierce. He loved his firehouse family and had made her feel at home. Like she was part of something. Basically, she was starting to crush hard on her widower friend, and she was trying to find reasons to leave him standing there and go off to bed.

But everything in her was telling her to do it. Throw caution to the wind. She was supposedly dating him anyway. He knew the score, right? 'If we do this, we both need to be okay with it just being this. No weird aftermath. I... can't leave 17. It's my dream, Alex. It's bad enough having John there.'

'I get it.' He pulled her closer. 'No feelings, no expectations. No weird aftermath. I know what this is, and what it's not, but ever since John came along, I don't know, I just want to be there for you, and that's a new feeling for me. You're my friend, Lexie. I got you.'

'I know that.'

He scanned her face as if he was trying to find the answer to something, and then stepped away. 'It's late. You should get some sleep.' He leaned in, his stubble tickling as he brushed his lips against her cheek. 'Night, Bug.'

She didn't sleep that night. *Kissing or no kissing* replayed in her head over and over. She needed to talk to Win, and fast.

'Wait, so he's pretending to be your boyfriend to chase John off, but he wants to get it on too?'

'Get it on?' Lexie gagged. 'How old are you?'

'Hey. I'm practically an old married woman. You wouldn't send me the pics, but this is far better. So, what did you say? How did you leave things? Was it weird after?'

She picked at the comforter on her bunk. 'No, it was... normal. We just sort of hung out the day after, I read a book on the couch. He was out in the garage working on his truck. He went out with Kyle last night, and I was asleep before he got home. He made me breakfast this morning, and we drove to work.'

'You sound like a real couple, Lex. He made you breakfast? Wait, like Pop-Tarts and juice, or…?'

'Omelettes, from scratch. Coffee and juice.'

'Man.' Win was positively swooning down the phone. 'We need to double-date. He could teach Hunter a thing or two.'

'Hunter is amazing, Win. The man works his behind off and still puts smiley face notes in your packed lunch. Which, might I add, he prepares for you every night for when you're on shift.' Lexie could hear the pout when her friend spoke again.

'Fine, Hunter is perfect,' Win agreed readily. 'I guess you forget that stuff when you've been together awhile. Maybe Alex can start doing little notes for you too. After you bone him.'

'Win! I haven't decided yet!'

'Oh, shut up! You so have, and you know it. If it was a no, you wouldn't be talking about it like this with me. You would have turned him down already. I know you, remember? You don't do all this flip-flop stuff. When John cheated on you, it was done. Like, so done in one night. You ghosted the guy, moved your stuff out the next day and it was over. Instagram unofficial. Thank you, next. You were barely at my house before you'd got your own place. The fact that you stayed with Alex when he offered instead of coming to us is enough evidence for me. You could have moved place again by now if you really put your mind to it. You want to stay with him, admit it! You are so going to do this, and you should. Get yours.'

'It's not that easy. The guy is an adult. Like, a real adult. With a house and a dead wife, and… I don't know, he's just put-together. He doesn't scream "friends with benefits," he's more "get you barefoot and pregnant," you know?'

'Lex, you're a lead paramedic in one of the best firehouses in the state. He's not asking you to quit saving lives, marry him and have his babies. It sounds like he's on the same page as you. He's had a rough ride and wants to spend time with you, have some fun. He obviously likes what he sees, and rightly so!'

Win sighed loudly. 'Just because you dated John Coxley doesn't mean you're failing at life. You've been looking after yourself for far longer than most people do. John just made you forget that. Exes are the worst for stripping away how people were before them. That's the point. Everyone's kissed the odd frog, now go jump on your fake prince while you can. Seriously.'

The alarm sounded.

'Road traffic collision. Truck and ambulance required.'

'Saved by the bell,' Lexie muttered. 'Speak soon.'

'Go get 'em, tiger. Stay safe. Love you.'

'Love you too.'

CHAPTER SEVEN

THE ATMOSPHERE WAS off in the truck, but Alex didn't let it dim his mood. He was shattered after the other night, yet he felt like he was high on caffeine. He'd kissed Lexie. Finally, he'd got to touch those plump pink lips of hers, feel her curves under his fingertips. She hadn't given him a definitive answer, but it hadn't been awkward after. Yesterday, they'd done their own thing, but it had felt good, having her in his space. She hadn't mentioned going back to her place again either. Which he was glad about because the thought of her staying there made his stomach hurt. He wanted her in his place, where he could look after her.

Man, I am so gone for this woman.

A voice made him start. Kavanagh was looking at him quizzically.

'What?' he asked. 'You say something, Kav?'

They were in the front of the truck, Kavanagh driving. He turned the wheel with a low chuckle.

'Yeah. How come you never told me about you and Olsen?'

Alex couldn't help it, he smiled at the question. He liked the two of them being used in the same sentence, even if it was fake. 'I guess we were just seeing where it was going before everyone knew about it.'

'Mmm...' Kav wasn't buying it, he could tell. 'Makes

sense, but I thought you might have told me all the same. And you've been avoiding me.'

'Not avoiding.'

Totally avoiding.

'I've just been busy with Lex, that's all.'

At least that wasn't a lie. She had been taking up his time. Watching movies on the couch with her was becoming the best way to spend his time.

'That's fair.' Kavanagh levelled another assessing gaze his way. 'Why come out now? Seemed a bit odd, the timing.'

'Yeah well…' He nodded his head behind him. Coxley was in the back of the truck but he didn't want him overhearing.

He didn't miss the way he kept shooting glances at Lexie when he thought no one was looking. Didn't like it either. He'd backed off, but Alex could tell that the guy wasn't going to give up without a fight. Why he'd ever hurt a girl like Lexie in the first place didn't make sense. Alex hated cheating, always had. He didn't like smug men much either, and with the way Coxley felt so entitled to her, it wasn't something he ever wanted near her.

So keep her, then.

He silenced the thoughts in his head, like he always did lately, and lowered his voice to answer his friend. 'With the new team member, we figured it was time, you know.'

'Yeah.' Kav nodded, a knowing look in his eye. 'I think I do. Question is, do you know what you're doing? After Holly…'

The two men locked eyes for a second, before Kavanagh turned back to the road. Kyle Kavanagh was his best friend. He'd been the first person that he'd called when everything had happened, after Holly's parents. Kavanagh had driven straight to him, held him while he sobbed. Helped him arrange the funeral. Stood by his side through everything. He knew how much losing Holly had affected him. If it wasn't for Kav and the guys, he would probably have just sat on the couch in a crusty pair of sweatpants and given up completely. He'd even helped him move house, saying a fresh start would do him good. It had, but now Lexie was here, he realised he'd just been on autopilot. Now, he was fully awake and back at the controls.

Only thing was, he was Mr Commitment and Lexie was more than a little gun shy. He was hoping she was going to agree with everything he wanted for this arrangement, but the expiration date, and what it would mean, was something he didn't like to think about. A part of him was hoping she'd change her mind, he realised. Either way, Lexie Olsen was not someone he could walk away from. He wanted whatever pieces of her she was willing to give.

'I'm good, Kav. You don't have to worry about me.'

'I know, but I do anyway. That's how this works, with us. Just be careful, okay? You're not the kind of guy to do things half-heartedly. Especially when it comes to women. I'm not sure Lexie is that kind of woman.'

Alex knew what he was getting at. He'd been trying to talk himself out of this whole thing since this had started, but whenever he was around Lexie, he couldn't help himself. He'd been powerless. Every time he was near her he just wanted to make her life easier, make her smile. And moan.

He felt himself stiffen as he remembered the little noise she'd made when he'd touched her the other night. He would walk through fire to hear that again. It was like a drug, and he was fast becoming a needy addict.

'Lexie's different,' he said, more to himself than anything

else. 'Our friendship is solid, Kav. No matter what happens.' And he would make sure that he kept that, if nothing else, at the end of this. She was part of his life now.

'I know,' Kav said, patting him on the shoulder. 'Like I said, she's good for you.'

'I think we're good for each other. That's what I want to focus on. The rest of it, it's just noise.'

'All right, brother. I hear ya. Just make sure your eyes are open, that's all I ask.' He raised his voice, addressing the others. 'Heads up, boys, looks like a busy one.'

The sirens were blaring as both vehicles pulled up at the scene. Right outside Benny's coffee shop, the junction was closed off. Debris all over the road.

'Okay, guys, let's go!' Alex called out, jumping from the truck and running over to one of the attending police officers. Lexie and Taylor pulled up in the ambulance and grabbed their kit. 'What's the situation?'

'The SUV ran the red light, hit the Chevy side on. The driver of the SUV was dead when we arrived. Suspected heart attack. Had heart meds on his person. Two passengers in the Chevy, a Mr and Mrs Monaghan. Both in their sixties. The husband was driving, and we can't get the wife's door open. She's pretty messed up. Coroner is en route to collect the body of the other driver.'

'Copy that,' Alex confirmed, turning to see that Kav was already going for the equipment they needed. He ran over to the driver's side, assessing the cars as he went. The SUV was turned off, the whole front end crumpled like corrugated cardboard against the Chevy. 'Hodgens, ready with the Jaws of Life once the patients can be moved? Olsen, what's the status?'

Lexie was in the back of the car, leaning over the centre,

fitting Mrs Monaghan with a collar. Alex came in beside her, as his team outside started to prep for moving the SUV. The body had been removed there and was on the side of the road under a blanket, watched over by a police officer. 'Trudie here can be moved. She has a three-inch-deep laceration on the forehead from the dashboard. Glass embedded in the wound from the window. Her right arm is broken below the elbow. Her wrist is fractured. I've strapped it up for now till we can get her to the hospital. She's had some pain relief but we need to get her assessed when we get her out of here. Her blood pressure's a little too high. One-fifty over ninety-five.' She leaned in closer, securing the collar before shining her pen torch into Trudie's eyes. 'Pupils are responsive. Trudie, are you on any medication?'

Trudie didn't answer, she was in shock, babbling under her breath. Her husband answered for her. 'No, she's not on anything. Neither of us are. We walk a lot, keep fit. We were only in the car today because we wanted to get some groceries. I can't believe this is happening. That car came out of nowhere. They didn't stop. I didn't hear brakes, or a horn. They just didn't stop.'

'I know, Charlie, but everything's going to be okay. The other car had a medical emergency unfortunately, which is why they couldn't stop. Trudie, can you follow my light with your eyes?'

'Yes,' she croaked, her hand clasped around her husband's. 'I'm okay, dear. Just get my Charlie out first.'

'Not a chance,' her husband refuted, holding her hand that bit tighter. 'I'm staying right here, darling.'

Lexie met Alex's eye. 'He has superficial injuries to the face. Her side of the car took the full impact. Prominent bruising on the right-hand side of his arm. Complaining of pain in his shoulder, but it doesn't appear to be dislocated. Query possible collarbone fracture.

'Charlie?' She addressed him with a smile. 'We are going to get your wife out now, but we need you out first, okay? Give us all room to work while we get this door off. Will you let Alex here take you out?'

He was already wearing a collar, but he shook his head. 'No, I'm not leaving her in here alone.'

'What happened to the other driver?' Trudie asked, crying again. 'Are they okay? I don't understand what happened. Charlie, what happened?'

'It's okay, it's okay. We're fine. It was just an accident. We're going to be fine.'

Kav shouted to Alex. 'Ready with the Jaws!'

Alex took off his jacket, using it to shield Trudie and Lexie, who was still right there in the centre of them. 'You ready? I'll talk to Charlie.'

Before he could do anything, Coxley appeared at Charlie's door. 'Hey, Mr Monaghan. We really need you to exit the vehicle now. We have a paramedic waiting to have a look at you.'

'No.' Charlie gripped onto Trudie tighter. 'Not without her!'

'Sir, we don't have time for this—okay? You need to leave, now. Come with—'

Alex's voice was terse when he cut him off. 'Coxley, leave him. Priority is getting the door off. Go help Taylor get ready with the gurneys.'

'But—'

'That's an order, Coxley. Move.'

Lexie flashed him a look.

'There's no point stressing everyone out further,' he

explained. 'Him being in here keeps her calm. It's not about John.'

'I know,' she said, the corners of her lips tipping up. 'I agree, they need each other. Sometimes, you just need someone there, right?' His chest felt like it was going to crack wide open.

You're that for me. He wanted to say it badly, but it wasn't the time.

'We're good to go, right, Charlie?'

'Just get her out, please. She's my life.'

Alex put his hand on the man's arm gently. 'We've got this. Kav! We're ready!'

It took mere minutes to free Trudie. Kav had the door off in seconds, and Lexie didn't hesitate. Taylor and Coxley were ready with the gurney, and Lexie assessed her again. Her wrist was broken, and her ulna. Lexie chatted to Trudie and Charlie the whole time, helping her husband into the back of the ambulance with her. Alex closed the doors, banging on them twice once they were closed up. It hadn't even reached the end of the block before John was in his face.

'What was that about?'

Alex turned to face John, who was glaring at him like he was waiting for the first punch to fly.

'Excuse me?' The rest of the guys were packing up too, dealing with the removal of the cars, the police. Managing the crowds. 'Do you have a problem?'

'Yeah, I have a problem. I was trying to move that casualty, and you stopped me.'

'I stopped you because he wasn't in any immediate danger, but his wife was very anxious and disorientated. In pain.

She wanted him there, and her blood pressure was already high. I made a decision for the benefit of both of them.'

'For the benefit of them, or because your new girlfriend was making moony eyes at you in the back of the car? Is this how you get her all hot—'

'Don't.' Alex hadn't realised he'd stepped up to him, but they were toe-to-toe now. 'Don't finish that sentence. I am your lieutenant, Coxley, and I will write you up. If you have an issue with my command of the scene, then I suggest you take it up with the chief. Now get back to work.'

Coxley looked like he was going to spontaneously combust, his lips pulled back in an ugly snarl. Fists clenched; he chose to walk away. Which was a good idea, because it was taking everything Alex had not to smear him all over the street. Coxley was still muttering to himself when Alex called his name, stilling his retreat.

'Yeah?' he growled.

'Taking my lieutenant hat off for a second, I just wanted to be clear on something.'

Coxley's eyes narrowed, the indignation shining through his baby blues. 'And what's that?'

Alex closed the distance, crossed his arms to stop himself grabbing this petulant a-hole by the collar. 'Talk about my girl like that again, and we'll have a problem. In fact, I hear her name in your mouth again in any capacity other than professional, I'll make you my personal problem. And I have a very definitive way of solving problems, believe me. When I check you, you will know about it. Copy?'

His jaw clenched, but Alex kept his face straight. He knew full well that Coxley was having all his feelings right now. Deciding on which way to go with this. Alex wasn't a violent man, just the opposite in fact. The guy in front of him challenged the hell out of him. Like a magnet affecting his moral compass. Gone was the quiet, brooding Alex. His true north was Lexie now, and he wasn't going to let anything or anyone get to her. Holly flashed into his head.

Something got to her. You were right there and couldn't stop it.

He pushed the thought down. Lexie was a friend; the rest was fake. He wasn't in a relationship; he told himself for the tenth time since he'd started all this. The problem was, it was getting harder not to want the whole thing with her.

With Lexie, it was fun. He needed her brand of sunshine. He might have been lost forever if not for her, and he was out there taking risks. Standing up for her, doing things to make her day easier. When danger loomed, she was right there with him. Walking into the thick of it with him. At the building site, when the dust swallowed her up, he'd felt it. That hopelessness. Just for a moment, until she'd strode out of there with a life she'd saved. He hadn't been able to stop thinking about it since. A canon moment in his head.

Bad things happened, but without love, and reaching out to another person, life had been just as painful as revelling in the loss. Having someone who saw the pain, the loss and still found the humour, the good? That was worth fighting for.

Coxley was still standing there, looking like he wanted that too.

'Do I need to repeat myself? I said...' Alex leaned closer, his lip curling '...my girl is off-limits. Just do your job and leave the rest out of the house. Do you copy?'

'Copy, Lieutenant. Message understood.'

Alex threw him a curt nod. *My girl.* It had rolled off his damn tongue so easily, and he didn't even know whether

Lexie was going to take him up on his other offer. She hadn't mentioned backing out of the arrangement, or about staying at his place. Right now, he wanted three for three so badly he could taste it.

How bad was it going to be when this ended, and he had to watch her with someone else? Would they drop her off at the firehouse, open her door for her, hold her hand until they absolutely had to tear themselves away from her touch? Unbearable. Unthinkable. There also wouldn't be a damn thing he could do about it. She wouldn't be his.

Just like now.

He'd never wanted to feel vulnerable like this again, and the constant push-pull in his head was draining.

When he got back into the truck to leave the scene, Kavanagh was laughing.

'What?'

'Nothing,' he said, starting the engine. 'I'm just looking forward to seeing how all this plays out for you, brother.' He smirked at him before pulling out into the traffic. 'Never seen you so wide awake. Nice to have you back, man.'

Alex didn't say anything, but he couldn't help but agree in his head. Lexie had well and truly stirred him up, and now—he didn't want to go back to antipathy. Ever. Temporary or not, he wanted more of her. And the more he had, the stronger the feeling grew that not having her was scarier than losing her later.

The look of pleasant surprise on his face when he saw her waiting by his truck after shift made her stomach do that stupid flippy thing. He looked so handsome, lit up by the morning sunlight. She'd taken her hair down so it hung in loose waves around her shoulders, and she knew Alex had noticed. His eyes were hungry as he scanned her form, and she stood there and let him. Wanting him to see her. In his eyes, she felt beautiful. Perfect just how she was.

'Hey. Ready to go home?' he asked, that cheeky smile lighting him up from the inside.

Ah... Home. Her place? Was he regretting his actions?

It had been pretty weird when she'd come back to the firehouse after the hospital. John had kept his distance, which was welcome, but so had Alex. Which wasn't. The vibe had felt different after that call-out, but she didn't know why.

'Er...yeah. Sure.'

He frowned a little as he reached her by the passenger door. Some of the guys were leaving too, chatting away as they headed to their cars. The sun, peeking out from behind the huge, white clouds illuminated his face as he came to a stop right in front of her. 'You okay?' He brushed his fingers along the side of her face, pushing a loose strand of hair behind her ear. She nodded dumbly, mesmerised by the way he was looking down at her. Someone wolf-whistled behind him, but Alex didn't acknowledge it. 'I was thinking we could fire the grill up for lunch. I have some nice steaks. I figured we have a bit of a nap, sit out on the deck later?'

'At yours?'

'Er...yeah?' His brows knitted together, causing the deep ridge to form. She wanted to smooth it out. 'Are you not staying with me?'

Staying with me. Geez, he had a way with words. Was he even aware of it?

'Yes. Sorry,' she stammered. 'When you said "home," I just...'

He chuckled, reaching for her hand to pull her away from the door. '*Mi casa es su casa*, Bug.' He opened the door, taking her bag off her shoulder as she went to get in. He waited till she was buckled in before stashing both their bags in the back and sliding in beside her. 'So, my place, then? Steaks?'

'Steak sounds good.' Her stomach chose that moment to agree loudly, making him laugh again. 'Sorry. I'm starving. I didn't get much chance to eat today.'

'That's okay. We can hold off on the nap, have steaks for brunch. How were the Monaghans when you left them?'

'Good,' she said, smiling at the memory of the sweet older couple. 'He pretty much demanded to stay with her the whole time. They were so cute it made my teeth hurt.'

'It was nice, seeing that. Him not leaving her side.'

'Yeah, he reminded me a lot of you, actually.'

'Oh, yeah? You think I'm cute?'

'No.' She blushed. 'I meant the protective side.'

'I thought you hated all that,' he smirked, his arm coming over the back of her seat as he put the truck in Reverse and pointed it towards his house. 'The whole "knight in shining armour" thing.'

'I do—' she shrugged '—but it does kinda look good on you.' She drew in a deep breath. 'I've been thinking about what you said the other night too.' He didn't say anything, his eyes on the road as he drove them home. 'And I think, as long as we both know what this is, then we should do it. Ah! Not *it*, but…well…yes it, but also the kissing thing, and the…oh, man, you know what I mean.'

She pretended to open the car door, groaning. 'I'm going to throw myself onto the asphalt now. Bye.'

He reached for her hand, pulling it away from the handle and chuckling. When he changed gear, he linked his fingers with hers and placed them onto the gear stick.

God bless manual trucks. My fingers thank you.

'No need to end things, Bug. Not when things are just getting good.' He brought her hand up to meet his lips, kissing along the back of her hand from knuckle to wrist. 'You have the day off Saturday, right?'

'Yep. Same as you. And Sunday.'

'Nice. We can go to the party together. Hodgens is hosting that cookout. Saturday, I think we should go to your place, start clearing it out.'

'Alex!' she started to protest, 'I haven't said I would move into your place yet.'

He squeezed her fingers. 'Fake or not, no woman of mine is staying in some cold hell-hole when I have a home plenty big enough. Addendum to the arrangement.'

'What? You can't add a—'

'Sure I can. If you need a fake boyfriend, then he's one you also happen to live with.'

'People won't think that's weird, me just moving in two seconds after we—' she made quote marks with her free hand '—got together?'

'No, they won't, because as far as they know, we've been hot for each other since you came to 17. They bought that part, I think they'd buy this, and it will keep John off your back. Once I let it slip that our toothbrushes share the same mug.'

John. Of course. Somehow, she'd forgotten about her ex for a moment. 'Actually, he kept his distance when I got back. Maybe he's getting the message.'

Alex made an 'mmm-hmm' sound, flexing his fingers around hers in a distracting way.

'Okay.' She nodded. 'Let's do it.'

His grin was devilish when he looked across at her.

'Shut up!' She went to pull her hand away, but he held it

fast. 'I meant the moving in thing, but I pay my way, and only till I find a decent place. Deal?'

Pulling into his drive, he pulled her hand to his chest, tilting his head down to drop a soft kiss onto her skin. 'Addendum approved, Bug.' He cut the engine off, but neither made a move to leave. She could feel his heart hammering under their twined hands.

'I'm going to give you the full boyfriend experience, you know.' Another brush of his lips.

'Oh, yeah? What does that look like? Steaks and packing my stuff up?'

'Oh, that's just the basics. I'm a full-time protection detail at work and at home too.'

'Like Kevin Costner?'

He snorted out a laugh.

'Yep. Coxley won't get near when I'm around. I'd bend him like a pretzel before I let him hurt you again.'

She barely, barely managed to repress the little feminine shudder at that one. Her hard shell was starting to goo up. She needed to remember that this was just temporary. A little adventure out of her normal life. Something she'd remember when she was old and grey, sitting in her rocking chair with her cats and thinking of her fling. The time when she was a young, wild thing.

'Good to know,' she breathed. Her voice was practically a heated pant, and the turn of his head let her know that he'd clocked it. 'So, what does the fake girlfriend do, to deserve all these special treatments?'

His grey eyes turned darker as they zeroed in on her. The slightly heaving chest under her sweater, the way her tongue flicked out to moisten her dry lips. She knew he was taking in every detail. He always made her feel the centre of his attention, seen in the best way possible.

'Well, kissing would be a good start.'

'Oh, yeah?'

'Hell, yeah,' he rumbled, his brows waggling comically. 'I haven't been able to stop thinking about that kiss in the kitchen.' He moved closer, still holding her hand to his chest. She could feel his muscles shifting beneath as his face came to meet hers. 'Those lips of yours are addictive.'

'Oh, really—'

She soon stopped her teasing when his mouth moved closer. He brushed his lips against hers, the stubble tickling her skin as he rubbed from side to side. His eyes still on hers, so near and intense her vision swam. 'Alex,' she breathed, before grabbing the back of his head and well and truly closing the distance. All pretence of their banter was gone now, replaced by pure, unadulterated exploration. He tasted of mint, fresh and warm as she slid her tongue inside his mouth. He groaned, meeting it with his and tilting her head to deepen the kiss. After a few moments, he groaned again, as though frustrated, and pulled away.

'Stay right there,' he rasped, dropping a kiss on her mouth as if he couldn't help himself before stepping out of the truck.

She was just wondering what the hell was going on when he opened her door and reached into the truck to pick her up. Her legs wrapped around his waist automatically as he lifted her up, kicking the truck door shut with his foot as he carried her towards the front door. His lips dipped to her neck, tasting her, and she felt the hard length of him right against her core, making her gasp.

'Lexie. You smell amazing.' He breathed her in, running

his nose along the length of her neck, his hands under her ass, holding her to him as he strode up the steps to his house like she weighed nothing.

She reached up, grasping his hair between her fingers as she pulled his mouth back to hers. Kissing him with everything she was worth and feeling the heat between them. He adjusted her in his grip, shoring her up as he tried to put his key into the lock. She giggled when he cursed, wiggling out of his grasp so he could open the door. The second he'd gotten it open, he turned and scooped her right back up again, pinning her against the wood the second it closed behind them.

'We should have been doing this the whole time,' he added, making her smile between frantic kisses. 'I haven't stopped thinking about this.'

'Me neither,' she panted, pulling at his shirt to feel more of him. 'Off,' she urged, feeling him smile against her lips.

'So needy, my girl,' he huffed, stepping back and pulling his T-shirt up over his head. He was…beautiful. Like no calendar in the world would ever do him justice. She'd seen him shirtless before, it wasn't a total shock.

This was different. Just for her. Standing there in front of her right now, his grey eyes full of lust, his lips swollen from her kisses, hair tousled from her fingers running through it. This was next-level hot.

'You're gorgeous. Come here.'

His grin was lascivious but then he suddenly stilled her hands. 'Wait,' he murmured. 'I might regret this, but I kind of want to slow this down a bit.' He looked a bit sheepish, running his hand along the back of his neck. 'It's been a while.'

Lexie's libido felt the icy sting of his words. 'Oh, wow. I'm sorry. I got a little carried away.'

'No, Bug. I want this. You don't know how much I want this.' He dropped the T-shirt to the floor, stepping back into her space. 'I just want to savour it. Do things right. Is that okay?' he asked, and she saw his vulnerability then.

He was nervous, and her heart skipped a beat. This man had always been there for her, making her laugh when no one even realised she was down. He'd stepped up to the plate without her asking or even thinking she needed help. And now he was asking something from her.

'Just tell me what you need.'

'I really fancy you, Lexie. You're just…beautiful. I just need to take this at my pace, that's all. When we finally do this, I want it to be right.' He huffed out a laugh. 'And last longer than five seconds.'

'Oh, I thought you were…'

'You thought I was all in my head.' He shook his head. 'I know what I'm doing with all this, it's not about my past. I just don't want to embarrass myself by acting like a horny teenager. I've been wanting this for a while, Bug. If I'm honest, since you first walked into the firehouse with those sweet little cupcakes.'

She laughed then, feeling the relief as she brushed her hands along his chest. 'Okay, I get that.' She gave him a swift kiss. 'How about we eat?'

'Too early for the grill?'

She dropped a kiss onto the bridge of his nose. 'Not for me. I'm famished, and you just worked up my appetite.'

I'm such a cliché, Win.

Why? Oh, Lord. Don't tell me John talked you round. I will come down there and beat you with the firehose.

No, not him. Eugh! Alex. I'm at his place. He made us steaks and salad for breakfast, and now I'm on his couch while he washes the dishes. I swear, the man knows how to use a grill.

She sent Win the photo she'd snapped out on the deck. A shirtless Alex, wearing a long apron and turning a steak on the grill. The light had caught him just right, making his blond hair look lighter.

That's Alex? Lucky girl! He is hot. Smoking hot. As in my phone just melted.

I know, right? I swear—I could get used to having a man take care of me. He wouldn't even let me help him clear up. He sent me to the couch to read, and then he wants to watch a movie before we get some sleep. See, cliché? I am becoming one of those women we hate.

What, a woman who lets a man do stuff for them? Just because we have boobs doesn't relegate us to the kitchen. That's not cliché, that's being modern. Although, I swear being a kitchen servant doesn't sound too bad—if he brings that apron.

I said I'd move in, till I find a place. We're clearing my place out on Saturday if you and Hunter want to come help.

Sure, I'm off shift. You do realise you just did the 'we' thing, right?

See? Cliché. Although moving in with a fake boyfriend

isn't totally new for me. At least both of us are aware of it this time.

Alex is not John. Pretty sure he wouldn't be going to all this trouble to help you if he was. Do they get on? Must be weird at work. So glad Hunter isn't in medicine.

Well, he said earlier that he would pretty much fold John into baked goods if he didn't pack in the longing looks and fake pining.

Lexie laughed at the eye-roll emoji that popped on-screen. He's such a loser. Also, if that happens, send pictures. I could use a laugh sometimes on shift. It's my day off and I am already dreading tomorrow.

The whole point of this was to keep my career clear of scandal. A low-key fake relationship, not igniting World War Three. Alex has been pretty cool though. I think he likes getting under John's skin, but he's very low key about it. It's pretty hot, I just hope John moves on to his next victim soon.

Something in the back of her mind, however, didn't want that to happen too soon. Not because of her ex. He was nothing more than a bad memory and an inconvenience at work now. But because if their plan worked out how they'd planned, then John would leave her alone for good, start dating someone else, and then there would be no need for a fake relationship. When she thought about that, it didn't feel good.

Would she still stay here after they broke it off? That

would be beyond weird, right? And more to the point, if she got a taste of what it was like to be in his bed, as well as his house, how would it feel to go back to living alone again? Her phone beeped, cutting off her inner soul-searching.

Just enjoy it, girl. I mean, he's hot. He wants you at his place. He obviously likes you, and you need some fun in your life. Seriously, you've been working so hard to get where you are you forgot to lift your head up and enjoy the ride. And speaking of riding…have you opened his hydrant yet?

No. Not yet.

Not greased his tool? Stoked his embers?

No. And keep this up and I won't tell you anything ever again. I swear, you get one more phallic firefighter joke and I'm cutting you off.

I wonder how big his pole is. Do you think you can fit one hand around it when you slide down?

And you're done.

Totally worth it. See you Saturday. Stop thinking and start doing. Him.

'Something funny?'
She hadn't heard him come into the living room. Her book was open on the arm of the chair, so she couldn't pretend it was her novel that had her giggling.

'Just messaging Win.' He quirked a brow, but no way in hell was she telling him about their conversation. 'She and Hunter said that they can come and help with the move, if that's okay.'

He flopped down on the couch next to her, passing her one of the soda bottles he was carrying. 'Sure. I mean, I'd like to meet them. Do they both know…everything?'

She shook her head. 'I'm pretty sure Hunter doesn't, but I haven't really seen either of them lately what with work and everything. Win knows the truth though.'

'*Knows* knows?' He reached for the remote, leaving Lexie distracted by corded forearms.

'Yep.' When he shot her an amused look, she shrugged, taking a drink to quell the blush in her cheeks. 'She's my best friend.' He gasped dramatically, and she nudged him with her elbow. 'Best female friend, Touchy. I tell her everything, but she's cool.'

'She is? No worrying about me corrupting you?'

She snorted. 'No. She's not worried. I'm sure she'll interrogate you anyway.'

'That's cool. What do you feel like watching?'

The yawn escaped her as she looked at the movies he was scrolling through. 'I don't watch a lot of television. I swear, the most films I've watched have been with you.'

She yelped when he tugged her across the couch, until she ended up in his lap.

'Fine, no movie. Let's make out.'

CHAPTER EIGHT

WHEN SUNDAY CAME AROUND, the day of Hodgens's cookout, Lexie was so nervous, but the second she walked in with Alex, she relaxed. It felt good, having him to walk in with. Holding her hand as they walked over to greet the rest of the squad. Hodgens's place was just like Alex's, but his wife was the biggest surprise.

She was like a whirlwind compared to Hodgens, who loved to tell long-winded stories about nothing, and always napped in front of the TV in the firehouse. Matilda didn't stop once, throwing more food onto the already groaning table. Slapping Hodgens on the butt when she passed him. Scooping up their five-year-old son for a dance around the garden when the music started playing from a speaker sitting on the kitchen windowsill.

Meanwhile, Hodgens looked so happy in his element, telling his stories and cooking sausages, burgers and huge slabs of meat on the grill.

John was the only fly in the ointment, really.

Lexie had worn a pretty blue dress, little white flowers on it. Feminine for her. She'd felt so awkward in it, at first. Had almost changed for her trusty staple of dark blue jeans, cute top and black worn leather jacket. Until Alex had come downstairs and seen her outfit.

'You really are trying to kill me, Olsen,' he'd breathed and she'd revelled in his hungry gaze washing over her. Head. To. Toe. The man practically drank her in, nuzzling at her neck when he crossed the room to put his arms around her. 'You look edible,' he'd growled before nipping her neck gently. 'I love you in a dress.'

'Girly, huh?'

He'd shrugged, drugging her thought process to stupor levels as he kissed the life out of her. 'You'd look sexy in a damn sack. Wear what you want. It's all gravy, baby.'

She reminded herself of his little joke when John took his chance to talk to her. Alex was chatting with the others at the bottom of the garden, and she'd gone to wash her hands after she'd tackled some ribs with gusto. Another thing that Alex had appreciated—watching her with wonder as they'd sat at one of the many tables set up outside. She walked out of the bathroom and collided with a solid chest.

'Oh, sorry— John! What do you want?'

He took a step back, holding up his hands and leaning around the far wall. She should have known he'd ruin this. She'd been having such a good time with everyone. After their movie night, Alex had wordlessly turned off the TV, whispered, *time for bed* to her and lead her right to his bedroom door. When she'd looked at him quizzically, he'd shrugged. *Just to sleep. I don't want to say goodbye to you yet. I need more snuggles.* No sane woman would turn that down.

I, Lexie Olsen, being of sound mind and body...

She'd woken up wearing his T-shirt, the material bunched up above her panties. Alex's hand spanning her stomach, his breath skittering across her cheek. Front to back, connected together. Right. She had a feeling her bedroom wasn't going to be used much, if that human blanket was on offer.

'You know what I want.'

A voice pulled her out of her thoughts of warmth.

Oh, right, John. Of course he's cornering her here. Chicken.

'But Sarachek said you've moved in with Morrison. What the devil are you playing at, Lex? You have a place.' His brows crashed together. 'Did you get evicted or something? You could have stayed with me. At our place.'

She snort-laughed, making his face darken. 'I meant I would have taken the couch. I know you're with...*him*.' He spat the word out as if she was dating Nosferatu. 'Don't you think it's a bit fast?'

'No,' she surprised herself with the speed of her answer. 'I don't at all. My lease was up in two months anyway, and it made no sense getting a new place when I'm at Alex's house all the time anyway.' It was the truth, not that she needed to explain herself. 'Look, I need to go. If Alex sees you there will be a scene.'

'I don't care about him; we are not at work now.'

'No, but the answer is the same, John.' She sighed, and when she went to pass him, he didn't stop her. Which was a good thing because she needed to practise her self-defence skills. It had been a while since she'd thrown a punch.

'I have moved on. I am happy with Alex, and even if I wasn't, we were never right for each other. Not really.'

John looked downcast, but he surprised her by nodding slowly. 'Yeah, seeing you two together clued me into that one.' He straightened up, rolled back his shoulders. 'He'd better take care of you.'

'I will,' a deep, growling voice came from behind her. Turning, she saw Alex standing there. A couple of bottled beers in his hand. His eyes were locked on John behind her, his lip curved into a 'touch her and die' snarl.

Ovaries, don't explode on me now.

His eyes dropped to meet hers, and she watched them thaw, and melt. 'I missed you,' he said simply, and something in the way he looked at her screamed that it wasn't for John's benefit.

'I missed you too, Kitten.' She took the beer from his grasp, reaching up to kiss his luscious lips.

'Caveman,' she whispered. His mouth lifted in one corner.

'Woman, mine,' he whisper-growled, making her whole bottom half shiver.

'Drink beer, go home to bed,' she whispered back, matching his Neanderthal voice. The rumble from his chest as he pulled her to him while walking them both back to the garden was all she needed by way of answer. It had put John in his place too, because he kept his distance after that. She spotted him looking her way a couple of times, but it was like Alex knew too. Every time she felt John's eyes on her, Alex was there with a touch of her hand, an arm pulling her closer. She felt…protected. Drunk on the care the man on her arm showed her. Before long, she'd almost forgotten her ex was even there.

It was dusk when the cab pulled up outside his house. She'd spent the whole ride in his arms, his hand on her chin as he kissed her home. It wasn't pure lust, it felt like something else. Making out in the back seat conjured up horny teenagers, but this was more than that. Like he was cherishing her with his lips.

He paid the driver, pulling her out of the back seat with him and shutting the door behind her. As the taxi pulled away, he turned and claimed her again. Dipping for a moment, he wrapped his arms around her back and the backs of her thighs as he lifted her into his arms, lips locked the whole time. The only moments he let her down were to open his front door and when he lowered her down to his bed.

'I can't wait any longer to have you, Lexie.' He stood in front of her as she lay, hair fanned out on his bed. 'You looked beautiful today.' He blushed,shaking his head in wonder. 'You always do.'

She didn't say anything. She needed to be with him too. Shrugging her jacket off her shoulders, she started to take off her kitten heels, but he sank to his knees before her. His touch was like a molten caress against her ankles as he took them off, one by one, and dropped them to the floor. She leaned forward, lifting the skirt of her dress from under her and taking it off. Relished the sucking in of his breath when she bared herself to him. He leaned in, kissing the tops of her breasts as she made light work of the buttons on his shirt.

He grew impatient, growling in protest as he stood to remove his clothes. She took off her bra, and he laid her back on the bed. Just their underwear between them as he lifted her like a feather higher up the mattress.

'I'm…er…safe,' he murmured, brushing her hair away from her face. 'It's been a long time.'

'I'm on birth control, and clean. I got checked…after—'

He placed a long finger against her lips, and she kissed it. 'There's no one else but us in this bed, Bug,' he smirked, before shuffling down and taking one of her nipples into his warm, dirty mouth. 'Mmm…' His low voice rumbled right out of him into her.

The sensation of him sucking and licking at her shot right

to the core of her, and she reached for him. Had just got her hand into his pants, onto his length, when his hand shot out.

'Easy there. I need this to last, and you're so fricking hot, it's not going to be easy.'

He pushed her hand out and up onto his chest, over his heart. 'You feel that? You're wrecking me, Lex.'

'I need you,' she told him. 'I don't mind the wait.' He raised a brow.

'Oh, darling, we're not waiting. I'm going to have you. I want you all around me.'

He cupped her sex and slipped into her underwear. Rubbing his fingers right where she needed him to. The little bundle of nerves in her pants had a party. She could practically hear her libido cheering as he kissed her again, and sank one finger into her.

'Alex,' she half screamed, as he hooked one, then two fingers against her wall and damn near made her come on the spot. Her vision was blurring as his fingers worked, his mouth everywhere. Breast to breast, lips to neck. He nipped her collarbone with his teeth, laving the spot right away with his tongue. 'The deal is you come first. Then I'll give you everything I want to.'

She moaned. Alex Morrison was a dirty talker. She knew that, but hearing it from his lips as he made her climax with his hand? There needed to be a new word for *hot*, because it just didn't cut it.

'Come, baby,' he urged when she started to shake. Upping his tempo, his breath ragged. She could feel him hard against her body as he pumped into her, twirling and teasing. It built, built, built inside her, until…

'That's it. Now, sweetheart. Show me how you come. God, I've been waiting for this. Look at me, darling.'

She locked eyes with him, and jumped right over the edge. He moaned low in his throat, his free hand coming up to caress her cheek as she rode out her orgasm, rocking on his fingers and grabbing his hand as she moaned out his name. 'Alex, Alex. Oh, yes!'

All the bones in her body disappeared. Her vision swam. Geez, she had been missing out on the sex front. It had never been like this. He played with her as she came down, her body feeling empty as he slowly slid out of her. Looking her right in the eye, the dirty animal licked his fingers clean of her.

'Delicious,' he rumbled, and she almost came on the spot again.

'Alex,' she managed to get out. 'Take those pants off. Now.'

He chuckled, doing what she asked and coming to rest in between her thighs. 'Bossy woman,' he teased.

'Shut up and get inside me,' she begged, and his eyes turned dark. Flicking his arm under one of her legs, he hoisted it onto his shoulder, lined himself up and…stilled. She was just about to ask what was wrong, when she locked eyes with him and saw that he was trying to get control of himself. She waited, beyond turned on, beyond gone for this man. She could feel his tip just nestling inside, feeling the girth of him even through her slick heat.

'That's it,' he praised, dropping his lips to devour her once more before pulling back. His free hand was behind her head, fingers spanned around her nape loosely. 'Don't take your eyes off me.'

'Who's bossy now?' she breathed, and he grinned devilishly, before pushing inside.

He felt like silky steel as he slowly slid home. His neck

muscles straining, his biceps rippling, he took her, inch by gloriously sexy inch. Not taking his eyes off her once, hooded lids and kiss-swollen mouth open in a silent O...

They both groaned when he was finally sated.

'This is how I die,' he murmured, and she felt her lips curl into a smile that ignited his own.

They lay there, connected in every way. Smiling at each other at how easy and comfortable this moment was. How utterly, irrevocably erotic it was to be so in sync. Best friends, lovers. There were no lines now. 'You feel so good, wrapped around me.'

She huffed out a ragged breath. 'Give me more, Alex. Please.'

He shuddered, the shiver rolling through him as he pulled back, so slowly she barely felt him move, and then thrust back in. Hard and sure as he pulled her tighter to him. 'Yes,' she breathed. 'Eyes on me, please.'

He locked eyes with hers, and built up a rhythm. Every thrust bringing her closer to another wave of pleasure, and she was lost to it, to him. 'You're so wet for me,' he rasped, his movements less measured with every thrust. 'I'm so gone, Lex. You've wrecked me.'

She barely heard him as wave after wave rolled through her. He moved his hand from her leg, bringing it down between them to caress that nub once more, and stars exploded behind her eyes. He knew, of course he knew. His smile of victory was written across his face.

'That's it, Lexie, come for me, sweetheart. Let me feel it.'

She exploded around him, her arms reaching for him as she kissed him, moaning into his mouth as she came and came. He never stopped, his fingers, his hips, and then she felt it. He tore his lips away from hers, burying himself in her neck as he roared his own release, thrusting his hips against hers at a bruising pace as he shuddered and pulsed inside her. His thrusts grew shorter, slower, as he breathed hard into her neck.

When they had both stilled, breaths ragged, he pulled out of her slowly, turning her to face him as he reached for her. Sticky and sweaty, he didn't care. He locked his legs around hers and rubbed one hand along her back, not breaking his gaze as she lay her head on his arm. He looked…satisfied. Utterly wrung out, and she felt so proud to have been the one to do that to him.

He was hers, if only for a short while. She tried to ignore the pang in her heart, but as she lay there, listening to his breaths grow shallow, she wondered if what she had done had wrung her out too.

She'd never expected it to be like this. So…hot, but also personal. Meaningful. Alex Morrison didn't make love like a caveman. He was sexy as hell, strong and tender, but it was more than that. He had just made love to her. And she him. This wasn't some agreement addendum. Alex had claimed her, in every way a man could a woman. And the thought of losing this, losing moments like tonight, scared the living daylights out of her.

Oblivious to all this, his eyes closing as he held her tight, he didn't see it. Couldn't see the panic in her eyes as she buried herself deeper into his chest, wishing that she could get rid of the bad thoughts just by being in his arms.

'That was amazing,' he mumbled, his words thick with sleep. 'So tired. You're amazing, Lexie. That was everything.'

'I thought so too,' she whispered back. 'I never thought it would be like that.' Truth. Or as much as she could admit.

Something had shifted deep within her, but the default fear she harboured was choking the life out of it.

'I did,' he said, his voice low and slow as he drifted off. 'I knew you were it.' And then he said something that flicked the panic button in her brain. The one with the alarm attached, telling her to run. 'Love you, Lexie. Love you… so much.'

That was the moment she left him lying in the bed, grabbing her clothes and running for the door as if the room were the flames of hell.

He was hot on her heels, catching up with her in the kitchen.

'I don't understand,' she blurted out, even though she did. She'd been right there. In that moment. It wasn't lust, the sex they'd just had wasn't some hookup. It was lovemaking, period. She'd felt the words herself, prickling the back of her throat like needy, stabby knives.

She'd wanted to say them. Badly. She wanted to be the type of girl who heard those words and only heard the joy in them, the hope in his voice. She wasn't though. She was a jaded, closed-off woman who should never have gone down this road in the first place. This was meant to be a way of getting rid of John, killing his plans for the two of them once and for all.

Now Alex was here, telling her how he'd fallen for her. The man who'd loved his wife so much that he'd locked his heart in a box after she'd passed and melted down the key. She'd changed that. Changed him, just as he'd changed her. It wasn't enough. She'd been here before, letting someone in, and it had hurt.

John had ripped that sense of security she'd secretly longed for all her life into pieces. He wasn't half the man that

Alex Morrison was, which meant that when this ended, and it would, one way or the other, it would hurt twice as much.

She cared for Alex so much, trusted him, wanted to be there for him like he was for her. When that ended? She'd be alone again, but this time she wouldn't be able to squash it down and go through the motions. This, ending? It would destroy every part of her. Her career, her sense of self. Her heart. And his. He'd done this for her, and she'd ruined him. He'd learned to take that leap, but he was jumping alone.

Alex was looking right at her, as if he knew she was processing everything and giving her the time to do it. She wanted to scream at him, tell him to stop being so nice to her. That she didn't deserve his patience. She'd done this, it was her fault. She'd moved in here, allowed him to let her into his home, his life, his heart. And now she had to leave them all.

'Say something, Lex. I know you're all in your head right now, but you don't have to be. Not with me.'

That was the point though, wasn't it? She might never be that girl who said yes to love, not fully. Alex deserved better, and she figured that eventually, he'd figure that out too. He knew what real, giving love was. Sooner or later, what she could offer to him wouldn't be enough, and then she'd be at 17 avoiding an ex all over again. She should have walked away so much sooner than this. She hadn't needed a fake boyfriend for a while, she should have stuck to the plan and ended all this while they were both emotionally intact.

Now he was in her heart, and it was torture to rip him out.

'I...we had a deal, Alex. This was meant to be no feelings, remember?'

His brows crashed together, that ridge in his skin deepening. It took her breath away, knowing that she had put it there and now she'd never be able to smooth it away.

'I know, Lex but that was before.'

She had to swallow to get her words out. Her legs felt like jelly, but she managed to stand tall just the same.

'Before what?'

'Before I truly knew you. Before I kissed you. Before we lived together, before we were us. Before we made love to each other like we did. It wasn't just sex, and you know it. I can't go back to being friends, Bug. I want more than that. I know you have doubts, but I'm not pushing for anything. I just want to know that you are in this, for real. No more fake boyfriend and girlfriend. I think we both know we've been more than that for a while now. I know I have.

'We're good together. I don't want you to go get your own place, if you don't want that. I would love nothing more than for you to stay here, with me. We can make this our place, or buy somewhere new together down the line, if you want that.'

Alex smiled tentatively at her and shrugged. 'I'd be happy to do anything you want to make this work, Lex. I don't need a ring, or a plan. I am not asking for anything you haven't already given me. I just want to be in this, with you. Fully.'

He came forward, and she could feel the tremor in his hand as he cupped her cheek. 'I don't want to freak you out. I love you, Lexie Olsen. So much sometimes I can't breathe without looking at you. Knowing you're close. I wasn't living, before. When I lost Holly, I shut down. Figured I'd had love, and that was that. Till I met you, Bug. I fought against it, told myself we were just friends, that I was doing this fake thing to protect you. Help you out, but I know that wasn't true. I couldn't think straight when Coxley was near you.

I wanted to tell him he was an idiot for not seeing what he had, because I saw it from the first second I saw you.

'I loved Holly,' he went on, 'but what I feel for you? There aren't enough words to tell you how much I adore you. I feel like you were sent to the firehouse for me, baby. To show me that life was still good, that I could know a new kind of happy. I'm head over heels for you, Lex. I swear when you walked into 17, you shook me right out of my head. You were good for me, so good. I want to be that for you. I want to be your one. The one guy you never have to doubt, or worry about, or not be yourself around. I know you, Bug, and I love what I see. I… I love you. So much I think I might lose my mind if you're not mine.'

He was cradling her now, his thumb running along her flaming cheeks as she reeled from the depth and emotion of his words. She'd felt her heart skip, stutter, race to catch up and then hyperventilate all in the space of his heartfelt speech. This man was utterly perfect. She didn't deserve him. She didn't know a woman on the planet who did.

Even as she looked into his eyes, memorising every detail of his stunning grey eyes, she knew whoever he chose was the luckiest girl in the world. Because Alex was a forever guy.

She just wished she had the courage to be a forever girl.

For him, she wished it so much. But life had taught her that nothing was forever. He'd already lost a wife. It was better to break his heart now, instead of down the line when it would be much, much worse. For both of them. People left; they changed. She couldn't bear that again. Her career wasn't the only thing she'd mess up forever.

'Say something, please?'

This was it. This was the moment. He'd told her how he felt, had been brave enough to put it all out there.

I'm such a coward.

She drew in a shuddering breath, blinked away the tears that threatened to brim over, and she ended it.

'I can't.'

He winced, as if her words were steel blades sliding past his ribs. She felt his fingers flex around her face, not releasing her. 'I'm sorry, Alex, but we knew what this was. I have feelings for you, but everything we agreed still stands. I can't be with you like that, not fully. I don't have it in me. We'd end, and I belong at 17. The whole point of this was to keep my career going, and when we're over, it would be awful.'

His shoulders stiffened before he took a small step back, dropping his hands. She mourned his touch, knowing she wouldn't be feeling it again. It struck her like a bolt of lightning. 'So that's it? You don't want to try?'

'I just think we should stick to the plan.'

Folding his arms, Alex looked down at his feet, the breath puffing out of him in a huff. 'The plan was from before we knew what we mean to each other, Lex.' He lifted his head, meeting her eyes. 'Or am I alone in this? I'm not expecting you to love me right now. I know I kind of blindsided you—'

'Blindsided me? We agreed we wouldn't do this!'

'I know.' He started to pace in front of her, rubbing the heel of his hand on a spot on his chest as if he felt pain there. 'I know that, but I couldn't help it. I fell in love with you, and I don't regret it.'

'It won't last,' Lexi rebutted, shielding herself by folding her arms around her chest. To hold herself together. To stop her from running right into his arms. 'We both know that. This is just…you know, lust. Proximity.'

'Proximity?' His face dropped into a scowl. 'So if I had offered this deal to another woman, asked her to live with me, the same thing would have happened. Right?'

Wrong. We are different, but I can't trust it to be forever.

'I don't know.'

'Yes, you do. It wouldn't have happened with anyone else. I didn't look at another woman after Holly, but I had the chance. I had offers. I didn't meet anyone worth it till you. I can't believe you could think that. You knew the old me, the man I was when you came to 17. Do I seem like the same man to you?'

Yes. No. I liked both versions.

'No, but—'

'Exactly. My life started again with you, Lexie. I want to look after you, as much as you'll allow me to. I want to be the man in your corner, forever. I don't care how we define this. I've always known that you have commitment issues, but I don't care. I just want to know that you are mine. The rest, we can deal with together. When and if you are ready for it.'

He came back into her space, his whole body agitated, antsy. 'Can't we at least try? It doesn't have to be some big thing.'

'Of course it does! It's too much. We live together, Alex. Everyone thinks we're some dream couple. It's a lot of pressure to live up to.'

'Screw what people think! We don't have to change a thing. We just drop the fake part, which is the only difference now! We can even keep separate rooms. I'm not going to suffocate you. We do this our way, like we did from the beginning. What matters is what *we* want, right?' He lifted his hand as if he was going to reach for her, but it stopped mid-air before he dropped it to his side. 'Is it because I said I loved you?'

The pain on his face was evident now, it loomed large in the space between them. 'Tell me, Lexie, how do you feel about me? Because I think you feel the same way.'

No. Don't make me lie to you.

She loved him so much she couldn't bear it. Every cell in her body was screaming at her to reach for him, to show him how much she wanted this. Wanted him.

From the first moment she'd seen him, the angry closed-off newbie she was had noticed him. Gravitated to him. Thought about him when he wasn't around. Her eyes searched for him at 17, knowing just being near him made her feel better. He lit her up from the inside, knew her so well. He accepted every flaw, every stubborn bone in her body. She would never find another man like him. Knew she wouldn't bother trying.

Why can't I just do this? Be with him? Why does my whole body just want to run in the opposite direction and reach for him at the same time? My head is telling me to run, that this will end with him being hurt. All while my heart wants to leap out of my chest towards him. I suck.

She didn't deserve his love. She knew she'd never keep it. 'I care about you,' she said instead.

Wow, Hallmark-card fodder right there.

She might as well have just said thank you when he'd declared his feelings. Years of being let down, relying on herself had hardened around her like a shell. If she let it fall away, she wouldn't survive losing him. It felt too…big, being loved by him. The pressure was too much.

Flight or fight, Lexie.

She was so tired of fighting.

'I… I like you, Alex.'

'You like me.' His voice was flat. 'That it?'

'Well, no. I really like you. I've enjoyed being with you, but…'

'But you don't want this to carry on, do you?'

'Alex, you're pushing me. I can't just say how I feel on the spot. We never said that this was going to be anything but what we'd agreed. You say you love me—'

'What?' The pacing started again. 'I don't just say that, I do! Are you really not getting this?'

'I get it, yeah. I just…can't. I don't want to fall out with you, but I…just don't see this going where you want it to. I think we should end things, like we agreed. We can tell people it just didn't work out. I'll go to Win's till I find a place.'

'No, I don't want you to leave. You belong here.'

You belong here. He was so steadfast, so certain. Of his feelings, of them. He didn't deserve this, and Lexie couldn't help but feel like she was running scared. For someone who was fearless at work, she sure was being a coward now.

'I'm sorry if this is too much for you. I just wanted to tell you where I stood. I never meant to scare you. I know that you have trust issues. I just thought we were past that. I can back off, take things at your pace. If you really want to move out, I'll help you find a place, but you have to know it's not what I want. The agreement—'

'Is over, Alex. We did what we needed to do. I think it's time to end this, before we hate each other. I never meant to hurt you. It kills me that I have, but I can't do this. I just can't give you what you want. What you deserve. It's not possible for me.'

He didn't say anything for the longest time. He just stood there, shaking his head and looking down at the floor. Eventually, he released a sigh that came from the depths of him, and met her eye once more.

'I understand. I won't make this any more difficult than it has to be.' After a long look, he straightened up, rolling his shoulders as if the tension was painful. 'I'll stay out of your way at work. However you want to spin the break-up is fine with me. I'm going to stay at Kav's, give you some space.'

'You don't have to do that, it's your place.'

'It's fine.' His throat worked as he tried to keep himself together. 'I don't want to lose you from my life. If friendship is all I can have, then I'll take it.' His smile was so sad, his eyes wet with unshed tears. A weak laugh huffed out of him. 'It might just take me a minute.'

The tears rolled down her face unchecked now. She'd ripped his heart out, and he was still thinking of her. Asking her to be patient with him while he recovered from what she had done to him. She'd caused this, she'd been right there with him the whole way. Every kiss, every touch, every moment. She'd felt it. Truly felt his love, and rejecting it was the hardest thing she'd ever had to do. Even now, as he came back to stand right in front of her, it took everything she had not to tell him that she was full of it. That she wanted him to stay, see where this went.

She just couldn't stop the fear and worry from choking off her words. Alex meant forever, and she'd been taught in life that nothing was. Everything and everyone in her life ended. They walked away, hurt her. Took her for granted, and even with everything Alex was, she wasn't brave enough to risk it.

'I'm so sorry,' she sobbed. 'I never wanted to hurt you.'

Her eyes were closed when she felt him take her into his

arms. Run his hand down her hair while he shushed her, wiped her tears.

'It's okay,' he soothed, which made her feel even worse. 'I moved too fast. I should have known, Lex. I knew what this was. I just… I don't know. I just hoped that if I kept loving you like I want to, it would be enough. Don't cry, please. It wrecks me.'

She sobbed harder, clinging to him selfishly so she could breathe him in one last time. Savour the feel of the man she didn't deserve. She told him as much. She could be honest with him on that at least. 'I'm so sorry. I don't deserve you. I wish I could be the person you want me to be. I want that for you.'

He shushed her again, wiping another tear away. 'You are the person I want, Lexie. Nothing you can do or say will change that. I get that you're scared of this. You don't trust it, but I know how I feel won't change. We're okay, Bug. You won't get rid of me that easily. I'm still here for you, sweetheart.' When he finally pulled away, she mourned the loss. 'I'll see you at work. I have my phone if you need anything.'

'You're really going?'

Stupid question. You just crushed him, and now you're sad he's leaving when he already told you he was.

Dropping a kiss on the top of her head, he nodded. 'Yeah. I'll just be at Kav's. I think we both need a bit of space right now.'

'Oh, okay. I can go to Win's though.'

He was already shaking his head. 'No, you stay here. Eat something, okay? I'll see you soon.' He bit at his lip, a rueful smile on his beautiful face. 'I do love you, Lexie. Whatever that's worth to you.'

She watched him head to the bedroom to dress, and she

didn't move. She was pretty sure her legs wouldn't work if she tried. She was still standing in the same spot long after the front door had closed and the noise from his truck had stopped. He was all around her. His scent on her clothing, the echo of his touch on her skin. Standing in his house alone was the loneliest she'd ever felt in her whole life, because she hadn't been left behind this time.

She had caused this. She was a coward, not able to take the leap with the one man she couldn't imagine ever letting her down. She could blame her upbringing, her parents, her past relationships for making her this way, but so what? People had trauma, real painful trauma. They moved on, they took that leap.

Alex had watched his wife leave this world right in front of him, and he was all in with her. Had been there for her since the minute she met him.

Why couldn't she just say yes? Risk it? She had before, with John. And that was the problem. She had just gotten her life back together from that, and she hadn't cared for him as much as she did for Alex. She'd recovered, survived. One thing she knew was that she wouldn't survive Alex Morrison. Not being with him was heartbreaking, but being in love with Alex, openly? Living together and being a proper couple with dreams and plans? Losing that was just not something she could get through. She didn't trust life not to pull them apart, and then what? Alex would be worse off. Breaking things off now was better for them both.

The one thing she was sure of was having Alex Morrison in her life. This way, she could guarantee never losing him. She just wouldn't be the one with him. Even as she lied to herself about that being okay, she didn't fool herself into feeling any better. At her core, she was pretty damn sure that she just let the best person she'd ever met walk out without even trying to put up a fight. So, she headed to her room and called her second favourite.

'Win, I need you. I think I really messed things up this time.'

CHAPTER NINE

KYLE KAVANAGH'S HOUSE was a few blocks from where Alex lived. The lights were on when Alex pulled his truck into the drive next to Kyle's car, and his huge dog was lying out on the front porch.

'Hey, Brody,' he called out to the cane corso, who didn't bother to get up but wagged his tail half-heartedly. The door opened before he got to the steps. Kyle was wearing sweats, and a quizzical look on his face. Alex could hear the football game coming from the lounge. 'Hey, bud.'

'Hey,' Kav said, stepping aside to let him in. 'Judging from your face, we're going to need alcohol. Is this a beer kind of talk, or do I break out the whisky?'

'Ice in mine,' Alex muttered, heading through to the lounge and slumping onto the couch. 'How come Brody's out on the porch?'

Kav came back from the kitchen with a bottle of whisky and two tumblers filled with ice. Alex took the bottle from him and poured out two strong measures.

'He hates sports,' Kav said, nodding to the dog they could see lounging beyond the screen door. 'Prefers it out there on a night till bedtime, even in the winter.' He settled back into his armchair with the whisky. 'So?'

'So.' Alex drained half the whisky and topped himself up. Kav raised a brow.

'So you going to say any words, or just get blasted on my couch? I figured you might have come round to finally tell me that your little subterfuge with Lexie was real.'

Alex felt his jaw drop. 'So, you knew, this whole time?'

Kav chuckled, shaking his head in his usual easy way. 'I didn't come down in the last shower, Morrison. I had it pegged from day one.' He shrugged, flashing him a rueful smile. 'I just figured that the two of you would work out that you had the hots for each other for real.' He pointed a finger his way. 'From the look on your face, something went wrong. Am I right?'

Alex released the groan of despair he'd been holding in since he'd walked out of his house, leaving Lexie behind. 'Yeah, well with your intuition, you should play the lottery.' He swallowed down the lump clogging his throat. 'It just snuck up on me, I don't know. I never expected to feel like this again. I didn't go looking for it, but she was there, man. I couldn't look away. Maybe I should have.'

'What happened?'

'I told Lexie I loved her. After we had the best sex of my life. It just slipped out.'

'That's what she said,' Kav quipped. Wincing when Alex shot him a death glare. 'Sorry. How soon after?'

'We were falling asleep and it just came out. I've been holding the words in for too long. I…thought I had felt a shift in her. I don't know. I thought she might have felt the same. Dumb move, I know. Anyway, she shot out of bed right after I said it. It was…brutal.'

Kav whistled through his teeth. 'I understand the drinking now.'

'Yeah,' Alex sighed. 'She ended it. She's moving out. I need to crash here tonight.'

'Well, you sure as hell aren't driving home. Did she not say anything back?'

'She says she likes me, but it was time to end it.' Saying it out loud really brought it home. She wasn't his anymore. If she was ever his in the first place. 'She's leaving. I just couldn't be there tonight. I didn't want her to leave either.'

'I get it. Lick your wounds tonight, go see her tomorrow.'

'I don't think there's any point. She was pretty clear on what she wanted, and it's not me. She dumped me the second I said it.'

'She doesn't mean it though.' Kav turned the TV down when the Giants scoring made the crowd erupt. 'I'm pretty sure she feels the same, dude. I've seen the two of you together. Nothing about the way she looked at you seemed fake. Is it Coxley?'

Coxley. God, I hate that guy.

'No. It's not him. But the fact she said yes to him, lived with him? It sucks.'

'Come on, man, we know how much of a douche he is.'

'Exactly, yet she was with the guy almost a whole year. He messed that up, not the other way around. She'd still be with him if he didn't step out on her.'

'And you'd still be with Holly if things had been different. The universe works in mysterious ways, my friend. We have no control over that, just what we do with what we have.'

'Yeah, well, I don't have her, do I? I scared the hell out of her, I think. I should never have told her I loved her. I just couldn't help it. It came spewing out of me. She was crying and everything.'

'Crying because you love her? Does that sound like a girl who doesn't care? Come on, man. Get some sleep here, and then go fight for her.'

'She doesn't want it, Kav. I don't want to be the next Coxley, all up in her face trying to force something that isn't there. I have to leave it up to her. She wants things at 17 to be normal, and so do I.'

'Totally normal, watching the woman you love from afar. Maybe you should ask Johnny Boy for some tips.'

'Not funny.'

'I'm not trying to be funny; I'm sitting here listening to you let the only woman who's made you feel anything since Holly, walk away without doing a thing to stop it. Is this what you want to be, Al? Back to your old lonely grumpy-ass self? 'Cause I'm telling you, the guys and I can't stomach it again. The house won't take it. You have to wake up to this, man, and fast.'

'What do you want me to do, hog-tie her in my house and hold her hostage till she falls in love with me? Do you know how this feels? I'm broken-hearted, man.'

'Finally!' Kav did something Alex didn't expect. He smiled.

'You're smiling at me? Cheers, bud! Appreciated.'

'Oh, shut up, man. I'm smiling because I just saw some fire in you again. Use it, dude! Fight for her! She's scared, right? We all know Lexie is a complicated woman. She's tough as hell on the outside, but she still wants someone to be with her, right? Everyone wants someone to come home to, bud.'

'You don't.'

Kav shrugged, turning up the television and staring at the screen. 'I have Brody, that's enough for me.'

'Liar.'

Kav snorted, draining his glass. 'Yeah? Well, that makes two of us. Get it together, Morrison. If you let our Lexie get away, the guys won't forgive you for it. You need each other, man. Make it work. She's scared, sure—but you're not. Not anymore. Be the thing she clings to when she needs something to hold her up. You've always been that for her anyway. Lex is not the damsel type, but whatever she sees in you, I know you have her back. She just needs to realise it for herself, that's all.'

Alex couldn't drink from his refilled glass because he was too busy gaping at his friend. Kav must have felt him staring, because he turned from the game with a questioning look.

'What?'

'Nothing.' Alex rumbled out a laugh. 'Just wondered when you got so good at this. Pretty philosophical for a jock.'

Kav turned back to the game. 'Yeah, well… I might not have my own dating life but I've seen enough of you guys messing up to figure out what works and what doesn't. Don't give up, Alex. That's all I'm saying. You guys are good together. The forever kind of good. She'll come around, I'm sure of it.'

Alex wanted to believe his friend more than anything. He wanted to go back home and cuddle up on the couch with Lexie like they used to. Laugh at her dancing while they listened to music in the kitchen, put food in the oven they'd made together. He wanted to not have said anything in the first place, but he couldn't hold back. Not when there was a chance that he could have kept her forever.

The look on her face when he'd spilled his guts. It wasn't horror, or revulsion. What he'd seen on her face was fear. Would she ever get over that? Would she ever take the leap, when she was so closed off?

The thought of not having her in his life was unbearable. More than anything, he knew that he needed her. He just wished that the prospect of being her friend didn't make him feel like he was being ripped apart from the inside.

'Maybe' was all he said to Kav. 'Good to crash here, right?'

'Of course. Just try to keep the wailing and gnashing of teeth down. I like my sleep.'

They spent the rest of the night eating pizza and watching the game, but Alex didn't remember a thing. He couldn't stop thinking about the woman who was back at his house. Wishing he could prove to her that being there, with him, would be worth all the fear. That he would take all that away, if she jumped into this with him.

CHAPTER TEN

'Morning, Olsen!'

Hodgens passed her a plate of scrambled eggs, buttered toast and crispy bacon.

'Morning. Thanks, I'm starving.'

She wasn't, but she didn't want to bring her personal stuff into work. It had been almost two weeks, and things were weird to say the least. Add to that the fact that she was sleeping in Win's spare room when she was off shift and wasn't eating or sleeping much, and life was pretty much a party. The worst of it though, was Alex. He was being so nice. So…normal. It hurt her to see him like that, as if nothing had happened. He'd been cordial, less jokey than usual and further away, but still the Morrison she knew and… had thrown away.

Win had been less than enthusiastic about her choices. Her best friend had basically chewed her out for not telling Alex the whole truth. But the reality was, Lexie herself didn't even know how she truly felt. It was all choked up with the fear of the future, the unknown. She couldn't stop herself from remembering the bad things from her past.

When Alex had declared that he loved her, she'd been right back there. Listening to her parents argue, and drink and swear at each other. Shouting about how they hated each other, that they never should have been together in the first place. Her mother always told her that choosing to be with her father was the worst decision of her life. She'd always wanted more out of life. For herself, a career of her own. A chance to make her time worth something other than being a wife. A mother. That resentment had trickled down from them to her own existence. She'd left as early as she could, not wanting to ever feel like that again. Not wanted, cast aside. She'd learned from an early age to rely on herself, and then that would never happen again. She could live her life.

Until the night she was on that sidewalk, in the cold, watching John grapple with his bit on the side. And then the feelings had slammed right back like a gut punch: the feeling of trusting someone else, allowing yourself to be vulnerable with that person. Watching as they'd held your vulnerable heart in their hands and then crushed it between their cold, untrustworthy fingers.

The old feelings of not being enough had come flooding back, and when Alex had declared himself to her, it was there again. Not all-consuming, or loud in her ears, but there all the same. The old her had come rushing back, and she just couldn't risk it. Couldn't risk being the one who wouldn't be enough for him, especially after his wife. Holly had been his world, and he was telling her that she would be his new one. If they didn't work out, it would wreck both of them and she couldn't risk it. She just hoped that the feelings would dwindle. That eventually they would be them again, and she could cope with the rest of it.

Since she'd turned him down, it had been pretty obvious that she couldn't forget. Every time she was anywhere near him, she wanted to touch him. Smooth down the divot in his brow that he seemed to have in permanent residence now. She'd put it there, and she knew it. He was putting on a brave face, and her mask was slipping further each day. It was so hard to be normal around him.

Sitting down with her breakfast at the long table in the dining hall, she forced herself to take a bite of eggs while she listened in to the chatter around her. They'd had a quiet few days, no major incidents. Lots of patient welfare checks, the guys going out to do fire prevention talks at a couple of the local schools. The mood in the house was upbeat, easy.

She'd noticed Kav giving her a few looks, but he didn't say anything to her. She could tell that Alex had told him something, but she didn't know how much. Sitting across from him now, she felt his eyes appraise her.

'You okay, Kav?'

He finished his rasher of bacon and tipped his head. 'I'm good. You?'

The smile was already on her face, plastered there just like it had been since Alex had left her standing in his kitchen. She opened her mouth to lie, say that she was fine. All good. It didn't come out. The words were stuck there in her throat, making it difficult to breathe. Her face felt hot, and she knew her cheeks were blazing. She tried to speak again, and then Kav got to his feet.

'Actually, Olsen, I need to check something on the rig with you. Got a minute?' He nodded his head towards the door, and she nodded dumbly and followed him. Kav didn't say anything till they got to the back of the ambulance, and Lexie waited for him to speak first. She still couldn't get the words out. She didn't know if he was going to chew her out, tell her to leave 17 and Alex. Ask her what the hell she'd been thinking, destroying a man like Morrison by involving him in her daft and dangerous ruse. Folding her arms over her chest, she tried to dislodge the slab of pain that had taken up residence within, choking off her vocal chords.

'Do you know what you're doing, with all this?'

Do I ever know what I'm doing when it comes to Alex? No, that was the whole thing.

'I don't want to hurt him, Kav.'

'That ship has sailed, sweetheart. The man is in pain, but from the looks of things, he's not the only one. It's none of my business, but you two seemed perfect for each other. Is there no way it could work?'

'I…don't know. I ended it. I think I really broke him.'

'You did, but that's the best kind of love, right?'

She met his eye for the first time, and couldn't help but emit a teary laugh. Swiping at her eyes, she shrugged. 'I'm not built for it. It's just not in me to put that kind of trust in people.'

'People, maybe. Alex? Definitely you should. That man would never let you down.'

The tears came unchecked after that. 'I know. I do, I know that, and I want to be with him, I just can't risk it. After John—'

'John is a loser, Olsen. He's not in the same ballpark as my guy.'

'That's the problem. Alex is just *too* good. I am not made for long-term.'

'You lived with John.'

'Yeah, and look how that turned out! You can't talk either, I never see you with a woman.'

'That's because I don't want one. I do fine in the short-term market, if you get what I mean.'

'Eugh, Kav!'

'Hey! You asked. I have my own "friends with benefits"

thing, casual. And it suits me fine, but that's not you. Or Alex. Miserable is what you two are, and I am sick of the guy cramping my style staying at mine.'

'He's staying at yours? But I'm staying at Win's.'

'I know. The poor sap hates being at his place without you.'

Well, that was a slap in the face. She figured he'd be upset alone in his house, but she'd apparently haunted his house with the ghost of their fake-not-fake relationship.

'I didn't know, I thought he'd be okay.'

'Only other time I have seen him like this is when he lost Holly. I hate it. And we are all over this "pretending to be okay" thing too. Amicable break-up, my ass. The guys are not buying what you're trying to sell, sister.'

The alarm went off, and the team started running to grab their gear. Alex came striding out, spotting them. His expression grew dark.

'Lex, you okay?' He eyed Kav in a way that made the big lug squirm at the side of her. 'Kav?'

'I'm fine. We need to go.' She told Alex, flashing him a sorry smile. He nodded, his eyes dropping to the floor. 'But…can we talk, later?'

The wary relief on his face almost took her off her feet.

'Of course, Bug.' He flashed her a smile she'd missed so much and ran to the rig. 'Anytime.'

She squashed the nerves down and got to work. Taylor was already in the driving seat.

'I knew you two would kiss and make up.'

He peeled out, sirens blaring. As she checked the screen for details of the job, she let out a sigh.

'Jury is out on that one, but I'm going to try.'

And she was. Just a talk was nothing in the grand scheme

of things. They'd done it a million times. She had time to make this right.

As she followed the engine to the scene, the traffic came to a standstill. The engine got through, but the rubberneckers combined with the usual traffic held them up for a good few minutes.

The fire was already raging when the ambulance squealed up to the warehouse. Lexie had jumped out before the thing was even in Park, running to the back doors to grab her kit. All the way there they had heard how bad it was on the radio. The chief sounded stressed, and that was a very bad sign. He was normally unflappable, sturdy. Hearing the slight tremor in his deep voice was enough to make her want to move fast.

'What's the situation?' She shouted to the first firefighter she saw. John was pulling hoses, his movements swift as he glanced over his shoulder. 'Who's in there?'

'All of them, bar me and the candidate,' he shouted, not stopping for one second in his movements. 'It's bad. The whole building's a damn tinderbox. Mattresses, duvets, everything you can think of that lights up like the damn Fourth of July. We still have some workers in there, ground floor.'

'Triage area?' she shouted after him. He didn't reply, was already barking something at the candidate, who nodded, picking up a hose line and running over to the building. Taylor ran up beside her.

'Triage area has been set up by the other crew, I'm going to get more supplies from our rig.'

Taking in the scene before her, Lexie tried to focus. 'Good, I'll check in with the chief—see what's happening.'

She needed a second, just a split-second to scan the crowd. Firefighters were coming out of the smoke, people in their arms or being supported by them. She checked every masked face, every bit of uniform for the name Morrison. Nothing.

The radio trilled, Hodgens's voice coming through telling them there was an unconscious patient on the way out, and her training kicked in. Shouting to Taylor to bring a gurney, she hoisted her kit higher on her shoulder and ran over to meet the casualty coming out. It was a woman who looked tiny in the firefighter's grasp as he carried her in his arms. Her head was black with smoky grime, lolling back against Kav's arm as he carried her to safety. Even from the short distance away, Lexie could see the burns to her arms and face, the flesh black and red, bubbled up from the heat and lick of the flames. Taylor met them with the gurney, and Lexie got to work on her airway.

'She has soot in her throat, I have a pulse but it's barely there. We need to intubate her before we lose this airway altogether. The swelling is getting worse.'

As she passed the tube down, checking it was in position and bagging her, Taylor was checking the rest of her. 'No other injuries visible. The burns are second-degree, I'll let the burns unit know she's on her way. The other crew is taking the most serious to hospital.'

'Over here!' Another victim had been pulled out, and Lexie nodded to Taylor. 'You got this one?' Taylor nodded, and a paramedic came to help transport the patient to the ambulance. The whole place was organised chaos. Police were blocking off the road, keeping a wide perimeter around the huge brownstone warehouse. The car park was filled with emergency vehicles, a triage tent over in one corner treating the walking wounded.

As she moved from patient to patient, checking airways,

dealing with cuts and scrapes from their escape, and so many burns, she looked for Alex. She couldn't see him coming out with the warehouse workers, and she didn't hear his voice over the radio. He must be here. Which meant that he was in there, fighting the blaze.

She tried not to think about it. She'd seen him many times over the last few months in situations like these. Rappelling down the sides of buildings, climbing ladders and entering smoke-filled domiciles. Teaching kids about fire safety when they came on school visits to the firehouse. Even doling out bowls of soup at the homeless drive the station did once a month. She'd seen him do good in so many ways, walk right into danger to save other people. This felt different.

The atmosphere was charged with an urgent energy that even she hadn't felt before. The chief was just shouting something into the radio as she approached him. She didn't get a chance to process his words before the explosion.

It shattered what windows were left standing. The sound of glass hitting the ground amid the screams. She ducked as debris rained down on them from above, the heat from the fire bursting out like a sun flare. She could feel the heat on her face, hear the shouts on the radio. The chief was back on his feet in a second, barking commands into the radio. It was then she took in his words.

'Damn it, I ordered you to pull out. The whole building's going to come down! Morrison, status report. Kavanagh, do you have eyes on Morrison?'

No. No. Not him. Not now. Please. We were going to talk.

'No, Chief. We lost sight of each other. He heard shouting from the northwest corner of the basement storage. He went to check it out.'

Typical Alex, putting everyone before himself. It made her gut clench. She should have been the one that was different. That was brave enough to stand up and be his person.

'I... I can't see him, Chief.'

In the background, over the roar of the fire, was the faint but unmistakable beep of a PASS device. No one ever wanted to hear that sound. It meant that there was a—

'Firefighter down!' Kavanagh shouted. 'I can hear his alarm. He's down, Chief, but I can't see him! The boiler must have blown, there's debris everywhere! We need backup!'

The chief looked at her, and her heart sank. She knew the protocol. The building was toast, they were thin on the ground with the size of the building and the nature of the fire. Other stations were coming, but they weren't here yet. It would take time, seconds, minutes. All of which they didn't have. Alex was in there, on the ground. Hurt, or worse.

She rested her hands on her knees, trying desperately to suck air into her lungs. The air wouldn't hit her lungs, no matter how hard she tried to breathe. Even out here the smoke was thick, cloying to everything it touched.

'Can you locate him, Kav?' the chief asked, and Lexie desperately tried to listen. To hear anything other than what was playing through her mind in that moment. Smith emerged with another warehouse worker, and she made herself move. Made her feet step one in front of the other. Taylor caught her arm, stopping her. His face full of concern.

'I got this, Lexie. Stay with the chief.' He squeezed gently. 'They'll get him, okay?'

All she could do was shoot him a grateful nod. She didn't believe that. She knew the signs. It didn't look good. They were already ordered to pull out because the building was unstable. Risking more lives entering was not something they did lightly, even with their own in there. Running back over to the chief, she could hear Kavanagh. 'Got him! He's in bad shape. We're coming out now. Sarachek, let's move! Get his mask—'

The radio cut out, and the chief didn't stop barking commands. 'The second they're out, we pull back. This whole thing is coming down. I need a wider perimeter. Coxley, tell them to get everyone back further. We're going to need some room around here.' He took his finger off the radio button. 'They got him, Lex. You good?'

She nodded, the panic cutting off her ability to smile, to think. Alex was injured. He didn't have his mask on, which meant he'd been lying there, no protection to his airway from the smoke, the chemicals burning up in that fire. She just needed to see him for herself.

'I'm ready,' she told him, before preparing everything she would need. Oxygen, morphine, burn kits—she'd run to the ambulance and pulled half of it out. Stacking the supplies on one of the gurneys before racing hell for leather through the crowds and the chaos to where they'd be bringing him out.

The whole time she could hear her colleagues, her family, on the radio. A constant chatter of information as they spoke to each other, telling each other where they were, what the situation was. And then she was back there—waiting. Standing by the huge warehouse bay doors, trying to see something, anything, through the thick black smoke.

Kavanagh came through the radio, his voice different. The calm demeanour it usually contained gone without a trace.

'We're here! You ready, Olsen? We need to move fast!'

'I'm here,' she shouted into the radio. 'Ready. Just keep moving!'

It might have been Sarachek who broke through the curtain of darkness first. Or Kavanagh. At that moment, they could have emerged wearing clown suits and whistling a tune, she wouldn't have known it. Her eyes were on the man propped up between them.

She couldn't see his face; his helmet was nowhere to be seen. The protective head mask was still on, covering his hair, his face. It was wet, and she knew it was blood. Dripping onto his fire jacket, it marred the sooty yellow stripe running down it. His feet were dangling, no purchase on the ground below.

She met them with the gurney. Kav tore off his mask the second his hands were free. Their eyes met, and she saw shock and panic stamped across his features. Just as she knew they were written all over her own as well. That second seemed to last forever, and then all she saw was him. Blood came from a head wound on his right-hand side, the short hair she loved to run her fingers through streaked with blood. Bright red, a sharp contrast to the pale skin she could see that was untouched by the dirt and grime of the inferno.

'He's going to be okay, right? Olsen?' Kavanagh said between barking coughs. He spat onto the ground beside him, trying to clear the soot from his mouth. 'He was down too long…we couldn't get to him fast enough.'

'I've got him,' she said, meaning it. She would do anything and everything to save this man. She wished he was awake, just so she could tell him how scared she'd been. How glad she was to see him again, even like this. 'I've got him, I promise. Please, go with Taylor—both of you. Go get checked out.'

'No way in he—'

'Kav!' she shouted. 'I've got our guy, okay! Now go get checked out and let me work! He's going to be so pissed when he wakes up and you're not okay.'

Kav's lips pursed tight, and she knew she'd hit home. 'Fine,' he said. 'But I'm going to the hospital.'

Lexie nodded, already looking away, back to Alex. He had a pulse, strong and steady. His suit was burned badly in places, deep charred clumps of material where the fire had tried to eat away at him. The right side of his face had a burn on the cheek, the flesh angry and torn. He had cuts all around his face, and when her gaze slipped to the mask still attached to the suit, her vision swam. His mask had been shattered in the blast, cutting off his air and leaving his beautiful face open to the flames. Lacerations marring the features that she'd gotten so used to seeing crumpled with laughter, that mouth in a teasing smirk she pretended to hate but utterly adored.

'He's breathing on his own,' she announced, letting the team around her know what was going on. 'Head wound, possibly a fractured skull. Has he been conscious?'

'No,' Sarachek called out, before Taylor shoved the oxygen mask back over his face.

Lexie gently opened Alex's mouth, relieved that his airway wasn't singed. His position on the floor and the swift reactions of his team must have saved him from the worst of it. His breathing tube was still working even when the mask had been obliterated by the impact from the explosion. 'He was under some metal shelving, pretty sure that's how he hit his head. It sort of covered him from the flames.'

Small mercies.

Without a mask, his airway would have been open to the fumes and smoke.

Lucky, lucky, lucky repeated in her head.

Smoke inhalation on top of a head wound would have been catastrophic. The burn was first-degree on his face, he might have a scar but that didn't matter as long as he was living and breathing and moving around in this world. He wouldn't be any less beautiful. Especially not to her. Careful not to move him too much, she secured a collar around his neck and placed the oxygen mask over his face. 'His airway's clear, no need for intubation. We need to get him to the hospital now. He needs a CT scan—stat.'

Taylor came to her side, and the pair of them ran with the gurney to the rig.

'You drive, and fast. Hit every red light, make them move!' she shouted. She jumped in after him and slammed the doors closed behind them both, encasing them in their own metal reality. Getting to work, she cut away his clothing, needing to see his body. Have access if she needed to do extraordinary measures. When she freed his arm from the coat-sleeve, a flash of pink stilled her.

It couldn't be.

It was. There, around his wrist, was her hair tie. The tiny pink and red hearts were marred with blood and dirt. He'd kept a piece of her with him, even now.

If you're listening up there, she prayed silently. *Don't take him from me. Let this piece of fabric be a tether to the earth. A ward against death. We need more time.*

She thought of Holly, who was taken from him. She thought of how she'd broken the heart she'd mended. Did God care about time? He had his own plans for Alex. She felt herself turn to steel once more. This time, it wasn't armour, it was a shield she wrapped around the pair of them. If God wanted him, she was going to put up one hell of a fight to win.

'You can't have him,' she said, her voice strong. 'Not today.'

She was hooking him up to the monitors, checking his pupils again for dilation, any signs that a pupil had blown, when his eyelids flickered. The ambulance lurched forward, and she gripped the gurney. 'Alex? Alex!'

Grabbing dressings, she covered his head wound and taped it up. There were no debris in the wound, and she prayed that they could get him to the hospital. She wouldn't be able to rest until he had been scanned. Till she knew he would come out of this okay. Still Alex. They all needed that. Needed him to be able to be the man they all revered. His job was so important to him, she couldn't imagine him doing anything else. She checked his oxygen levels, they were coming back up steadily. He was hanging in there. All she could do was sit and watch, look after him while they raced to the hospital, sirens blaring.

Pulling his gloves off, inspecting his hands, she took one of them and placed them between hers. Felt the warmth of his calloused skin even through the latex encasing hers.

'Alex, just hang in there, okay? We're nearly there. You're going to be okay. I promise.' She brought his hand to her lips, dropping a kiss onto the back of it. His hand squeezed hers, and her eyes shot to his. He was looking right at her. He tried to lift his other hand to pull at the mask, but she stilled his movements.

'Alex, I'm here. Don't try to talk. We're on our way to the hospital.' He squeezed again and tried to pull at the mask once more. Pushing at the hand that tried to stop him even as the other was still linked tightly in hers. She let him this time. Needing to hear his voice, to answer whatever question he had on his mind.

'Alex, you need to keep that on. Your oxygen…'

'Kav…'

'They're all out. They're all pulled out. Safe.'

She was pretty sure he'd tried to nod, but the movement was barely there. 'You're here,' he mumbled, trying to smile. It didn't look right. Pained. 'I…didn't think I'd see you again. I thought…'

Her heart chose that moment to splatter across her chest, breaking into a million shards against her ribcage. She let the tears that came spill down her cheek unchecked.

'I'm here. I won't leave your side.'

His smile dimmed. 'You will,' he mumbled. 'You already did, Bug.'

'I won't leave you now,' she said again, wishing to all the gods in all the heavens that she hadn't been so damn weak. That the man lying before her knew her heart, instead of lamenting her absence. Even now, he was hurt in more ways than one. 'I will never leave you again.'

He narrowed his eyes, and she could tell he was trying to absorb her words, take in what she was saying. The pain meds would have taken hold now, numbing him to the trauma he'd survived. He looked so confused, but the one thing that was missing was fear. Imagine that. She'd gone and picked the one man on the planet who seemed to fear nothing. The only thing he'd spoken of was his team, and her.

She didn't deserve him. She'd *never* deserved him, but she had no intention of letting him go. Screw the tentative talk. She was in. She was all in the second she'd thought he was dead. Nothing was worse than that. She was going to heal him from this and keep him forever.

Damn being scared or allowing the past to take her future from her. He could have died in that fire, thinking that she didn't want him, not knowing that he wasn't alone in this. It ripped her apart from the inside as she tried to push the mask back to his face.

He resisted, but he wasn't making much sense now. 'Don't make me leave, Bug. Home. We need to be…home. Tell Kav I didn't stop the fight.' He gripped her uniform, pulling her closer with eyes that were flickering with the effort of staying open. 'Fight never stopped…'

His levels were dropping, his heart a little erratic. The adrenaline was wearing off now, letting him slide into the shock his body was succumbing to. As she fought to stabilise him, she couldn't stop her words from tumbling out. 'Taylor, how close?'

'Four minutes! I'm hustling as fast as I can, but the traffic's not moving!'

'Well move them! Get on the radio, get the police to step in if you have to. Taylor…' She paused, knowing that Alex could hear her. He was still mumbling, his words getting weirder, weaker. She could only make out random words. *Bug* and *fire*. She thought she heard him say "I love you," but she focused on every inch of him, and her skills to heal. She wanted to scream that they were losing him, but she wouldn't admit that to any of them, let alone herself. 'It's bad, Tay. Move!'

She tightened the mask around his face, trying to get his oxygen levels up. His hands were looser, the grip weaker. It made her think of how he'd carried her before, scooped her right off the couch into his bed. His legs sturdy, as sure as his grip around her with his strong, warm arms. After this, she would let him manhandle her all the time. She'd let him carry her around like a damn baby if he wanted to. 'Alex, I'm so sorry. I was wrong, just hang in there. Please. Come on, smoke eater!' She turned the tremor in her voice to a command. 'Open those eyes, Lieutenant. Come on, come pick a fight with me!'

Something was wrong. Really, really wrong. She knew it from her training, her eyes assessing the beeps on the monitors, the rise and fall in his chest. He was fading. She pulled back the bandage from his head, a spurt of blood shooting up and coating her arm. 'Oh, God, Alex.'

She stemmed the flow, packing the wound as best she could while desperately searching for something she could fix, right here, right now. Wishing she'd trained in neurosurgery so she could fix his head with her bare hands. She looked for the cause, all the while knowing that a knock on the head like Alex's was bad. Life-changing bad. Still, she looked. A shard of glass, a fragment of metal she could blame. A clot that she could scoop out with her own fingers and relieve the pressure she knew had to be building under his skull.

Nothing, just the jagged edge of the cut, brimming with blood that dripped from his soft hair down the gurney. A steady little drip on the ambulance floor.

He was moaning now, a low growl of pain. Grabbing her light, she checked his eyes for the thing she was terrified to see. His right pupil had blown.

'Pupil's blown!' The monitors were slowing, his breathing raspy. 'He's losing his airway, intubating now! Hold it steady, Taylor!'

'I got you!' he called, his hands tense on the steering wheel as his eyes constantly scanned for the smoothest, fastest route possible to the help they needed. 'I called ahead, they're ready.'

She didn't acknowledge him, she was too busy concentrating on pushing the clear tube down Alex's throat, her stethoscope whipping the side of her head as she yanked it off her neck, listening to his raspy chest to check she'd hit home. Alex was still now, his eyelids closed, his wet lashes fanned against his bloody, pale cheek.

She pulled herself around to his side, the rhythmic squeeze of the bag in her hands steadier than she felt as she pushed the air into his lungs. One Mississippi…two Mississippi. 'We're almost there, Alex. Hang on, baby. Please. Come on, you're not getting off this easy. I only just found you!' Her voice broke as she struggled to pin down the emotions threatening to take her over. His monitors were beeping, his chest moving. He was still here. Still a chance.

'Alex, I love you. I love you. I love you so much. I'll never be scared again, I promise. I will never walk away from you again, I will stick with you, baby. Sweetheart, you wake up for me, and I swear, I will bug you for the rest of your life. Hang on…please…hang on.'

The second they pulled up, everything was swift. So swift time itself struggled to keep up. The doors were flung open, and she could hear her voice. Strong, commanding. Giving them a rundown as they dragged out the gurney and raced to the OR.

'Responsive in the field. Normal pupillary response. Awake but drifting in and out of consciousness. Severe laceration to the head. Breathing grew erratic, oxygen levels dropping below seventy. Speech incoherent, not making sense. Bleeding from head laceration. Lacerations to the face and neck. Mask broken in impact. Blunt force trauma. Right pupil blew en route. Airway compromised. Intubated upon loss of consciousness.'

All the while her body moved, hands working to help, to touch the man fighting for his life before her. He was right there, touchable, but she couldn't reach him.

'Tell Kav I never stopped the fight.'

She hoped he would remember his rambled words, would pay attention to them now and do what he always did. Be a man of his word. Keep that big heart of his pumping in his broad chest.

The gust of breeze from the closing doors was the next thing she remembered. The doors to the operating theatres; when kind but firm hands had stopped her from being where she wanted to be. With him. Leaving her standing there, feeling the cold and the lack of Alex Morrison so badly she barely stayed on her feet.

You'll leave again, Bug.

His words pulsed in her ears, as erratic as the beat of her heart. She just hoped that she'd get the chance to prove him wrong again. It was one argument she would never survive losing.

CHAPTER ELEVEN

Something burned in her hands, and she jolted out of her head, where images of Alex were playing on a loop, his body caked in blood and surrounded by the sirens and the beeps and the thudding in her ears.

'Olsen!' Her head snapped up into a pair of familiar, warm eyes. 'Don't spill it. Drink.'

The fingers banded around hers loosened, only leaving when her own flexed over the cup of warm brown liquid contained in her grasp. There was a red tinge to her wrists, in a straight line that made the pale unblemished skin look like it belonged to a mannequin. It was only when Kavanagh took the seat next to her that she realised she was even sitting down. There was a blanket around her shoulders, her gloves must have been taken off. But when? She hadn't felt a thing. Still didn't.

She looked down at her boot-clad feet, peeking from under the soft white wool. Moved them, just to see if they were still connected to her limbs. They stirred, and she sagged a little further in her seat, registering fully for the first time that she could smell the coffee from the cup in her hands. She felt fingers wrap around her chin, pulling her head to the side. Kav's eyes were full of concern. His lips were moving. She frowned at them, wondering why he was messing around when Alex was probably dead somewhere close.

He took his hand off her chin to snap his fingers in front of her face, and it was as if that movement had turned the sound back on. She could hear the hospital move around her. The ringing phones. The shuffling and clacking feet along the floor. The low gruff mumbles all around her.

'Olsen, do I need to get you checked over again, or what?'

'What?' Her voice was a cracked whisper. 'No. I'm good.'

He lifted a brow and pushed her cup closer to her lips with a stubby finger. 'Drink, then. You're freaking me out.'

She forced her lips to form a seal around the rim, sipping the hot liquid and willing it to knock her out of her stupor. No, that was a lie. What she actually wanted was for the caffeine to reverse her consciousness. She just wanted to sleep. Be back in Alex's bed, in his arms. When everything was simple, and felt right. Before she'd well and truly screwed up and ruined them both.

'This is all my fault.'

'Cut that out. You did everything you could. The doctors said you'd done everything you could. Hell, Taylor had half the Brooklyn precinct moving the damn traffic out of the way.'

She didn't even realise she'd spoken out loud. It wasn't even what she meant.

'It is my fault. If I hadn't told him I wanted to end it, he wouldn't be here.'

Kav was already shaking his head, reaching for the hand that had landed in her lap. His touch was warm, causing a shiver to run through her. She realised even with the coffee and the blanket she was ice-cold. Like Alex had taken all the warmth with him.

'That's just stupid. He knew the job, we all do. Doesn't matter what or who we have to tether us to the earth, bad stuff still happens, Lex. He knows how you feel about him.'

'No,' she refuted, the tears finally choking her. 'No, Kav. He really doesn't. He...' Her words were punctuated with hiccups as the sobs took over. The adrenaline finally leaving her when she didn't need to save a life anymore. There was nothing she could do now but wait and fear the doors she could see in the distance. Wait for the surgeons to come tell her that he was gone. Out of her reach for ever. 'He told me, in the ambulance. He said—said I'd leave him again. I didn't mean... Kav... I—can't take this!' The coffee cup dropped to the floor as she tried to pull the blanket away, suffocating under its weight now.

'If he's gone, Kav...if I never get to tell him... I need to tell him that he can't leave me, not now when I just found him...'

She was leaning forward one minute, pulling at the blanket and then she was free of it, in the air. Kav had yanked it off and lifted her into his arms in one smooth motion. He kicked at the doors as he headed for the exit, all the while she was crying, sobbing now. Pulling at his clothes which smelled of smoke, and dust...and death. That's what that smell meant to her now. Smoke was death. The ending of everything good and pure.

He walked right out of the front doors as they opened for him, the squeak of their runners in her ears as he dropped right down onto the bench outside, with her still in his arms.

She felt him brush the hair out of her face, swipe at the tears soddening her cheeks. He cursed when the dirt from him streaked through the salty water. She couldn't get her breath, her vision was blurring, tinting black at the edges as panic clamped down on her windpipe and refused to let go.

'Lexie, stop! Just breathe!' He grabbed her face roughly between his, his voice almost angry. 'You're giving up on him, now? I don't think so! We're 17, and we never give up, we never stop. You hear me! Snap out of it! Look at me, right now, Olsen! Fricking breathe!'

She finally locked eyes with his, saw the determination covering his own fear, and that's what did it. She drew in deep breaths, filling her lungs with the sweet night air. They must have been there for hours. Night had fallen around them while they were suspended in time. 'Good,' he soothed, his voice softer now. 'Good, Lex. That's it. Stay with us.'

His words unlocked something in her brain, and an eerie calm settled. Alex's words to her, maybe his last words. They weren't just for her.

'He asked me to tell you that he was still fighting,' she told him, watching his brows rise in surprise. 'He said the fight never stops.'

'He said that?'

She nodded, her breath even but shuddery as she got control. His laugh rang out loud, rumbling around her as he pulled her closer. Laughing heartily as he hugged her to him, rocking them both back and forth on the bench. 'Oh, Olsen, he's still in there, girl. He's still there.'

'Do you think he was talking about the accident?' she asked, confused by the change in Kav's whole mood. He was almost…happy. Like it had loosened the terror inside him.

'No,' he rumbled, pulling her head into his chest and stroking her hair. 'No, Lex, the fight's about you.'

'Me?'

What?

She wanted so badly to understand, to grasp on to the joy that Kav now had.

'We had a talk, about you. I told him to fight, and never stop. For you, for what you had.' He pulled away, forcing her to look at him. 'That man is such a stubborn bastard that not even death will keep him from getting back to you, Lex. Trust me on that.' He laughed again, a disbelieving, joyful sound that shuddered through him to her. 'But when he comes to you, make sure you're ready. Don't break him again.'

She wanted to believe him. Believe that it wasn't just the rambling, confused thoughts of a man with a brain injury. That what he still wanted was her, and he was willing to fight everything for it. Because she was willing. She would have split the world in half to save him in the back of that rig. If he needed full-time care, would never be him again, it didn't matter. She would be there, good and bad. Pain and joy. Dark and light. If she got to be by his side ever again, she would glue herself to him and call it permanent.

He was the glue of 17, of her. The best thing John had ever done was cheat on her. She'd never been so grateful to her ex for showing up at 17, and pushing her and Alex out of the friendship zone into…this.

'I won't,' she said, knowing with everything in her that it was true. 'The Jaws of Life won't separate us, if I get the chance. I love him, Kyle. I just got scared, but I didn't know fear till this. I just love him so much. He has to live, right?'

'Right,' Kav said, patting her shoulder. 'Come on. Let's get back to the team before they come looking.'

They were just sitting down when the doctors came through the waiting room doors, and Lexie's heart stuttered in her chest.

* * *

'This really isn't protocol,' the nurse murmured as Lexie stood outside the door to Alex's private room. Hodgens tutted, and she could hear the chief talking to her, but she couldn't take in the words. The whole of 17 were here, and when they wanted something, they got their way. Her hand grasped the handle, and there he was.

She'd seen so many patients like this. Battered, unconscious, ravaged by trauma. Alex looked beautiful, even like this. He looked like he was sleeping, as if he might jolt himself awake like he did when they watched movies together at his place. The tubes and machines reminded her brain that this was different. He wasn't sleeping, or intact. He'd almost died. *Had died*, right there on the OR table. She remembered that the doctor said they'd had to resuscitate. The trauma of the head injury had caused his brain to swell, his body eventually trying to shut down as the injury took hold.

Stable, the doctor had said. They'd removed a clot, one she hadn't been able to see. Stopped the bleeding. His head was bandaged, his skull fixed back together like pieces of a dangerous puzzle. It had been touch and go whether a skull flap had been needed, an induced coma. He was responding well though.

The doctors said that if things stayed that way, they could remove his breathing apparatus. Once his brain had a chance to heal a little, and once he could be weaned off the drugs keeping him sedated and pain free. All signs were good. Tiny little pieces of joy like 'normal brain function' and 'response to stimuli' felt like presents to her. Facts that her medical-loving brain could compute, and cling to.

He was a fighter, through and through. She just needed him to wake up, lock those beautiful grey eyes on hers once more. Call her Bug and tease her mercilessly. Take her into his strong arms and show her that the world was back on its axis. Still spinning, with him a part of it. The centre of her world, if she got the chance. Yes, Lexie Olsen was now a girly girl, and she wasn't mad at it. Bring on the hearts and flowers.

The guys had been thrilled to hear the news, and with Kav telling them he'd been talking in the ambulance, but not the context, they were confident. She could see it in their faces as they railroaded the doctors to let her see him. Let her be by his side.

'She's his girlfriend, Doc,' Sarachek had told them. 'He'd want her there, and she's the reason he's still here in the first place.' That did the trick.

They took turns sitting with him over the next couple of days. Chief Maddison came in, telling her that she was on paid leave until further notice. The perks of being a not-so-fake fake girlfriend. A fake ex-girlfriend, at that.

Something I hope to God I get the chance to take back.

She didn't leave his side. Refused. The nurses brought her a cot, let her use the staff showers. She was pretty sure Win had pulled some strings. She'd been there too, checking in. Bringing her clothes. She'd brought her food so she didn't have to leave his side for long. She had just come back from a shower when she noticed it was John sitting in the chair at the other side of his bed.

'Hi,' he said, standing up when he noticed her in the doorway. 'I can go.'

'No, it's okay.' She didn't want to push him out. Whatever hassles they'd had in the past meant nothing now. He was 17 too. 'You can stay.'

He nodded, sitting back down and looking at Alex. His

bruising was out now, dark purples and greens as his skin healed. He was off the ventilator. Breathing on his own. She'd spent half the night just watching his chest rise and fall. 'How is he?'

'Good,' she said with a small smile, but it was an effort to even lift the corners of her mouth. 'Breathing on his own. His brain activity is normal. The swelling's under control. He should be getting weaned off the majority of his meds today. They're hoping he'll wake up.'

He nodded along. 'What about you?'

'Me? I think he will. He's strong—'

'No.' His smile was sad. 'I meant how are you? This must be hard.'

'Oh. Yeah. It is. But he's going to get through this. Be back bossing you lot around in no time.' He laughed, but it was short. Dying as soon as it started.

'Good.' He leaned forward in his chair, wringing his hands together. 'I never should have done that to you.'

'We don't need to—'

'I don't mean the cheating. I mean coming to 17. It was the wrong move.' He shrugged. 'I should have known that it wouldn't work. When I saw you two together, I knew why.'

'Alex was not the reason I said no to us getting back together.'

'I know. I just… You never looked at me like you do him. Seeing you two together, it's different. You're different. You love him, don't you.'

It wasn't a question. It didn't need to be.

'Yes.' She let the tears fall, heard the squeak of his chair when he moved across the room. A second later, she was in his arms. It felt…odd. Not Alex.

'It's okay,' he shushed. 'He'll come back to you, Lex. He's

a stubborn guy.' She laughed then, pulling away. It didn't feel right, sitting next to Alex in John's arms, even if it was just comfort. 'I'm going to go back to the house, okay? Ring us if you need anything. Kav is coming soon.'

She reached for his arm. 'Thanks, John. It's weird to say, but I'd like to be friends.'

'I'd like that too.' He nodded, then squeezed her shoulder as he headed for the door. 'Hang in there.'

Something was touching her hair. She stirred, brushing it away. Coming to, her back protested as she sat up, peeling her face off the blankets.

It had been a long day. Doctors had been in and out, making decisions. Adjusting medication. Tests, tests, tests. Kavanagh had gone home an hour after visiting time, and she'd taken up vigil in her usual hardbacked chair. She'd not made it to the cot this time, and her body knew about it. She felt it again, that brush. Glancing at Alex, she gasped when grey eyes stared right back at her.

'Alex! You're awake!'

He winced, but his lips were curled into that smile she loved. His hand was still mid-air, and she wanted to grab it, kiss it.

'Shh. Head hurts.'

'I'll get the nurse—'

She was halfway to the door when he stopped her with a croak.

'Don't go, Bug.'

She turned to look at him, and she was back in that chair before her feet registered the movement.

'I told you. I'm never leaving you again. I never have. I slept in a damn cot for you, Morrison.'

'Sexy,' he rasped. 'I'm glad you're here. I didn't think I was going to make it.'

There they were again. The tears. This guy had opened her up like an oyster.

'How bad is it?'

She licked at her lips, tasting salt water. 'You hit your head. How much do you remember?'

His eyes grew hazy as he plumbed the depths of his head. 'Chief told us to pull out, but I heard noises.' His eyebrows dipped, a wince marring his pale features. 'Did they—?'

'The building came down not long after you got out,' she told him as delicately as possible. 'They didn't find anyone, but three people got out of the back windows. Chief said they were in the basement. We think that's who you heard.'

He relaxed, that dent in his brow smoothing back down. 'Good.' His eyelids were slow, drowsy. She was about to tell him to go back to sleep when he spoke again. 'There was a loud boom, and I was hit. I came to on the ground, but everything hurt. I could hear Kav, but he sounded so far away, and I just wanted to take a nap. My head was killing me, and I couldn't breathe too well. My mask was shattered, but I managed to get to my reserve.'

He'd used the second mask, which had saved his airway. Lexie was grateful he was so skilled, even when all that was happening. They were so alike. Situations like that made their minds sharper, their training seeing them through the horror and the confusion. She kept the thoughts quiet, waiting for him to speak again. His hand squeezed hers.

'I could hear the fire roaring around me, my PASS alarm going off. My radio was smashed, I think because I remember trying to speak to you.'

'Me?'

He nodded but stopped when it caused him pain. 'I wanted to say goodbye, in case.'

She wasn't sure she was still breathing herself, right now.

'I would have been so mad,' she said eventually, kissing the back of his hand. 'You said you would never stop fighting, remember?'

'And I wouldn't have. I just knew that you would have blamed yourself. I didn't want you to bear that alone, without me there.' He was looking at her intensely, as if he was reminding himself she was real. 'You're my best friend, Bug.' He sighed, the sound deep and ragged. 'Now, how bad is it? I want the truth.'

She pulled her chair closer, not releasing him from her grasp for even a second. 'The truth, right?'

'I can handle it.' His lip curled into that cocky grin she adored. 'Big boy, remember.'

'Okay. When you hit your head, it caused a brain bleed.' His eyes widened, but he said nothing. 'You were talking in the ambulance, but then you lost consciousness.' She licked at her lips. Sugar-coating this was not what he wanted, and she knew him by heart. 'I intubated you, and you went right into surgery. They removed a clot. You had some brain swelling, but it wasn't dire enough to put you in a coma. You flatlined during the surgery, while they were taking the clot out. Your heart is fine. You were out for days, but you're stable now.'

She smiled then, tears silently rolling down her face. 'Doctors said that you are going to be fine, that if you woke up still having your capacities, you should make a full recovery.' She reached out to caress the bandage on his cheek. 'You burned your face, and it was all cut up and bruised from the mask. You'll have a neat scar there.'

He chuckled, and her heart raced. 'War wounds are fine. It means I survived.' His brows knitted together. 'And 17?'

She moved closer still, needing to be with him. 'They are being a pain, if I'm honest. Like clucking mother hens, the lot of them. They moaned to the nurses about my cot being lumpy, so I got a new one. They're all fine, they just want you back.'

His gaze had slid to the bed in the corner of the room. To her cot, which was looking more like a makeshift bedroom with all the comforting things their people had brought in.

'You slept here?'

'Yep. I never left you, not since the ambulance.'

His eyes widened. 'Never?'

'Well,' she smirked, 'I did take a shower or two.'

'Grateful,' he quipped. 'You do tend to stink the place out.'

She laughed, wiping at her tears. 'Yeah, well, laugh it up, mister.' She waggled her brows. 'Because I did your sponge baths, and you didn't smell so hot yourself.'

She expected him to laugh, but his gaze pinned her to the spot instead.

'Truth?' he asked, his voice hesitant. 'You stayed because you're my best friend.'

'Yes and no,' she breathed, wanting him to ask her more. His brow lifted.

'Truth. You stayed because I'm your best friend, and you felt bad about us ending.'

She shook her head vehemently. 'No truth.'

He blinked a few times, awake now.

'Truth...' he started. She finished it.

'You're my best friend. Truth. I stayed because I felt bad about running. Truth. I ran because I was scared of my feelings for you, and I was worried that I would mess this up. Truth.' She drew in a shaky breath. 'I'm in love with you, Alex Morrison. I love you so much it makes me want to fricking swoon and buy you flowers. When I thought you were gone, I couldn't believe how trivial my worries were. How damn stupid and stubborn I'd been.'

'Lexie...'

'No. I have to say this, please, Kitten.' His smile melted her. 'This is how things are going to go. I'm moving back in. I am going to take care of you. You are going to let me because quite frankly I don't think you ever really have. I am going to be your real girlfriend. I'm going to bake you cupcakes, and we're going to car-pool to work, and fight, and wind each other up. Every day, for the rest of our lives, if you still want that.'

She clenched her teeth, breathing hard for a moment as she spilled her guts to the beautiful man in the bed. 'Because I am in love with you, Morrison. The only thing in life that scares me now is living it without you letting me love you. For as long as we have left.' She folded her arms, feeling so vulnerable and seen under his warm gaze that she thought she might catch fire. 'So, what do you think about that?'

He nodded to the open door behind him, and her heart stopped.

'I think you should close that door, get over here and start the loving, Bug. Because it's about damn time you loved me back.'

EPILOGUE

'DID YOU REALLY have to wear that?'

Alex was the epitome of offended as he looked down at the medal of honour he'd received the day before. His quick actions in the fire had saved a lot of lives, and risking his life for the care of others had been well recognised by the NYFD.

'Of course I did, Bug. I'm going to wear this and only this around the house for the next month. Get used to it.'

Get used to him? This?

Oh, she would. It had been five months since his accident, and she had loved every minute of it. Looking after him, seeing his team well up when they came to the hospital in droves. Kyle Kavanagh, the big lug, had burst into tears the second he saw him awake. The lads hadn't let him live it down yet. John was even pleased to see him recovering. The two men weren't exactly buddies, but they had come to an understanding. Turns out, he wasn't such a bad guy after all. He'd started seeing someone new, and Lexie was happy for him.

'Get used to having your naked ass on the furniture? Eww!'

She squealed when he grabbed her, pulling her body flush with his in their bed. She felt the hardness of him, nestled between her thighs and groaned. 'Again? Really?'

'Really. We have a lot of recovery time to make up for,' he cackled, that devilish grin of his making his scarred cheek pucker. It was healing well, fading fast. A memory of what he had lived through. She ran her fingers through his peach fuzz hair. They'd shaved part of it in the hospital, and she gently ran her fingers along the surgery incision line.

'Okay.' She pretended to pout. 'I suppose I could live with that.'

He spun them around until she was under him. Making her gasp from his touch, the hard lines of his muscular form pinning her to the bed.

'Oh, you'll live with it. I want you naked in this bed, in the kitchen, the hall, the back porch.' He pulled a weak face. 'I still need looking after, you know. Cupcakes on demand. Feeding me beer while I watch the game, you know. The usual.'

She laughed, and something flashed in her mind. The second she'd had the idea she knew it was right. 'Sounds like you need a wife, Smoke Eater.'

He stilled, his arms tightening around her. His grey eyes searching the green of hers for answers.

'Don't joke about that,' he said. 'You can't threaten me with a good time.'

She closed the distance between their lips, kissing him till they both groaned. Pulling back, she sucked on his bottom lip, feeling him twitch against her. 'I'm not,' she murmured with a smile. 'You need a wife.'

She bit at her lip, pretending to think. 'I suppose I could do that for you. I could marry you. I'm pretty good at baking, and we are best friends.' His face was a picture. Eyes wide and shining, his lip curled into a grin.

'I propose an addendum to the agreement,' she said, kissing him again, because she never wanted to stop. 'Till death do us part. Just don't expect me to wear some flouncy meringue thing, and I want the reception to be held here. In the backyard, with Win, and Hunter. And all of 17.'

'You're serious,' he breathed, looking at her like she might just poof away. 'Truth?'

'Truth.' She beamed. 'Cross my heart and hope to—'

'Yes,' he cut in, pulling back with her still held to him. Sitting her up in his lap and kissing the hell out of her. 'God, Lexie, yes. Hell yes, I'll marry you.'

Hours later, when they had made love so many times she'd lost count, they lay together in the dark.

'I can't believe it,' he said, his low chuckle reverberating against her cheek as she lay on his chest. Naked, sweaty. Spent. And so happy. 'You actually beat me to something.'

She swatted at him, making his laugh all the louder. 'Yeah, well. Don't get used to it, Kitten.' She looked up, right into the face that once upon a time she'd almost lost. 'Because from now on, husband-to-be, I am going to take you down whenever we go at it. I am going to get a certificate printed up in the firehouse when I win that tally.'

Since their return, with Alex feeling the pressure of returning to command, she'd made a game of it. To pull himself out of his head when he needed it. Therapy helped, but it was his family that made the difference. The guys all set challenges for the two of them, daft stuff. Anything from chilli-eating challenges to seeing how many times they could jump scare each other. It had bonded the team back together stronger than ever, and the commanding force that was Lieutenant Morrison was well and truly back. Battle-scarred and ready for the world again.

He chuckled, leaning over and reaching into his top drawer. Slapping a black velvet ring box onto his chest.

Her jaw dropped.

'Oh, yeah? Well, you might be right there. Paper beats rock.'

When she looked at him, that sly little smirk was plastered all across his handsome face. Shaking her head, she giggled.

Game on, Morrison.

* * * * *

*If you enjoyed this story,
check out these other great reads from
Rachel Dove*

A Baby to Change Their Lives
How to Resist Your Rival
A Midwife, Her Best Friend, Their Family
Single Mum's Mistletoe Kiss

All available now!

SINGLE DAD'S FAKE FIANCÉE

DEANNE ANDERS

MILLS & BOON

CHAPTER ONE

Pale pink roses and white baby's breath filled tall crystal vases while twinkling lights lit the large barn that had been transformed into a rustic fairyland. A string quartet played softly in the background as almost a hundred guests, all the happy couple's coworkers and family members, raised their glasses to toast the newly married couple. It was a picture-perfect moment as everyone present smiled and laughed when the groom pulled his radiant bride, Midwife Skylar Benton, into his arms for a passionate kiss, something totally out of character for the reserved groom, Dr. Jared Warner.

Midwife Lori Mason tried her best to maintain her own smile as she was a part of the bridal party and it was expected out of her. But sitting there looking on as her friends stared into each other's eyes with an emotion she feared she would never get to feel was becoming harder and harder to do as the night went on. Maybe she would never find that? Maybe she didn't have whatever it was that other people had that could form a bond with someone? At what point did she give up on finding that elusive love and move on with her life, accepting that she was meant to be single? And then what? She'd wanted to be a mother as long as she could remember. If her biological clock was ticking any louder it would drown out the Miranda Lambert song the DJ was playing. Did she just give up on her dream of a family simply because she couldn't find a man who loved her? A man she could trust to always be there for her and their family?

Her old childhood memories of asking her mother why her father didn't love her resurfaced, but she pushed them away. She wasn't looking for a father figure. The time for that had long passed. She wanted someone to share a family with. She wanted children. A family of her own. Was that too much to ask for?

She looked over to where her friend Bree was curled up next to her fiancé with Knox's arms holding her close. They were probably discussing their own wedding just a few months away. It seemed that all her friends were moving forward while she was stuck in the same place she'd been since she had graduated with her midwifery degree. She was even still living in her childhood home, though her mother now spent most of her time where she worked at the Legacy House for pregnant women.

"What's wrong with me?" she asked, only realizing she'd spoken out loud when the man next to her turned toward her. Dr. Zachary Morales, the man who'd agreed to her last-minute invitation to the wedding when Donald, her "plus one," whom she'd been dating for over three months, had suddenly decided that attending a wedding with Lori was "moving things too fast" had been a surprise. After introducing him to her friends before the wedding, he'd quickly fit right in with the group, something her now ex-boyfriend, Donald, had never done. Whether that was because a lot of them shared a medical background she didn't know. What she did know was that when she'd seen Zach dressed in his tailored black tux sitting across the room as she'd walked in with the wedding procession, she had quickly forgotten about her no-show ex.

And what did that say about her? That she'd date a man for months when deep inside she'd always known he wasn't the man for her? And why had she done that? She knew the reason, though she wouldn't admit it to anyone else. She'd dated him because she felt safe with him, safe from giving even a small part of her heart to him. She told herself that if he'd been the right one, she would have taken that risk. But would she? How could she know that when she did meet the right man, she'd be brave enough to take that risk?

"I'm not sure what you mean," he said. "Are you not feeling well?"

"There's nothing wrong with you," Bree said from beside her, her friend instinctively knowing what Lori was asking. "Sky said she told you to get rid of Donald the first time she met him."

"She said he didn't look at me the right way. What does that even mean?" Lori asked. Sky always seemed to have a sixth sense about the men that Lori dated. Unfortunately, it was always the opposite of hers.

"Can you please explain what Sky meant?" Bree asked, turning toward her fiancé.

"I'm not an expert, but from what I have seen, when a man is interested in a woman, there can be a million people in a room, but his attention is primarily on that woman. Like the way Jack is looking at Lori's mother right now." Knox nodded his head to a table halfway across the room.

Lori glanced over to where her boss and her mother sat, laughing and smiling at each other. When the senior Dr. Warner raised Lori's mom's hand to his lips, Lori looked away quickly. It seemed that everyone in her world was pairing off. That was, everyone except her.

"Let's dance," Bree said, taking Knox's hand and leading him out to the dance floor. Lori watched the couple and smiled. If those two could find each other, surely she could find the right man for her.

"I feel like I'm missing something," Zach said, reminding Lori that she wasn't alone, even though at that moment she felt more alone than she had in her whole life. "Why do you think there's something wrong with you?"

A sudden thought crossed her mind. The only thing she had really known about the new doctor was that he had recently moved to Nashville in the hopes of making a new start in his life after losing his wife the year before. From everything she had heard, Zach had been very devoted to his wife and had taken a long sabbatical before deciding to move his practice from Memphis to Nashville. Lori's invitation to the doctor had been more of a coincidence as he'd just walked up on the OB-GYN floor after she'd hung up after Donald's phone call leaving her once again to be the third wheel with her friends. She'd explained to Zach that her boyfriend, make that ex-boyfriend, had canceled on her at the last minute. While making sure to keep the disappointment from her voice, she'd asked Zach if he'd like to come with her as a way to make some new connections with the staff. Lori had made it clear that it would in no way be considered as anything other than a chance for her to introduce him to more of his coworkers, and she'd been pleasantly surprised when he'd agreed.

Now, looking at him, pretty much a stranger to her and her friends, she realized she had the one person who might give her an honest opinion on what she was doing wrong.

"Well, let's see. Where should I start?" Lori looked around the room, then nodded, motioning to the head table. "So, the bride and groom over there, Jared and my best friend, Sky, they danced around each other a few months, then bam, head over heels in love. Then there's Bree and Knox. They met at our office while Knox was filling in for another one of our doctors that was on leave. They barely knew each other three months ago, now they're planning their own wedding. And then there's my mother."

"Your mother?" Zach asked as he scanned the room, as if looking for someone he would recognize as Lori's mother.

Lori pointed to where her mother and the senior Dr. Warner had taken to the dance floor.

"Isn't that Dr. Warner, the founder of the Legacy Women's Clinic?" he asked.

"Yes, that's my boss. Well, kind of. Jared is kind of my boss too now. And that's my mother dancing with him. My mom has worked for Legacy House for years, the home Dr. Warner founded to help pregnant women needing a place to stay. The two of them have a professional relationship. My mom was Dr. Warner's wife's best friend before she passed. Then two weeks ago I walk into Legacy House to find the two of them kissing like a couple of teenagers hiding under the football bleachers."

"You don't approve of your mother's relationship with your boss?" The look in Zach's eyes was one of curiosity. Good. If he was able to follow everything up till now, maybe he would be able to help her.

"It's not that I don't approve. My dad took off years ago. He was a long-haul truck driver who preferred the open road to being tied down with a family. I think I was five the last time he stopped by the house on his way through town. But after the way my father treated her, Mom has never dated. She was definitely not looking for a man in her life. Neither was Sky, at least not a steady one. And Bree? That story is too long to go into, but the last man she would have fallen for would have been Knox. Still, there they all are," Lori said, spreading out both her hands toward the dance floor that was becoming crowded. "And here I sit, the only one of them that has been actively looking for 'Mr. Right' so that I can start a family and I'm the one that will go home alone tonight."

She took a sip of champagne from her glass, needing the courage to ask her next question. Still staring into her glass, she said, "So, I ask again, what is wrong with me?"

She waited a few minutes, hoping he wouldn't give her the same nonsensical answers her friends always gave her. *"It's not you, it's them." "You deserve better than those losers."* And her all-time favorite: *"Your time will come. Just be patient."* But when Zach didn't say anything, she glanced up to find him staring at her with a curiosity that she wasn't prepared for, his brown eyes studying her so hard that she couldn't help but look away. He was probably thinking she was ridiculous and had just answered her own question by asking him, a stranger, such a ridiculous and personal question.

"Never mind, it's a silly question," she said, reaching for the bottle of champagne on the table and topping off her glass.

"No. It's not a silly question. I don't think you're asking the right question though." He held his own glass up for her to fill. "You say you are looking for Mr. Right, but then you say you want to start a family. So which is it? Do you just want a family? Or are you looking for the love of your life? That one and only true love?"

Now it was Lori's turn to stare at Zach like he was being ridiculous. And then she stopped and actually considered what he was asking. The love of her life? Her one and only true love? Did she even believe that type of love existed? It seemed a long time since she'd considered a man for anything besides his husband and father qualifications. Had she given up on finding that one true love he was talking about? If it wasn't for her friends' relationships, would she even believe in it? Had all her failed relationships caused her to focus only on her goal of having a family?

"I don't know," she said honestly.

"Well, maybe that's the problem. I'm not sure I can give you a lot of advice on finding a man to fall in love with. Things between me and my late wife happened when neither of us were looking to fall in love too. But

I can tell you that once you find that once in a lifetime type of love, you'll know it. I can also tell you that finding that great love doesn't guarantee that all your dreams will come true. It has a cost. You have to decide if you are willing to pay that price. I know it's not a cost that I want to ever have to pay again."

His wife. He was talking about the price of losing his wife.

"I'm so sorry, I know you must miss your wife terribly," Lori said, then wanted to bite her tongue off. Of course he missed his late wife. And this was a wedding, a happy occasion. She had no business bringing up what she could tell were painful memories to this man, especially here where he had seemed to be enjoying himself earlier. But then all she'd been was a downer all night.

"Would you like to dance?" Lori said, standing suddenly. Zach had been nice enough to agree to accompany her to the wedding of a couple he didn't even know, and so far all she'd done was whine about her own life. And then she had brought up the painful subject of his losing his wife. She had to do better than this. He deserved better than this. They both deserved better than this tonight. Sky and Jared's wedding was supposed to be a happy occasion about them, not about her.

She held her hand out to him.

He hesitated a moment, then stood and took it, giving her a reassuring smile. "I'd love to."

They joined the other couples and for the next hour they danced to everything from classic country to the current hits. They were both breathless by the time they made their way back to their table after line dancing to a popular bar song.

"I can't believe I used to be able to do that for hours," Lori said, reaching for her glass.

"I can't believe we were line dancing next to Mindy and Trey Carter," Zach said, his smile broad, his eyes wide. Something about that smile and his big brown eyes had Lori taking another large gulp of her drink.

"Sky and Jared delivered their son a few months ago and they've been good friends ever since," Lori said, looking at him from the corner of her eyes.

How had she not noticed just how good-looking the new pediatrician was until tonight? They'd worked together several times since he'd come to Nashville as one of the neonatal hospitalists, though tonight was the first time they hadn't been surrounded by crying babies and worried mothers. Still, somehow, she'd never taken a real good look at the man. Maybe because she'd known he was a grieving husband which meant he was off her radar? But that still didn't mean she couldn't appreciate all his tall, dark and deliciousness. She also couldn't deny that the dancing hadn't been all that sent her heart racing.

"Well, it was a lot of fun. I have to thank you for inviting me tonight. I haven't enjoyed myself this much in…" Zach's smile dimmed and Lori knew he was thinking about his wife. "Anyway, thank you for inviting me."

"Thank you for agreeing to come with me—you saved the night for me. I don't think I could have stood to spend another night feeling like the awkward third party."

"I understand. I've had some experience with that myself since I lost Katherine. My friends, they all meant well, but most of our friends are married. It seemed to make things even more painful to be out with them," Zach said, staring down into his half-empty glass. "And then there is the awkwardness that everyone feels when you talk to someone who has lost someone. I understood why they felt that way—I've been in the same position. You don't know what to say. You don't know if they want to talk about the person they lost or not. So, you pretend that nothing has changed even though you both know it isn't true."

Lori remembered the feeling she'd had when she'd brought up his wife. He'd been so good at listening to her problems, problems that were so miniscule when compared to losing his wife. "I didn't know your wife, but if you ever want to talk about her, I'll be happy to listen."

Zach's smile, though not as bright as before, returned. "I'd like that. Moving to Nashville has been a blessing in some ways, but I'd lived in Memphis my whole life and I do miss my friends."

Lori lifted the champagne bottle and found it empty just as a waiter strolled by offering them a new bottle. Bree and Knox had waved bye to them as they'd left the wedding reception, and it seemed a waste to open a new bottle just for the two of them, but she took it anyway.

She filled her glass and then Zach's. "A toast to new beginnings and new friends."

"To new beginnings, and new friends." Zach's glass touched hers and they both took a drink.

"I hope you know I mean that," Lori said. "If you want or need to talk about anything, just call me. Or if you need something, let me know."

"You really mean that, don't you?"

"Of course. Besides, after talking to you about my problems with men, you've given me a lot to think about. I'm not sure what I'm going to do, but I know I need to make a change. I've spent the last three years looking for a man that might not exist and it's gotten me nowhere."

Zach took another drink, then set his glass down and pulled out his phone from his suit's inside pocket. "I want to tell you something and I know it's going to sound a bit unconventional, but I think you'll understand when you see this."

Lori watched him as she opened his phone, trying to prepare herself for whatever he could be about to show her. When he finished scrolling on his phone and pushed it over in front of her, she expected to see a picture of the beautiful woman that he was still mourning over. Instead, the face of a darling little boy, around a year old with curly dark hair and big brown eyes stared back at her with a wide smile. She knew that smile. She'd seen it earlier tonight on Zach's face while they were on the dance floor.

"My son, Andres," Zach said as he took his phone back, staring down at the picture of the little boy, his smile proud though it didn't reach his eyes.

"I didn't know you had a son," Lori said. "He's beautiful."

"He's the reason I moved to Nashville—to make a new life for the two of us."

"Nashville is a great place to raise a family. We have a great children's museum and then there is the zoo."

Lori had always dreamed of family outings to places like the zoo and the museum with a family of her own.

"He loves the Memphis Zoo. I'll have to take him to the zoo as soon as I can get him here with me," he said.

"What do you mean? Where is he?"

"It's a long story. Right now he's in Memphis with my in-laws, but I'm hoping to get everything set up so that he can be here with me soon. I'm settling into our new home right now and getting his room set up. There's only one thing I need now, and this is where you're going to think my idea is strange." Zach paused, looking down at the picture a moment longer before putting his phone back in his pocket. "I need a wife. Any chance you're interested?"

CHAPTER TWO

WHEN LORI BURST out in laughter, Zach knew she hadn't taken him seriously. But who could blame her? She had no idea how desperate he was, how much he needed someone's help to fix a situation that he'd created himself.

After his wife's death his brother had warned him against letting his wife's parents take Andres home from the hospital, but at the time it took all he had to just get through the day. The shock of his healthy wife suddenly going into cardiac arrest, only two days after the birth of their son, had crushed him. Even now, almost a year after he'd received the results of her autopsy, he found it hard to believe that a simple, tiny blood clot could destroy all the dreams they'd made for their family. He'd been inconsolable for the first week as he'd navigated through the funeral arrangements. And after the funeral, when he should have taken his son home, it had seemed too cruel to pry the infant from his grieving mother-in-law's arms.

"I have to say, that was definitely not how I saw my first proposal taking place. I'm afraid I envisioned flowers, a bended knee and maybe a ring," Lori said, as she held out her bare ring finger for him to see. It was when she let out a very unladylike giggle, that Zach realized that her champagne glass was empty.

"I'm sorry," she said, her hand coming up to cover her mouth, before she let out another laugh.

Her humor was catching, and he held up a large golden napkin ring to her. "Will this do?"

"It might be a little big, but I think it will work," she said, reaching for it. Taking it in her hand, she placed it on her ring finger, though at least two fingers could have fit inside it, and held it up toward the twinkling lights inside the reception tent.

"It's perfect," she said, continuing to admire the napkin ring on her finger.

Zach noticed the crowd was beginning to thin out. Because Lori had been part of the wedding party, she'd already been there when he'd arrived and he wasn't sure what arrangements she might have made to get home. One thing he was sure of, neither of them would be driving home.

"It looks like the party is ending," he said. "Did you drive here?"

"What? Oh, no. I rode with Bree and Knox. I can call a service to pick me up," Lori said, looking away from the cheap napkin ring she still wore around her finger to where a crowd was gathering. "Oh, we have to go send Sky and Jared off."

Before he could stop her, she sprang out of the chair, almost falling face-first.

"Hold on," he said, taking her arm to steady her as they hurried to follow the bride and groom who were heading down the drive to where a limo waited for them as all their well-wishers waved colorful lights and yelled their congratulations.

Pulling out his phone, he pulled up the app he'd used earlier that evening and requested a ride. "I've ordered us a car."

"Thank you," Lori said, as she wiped at her eyes. "Why do people cry at weddings?"

Taking her arm, he followed the other guests to the center of the curved driveway where several cars were already waiting for the partying guests. He thought about an answer he heard on a sitcom once, but didn't think she'd appreciate it. "Sometimes happiness moves people to tears. There are a lot of emotions that go into a new marriage. First you know they're leaving their old life behind, and sometimes that means friends and family changes too. But at the same time, it's a new beginning for both the bride and the groom. New beginnings can be both scary and exciting too and everyone responds differently to both."

"Are you excited about coming to Nashville for a new beginning?" Lori asked, her head coming to rest on his shoulder, something that would have made him uncomfortable a few hours ago, but which felt perfectly normal after spending the last few hours with her.

"I'm excited about the possibilities, of course, but mostly I just want to have my son with me." His phone dinged letting him know their driver was only a couple minutes away.

"I still don't understand. Why didn't he move with you? I know that being a single dad in a new city has to be stressful. If you need the recommendation of a good nanny or daycare, I'm sure someone at our office could help you out. With all the mothers that go in and out of our office, I'm sure we could find someone you could trust."

He loved that she included herself in helping him. If only things were that simple. "Things are complicated. My in-laws back in Memphis have been caring for Andres since he was born and they are—" how did he say this without sounding like a bitter son-in-law "—possessive. But we're going to work it out."

Oh, yes, they were certainly working it out. At this rate he'd be lucky if he had his son in Nashville by the time Andres started kindergarten. Or even later.

But it's your fault, he reminded himself. He'd let things get out of hand immediately after his wife's funeral. Instead of standing up and taking control as he should have, he'd all but handed over his infant son to them, something that he was too ashamed to admit to Lori. He'd been a poor example of a father, but that was going to change. Once he had settled Andres home with him, he'd never let his son down again.

A small blue sedan pulled up and Zach led Lori to the car, settling her into the back seat before joining her. The driver repeated Zach's address and started down the driveway.

"Are you okay if we make another stop on the way?" Zach asked the driver.

"Sure, I can add it into the app," the driver said. "Where to?"

"Lori?" Zach asked, easing her back from his shoulder. With her eyes closed and mouth half open, a cute snore sounded in his ear. "Lori, wake up. I need your address."

Another snore escaped her mouth, before she turned toward him and burrowed into his suit jacket. Not sure what to do, he shook her once, but only got a wince and a mumble from her. There was nothing else for him to do. It looked like Lori wouldn't be going home alone after all.

Lori rubbed her face against her pillow. There was something jabbing her in the hip, but she just didn't have the energy to move away from it. Maybe it was time for her to get a new mattress. One of those that cushioned you instead of poked you until you had no choice but to change positions. Rolling over, she felt something cold and metal come to rest against her leg. Reaching down, she pulled out the object, ready to throw it off the bed. Only when the cold metal touched her fingers did she realize what it was. It was the ring. The metal napkin ring Zach had "proposed" with. She slowly opened one eye. Nope, this wasn't her bed.

So where was she? And what had she done?

Afraid of what she might find, she looked to her left side, but there was no one there. She was alone and from what she could tell by the smooth sheets and undented pillow next to her, she'd been alone all night. Pulling back the sheets, she was relieved to see that she still wore the tea-length bridesmaid dress from the night before. Only her shoes were missing.

The door to the attached bathroom opened, and Zach stepped out. Only this wasn't the white lab-coated Dr. Morales she was used to, or the black-tie–dressed Zach she'd danced with the night before. No, this was a hot, steamy, version of Zachary Morales that made her breath catch.

His dark hair was brushed back, still damp enough that a drop of water rolled down the side of his face. She bit down on her bottom lip before her tongue could sweep out as she felt an uncontrollable need to lick that singular drop. Instead, her eyes followed the drop as it ran down his neck before disappearing into a bare chest that had her biting down even harder. With only a pair of sweatpants hung low on his hips, the man was every woman's dirty dream come true.

But this wasn't a dream. This was real. And somehow, though the headache that had begun to throb behind her temples made it hard to think, she had to figure out how she'd come to spend the night in Zach's bed. Was this even his bed? His house? Her head throbbed again and she remembered all that wonderful champagne she'd drunk the night before and wondered exactly what trouble it had gotten her into.

She looked over to the other side of the bed again. Was it possible that Zach had made his side of the bed after he'd gotten up? And the ring, that stupid napkin ring? Why was it here? He hadn't really been serious about his proposal. Had he?

"Good morning," Zach said as he began to dry his hair with a towel she hadn't noticed. "How are you feeling?"

"Maybe a little like Alice in Wonderland, who shouldn't have drunk that potion?" she said.

"I'm sorry. I didn't realize you'd…enjoyed…so much of the champagne till we were headed home. I couldn't get you to wake up to get your address so I brought you here with me. I hope you're okay with that."

"Of course. I'm sorry I put you in that position. I guess I shouldn't have been complaining about being the only one of my friends going home alone." She thought about what she said. "Not that I did this on purpose."

Dropping the towel on his dresser, he opened a drawer and pulled out a dark blue T-shirt. He pulled it over his head, giving her a view of taut muscles that had her stretching her neck to get a closer view.

"I didn't think you did," he said, turning back toward her. "It's fine. I have four bedrooms, but this is the only one with a bed so far, so I took the couch."

He walked into the closet and came out carrying a white pullover. "I was about to start breakfast."

Lori pushed the sheets off and climbed out of bed, then began to look for her shoes, locating one beside the bed. "I've been enough trouble. I'll call for a ride."

"You weren't any trouble at all. Let me show you my appreciation for inviting me last night with some eggs and bacon. It will help you feel better too," he said as he headed out the door. "The kitchen is downstairs on the left."

Waiting till he'd left, she got down on her knees and located her other shoe. Slipping both of them on, she looked from the bedroom door to the bathroom. Scooping her purse up from where she'd seen it lying on the dresser, she rushed into the bathroom to freshen up. She just hoped that a cold splash of water would be enough to cool down all her overstimulated hormones that Zach Morales had just awakened.

* * *

The smell of bacon was working its way upstairs by the time she came out of the bathroom. Not being much of a drinker normally, she wasn't sure how her stomach would handle eating, but right then her stomach growled at the delicious smell, so eggs and bacon it would be.

"Have a seat," Zachary said when she entered the modern kitchen set up with a long island facing windows that showed a large fenced back yard with a small playhouse and a swing set. She suspected that it hurt Zach every time he looked out that window and thought of his son not being there.

"How do you like your eggs?" Zach asked. "I can do scrambled and scrambled."

"I guess I'll go with the scrambled. How about I make some toast?"

"Perfect," he said, pointing toward the pantry.

They worked in silence, neither feeling the need to talk. Then they sat side by side and there was no awkwardness there either, though Lori did find her eyes straying to him whenever he wasn't looking. Still, even with this new awareness that she felt around him, there was a comfortable feeling between them that Lori knew was rare. As rare as the friendships she had with Sky and Bree.

"Tell me about your son," she asked, wanting to know more about the cute toddler with the eyes and smile that matched his father's.

"He's a happy child, for that I'm thankful," he said.

"You were afraid he wouldn't be? Because of the loss of his mother?" she asked before standing to bring the coffeepot closer. "And what's this thing with your in-laws? Explain it all to me again."

She was afraid she'd crossed the line when she poured coffee into his cup and noticed the white-knuckled hold he had on it. Whatever it was, why ever he felt he needed to have a wife to bring his son to Nashville to live with him, she wanted to know. And if there was anything she could do to help him within her power, with the exception of marrying him, she'd do it.

His hand moved away from his cup, and he put his fork down before turning toward her. Any of the comfort she'd felt between them was gone. He had withdrawn from her, as if explaining about his son would change things between them. But why?

"When Katherine died, I was a mess. By the time I started getting myself together, my son had been with my in-laws for a couple months." He looked down at his half-eaten plate of food. "Andres was so little and I felt so alone and unable to cope without his mother. So, I took the easy way out. I let him stay with his grandparents, thinking that it was what was best for him to have us all around him."

He looked up to her, his eyes searching hers. For what? Did he really think she was going to judge him for his actions? Why? Because she'd told him how her own father had left her? He had to know that this wasn't the same. He'd just been through the trauma of losing his wife. How could she judge him? How could anyone? He was grieving. And the truth was, at that time it might have been better for his son to stay with his grandparents. Who was she or anyone else to judge that? Who else could know what he was able to handle at that time, but Zach?

"You needed time to grieve. I understand that. And it's understandable that you needed some time to come to terms with being a single dad. A new baby is a lot for anyone, especially someone who has just lost their wife."

"But I'm a pediatrician. I should have been able to handle it."

"No. You were a man who had just lost his partner. You were a new father that felt overwhelmed." She held her hand up when he would have interrupted her. "You were in shock. It's understandable and I'm sure it's not the first time that grandparents have stepped in and helped this way. I've had patients, couples, that go stay with their family members the first few weeks, just so they have that extra support."

"Besides, all of that is in the past," she went on before he could try to interrupt her again. It was plain to see that he was suffering a terrible case of guilt. It would take time for him to get over it. The only thing that would help was for him to put things right with his son now. Which meant he had to move forward. "Now, tell me the reason, the real reason, your son is not here with you now."

He looked at her, stunned. Was he so used to the people in his life judging him for what he'd done? "You don't understand. I did this. I wasn't the father I should have been."

"From what I can see, you did exactly what a caring father would have done. You knew you couldn't take care of your son, so you put him with people you trusted.

You were doing the best you could. You're human. Give yourself a break. What matters now is getting your son back with you, right?"

He stared at her, his brown eyes studying her as if he wasn't sure he could believe her words. "You understand."

"Yes, I do," Lori said. "Now, tell me what we need to do to get your son here with you, where he belongs."

They cleared the table as they talked, him explaining his relationship with his in-laws, which seemed to have been good until he'd told them that he was moving to Nashville to make a new life for him and his son. As could be expected from doting grandparents, the thought of not seeing their grandson daily had not gone over well.

"Did you consider just taking Andres to live with you instead of moving out of town?"

"Oh, I tried to do that just weeks after he was born, but there was always a reason that my mother-in-law didn't feel that it would work. First it was that my hours were too irregular—a baby needed consistency. My answer to that was to get a live-in nanny. Her answer to that was why do that, when I could just move in with them."

"Oh, no. Tell me you didn't do that." She handed him a plate to load into the dishwasher, then took a kitchen rag and began wiping down the stove.

"Of course I did. But even though I was still in the same house with my son, I was made to feel like a visitor. Like someone they were allowing to spend time with his own son. That's when I talked to my brother and decided to relocate my practice to Nashville."

It must have been really bad for him to go to the extreme of relocating his practice, which was not only a lot of work, but expensive too. He had to have felt that it was his only choice.

"I still don't understand why you don't just go to their house and take your son. You're his father."

Zach placed the last of the dishes in the dishwasher and turned it on before answering her. "My wife was an only child. They doted on her and she loved them very much. I know that I wasn't the only one that suffered a loss when she died. Over the years that Katherine and I dated, then married, I came to love them too. I lost my parents when I was nine. My older brother and I went to live with my cousins, but it wasn't the same. Katherine's parents came to be like a new set of parents to me. We were as close as families could be until now."

So not only had he lost his wife, now he feared he was going to lose the love of his in-laws, people who he'd thought loved him like a son. The longer his story went on, the sadder it was becoming.

"And you're right. When I let them take Andres home from the hospital, I had no doubt he was in good hands. But now, they aren't the same. It's like instead of accepting that they lost their daughter, they have used Andres to fill that hole in their hearts. Anytime I've mentioned taking Andres, made plans to move out on my own with him, they've countered with reasons why that wouldn't work out. Katherine's death changed them, especially her mother. This last time, when I explained that I was moving to Nashville, they threatened to take me to court. To say that I had abandoned my son. They're threatening to file for custody."

It was easy to see the hurt in his eyes. "If I have to go to court, I will. But I would rather find another way. Some way to counteract all their reasons for why a single dad with a demanding job can't give their grandson as good of a life as they can."

"So, you weren't joking about needing a wife?" The whole idea that he would just marry some stranger still sounded absurd to her. Of course, if you considered that she'd realized just the night before that she'd spent the last three years looking for a baby's daddy more than for a man that would love her, maybe she shouldn't be so judgmental.

"I know they're going to try to show that as a single dad with a demanding job, Andres is better off with them. They can probably use the fact that I left him with them after Katherine passed as evidence that I, myself, didn't even think I could take care of him."

She could see why he'd think that having a wife, someone to share in taking care of his son might help, but there were a lot of single moms doing fine raising their children. That reasoning wouldn't get them far. And it would be hard to argue that Zach wasn't moving forward, hadn't dealt with his grief and wasn't ready to be a fulltime parent to his son, if he was to marry. But Lori thought that what Zach needed more than anything was to have someone on his side. To show his in-laws that he had someone in his corner that was ready to go head-to-head with them and that would be there for Andres too. And Zach needed to know that he wasn't alone. Lori could tell with just the little amount of time that she'd spent with him that, though he did have a brother and cousins, Zach had been bearing this burden alone for a long time.

"You said you have a brother? He lives here?" she asked. Having family support nearby would be a plus too.

"He's lives in Hendersonville, so about thirty minutes away. He and his wife have three kids, the youngest is just a month older than Andres."

"Well, that's good. I'm sure Andres's grandparents want him to grow up around family." Lori washed out the dishrag and spread it out to dry. "And even if they don't, I'm sure a judge would take your having family support into consideration too."

"I'm hoping it doesn't go that far. I know we are at odds now about what is best for my son, but there was a time when I thought of them as family too." He turned to her, his eyes sober. "I don't want to hurt my wife's parents. She loved them and I know she'd never want me to hurt them this way. I have to find a way to make everything right between us, but still have my son here with me where he belongs. Does that make sense?"

It made perfect sense, and just showed what type of man he truly was. He was the kind of man she had been looking for, one that would make a great father.

Only he wasn't looking for a wife to love, he was looking for a wife to take care of his son. It would be a ready-made family, something that might have been tempting to her if she hadn't seen that sad look in his eyes every time he talked about his wife. It was one thing to give up on finding her Mr. Right. It was a whole other thing to live in the shadow of a woman who was no longer here in this world. No, that was not something that any woman should ever have to do.

And though she didn't agree with what his in-laws were doing, she had never met them. They might normally be perfectly nice people. Life had changed for all of them the moment Zach's wife, their only daughter, had died, and that had apparently changed the dynamics of their relationship too. But maybe there was still hope for them, if not for their sake, for the sake of the little boy who they all loved.

They'd busied themselves as they'd talked and the kitchen now was spotless. It was time for Lori to go, but her mind kept going over and over Zach's problem. Problem solving had always been something she enjoyed. It was one of the things that had drawn her into going to nursing school.

"So, what if instead of going to the extreme of marrying someone, which I think would be a terrible idea, you make your in-laws think you're getting married." She sat down on one of the bar stools. Her headache had retreated to the back of her neck now and though the food had helped her stomach settle, she was still feeling some of the effects of her over-partying.

"What do you mean?" he said, leaning against the island that separated them. "Make up a story about some woman I'm engaged to? And when they want to meet her? They'd be even more determined to keep Andres if they believed I would try to fool them."

"I'm not saying make up someone. Haven't you ever read a romance novel?"

One dark eyebrow went up at her question. Why wasn't she surprised?

"Okay, here's a quick tutorial. First, romance books are a great genre, and every man should at least read one before they count them out. Second, a lot—I'd say the majority—of romance books have tropes, certain themes or plots that readers love. One of the most popular ones, and one of my favorites, is the fake fiancée trope."

Zach leaned in closer. "You read those books?"

"I love those books. And I think they could hold the answer to your problem."

He took a seat across from her and waited.

"Okay, so how these books work is, someone, say a billionaire or a—" she pointed to him "—single dad, needs a wife. Sometimes it's because of family issues, such as nagging parents who refuse to quit matchmaking. Sometimes it's a business arrangement. Sometimes it's just to save someone from being humiliated, like when someone's ex is getting married and they've been invited to the wedding."

"I'd say they're all silly ideas, except I can feel where they are coming from. So, what exactly do they do to make people believe them? It isn't like you can suddenly show up with a fiancée and no one is going to be suspicious."

Lori looked at him before making a dramatic eye roll. "Your plan was to show up with a *wife* that no one had ever heard of. You didn't think that might look a little suspicious?"

Zach's lips parted in a smile. "I admit, it wasn't something I had thought out. It's just that we were talking about you needing a husband and a family and it just seemed like me having a wife would help out with my in-laws concerns about me being a single dad. But you're right. This sounds like a much better idea."

"Of course it does," she said, smiling back at him smugly.

"But those books you're talking about, with this fake fiancée trope. They're romances, so that means they always end with a happy ending, right? Boy gets the girl, that kind of thing?"

"Well, yes. But in this case, instead of a romantic happy ending, you'll have a happy ending with your son." Lori felt a little tinge of uneasiness. She knew exactly how those stories ended. The single dad not only ended up with the son, but also with the girl. Only from the way Zach had looked every time he talked about his late wife, the last thing he would want was to end up with the girl. He'd made it plain that he thought the cost of love was too high the night of Sky's wedding.

"So, you'll do it?" he asked, his smile so confident that she almost agreed.

"Why me?" She knew she should be shocked by his request, but it had been her idea and she had to admit she had been considering it the whole time she'd been explaining it to him. Her life was at a standstill and it didn't look like he had anyone else that could do that for him. Maybe just pretending to be engaged would help her discover what it was she was going to do with her life. She'd always thought that she would have that happily-ever-after that she read about. But right now she wasn't sure that would ever be in her future. At least it wasn't unless she made some changes and found some way to trust her heart, something that she had never been able to do.

And then there were those big brown eyes. Not only the ones that stared at her so hopefully right then, but the ones of the little boy in the picture Zach had showed her. In her heart she knew those two belonged together. And unlike her father, Zach was trying to do the right thing for his son.

But playing as Zach's fiancée? She was still recovering from her reaction to him this morning in the bedroom. Playing his fiancée, spending the amount of time with him that would entail, could be dangerous, at least for her.

"Who better? You seem to be an expert on this faking thing," Zach said.

"I'm certainly not an expert at faking it. It's not like it's something I've ever done." But hadn't she done just that through relationship after relationship? Pretending that she wanted to love and be loved, while the whole time a part of her was self-consciously waiting for the person she was involved with to leave her? She could even see now that she'd been the one to end relationships because of her fear that if she got too close to someone she was afraid they were going to leave her. Hadn't Skye accused her of running away from people when they got too close?

"But you know how to, you've read about it. You'd make a perfect fiancée," Zach said, so confident that she was beginning to believe him.

"I'm perfect because I'm the only woman you know in Nashville." She understood she was too close to agreeing with him. She needed to stop and think this out.

"You're perfect because you're the only one I trust," Zach said.

Somehow she realized, deep inside herself, that he meant those words. They barely knew each other, yet he trusted her. It sounded unbelievable after the short period of time they'd known each other, but she felt the same way. Too bad she trusted the one man that wasn't available. Or maybe that was why she felt safe trusting him.

That realization had her standing and walking over to the counter where she'd laid her purse. She needed to leave before she agreed. She needed to think things over and make sure that she was up to this. The last thing she wanted to do was to fail to help Zach get his son back. Or even worse, make things even more difficult for him. "I need to think about it. See if I can make it work."

"But you are going to think about it?" His eyes lit up with hope, making it even harder for her to walk away without giving him an answer.

Oh, she was definitely thinking about it, thinking how she could help him convince his in-laws that his son belonged with his father and his wife-to-be. If only it was that simple.

Because there was one thing she hadn't told Zach about those romance books that she had read, the hero and heroine always got their happily-ever-after. But with a man who was still grieving the loss of his wife, the only happily-ever-after she could hope for in this case was for the hero to get his son back.

CHAPTER THREE

ZACH WATCHED AS Lori walked up the sidewalk to her house. He wasn't sure what to think of the midwife. He didn't think he'd ever met anyone quite like her before. She had so much energy and she was so spontaneous, something she would have to be to consider his proposal of faking an engagement with him.

A fake engagement. What had he been thinking? He didn't even know if it would help him with his situation with his in-laws, but then it couldn't hurt. And he wasn't sure why, but for some reason, he felt that having Lori by his side was just what he needed. It just seemed right.

A pang of guilt rushed over him. It was supposed to be Katherine by his side, not a woman that he barely knew. The fact that he was even considering letting someone get close to him like this made him uncomfortable. He had no right to be forming a relationship, even a platonic one with Lori.

But how was he supposed to make this all work? How was he supposed to pretend to be in a relationship with Lori? A part of him had been frozen since the moment he lost his wife. He had no idea how to even act intimate with another woman now, though he had to say, he and Lori did have a surprising chemistry together. And there was that guilt again. He shouldn't be feeling an type of chemistry for Lori. But there it was. Would it make it easier to pull off this whole pretense?

After leaving the house, Zach headed to the nearest bookstore. Maybe Lori was right. Maybe he did need to read some of those romance books she was talking about.

Zach had just dropped Lori off at her home when her phone rang. It was her mother, not surprising since she'd already noticed her mom's car at the curb.

"Where are you?" her mother asked.

Lori looked down at the bridesmaid dress that she still wore and for a second Lori considered calling Zach and having him come back and get her. She knew her mother was going to assume that she'd spent the night with the new doctor Lori had invited to the wedding.

This was going to be as awkward as catching her boss and her mother play tonsil hockey on the family couch, a picture that would be burned in her brain for eternity.

Well, it seemed now would be as good a time as any to try out her acting skills. If nothing else, she could at least hint that there was something going on between her and Zach. That wasn't a lie. At least there could be soon if she agreed to help him.

Was she really thinking about doing this with Zach? Fake an engagement with someone she barely knew? What was she thinking?

Well, that was easy. She was thinking about helping a man who'd already lost his wife and was in danger of losing his son. She would hope that someone would have helped her father if he'd wanted to get back into Lori's life, though she'd given up on that dream years ago.

"I'm here," she said as she opened the door to their home. "I thought it was your weekend to stay at Legacy House."

Her mother hung up the phone as Lori walked into the foyer, stopping when she saw Lori as her eyes swept up and down her daughter. "You haven't been home since the wedding?"

"Since you would know that if you had spent the night here, I guess I could ask you the same question." Lori wasn't an amateur when it came to getting out of trouble with her mom. Changing the subject had always worked well for her. Putting her mom on the defense wouldn't hurt either.

"I've been here. Your car was in the garage so I figured you were home," her mother said, ignoring the fact that Lori knew her mother would have checked in on her in her room if she had actually come in during the night.

"Okay. You caught me. I spent the night at Zach's place." Lori realized her mom would read more into that statement than she should, but it was the truth. Her mother probably wouldn't even believe her if she told her there had been nothing but sleeping going on at Zach's.

"Jack introduced me to Dr. Morales before the wedding. He seems like a nice guy, especially compared to Donald."

Had anyone liked her ex? Now that she thought about it, she hadn't given the man one thought once she'd begun talking to Zach the night before.

"He is really a nice guy. I'm glad I invited him." Lori

moved past her mother, heading up the stairs to shower and change.

"Just be careful, Lori. Jack said Zach lost his wife just over a year ago. I don't want to see you hurt."

Lori stopped and turned toward her mom. Part of her wanted to tell her all about Zach's issues with his in-laws and his son. But that wasn't her story to tell, even though she'd love her mother's advice.

And if she did decide to play the part of Zach's fiancée, she wouldn't be able to tell anyone, not even her mother. For all practical purposes, she'd be his fiancée. It had to be that way if they wanted to make sure he got his son back. "Don't worry, Mom. Things are good between us. I feel like I've known him all my life, and I think he feels the same way."

And that part wasn't a lie. Hopefully, that would just be one more thing that would help them be successful if she agreed to help him. Lori started up the stairs then stopped.

"Mom, is that why you haven't dated anyone till now? Because you were grieving over Jim leaving?" She'd refused to call her father by anything but his given name since she'd been a teenager and sent him a letter he'd never answered back.

"Grieving? No, I wouldn't say that. I think it was more that I lost the ability to trust someone not to hurt me again."

Lori hadn't been sure how she felt about her mother dating her boss until then. If there was anyone she knew that would never hurt her mother, it would be Dr. Warner. But it had taken her mom twenty years to get to the point that she could trust another man. Lori couldn't help but think of herself twenty years from now, still single, still childless. Still waiting for a man she could trust enough to have the kind of relationship her friends had. "I'm happy for you and Dr. Warner. And I know that you can trust him."

The office was short with both a midwife and a doctor being off and it would stay that way until Sky and Jared were back from their honeymoon. But while everyone had their hands full, there was still talk of the weekend wedding. Lori wasn't surprised when she was stopped by several of the staff with questions about the new guy she'd brought to the wedding. Their office was a close group, but they also had their share of gossips so she'd prepared herself with noncommittal answers concerning her and Zach, while still leaving them with a hint that she was interested in getting to know the new doctor at the hospital better. When she found herself cornered by the office receptionist, the lifeline to the office rumor mill, she more than hinted that she and Zach planned to be seeing more of each other.

"I hear he lost his wife last year," he said. "Don't go and get yourself hurt, girl."

She'd just laughed and brushed off the comment. The people she worked with knew her record of picking the wrong man almost every time. "He's a nice guy and he's new to town. I just want him to feel…welcomed."

She winked at him and walked away. That would surely cause some whispers around the clinic. It might even become more popular than the one concerning her mother and the senior Dr. Warner. Besides, it couldn't hurt to have the staff thinking of the two of them as interested in each other.

Because though she still hadn't given her answer to Zach's request, she knew that she was leaning toward agreeing to play his fake fiancée. Zach needed her help. So did the little boy who had no mother. And it wasn't as if she had anything else going on in her life. She had no love life. And after talking with her mother and looking back over her history with men, she wasn't even sure now that it was something she would ever be ready for. Still, accepting the possibility that she'd never meet her Mr. Right was hard for her. Just as hard as accepting that she might never have the family, the children, that she'd always dreamed of having.

Her workload was heavy that morning, so it was lunchtime before she could round on the patients that had delivered over the weekend and she was nervous about the possibility of running into Zach. He would want an answer soon and she still worried that she wouldn't be able to do what he needed her to do. Just the fact that the clinic's receptionist had considered that Zach would be interested in her surprised her.

Because, while Zach with his dark and mysterious vibes would draw women to him by groves, she was just a plain Jane, nothing special at all. With her pale skin and light brown hair, she definitely wasn't the type of woman that a man would suddenly declare his undying love for or his plans to marry her. How were they supposed to make anyone, especially his in-laws, suddenly believe in their love at first sight?

She was so busy thinking about Zach and his in-laws, that she didn't hear the nurse's call for help until the nurse passed Lori with a woman in the wheelchair. The woman's panting and white-knuckled grip on the arms of the wheelchair was proof enough for both of them that this woman was in labor.

"What room?" Lori asked, running in front of Sandy, one of the more experienced nurses on the unit.

"Room eight, it should be set up for an emergency delivery," Sandy said.

Lori ran to the room and opened the door, holding it open for the nurse. It took both of them to help the woman into the bed. And as Sandy began to undress their patient, Lori pulled the emergency call light, then returned to the woman's side.

"My name is Lori. I'm one of the midwives here on the unit. Can you tell me the name of your OB doctor?"

"I haven't seen one," the woman said before her hands grabbed ahold of the bed's side rails and she began to bear down.

"Try not to push," Lori told her, though she knew the woman was too far into the contraction to listen to her.

Another nurse rushed into the room as Lori grabbed a pair of gloves. It took just a moment for Lori to confirm that not only was the woman in active labor, but she was only minutes from delivering. The good news was that Lori was sure that the baby was coming headfirst, as she could already see a dark cap of hair as it began to crown. "Call and see if there is an OB doc on the floor."

Without any prenatal care, Lori had no idea what complications she could be facing with the delivery or with the baby after delivery. She didn't even know if this baby was term. "And call the nursery, have them send down the NICU team."

"I know this is hard—" heavens, Lori didn't even know this woman's name "—but it's almost over. We're trying to get one of the doctors into the room in case there are complications, so try not to push if you can."

The woman took a breath and began to bear down again and Lori knew there would be no waiting for a doctor. She'd be the one delivering this baby.

"What's your name?" Lori asked the woman when she stopped to take a breath.

"It doesn't matter," the woman said, her eyes avoiding Lori's, causing a chill to run down her back. Something was definitely wrong here.

But as the woman bore down again, Lori had to put everything else aside as she carefully delivered a small dark-haired head, then one shoulder and then the other one. The NICU team arrived just in time as she delivered the rest of the body, then held the tiny newborn only a moment, drying it off, before it let out a weak cry. Quickly clamping and cutting the cord, Lori handed the baby to one of the NICU nurses. By the small size of the baby girl, weighing no more than five pounds if she had to guess, the baby looked to be at least six weeks premature.

The door opened and Zach came into the room. Their eyes only met for a moment before he headed toward the neonatal unit where he took control of the assessment. While Lori finished with the delivery and a small repair, she listened to Zach as he began his assessment.

"One-minute Apgar?" he asked one of the nurses assisting him.

"I gave her a seven, counting off for her tone, reflex and color."

"Her Dubowitz is coming out at around thirty-four weeks. Lori, what was her due date?" he asked.

Lori looked at her patient, but the woman turned her gaze away from her. Whether from guilt about not getting any prenatal care or simply not caring, Lori wasn't sure. Something was definitely wrong with this situation and Lori would be having a conversation with this mother as soon as they had more privacy. "There was no prenatal care, so I'm not sure."

A buzzer went off and one of the NICU nurses silenced it. "Five-minute Apgar score of eight. Still some cyanosis, but she has a heart rate of one hundred and forty, good flexion and respiratory effort with a good cry, though she's breathing a little fast and her tone could be better."

"Breath sounds are good, and I don't hear any murmur. Let's get her to the NICU and get a preterm blood panel," Zach said.

As Lori and Sandy repositioned the patient, who still hadn't disclosed her name, Zach walked over to the bed to join them. "I'm Dr. Morales. I'm the pediatric and neonatal hospitalist here at the hospital. It looks like your little girl came a few weeks early, but she seems to be handling it well. We're going to watch her closely in the NICU for the next few hours. Do you have any questions for me?"

When the woman didn't say anything, he went on,

"Lori and the nurses are going to want to get your medical history so that we can know if there is anything we should be worried about. Some of those questions might be personal, but they're important for us to care for your baby. We're not here to judge you. We just want you and your baby to get the best care possible." Zach nodded to Lori and Sandy before leaving the room. Whether he'd seen the marks on the woman's arms or whether he just had good intuition, Lori knew he suspected the same thing as she did. The most probable reason this woman hadn't gotten prenatal care was because she was using drugs. Which meant the little baby girl that Lori had just delivered was not only a few weeks premature, she would probably also have to go through drug withdrawal.

"Sandy, if you could get…?" Lori said, hoping to force the woman to give them some type of identification.

"You can call me Christy," the woman said before turning away from them. "I don't need anything. I'm just tired and need to sleep."

"How about we let you rest for an hour, and then I'll be back to check on you? We'll get you some food brought up too. Sound like a plan?"

The woman shrugged her shoulders and Lori and Sandy slipped out of the room, closing the door quietly behind them.

"Do you think her name is really Christy?" Sandy asked.

"I don't know," Lori said, "but I hope to find out. She has to realize that we aren't going to send that baby home with her without getting her information."

"From the needle marks on her arms, I don't think that

baby will be going home with her at all. I don't know if she noticed that I drew some blood when I started her IV. I'll add a drug toxicology screening to the prenatal panel."

"Let me know when you get the results. I've got three postpartum patients to see on the floor and then I'm going to go by NICU and check on the baby before I head back to the office." While Sandy headed toward the nurse's station, Lori stopped at her first patient's room.

In forty minutes, she had seen all three patients and written discharge orders on two of them. By the time she made it to the NICU department, she had fifteen minutes left. She knew there was nothing she could do for the little girl she'd just delivered, but she felt this overwhelming need to make sure that the baby was doing well. Maybe it was because the baby's mother had shown no interest in her. The thought of a baby all alone in this big new world without her momma's arms to comfort her tore at Lori's heart when her own arms ached to hold a child of her own.

"How's she doing?" she asked Zach as she came up behind him. While there were several babies in warmers and isolettes, she recognized the baby she had just delivered immediately. She had a tiny nasal cannula in her equally tiny nose and another tiny intravenous catheter had been inserted into her arm with a small two-hundred-and-fifty-milligram bag of fluid running into it. While the baby's color had improved, Lori could see that she was still breathing too fast.

"Did the mother tell you when her water broke?" he asked, all his attention on the baby.

"No. She's not cooperating at all. I couldn't even get a last name from her. I do know it had broken before she came into the hospital. We agreed to let her sleep for an hour and then talk. We ordered a toxicology screen with the regular labs and I'm sure it will come back positive, I just don't know with what." Lori leaned over the warmer and placed her finger in the baby's hand. When her little hand grasped her finger, hanging on tightly, Lori's heart broke. This little one would be a fighter whether her mother cared or not. Right then, she decided no matter what, she was going to make sure this child got the love and the care she needed so badly.

Lori carefully removed her finger from the delicate little hand. "I'll let you know what I find out as soon as I finish talking to her."

The door to the NICU unit opened and Sandy rushed in. One look at her strained face and Lori realized something was very wrong.

"She's gone," Sandy said, her face pale and her breathing labored as if she'd run all the way from the patient's room.

It only took a minute for Lori to realize who she was talking about. "Christy? Do you have security looking for her?"

"I can't," Sandy said, holding out a piece of paper to Lori.

Lori recognized the sheet of paper as one of the information letters that the hospital had placed in every patient's room, but when she turned it over, she saw what it was that had upset Sandy.

"'To whom it concerns, I am leaving the hospital and

I am leaving my baby under the Tennessee Safe Haven law. Please take care of her. I am doing this of my own free will and according to this law I cannot be prosecuted,'" Lori read, then handed the letter to Zach.

"She can do this?" one of the NICU nurses asked.

"Yes, within two weeks of birth," Zach answered. "The law was put in place to protect the baby and also the privacy of the parents."

"Better that a baby is given up somewhere safe, like a hospital, than just abandoned on the street," Sandy said, though you could tell she was still upset.

"It's okay. It's not your fault. I should have insisted that she talk to me right away instead of waiting," Lori said. "Maybe I could have found out what was going on and found her some help before she did something this desperate."

"It wouldn't have mattered. She never intended to answer your questions when she came into the hospital. This was probably her plan all the time. The good thing is we did get some lab work before she left. And so far, this little one seems to be holding her own. All we can do is take care of her for right now," Zach said.

"I'll call DCS," Sandy said. "They can open a case immediately and hopefully there will be someone special out there who will love that little baby just as if it was their own."

"No, I'll make the call," Lori said, her mind already spinning with possibilities. Possibilities that had her heart beating fast and her hopes soaring to the sky. Here was a baby that had been abandoned. A baby that needed a mother to love her. Lori knew how it felt to be abandoned. No child ever deserved to feel unwanted. It was as if all the puzzle pieces of her life, the ones she had been struggling with, were suddenly falling into place. She'd thought about adoption before and had been involved with several patients that had chosen adoptive families for their babies. She'd considered that it might be something she wanted to do in the future. But delivering this baby and then just as fast discovering that the tiny girl had been abandoned—it was as if it was meant to be now.

"How about coffee later?" Zach asked as Lori was heading out to make the call. She could tell he wanted to know her answer about helping him.

For just a moment, she studied him. She knew so little about the man, yet it was everything she needed to know.

She'd seen how gentle he could be as he had carefully examined the newborn. She'd seen how patient he was with the mother of the newborn, showing no judgment for the fact that the woman hadn't received the proper maternity care. And she'd seen the way his eyes lit up when he talked about his son.

How could she not help a man like Zach, one that would be there to help her if she ever needed it? "How about we meet as soon as I finish at the office? I think the two of us have a lot to talk about."

CHAPTER FOUR

AFTER RECEIVING A text saying that she was free to meet him, Zach waited in the hospital café for her to join him while he went over the call he'd just received from his mother-in-law inviting him down for the weekend. Inviting him to see his own son? He felt anger boiling up inside him.

He'd been a patient man. Oh, he'd messed up by not taking on the responsibility of his newborn son when his wife had died, though what else was he supposed to do when his grieving mother-in-law kept reminding him over and over that his son needed someone who'd had experience with a newborn? Somehow between his own grief and her assurance that it was the best thing for Andres to go home with her, the fact that he was a pediatrician seemed to be ignored.

But his anger cooled when he remembered his mother-in-law's silence when he had told her he might be bringing someone with him, someone he wanted her to meet. It took a lot to shut the woman up, but that had done it. She'd had the same reaction when he'd told her he was moving to Nashville and would be taking his son with him. For a day or two there had only been silence from her, until the week before he was supposed to move and she'd informed him that taking Andres with him while he was starting a new job would be harmful for the child. And when he had protested? That had been when the not-so-subtle threats had started and he knew he had to do something drastic to convince his in-laws to let his son go or there was going to be an ugly trial. One that would have broken his wife's heart if she was still alive.

So, it was because of his love for his son and his respect for his wife's memory that he sat there waiting for someone he'd only known for a few weeks—and that had been mostly work related— to decide if she would be willing to help him convince his in-laws, and the courts, if necessary, that his son belonged with his father. Even if that father had made some mistakes before.

Realizing he had been staring into a cup of cold coffee, he glanced up and saw Lori at the cash register with her own cup. Laughing at something the man taking her money had said, she looked like she didn't have a care in the world.

But he'd seen those eyes as they had gazed at the little abandoned baby. She'd been beating herself up for not doing something to keep the mother from taking such a desperate action, though they both knew in the long run it was best for the baby.

Though wasn't that what he had thought he was doing when he'd left his own baby boy in his in-laws hands? Hopefully, the mother of the baby now known as Baby Girl Doe wouldn't have those regrets, though their two situations were nothing alike.

"Sorry, I was so backed up at the office after the

delivery this afternoon and my last patient was a new mother-to-be with a lot of questions I needed to answer."

"No problem. I was behind too."

"Is there a problem? Is the baby doing okay?" she said, stopping across from him. The worry in her voice showing just how taken she was with the little abandoned baby.

"She's doing okay so far, but we're watching her closely."

She took a seat across from him, brushing back the hair that had fallen into her eyes before lifting her cup and taking her first sip. She appeared tired with shadows below her eyes, but she still had a smile when she looked up at him.

Green, her eyes were green. He'd tried to remember the color of her eyes—it seemed like something you should know if you were engaged to someone—but all he could remember was the way they'd seemed to sparkle as the two of them had danced the night of the wedding. But these weren't just any green, Lori's eyes were the color of new grass as it broke through the dead brown grass that covered the yard after winter. The color that reminded you that the world would soon be awakening, it was the color of hope.

And that was exactly what he saw in her, the hope of a better future for him and his son. And if maybe he saw a little more, the hope that she might help heal the pain he'd felt since his wife had died, that was something he knew he needed to ignore. Friendship was something he was comfortable with. Anything more with Lori wasn't an option. She deserved to have a man love her like he had loved Katherine.

And that was a love he never wanted to feel again.

"Are you okay?" she asked, leaning over the table toward him. Had he missed something?

"Sorry," he said. "Long day topped off with a call from my mother-in-law."

"Is everything all right with your son?" she asked.

He could see the true concern she had for a little boy she'd never met. She was just that much of a caring person. What had all those exes of hers been thinking to let her get away?

"He's fine. I got to talk to him and listened to his jabbering for a few minutes. She 'invited' me to see my son this weekend. I told her I might be bringing someone for her to meet."

Lori went still, her eyes studying him as if she was trying to come to some type of conclusion.

He'd pushed too hard, too fast. "Don't worry, I didn't tell her anything definite. I'm not trying to pressure you into doing something you don't want to do."

She blinked and a very mischievous grin formed on her lips. "It's okay. I think I'd like to meet your in-laws. And I'd definitely like to meet Andres." The smile on her face relaxed into the more genuine one he was used to. "Fortunately, I'm off after clinic hours Friday so my weekend is free."

"So, you've decided to help me?" His whole body unwound for the first time since she'd told him she'd consider playing the part of his fiancée.

"Yes, but I need something from you in return. I spoke

with DCS about the baby. They're aware the baby is preterm and is still on oxygen and nowhere near to being ready to be discharged. I know the case manager that's been assigned to the case, so I called her too. I told her of our suspicions about the mother's drug use. I told her I'd let her know as soon as we got the toxicology tests back. I also told her that I was interested in fostering and later adopting the baby."

Her words should have shocked him, and at some level they did, but he'd seen just how taken she was with the baby. And he'd seen the pain in her eyes when she'd had to pull her finger away from the baby's grasp. It was almost like the midwife and baby had formed a bond stronger in those few seconds then the mother had formed with the baby she had carried for nearly nine months.

"What did the case manager say?" he asked, hoping that if this was something Lori truly wanted the state would at least consider her.

"There is a lot of red tape, and there's an application and a background check to begin with. I'll need to go through a training program and of course have a house inspection. And I'll need five letters of reference."

The list seemed daunting, but Lori had a positive nature and it showed as she went through the long list of requirements. "I'll be glad to give you a letter of recommendation. I would think as the baby's hospital provider it would carry some weight."

"I appreciate the offer, but I don't think that they'd take the letter from my fiancé. I think having a pediatrician that knows the baby being that fiancé might actually carry even more weight."

"You told them we were engaged?" Zach asked. Lori was definitely a woman who didn't waste time going for what she wanted.

She leaned over the table and laid her hands over his, then said quietly, "Yes. And don't look behind you, but it appears like we are about to have to tell someone else tonight before it gets out to anyone else."

She tightened her hands over his and leaned closer, "And please try to look a little happier at the news. Because if you don't take that shocked expression off your face no one is going to believe us."

He made his face relax and he pulled one of his hands away to cover both of hers and smiled. Far be it for him to mess things up now that she had put everything into motion.

His smile almost shattered when she looked above where he was seated and said, "Hi, Mom."

Lori had been running on empty for over four hours. The busy office, the delivery of the baby, and then being informed of the complicated process she would have to go through to be able to bring home Baby Girl Doe, a name that was wrong for so many reasons, had taken every bit of stamina she had stored up. All she wanted to do was have a few moments to make plans with Zach and head home to her bed. Telling her mother that she and Zach were engaged could have been left for tomorrow, except her mother was here now.

"I'm so glad you're here. You've met Zach."

"We met at the wedding. Jack introduced us." Her mother took a seat at the table, looking over at Zach, but he appeared as frozen as an ice statue sitting across from them. Was he even breathing? She knew that some men were afraid of their future mother-in-law, but this would never do.

She pulled her hand out from under his then entwined their fingers together, something that had her mother's eyebrows lifting. When his fingers tightened on hers, she felt a warmth inside herself, an awareness, that she wasn't faking. "Can you believe my mom's showing up right now? Right after I'd just said I needed to call her?"

With the squeeze of her fingers on his, he seemed to recover some. "Um, no. What great timing. And it's so nice to see you again."

"So what are you doing here?" Lori asked, hoping to give Zach a little more time to come to himself.

That was better. Now he just looked like a nervous man about to meet a future mother-in-law. And maybe that was the problem. Though they both knew this was just temporary, he'd been traumatized by his first mother-in law and what she was doing to him. It looked like she'd have to carry the brunt of this announcement.

"We had a meeting with the hospital board. You know they have a foundation that contributes to Legacy House. We were hoping that we could get some extra funding." Her mother stood and waved to where Lori could see her boss, though he was only her boss in a part-time capacity now that Jared had picked up most of the administration duties of the practice.

"Stop looking like I'm holding a gun to your head and start looking like you've suddenly fallen happily in love," Lori said to Zach when her mom stepped away to join Jack in the order line.

"I'm sorry, I just…it's your mother," he said.

"I know it's my mother. If anyone can sniff out something fishy going on, it's her. I'm going to let her know you've proposed. You need to help me convince her that we truly have fallen in love." Lori hated lying to her mother, but her mother would understand if she knew everything that was going on with Andres and she'd be thrilled if Lori was able to foster and someday adopt the little baby that had been born today.

"It's nice to run into the two of you," Jack said as he set down the tray that held his and her mother's drinks. "But shouldn't you both be off by now?"

"Lori had a complicated delivery and the baby has had some struggles," Zach said.

"We'd planned a date night, but it was too late by the time we finished," Lori said, turning toward Zach. "Isn't that right?"

"Oh, yeah, we've both been busy. Work and all." Then as if a switch went off in his head, his body seemed to relax and his smile went fluorescent bright. "I plan to make up for it tomorrow night."

He looked so proud of himself that Lori wanted to kick him under the table, though kicking her mother or her boss by mistake wouldn't be a good idea. Instead, she beamed at him. Maybe her mother and Jack would put their reactions down to them just being foolishly in love, though she was beginning to think the two of them were foolish to think they were going to be able to convince anyone that they were serious about their relationship.

"You said you wanted to talk to me?" her mother said, looking suspiciously between the two of them.

Lori took in a breath, ready to spill out their announcement, when someone, she assumed it was Zach, really did kick her under the table.

"I'm so sorry, Ms. Mason. I really should have handled this different. I hope you'll forgive me for not getting your permission before I spoke with Lori." The sincerity on his face was enough to even convince Lori though she knew it was all an act. Where had his acting skills been a few minutes ago?

"My permission? Lori's certainly old enough to decide who she wants to date," Lori's mom said, looking even more confused.

"I think possibly he had something else he wanted to ask permission for." Jack sat back looking at the three of them as if they were the entertainment for the evening.

"What Zach's saying, Mom, is that he should have spoken with you before he asked me to marry him."

"He asked you to marry him? But you…"

"And I said yes," Lori said, watching as the words stunned her mother. "I'm so happy. We both are."

"Yes, we are," Zach said, raising her hand to his mouth and pressing a kiss to it, causing an unexpected shiver to run down her body. "We hope you will be happy for us too."

When her mother found her words again, the questions, also known as an interrogation, began. Only the reassurance that they were planning to take their time to set a wedding date seemed to calm her mother. Surprisingly, Zach, who had been slow to begin with, managed to answer all her mother's questions. Lori would think he was a romance author the way he spun a story of the two of them being attracted to each other from the moment they met, but the time they had spent together at the wedding had only made those feelings grow stronger.

And when her mother had asked to see the ring, Zach had an answer for that too. He'd planned a night out with a trip to a jewelry store, but work had gotten in the way.

By the time Lori's mom had left the cafeteria with Jack, her mom might still have doubts about the two of them being ready for marriage, but Zach had charmed her enough that she was considering the possibility.

"Wow, that was a lot," Lori said, pushing back her chair so she could prop her feet up on one of the empty chairs. "I don't think we were prepared for that."

"I think we did pretty well," Zach said, looking very pleased with himself.

"You almost blew it the moment my mom walked up."

"I wasn't expecting your mom to show up in the hospital cafeteria. I still don't understand what she was talking about with Legacy House. I remember reading that new country music couple, The Carters donated a lot of money to the house."

"They did. And it helped cover the budget and some of the renovations that needed to be done. But the house is having to turn down women weekly. They need to expand."

"Your mom and Dr. Warner are doing some great work there. Let me know if there's anything I can do to help."

"Oh, don't worry. As my fiancé, you'll find yourself volunteered for lots of projects."

"So we're really going to do this? And you're coming to Memphis with me this weekend?" Zach asked, still sounding as if he didn't believe her.

"I wouldn't miss it. I'm looking forward to meeting Andres," Lori said as they stood and cleared their table. "And his grandparents."

CHAPTER FIVE

THE NEXT MORNING, Zach texted Lori while she was getting ready for work to let her know that Baby Girl Doe had been started on morphine. Not that this was a surprise to either of them after both the mother and the baby's lab work had come back positive for multiple drugs. Though Lori wished there was something else she could do, all they could do now was watch the baby's neonatal abstinence score carefully and treat as needed.

Lori rushed through the rest of her morning routine so that she could stop by the NICU before going into the clinic. Because she was so early, only a couple of family members were visiting the unit. She looked for the baby she was already beginning to think of as her own, a dangerous thing she knew but one she couldn't stop. When that little baby girl had wrapped her hand around Lori's finger, she might as well have been wrapping it around her heart.

And now her heart had to think of that tiny baby she'd bonded with so fast having to go through the painful process of drug withdrawal. All she could do now was try to let the baby know that she wasn't going through that alone.

She immediately went to the back of the NICU to

where the babies that needed to be isolated from the constant noise of the unit were located. Placed on the only warmer there was the label Baby Girl Doe, which for some reason bothered Lori more than it should. Every baby deserved to have a name even if it was a temporary one. She knew some of the nurses yesterday had been calling the baby Jane, because of her last name now being listed as Doe since the mother had never given them her whole name. Lori bent down over the sleeping infant and whispered, "Right now we'll call you Jane, but soon you'll have your own name. And it will be one that will let the world know just how special you are.

"How is she doing?" Lori asked when one of the NICU nurses joined her.

"She's doing okay. Still some tremors and her respirations are still too fast, but you know how this goes. It's going to get worse before it gets better."

"I know," Lori said. She'd seen these babies go through the tremors, high-pitched crying that couldn't be comforted, and even seizures. She wanted to touch the sleeping baby to reassure her that she was there, that she wouldn't be alone through it all, but she held herself back. It was better to let her rest when she could. "The case manager, Jessica, from DCS is coming today. Can you call me when she gets here, please?"

"Sure, I'll be going off soon, but I'll pass it off in my report." If the nurse thought it was an odd request, she didn't show it.

"Has Dr. Morales been in yet?" Lori asked.

"He stopped by here to check on Baby Jane, then he went to make rounds on the babies in the regular nursery."

Lori stood and watched the sleeping baby until her watch told her she'd be late for her first clinic appointment.

"I'll be back soon," she told Baby Jane, then reluctantly left the NICU.

She knew she was already getting too involved with the baby and if things didn't go the way she was hoping with DCS, she was setting herself up for a heart break like she had never experienced before. But what else could she do? It was like the decision to help Zach. What else could she do but help him get his son back? Once her heart was involved, she had to do everything she could for the people she cared about. And all of this was happening so fast, giving her no time to protect herself.

She had immediately felt for Zach when he'd told her his story. Now getting to know him and realizing that she might go through the same pain, she was more determined than ever to help him.

She took the back way into the clinic and hurried to her office. She didn't think the senior Dr. Warner would say anything about her and Zach's announcement last night. Her mother was a different story. And with her working at Legacy House and sometimes escorting some of the younger pregnant mothers into the office, she knew a lot of the staff personally now.

But as the day went on, Lori relaxed. Tonight, she and Zach would plan out their story which was important if they wanted everyone to believe their engagement was real. Zach had managed to charm his way through her mom and Jack's questions the night before, but she had no doubt that his in-laws wouldn't be so easy on them.

She was just leaving the clinic to make rounds and check on Baby Jane when her phone rang. "Sky, you're on your honeymoon. What are you doing calling me?"

"What are you doing getting engaged and not telling me?" Sky asked back.

"How did you find out when you're on an island in the Bahamas?"

"So, it's true?" Sky asked. Her friend's voice held all the disbelief Lori had expected. There had never been a man in Lori's life, at least not since they'd met, that Lori hadn't told Sky about.

Their volleying questions back and forth was getting them nowhere. Lori had to answer the question, even though she didn't want to lie to her best friend. "Yes, it's official. Zach and I are an item."

"An item I can believe. I saw the way the two of you were connecting at the wedding. But engaged? Isn't it a little early for that?"

"A lot of things have happened since you've been gone." How did those romance novels make it look so easy for the couples to fool everyone?

"So what, the two of you just suddenly fell in love and decided you needed to rush into an engagement?"

"It's an engagement, Sky. We haven't even discussed a wedding date." Lori entered the back wing of the hospital and headed to the elevator. "Look, I can't talk right now. I'm making rounds and then I need to check on one of the babies in the nursery."

She started to tell her friend about Baby Jane, but she knew Sky would start worrying that Lori might be setting herself up for another disappointment.

"Don't think you're getting away that easy. When I get back this weekend we need to talk."

"I'm going to Memphis with Zach this weekend to meet some of his family. We'll talk when you come back to work next week. Have fun and don't worry about anything here. I've got this." The elevator door opened. "Got to go. Love you."

When her phone rang next, she was relieved to see that it was Zach. "What's up?"

"I just wanted to check and make sure we're still on for tonight," he said.

"Yeah, I was wondering if maybe I could just pick up some food and come over to your house." She didn't want to take a chance of her mom being home.

"If you're sure, that's fine with me. But let me order something. Do you like barbecue?"

"I love it." And that was just the kind of thing the two of them needed to know about each other. "Have you ever done one of those speed dating things?"

"No, why?" Was that laughter in his voice?

"Well, I have, so don't even start making any jokes about it," she said.

"I wasn't," Zach said.

"Yes, you were. It really isn't as dumb an idea as you think. You can learn a lot about someone if you know the right questions to ask." The elevator doors opened and she headed to the OB hall.

"And why are we talking about this now?"

"Because tonight is going to be the most intense speed dating event ever. By the time we're finished, we should be able to answer all the questions your in-laws could possibly ask."

"Sounds like fun. I'll see you at six then?" Zach said.

Lori had hoped to spend some time in the NICU after she finished at the clinic, but tonight was the last night she had before the weekend that she wouldn't be covering deliveries. "I'm still waiting for the case manager from DCS. If I'm going to be late, I'll let you know. How's she doing?" She knew she didn't have to tell him who she was asking about.

"She's tolerating the morphine, but she's still not eating well. She's getting IV fluids, but if she doesn't start eating soon, we might have to start tube feedings."

For the next hour, Lori rounded on the clinic's hospital patients. Answering questions and helping the new mothers as they were breastfeeding. She was ashamed to say that she had always felt a bit jealous of her patients as she waited and waited for the right person to come into her life to start a family with. And now she was giving up?

No. She wasn't giving up exactly, she was just taking some time off. Right now, her focus needed to be on getting approved to be a foster parent for Baby Jane. Besides, it wasn't like she would be doing any dating while she was playing fake fiancée for Zach. She'd be too busy keeping herself from falling for the handsome doctor to even think about another man.

It wasn't until she was headed back to the office to catch up with some of her charting before her next appointment that she finally received a call from the NICU that DCS was there to see Baby Jane. She started to text Zach, but this meeting wasn't a formal meeting.

It wasn't until she entered the NICU that a case of nerves hit her. She knew in her heart that she was the mother that Baby Jane needed. Now she just needed to convince the case manager.

"Hey, Jessica," Lori said, greeting the petite woman that was going over Baby Jane's chart.

"Lori, it's nice to see you. I have to say I was surprised when you called. I didn't know you were interested in foster caring."

"I hope you don't mind. I understand it's a little irregular to call the case manager directly. But this case is a little irregular too."

"You're right. We do see a few abandoned infants each year, but this was a little different with the mother delivering at the hospital and not giving any information, then leaving right after her delivery, abandoning the baby."

"I can't say we've had anything like it in here before," Lori said. She still wondered if there had been anything she could have said or done to keep Baby Jane's mother from leaving. There were so many things that could go bad after a delivery. The woman could have hemorrhaged to death after she'd left the hospital and they wouldn't know it. But all she could do now was hope for the best for the young woman. And give the baby she'd left behind the best life possible.

"I've talked to the nurses and it looks like with the prematurity and her Neonatal Abstinence Syndrome that she will most likely be spending several weeks here before she's ready to discharge. I understand that you have an interest in fostering her, and I'm sure you're aware of the complications and struggles you could face with this baby down the road. Her going through withdrawals could be just the start of a long ordeal."

As they discussed all the complications and challenges and the long-term effects of drug use in pregnancy, Lori became even more determined to apply to foster Baby Jane. She would need a strong mother and Lori was determined that she could provide the care and love she would need.

It wasn't until after the case manager left that Lori noticed that the nurses had taken a lot of interest in their conversation. When one of the nurses came up and hugged Lori and told her she knew that Lori would be the perfect person to care for the abandoned baby, Lori had to fight back tears. Bending down, she brushed the tiny bit of soft dark hair on Baby Jane's tiny head. Her eyes blinked open for a moment, and a grimace crossed her face before she wiggled her tiny body, then relaxed back into sleep. "That's right, little Janiah."

The baby's eyes blinked open again, this time remaining open for a few seconds squinting against the bright lights above her.

"Oh, do you like the name? I do too." Lori had always felt that the generic name of Baby Jane was wrong. Even though Janiah was a version of Jane, it was unique. And every child should have their own name, a unique name that fit them.

"It means God is gracious or gift from God. I hope you always feel that way. That you are a gift." Lori hoped that when this baby grew up and learned that her mother abandoned her, she would never feel unwanted. Instead, Lori hoped that she would know she was considered a precious gift that was loved from the day she was born. "Now, just relax and sleep. It's going to be okay. Someday soon you'll be coming home with me and I'm going to make sure that you have all the love that you deserve."

CHAPTER SIX

As Lori waited for Zach to come to the door, she caught herself worrying about the fact that she had chosen her comfiest and most worn jeans and an old volunteer's T-shirt to wear. It wasn't that she hadn't cared how she looked, she'd just used all her time on her computer searching for the most common questions asked at different speed dating events and she'd run out of time to do anything except grab a change of clothes and touch up her makeup.

Not that it should matter. It wasn't like Zach was interested in her, not that way. He had made no secret that he was still grieving over his wife. There was no reason to dress up for him. She was wearing what she would have been wearing when hanging out with friends. And that's what they were, just friends. Though, the fact that she had to keep reminding herself of that did worry her.

She pushed that thought away as soon as Zach opened the door. It seemed there were many versions of Zach that she hadn't seen yet. This Zach, dressed in dark denim jeans and a navy blue fitted T-shirt was just another one. As her heart sped up and her breath caught, she decided that this one might be one that she liked a little too much.

That worrying thought returned. Never in her life had seeing one of her friends made her want to fan herself, nor had they ever made her feel like her heart had dropped to her toes.

"Hey, come in. I was just unloading the food," Zach said, totally unaware of the affect he was having on her right then.

She followed him to the kitchen without saying a word, afraid it would just come out in an embarrassing squeak.

"I didn't have a chance to ask what kind of barbecue you preferred, but I figured I was safe with pulled pork sandwiches."

She took a seat and a plate was placed in front of her. When she opened the foiled-wrapped sandwich, the tangy smell of sauce and smoked meat hit her. She took a bite, not even waiting for Zach to join her. With her mouth full she wouldn't have to worry about saying anything silly. With that first mouthful, she remembered that she hadn't had time to eat at all that day. That was the problem. It wasn't how delicious Zach looked tonight. It was just hunger pangs.

"This is good," she said, before taking another bite.

"I always thought Memphis had the best barbecue, but Nashville seems to hold its own with them," Zach said.

Then he picked up his napkin, bent over the counter and wiped the side of her mouth. For a moment they both froze. Zach's eyes had gone wide, as if he was surprised that he had been so bold, so intimate. There was suddenly an awkwardness that had never been between them before.

Unable to let the silence go on any longer, Lori took the napkin from his hand and wiped again at the spot where some sauce had dripped. "But is our BBQ messier than Memphis's?"

"It seems so," Zach said as he moved away from her. And though she could tell he was still bothered by his actions, his body relaxed back into his chair and he picked up his sandwich and began eating.

"See, these are the things we need to know about each other. We both like messy barbecue," Lori said, hoping to put Zach more at ease.

For the next few moments, they ate in silence, then cleaned everything up.

"Where do you want to do this?" she asked.

"Follow me," Zach said, leading her to a room off the side of the kitchen where there were deep cushy sofas, bookshelves and lots of toys. Toys for a little boy who had never gotten the chance to play here in the room his father had designed just for him.

She took a seat on one of the sofas and reached into her bag, pulling out a stack of papers she'd printed off one of the speed dating websites.

"What's that?" Zach asked as he took a seat on the sofa across from her.

"I printed out some questions to help us to get to know each other better." Reading over the papers, she found a question that she wanted to ask. "Like this one. What was your favorite game to play when you were a child?"

"Baseball," Zach answered.

"Okay, like, did you play in high school, college?"

"I played high school ball. I wasn't good enough to play college ball. Besides, I was busy with premed classes."

"Now we're getting somewhere. So, how old were you when you decided you wanted to be a doctor?"

"I don't know. I guess when I was in high school. I took one of those tests they give you to help decide what your strengths are. How about you? When did you decide to become a midwife?"

"I worked labor and delivery when I got out of nursing school. There was a midwife there that I really admired. She had a way with her patients that made me want to be like her. So, I applied to midwifery school here in Nashville." She smiled. "Now you ask me another question."

She handed him a copy she'd made then waited as he read through some of the questions. And waited. And waited. "It's okay. Just pick one."

"I'm sorry, I just don't understand how knowing your favorite season is going to help us make people believe that we're in a relationship."

"Well, my favorite season is spring. That should tell you that I like new beginnings, which helps you understand something about my personality. If this was a real speed dating event and I asked you what your favorite season was and you answered that it was winter, I might believe that the two of us wouldn't be a good match and move on to the next person."

"But there isn't anyone else to move on to and learning that I played baseball or that I also would pick spring as my favorite season is just superficial information. If you really want to know someone, I would think you'd need to ask more personal questions."

"Some of the questions are more personal. Just give it a chance." She was a little put out by his reaction to her plan for them to get to know each other, but she wasn't about to give up. She turned the page and asked the first question there. "What are your top three turn-ons?"

Her mouth fell open as Zach's eyes went wide. When he busted out laughing, she couldn't help but join him. "Are you telling me that two strangers sitting across a table from each other that have never met before ask those type of questions?"

It took a moment for Lori to answer as she was caught somewhere between the ridiculousness of the question and the fact she'd actually read it out loud. She had managed to embarrass herself at the same time as make herself laugh so hard that her stomach was beginning to hurt.

"I promise I've never asked a stranger that in my life," she said when she could finally get in enough oxygen to breath and talk at the same time. "I'm sorry. This isn't going anything like I had planned."

"Okay, so why don't we just throw these papers in the trash, and start over," Zach said as he reached for her copies of paper and left the room to dispose of them.

Zach was still laughing when he made it to the kitchen trash can. He hadn't laughed so hard in months. There was something about Lori that brought out a happiness that he had honestly thought he'd never feel again.

He saw a napkin lying in the trash can, reminding him of earlier when he'd reached up to wipe the sauce off Lori's face. It had been instinctual, but at the same time had seemed intimate. Too intimate for a man who'd just lost his wife a year before. Too intimate for a man who didn't ever want to feel the joy, and pain, of loving someone again. He'd crossed a line that he needed to keep between the two of them if they were going to go forward with their plan of a fake engagement. Maybe it was time he read one of those romance books with the fake fiancée to see just how the people in those books handled it.

He returned to the family room and handed Lori a glass of tea. "Sweet, very little ice."

"Thanks," she said. "I'm sorry if I messed this all up."

"You didn't. It's just…look, whatever your favorite movie is or your favorite color is isn't what's important right now. I mean, any of that stuff wouldn't really matter if we really had fallen in love as quickly as we want people to think we did. Wouldn't part of the fun of a new relationship be finding out about each other as we grew as a couple? Maybe, not knowing everything about each other is a good excuse for why we're not rushing into a wedding. We're taking our time. Enjoying this part of the relationship."

She smiled and nodded at him. "Okay. I give in. You're right. You don't need to know my favorite color or movie. Especially if you can remember things like how I like my tea. So, what do we need to know?"

"I think we did really good with your mother. We told her mostly the truth. We'd liked each other from the time we met, which is true for me. And we got better acquainted at the wedding."

"It was a little easier for her to believe because she thinks we slept with each other that night."

Zach choked on the swallow of tea he'd just taken. "What? Why would she think that?"

"She was at the house the morning after and caught me coming into the house with my bridesmaid dress still on. I told her I'd spent the night at your house. She assumed we had slept together and I didn't see any reason to deny it."

Zach wasn't sure what to say to that. No wonder the woman had been giving him the once-over. "That's not something I would ever do."

"Let my mom think that we'd slept together? I have to say she was pretty shocked."

"No. I wouldn't sleep with someone the first time I'd gone out with them. I have to know someone better than that." Which was one of many reasons he'd not slept with anyone since his wife had passed.

"I wouldn't do that either. I hadn't even slept with my last boyfriend and we'd dated for three months. Which was why my mother was shocked." The defensiveness in her voice was apparent.

"I didn't mean to suggest you would. And even if you did, I wouldn't judge you. And if you and your ex hadn't slept together by that time, it seems that one or both of you knew that you didn't belong together." He didn't like the fact that a part of him couldn't deny that he was glad that she hadn't slept with that jerk of an ex of hers. He hadn't even known her then. Had never even met her ex, but he had to be a jerk if he hadn't seen what he had in Lori. Couldn't the man see how amazing she was? She was beautiful and kind, and even Zach was feeling an attraction for the woman, though he knew the last thing he needed to do was to get involved with someone like Lori. Someone who'd want a man to give all of himself to her. Unfortunately, there wasn't a lot of Zach left after losing his wife.

So he told himself that it was just the protectiveness for a friend that he was feeling, but he knew it was more. It was jealousy and possessiveness which he had no right to feel. But it seemed no matter how many times he told himself that all he wanted was friendship, everything changed whenever he was around Lori. He could deny it all he wanted to, but his body was aware of her every time she was near. It was as if there was a magnetic pull between the two of them that kept inching him closer and closer to doing something totally irrational like kissing her, something that would surely lead to even more of a temptation that he wasn't ready for. Not now. Maybe not ever. Especially not when he knew that he would not only be betraying Katherine, but also he would be betraying the trust he was building between him and Lori.

She was helping him out, doing him a favor so big he would never be able to repay it. It would never be fair to ask her to give up on her search for that happily-ever-after that she so wanted for a man who could never promise to feel the love that he knew she deserved. And she'd just broken up with that Donald guy. No matter how much she might deny it, she was vulnerable now. He should be protecting her from any more pain. Instead, he was finding that he needed to protect her from him.

No, from now on he had to ignore even the smallest

acts of touching her. Hadn't just brushing her mouth with his napkin stoked a burning desire inside his chest? He could try to blame it on the barbecue they'd been eating, but he knew better.

"Speaking of your ex, is this arrangement with me going to cause any problems for you? With your search for this Mr. Right you've been looking for?"

He found himself becoming more and more anxious when she didn't answer him right away.

"You know, I think I'm going to take some time off from that. Right now, I want to concentrate on my application to foster Janiah. Then there will be the two of us settling in to a routine together. It's not like I was getting any closer to finding what I was looking for. I'm not even sure what it is that I want anymore. Maybe for right now I just need to spend time with my friends." She smiled at him, a bright smile that dazzled him with the happiness it contained. "Besides, this fake fiancée act is kind of fun, even if our speed dating hasn't worked out like I planned. Any suggestions to fix that?"

With that statement, Zach let some of the guilt he was feeling go. Lori was enjoying herself, enjoying spending time with him as a friend. All he had to do was keep things between the boundaries of that friendship and things between them would work out okay.

"How about we just talk, like two people wanting to learn more about each other? The rest will follow. If we have questions that we can't answer, we just put it down to we're still learning about each other."

"There's one thing we do need to discuss before we

meet your in-laws this weekend, but I'm afraid it's going to be painful."

"It's okay. I've admitted to you how I basically abandoned my son. What could be worse?"

"You didn't abandon, Andres. You love your son and you are doing everything you can to get him back without hurting your in-laws. What my father did was abandonment. He just took off and didn't look back. You would never do that. You're a good man, Zach. That's why I think your in-laws might think it's a little strange that you've never told me anything about your wife."

Zach took in a big breath, then let it out. He knew this was coming. At some point he'd have to tell Lori about Katherine. He just didn't know where to start.

And then he suddenly did. "You remember how you've talked about love at first sight?"

"Is that what happened?"

"Absolutely not. We were both in the premed program and to begin with we barely noticed each other. It started with a project for one of our classes and then there were the study groups we were both involved in. Before long, it seemed we were together all the time, either studying or going to concerts with our friends. We moved in together our last year of college." He could still remember their first place with its mix of his and hers furniture they'd assembled. They'd studied late and made love even later. "It wasn't until we'd both started to apply to medical school that we realized we might be living in not only separate homes, but possibly separate states. That's when we began talking about marriage."

"Did you have a big wedding?" Lori asked, her eyes

full of so much genuine interest that he couldn't help but wonder if she was thinking of his and Katherine's romance like it was one of her romance books. If so, she was going to be very disappointed with the ending.

"No, not really. Just friends and family. We were both lucky enough to get into Emory, but between Atlanta's rent rates and our tuition, we were broke." They'd both had to take out loans while they were in school. "Those were years of hot dogs, noodles and too little sleep. But now, when I look back on them, I realize how precious they were. We grew together so much that year because all we really had was each other."

"It does seem that we don't appreciate the things we have while we have them, doesn't it?" Lori said. "But then you had Andres."

"Yes, then we had Andres." It seemed like he'd been on an amazing ride for all the eight years of their marriage. They'd had good times. Hard times. Good times again. And then there had come the worst of times. "We had been so excited about having a baby. We'd barely gotten our practices off the ground, but neither of us wanted to wait any longer before we started a family.

"When Andres was born, we were both so happy. I never dreamed that in less than forty-eight hours she'd be gone." How could he have known? She'd looked so beautiful holding his son, her hair damp with sweat, her eyes bright with tears. The next few hours had been the happiest they'd ever had together.

And then she'd just been gone, taking all that love and happiness they'd shared with her. "She coded right before we were being released from the hospital. The autopsy showed that she'd had a blood clot. I still don't understand why. I guess I never will."

"I'm so sorry that things ended that way for the two of you," Lori said.

He saw her brush a tear from her own cheek and then realized for the first time that he'd been crying too. His story had started with so much hope and happiness, then ended so badly for both Katherine, him and her parents. "I didn't mean to make you cry."

"Don't apologize to me. I'm the one that made you go through all of that again," Lori said.

"You know, I think you're the first person I've ever spoken to about Katherine like this. Thank you for listening."

Later that night, when he watched Lori walk out to her car, he was still surprised by the fact that he'd been able to talk so openly about his marriage and the loss of his wife with her. He'd kept so much of his pain locked up inside him, yet it had seemed so easy to open up to Lori. While he still felt drained from talking so much about his marriage, he felt as if a weight had been lifted too. As if processing everything that had happened to the two of them had helped heal something inside him. He realized he'd been forced to remember the good times they'd had instead of just the end when he'd lost her. Was it possible that he was finally healing?

Looking around the home he'd worked to make for him and his son, he felt a new spark of hope.

And it was all because of Lori, a woman with a big heart that wanted to not only help him and his son, but also a tiny baby that lay in the nursery waiting for someone to claim her. He just had to make sure that when this was all over, that big heart of hers wasn't a shattered mess, like his own.

CHAPTER SEVEN

FOR THE REST of the week Lori and Zach communicated mainly with texts, with Lori covering the deliveries at night and Zach busy with the Well Baby nursery and the NICU. In between deliveries and clinic hours, Lori worked on her application for foster parenting and registered for the training classes starting the next week. They occasionally ran into each other on a delivery or in the nursery where Lori had begun to spend time between deliveries with Baby Jane. Lori knew that babies withdrawing from drugs could take weeks before they were weaned off their morphine drips, it seemed that the baby's abstinence score was slowly creeping up over the last couple days, requiring more medication to keep her tremors and respirations at a safe level. As Zach had feared, he'd had to order tube feedings on Baby Jane though the good news was that she was tolerating the feedings well.

By the time Lori climbed into Zach's car on Saturday morning to make the trip to Memphis, she was a nervous wreck. She'd spent the week either worrying about Janiah or worrying that she wasn't going to be able to help Zach as much as she hoped. What if Zach's in-laws took an instant dislike to her? While she wanted to make sure that they were aware that Zach wasn't alone, that there was someone beside him ready to fight for custody of his son, she was also hoping that things wouldn't come to that. She hoped that meeting her and seeing her and Zach together would ease them into thinking of Andres belonging with the two of them.

Zach handed her a soft velvet black box, dragging her from thoughts that were getting her nowhere. She stared at it then looked back at him. "What's this?"

"If we want my in-laws to take us seriously, I figured we better make it official with a ring," Zach said, never taking his eyes off the road. "I didn't know what you liked, so I hope it's okay."

Lori held the box like it was a bomb about to go off at any moment. She eased the box open and found a gold band with a large teardrop diamond surrounded by smaller diamonds. She shut the box, her hand beginning to tremble.

"What's wrong? If you don't like it, we can exchange it after this weekend." The nervousness she heard in Zach's voice matched hers.

"What if this is a mistake? What if I mess up and make things worse between you and your in-laws?" She opened the box again, then shut it quickly. Were they really going to do this? The sight of the ring made things seem more real now.

Zach pulled over into a fast-food parking lot. "If you don't want to go through with this, I'll understand. I can take you home right now and everything will be okay."

"Everything except your in-laws will give you an even harder time when you show up without me. They have to suspect that it's a woman you're bringing for them to meet. Besides, this was my idea."

"Which was a lot better idea than mine, to get you to marry me," he said.

"You're right. That wasn't a good idea. But is mine any better? At some point, the truth will come out."

"And by that time Andres will be living in Nashville with me," Zach ran his hand through his hair and looked back at her. "It's up to you. I understand. It's hard to fake something like this."

She opened the box again. The ring was beautiful, but the feeling in her heart that secretly wished that this was real was not. But how could she admit to Zach that the feelings she was having for him were seeming less and less fake? That the more she got to know him, the more she wished that she had met Zach later. Much later, after he'd gotten custody of his son and really started the new life he planned, maybe then he'd be ready to move on with his life.

She remembered the way he'd looked when he'd told her about his wife, the smile he'd had when he'd talked about their first years together, then the tears he'd shed when he'd talked about losing Katherine. All his emotions for his wife were still so strong that Lori wasn't sure that Zach would ever be able to move on from those. And risking her heart for a man that didn't love her wasn't something she would ever be willing to do. She'd had her heart broken by a man when she'd only been a child, a man who should have protected her instead of abandoning her. She wasn't about to let that happen again.

Still, she couldn't help but stare at the ring that was no more than a prop for their performance as if it was the most beautiful thing she'd ever seen. Taking the ring out of the box, she carefully slipped it on her finger. It slid on smoothly and fit perfectly.

She held her hand up and let the sunlight bounce off the facets of the diamonds as she admired the ring. For a moment she let herself daydream that the ring was really hers, that the romance they were going to pretend was real. Maybe it was because of all the romance books she'd read, but she'd always thought engagement rings held some kind of special magic. Or maybe it was the love that was supposed to go along with the ring that was the real magic. She couldn't help but wonder if she'd ever feel that magic.

Suddenly, unable to stand the sight of the ring any longer, she placed her hand down by her side and forced her eyes away from it. She needed to concentrate on what was really important instead of letting her mind be filled with dreams that might never come true. Right now, this wasn't about her.

This was about doing what was right for Zach and Andres, though she couldn't deny that her own history with her father made her want to help the two of them be together even more. It wasn't fair that a man who wanted to be with his child wasn't allowed to. Not when there were children that dreamed of having a father who didn't have one. And if it meant playing a part to help make that happen, then that was what she would do. "Okay, let's do this."

Traffic had lightened by the time they hit the interstate and in three hours they were pulling up outside a tidy brick home inside a quiet neighborhood.

When Zach took her left hand and she looked down at the ring that now sat there, her hand shook. Then she reminded herself of why she was doing this. There was a little boy in that house that deserved to be raised by a dad that loved him very much. Not that Lori was an expert on good dads. Hers surely hadn't deserved her or her mother. But Zach, he would be a great father. That she knew for sure.

It was only a moment after Zach rang the doorbell before the door opened. Lori wasn't sure exactly what she was expecting, but it wasn't the jolly-looking man that griped Zach's hand and welcomed them into the house.

"Lori, this is Butch Harrison, my father-in-law," Zach said. "Butch, this is Lori Mason."

Lori had noticed that Zach still referred to his late wife's parents as his in-laws, a sign that he still respected the older couple even though they were at odds where his son was concerned.

"It's nice to meet you." Lori held her hand out to Butch, and instantly thought that in any other circumstance it would have been.

A squeal came from down the hallway and then a brown-haired toddler, wet and naked, came running into the room. Before Lori knew it, the child had darted behind her, clinging to her legs. After the toddler came a beautiful older woman. With silver hair, blue eyes and a flushed face, no doubt from chasing the toddler, Zach's mother-in-law looked just like any other grandmother who'd come to the end of their patience with a certain little boy would look. Then in front of her eyes, the woman who appeared to have fought a war, and lost, straightened her back and wiped away all signs of defeat. Her tired eyes went on alert as if readying for another battle.

"Oh, Zach, I wasn't expecting you so early," the woman said, before turning her eyes toward Lori.

Lori gave the woman her warmest smile, before glancing down at the toddler still hiding behind her, his wet body soaking through the dress pants she'd worn. "You must be Andres."

The little boy stared up at her, his brown eyes merry with mischief and his smile wide with two little teeth peeking out at her.

Lori reached out for the towel Andres's grandmother held, surprising the woman so much that she handed it to her.

"Oh, you don't need to do that," the woman said when both Lori and Zach bent down to dry Andres off. "I can do it."

When Andres saw that it was his father beside him, he let out a yelp, abandoning Lori as he tried to climb up his daddy's legs as Lori attempted to dry the wiggling toddler. In seconds the three of them were kneeling on the floor all of them laughing, the little boy not even acknowledging that she was a stranger.

But when Lori looked up, it was the expression on Andres's grandmother's face that killed her enjoyment of the moment. Lori had heard of looks that could kill and she had no doubt that if this woman's eyes could shoot daggers, Lori would be lying in a pool of blood right then. But she'd been prepared for this and she wasn't going to let this woman's attitude ruin Zach's moment with his son.

"Kelley, this is Lori, Zach's friend from Nashville. Lori, this is my wife, Kelley," Butch said, the smile on his face reassuring Lori that, at least for now, she was safe. "Zach, why don't you go get Andres dressed while Kelley and I get to know Lori. We'll meet you in the family room."

It wasn't that she thought the woman would actually hurt her. Lori spent most of her time around mothers. She recognized a protective mama bear when she saw one. Andres was actually a very lucky boy to have all of these adults care so much for him. It was just too bad that at least one of the adults was putting their own needs ahead of his.

Zach looked up at Lori, soundlessly asking her if she would be okay. Lori nodded and smiled at him as he picked up his son, now wrapped securely in his towel. Lori stood and started to follow Butch, then saw something on Kelley's face that surprised her. Fear. It was then that Lori realized that the woman feared losing her grandson as much as Zach feared never getting his son back. Did Zach know this? Looking from the outside, it might be easier for her to see than for Zach with his history with his in-laws.

Lori followed Butch deeper into the house until they came to what looked like had once been a formal living room with its floral straight-back sofa and loveseat. Only now the room was scattered with toys. A lot of toys. Too many, it seemed to her, but grandparents were known for that.

"Please, have a seat. Would you like something to drink? Coffee? Tea?" Butch asked her, still showing none of the signs of hostility she had expected.

"A cup of coffee, no milk or sugar, would be great," Lori said. Though she usually preferred tea, she felt the need for something stronger today. She needed to be ready for all the questions she knew were coming.

"So, I take it you and Zachary are coworkers?" Kelley asked as she took the seat beside her after Butch left the room.

"We work at the same hospital," Lori said, not answering the question directly. Kelley would know soon enough that Lori and Zach were more than coworkers.

At least that was true. They were more than just coworkers. They were friends. Good friends. More than good friends. They were…what exactly were they? She couldn't say she'd ever had a relationship with anyone quite like the one she had with Zach. There was an intimacy with sharing all of this with him that she'd never experienced before. She had trusted him more with her feelings and fears than she'd ever trusted anyone. Just admitting that should scare her.

But that wasn't what was important right now. Right now, she had to win this woman and her husband over any way she could and pointing out what a great father Zach was would be a good start.

"You have a lovely house," Lori said.

"Thank you," Kelley said. "We've tried to make it a home for Andres, and of course, Zach while he was here."

"Zach has told me how much he appreciates you helping with his son while he gets settled in Nashville."

When the woman didn't say anything, Lori continued. "I know he's anxious for you to see his new home. We'd love to have you come see it."

Before the woman could respond to the invitation, Andres ran into the room, followed by a laughing Zach.

"Aren't the two of them so cute?" Lori asked, nodding to where Zach and Andres had settled down to play with a wooden train set. Then Zach made a choo-choo sound for the engine he held and Andres copied him, and Lori's arms came up and crossed over her chest, covering a heart that she felt would explode from the joy of watching the two of them together. Mistakes had been made by both parties when it came to Andres, but anyone watching at this moment would see that the two of them belonged together.

"Being cute won't help him when he's got a toddler fighting to stay up after their bedtime," Kelley said, looking away from where the two Morales males were laughing as they made the train roll on the plastic track they had made.

Lori wanted to tell the woman that there were more important things then being on time for bedtime, but one look at the woman's pinched face told her she'd be wasting her breath. Talking to the woman would be like talking to one of those knightly armors of steel. There would be no getting through to her. Kelley had decided a long time ago that the best place for Andres was with them. Whether that was still true or not, she wasn't willing to consider any other possibilities. How Zach hadn't seen this, Lori didn't know. Unfortunately for Kelley, Lori was just as stubborn as she was.

Maybe it was because of her determination to claim Janiah as her own that Lori could see that there was no compromise in Kelley's mind. Now Lori just had to figure out what to do about that.

She was so busy trying to figure out a plan that she jolted when Butch leaned over her to hand her the coffee.

"Be careful, it's hot," he said, handing her the cup then taking a seat beside his wife. "I guess I should have asked Zach if he wanted something."

"He's fine." Lori said. She was willing to fight an army bigger than the two of them to keep them from interrupting Zach and his son right then.

For a few moments there was a silence between the three of them, the noises of the father and son playing the only sounds in the room. Then Lori lifted her cup and took a sip.

"What is that?" Kelley asked, her voice an octave higher than it had been before.

Lori looked down to where the woman was staring, where Lori's left hand held the saucer Butch had given her. And where a beautiful shiny diamond sparkled on Lori's finger.

"I…" Lori let herself stumble over the words. "We were going to tell you. Zach wanted to do it himself, but then there was a wet toddler running up to us. That just didn't seem the time for it. We're engaged."

Lori held out her hand to show off the ring to Kelley and Butch. "It's beautiful, isn't it?"

"It's lovely," Butch said. The man might have been surprised by the announcement, but his eyes lost none of the kindness, though she could see a few tears gathering.

Lori had known this would be hard for the couple. They'd lost their daughter and now their son-in-law was moving on with his life. Or as far as they were concerned, he was. But Lori was beginning to accept that as far as his late wife was concerned, Zach might never be ready to move on. For a moment the thought made her sad. For her because she felt that there might have been something between the two of them if things were different, but also for Zach, as living with only memories seemed to be a lonely way to live. Then she remembered that none of that mattered. Not now. Now it was time for her to sow some seeds to help Andres's grandparents to come to terms with the fact that Zach was planning on building a family with his son.

"I told him you would be happy for him. I know it had to have been hard for him losing his wife, and for you losing your daughter. But I told him that you would understand that he, and Andres of course, needed to continue with a life that Katherine, your daughter, would have wanted them to have." Lori said the words, somehow knowing that this was true. From everything Zach had told her about his wife, she would never want things for Andres, or Zach, to be like this.

She felt a bit of guilt when she looked at the couple. While Butch's face hadn't changed, making her think he had accepted that someday this would happen, Kelley sat up, her back ramrod straight, her eyes still fixed on the ring Lori wore as if she was trying to find some way to remove it.

"I'm happy for…" Butch said, before being interrupted by his wife.

"We will talk about this later," Kelley said. She stood, then shot the two of them a look daring them to stop her. "Right now, it's Andres's lunchtime."

Butch didn't say anything when his wife walked away, heading straight for Andres. They both watched her as she said something short, and Lori imagined sharp, before picking the little boy up and walking back toward the kitchen.

Lori watched as Andres turned toward his father, the longing to stay and play with Zach clear for her and Butch to see. But it was the longing, and pain, in Zach's eyes that caused Lori to take a chance and speak quietly to Butch. "You know the two of those belong together, don't you? You know Katherine would have wanted her son to be with his father."

She waited for Butch to agree with her, to admit that he knew what he and Kelley were doing, keeping Andres from his father, was wrong. When he didn't say anything, Lori looked over at him to see him glance at Zach and then back over at her, before standing. He shook his head, whether to them or to himself, she didn't know.

How did he do this? Where did he find the patience to deal with his in-laws when it was plain to see that they were taking advantage of his feelings for them? That had to be the reason that he was putting up with the way they were treating him.

She felt the anger inside her begin to boil. Zach shouldn't have to deal with any of this. He deserved better than to be treated like this. He'd lost his wife, and now they wanted him to lose his son?

As Zach came to stand next to her, Lori watched

Butch follow his wife out of the room. She knew that Zach's father-in-law wasn't happy about the situation between themselves and their son-in-law. When Zach opened his mouth, no doubt to ask what had happened, Lori just held up her left hand showing him the ring.

Whether it was because of the defeat that must have shown on her face, or whether Zach was feeling the same disappointment, Lori didn't know, but he took her hand and gave it a gentle squeeze. Looking down to where their hands were joined, she immediately felt better. This was just one battle. There were more to come.

And Lori understood that in the end they would be successful, because after what she'd just seen, she wouldn't stop fighting until the Morales family was back together, father and son, as it always should have been.

CHAPTER EIGHT

ZACH WATCHED AS his son stood at the top of the stairs of the porch with his in-laws, taking a piece of his heart with him, just as his son did every time Zach left him. Maybe that was part of the reason he spent most of his time feeling numb and hollow.

But that wasn't how he'd felt today. Today, with Lori beside him, he'd felt hope for the first time since he'd moved to Nashville.

He waited until the three of them went inside before driving away. He tried to ignore that he'd seen Andres turn around and look for him before the door had shut. It was so wrong. So wrong to be leaving his son once more. Only the fact that Lori sat beside him kept away the tears that usually fell when he left his son. He reminded himself that the two of them had a plan. One that they'd begun today.

Not much longer, he promised himself and his son.

It wouldn't be much longer till he would be taking his son home for good.

"I think that went well," he said as he headed to the hotel where he'd reserved rooms for the night.

"What?" Lori asked, staring at him like she didn't understand him.

She'd been quiet for the last couple hours that they'd spent at the park, though she'd seemed happy to play alone with Andres on the gym equipment. And she had joined in to help chase his son around the park when the little daredevil had decided he needed to climb on every surface available.

"I said, I thought things went pretty well today. Maybe not as well as I hoped, Kelley did seem very skeptical of our engagement, but thinking they'd just hand Andres over when I presented them with the idea of our new family coming together had probably not been too realistic."

"Realistic? Zach, do you really think it's okay for them to treat you this way?" Lori asked, the anger in her voice something that he had never heard before. "Maybe it's time you were more realistic about what is going on all around you. Maybe you need to open your eyes and see what's really happening."

"I don't know what you're talking about." Glancing over at her, he saw that she was really upset. At him? At his in-laws? He didn't know which, he only knew he didn't like it. Because while there was anger in her voice, there was also pain in her eyes.

"I can't believe that they wouldn't let us take Andres to the park by ourselves," Lori said, then continued before he could interrupt her. "He's your son. Your son. Not theirs. Yet when you told them we wanted to take Andres to the park, they insisted that they come with us."

He understood her anger now. He hadn't been happy either when Kelley had insisted that they tag along "in case Andres needed them" even after Lori had very sweetly questioned what the child could possibly need them for. He'd thought Kelley would have an aneurism when Lori had pointed out the fact that Andres would be as safe as possible surrounded by a doctor and a nurse. But he didn't need Lori to tell him that his in-laws were overbearing, well at least Kelley was. What did the woman think he was going to do, steal his own son? Not that the idea of running off with Andres hadn't crossed his mind many times. Many, many times. But was that really the right thing for his son? It would fracture the only family that his son knew. It was important to everyone involved that he did this right. The last thing he needed to do was anger his in-laws and have his son involved in a court case that would get ugly. He just needed to be a little more patient.

No, he had to handle this, if at all possible, without causing problems with Katherine's parents. It was what his wife would have wanted.

But Katherine never would have wanted you to get yourself into this mess. Katherine would have depended on you to take care of her son if something happened to her. But you didn't. You took the easy way out then. You can't take the easy way out this time. You can't hurt Katherine's parents.

"This is all my fault. I shouldn't have let things go this far." He kept his eyes on the road until he pulled into the hotel entrance.

But when he started to get out of the car, Lori grabbed his arm. "The only way that you are at fault is that you let them convince you over the last months that you aren't able to take care of Andres on your own. Maybe that's what they really believe. Or maybe they're just using this as a way to control you. They're playing on your guilt, Zach. Well, at least Kelley is. She's been doing it since Katherine, I bet. Didn't you notice that every time you brought up moving into your new house and our making plans for Andres to join us there, she brought up something about Katherine. She thinks if she stalls enough, you'll move back in with them."

Yes, he'd caught the digs his mother-in-law had made about Katherine always wanting to raise a family in Memphis. And later, when she'd asked Lori if she'd be quitting work after they married, Kelley had gone on and on about how Katherine had dreamed about staying home with her children, though they both knew his wife had always planned to go back to work.

"I'm sorry. I know I shouldn't have said anything, but it makes me so angry to see them treat you this way. I know it has to hurt to have the people you trusted and loved try to manipulate you the way they do. I just wish there was something I could do about it."

"You are doing something. You're here with me. And you're supporting me. That means a lot to me."

She removed her arm, and they both got out of the car. He could still feel the tension in her as they walked to their rooms. Her anger being directed at his in-laws in defense of him felt strange. She was mad because she felt he had been wronged. He couldn't remember the last time someone had been this protective of him. His brother agreed that Andres belonged with Zach, but he was very open about the fact that he had warned Zach at the beginning against letting his in-laws take over Andres's care.

Stopping in front of Lori's room, he tried to find the words to make her understand how much he appreciated her defending him while explaining why she couldn't blame everything on Kelley and Butch.

"How about a drink in the lounge downstairs?" he asked. He knew they both were drained from the stress of the day. Kelley had insisted that they stay for dinner after they'd come back from the park, giving her more time to question Lori and his relationship. While they'd managed to keep their story together, it hadn't been easy.

For a moment she seemed to hesitate. Maybe she'd had enough of not only his in-laws, but of him too.

"Sure, but I want to wash up first. Meet you down there in an hour?" she finally said.

It would probably be best if they just went straight to bed, but he wasn't ready to face the lonely hotel room. And he wasn't ready to say good night to Lori. Even when she was angry, she was easy to talk to, easy for him to relax around. She'd even managed to make him laugh a few times in the last week, something that he hadn't done much in the last year.

Lori saw Zach the moment she stepped into the room. He sat at a small table for two, a drink in his hand and his elbows resting on the table with what looked like the weight of the world on his shoulders. She watched as a waitress stopped by and he glanced up at her and smiled. But even across the room Lori could tell his heart wasn't in it.

She was responsible for that, or at least part of it. She'd been so angry at having to keep her mouth shut as she'd watched Kelley do everything she could to make Zach feel like an incapable parent. Couldn't the woman see how much Zach loved his son? Couldn't she see how much Andres loved his father? And all of her concerns about Zach being busy at work and Andres needing a full-time parent, those were all just excuses. Now with Lori in the picture, she had even fewer reasons for her concerns.

And Kelley knew it too, because Lori had seen the fear in her eyes when Andres had hugged both Zach and Lori before they'd left tonight. They'd shown Zach's in-laws the family they could offer Andres as they'd played together in the park. There had been times when Lori had even forgotten that they were supposed to be putting on a show for Kelley and Butch. Once, as the three of them had been running with the toddler, each one of them holding one of his hands, she'd looked over at Zach and seen him smiling at her with such joy that she'd thought her heart would explode from the pleasure of sharing that special moment with him.

And that was when she realized what she had done. For the first time that she could remember, she'd opened herself up totally to someone. The thought had her stumbling, almost causing the three of them to fall down. But when Zach had looked over at her, she had hid the fear she felt at the realization. For the rest of the day, she was careful not to lose herself in Zach's smile again.

Now, looking across the room at Zach, she couldn't deny that something had changed inside her. For years she'd been careful to protect her heart from others, only to have this man tear down all the walls she'd kept between her and the rest of the world. And that scared her more than she wanted to admit.

"Hey," Zach said, standing as she joined him. "I was starting to think you weren't coming."

"I'm sorry. I called to check on Janiah," Lori said. She was glad she had come and seen for herself the situation between Zach, his son and his in-laws. She understood so much more of what he was going through now. But she'd missed her daily visit in the NICU.

"Janiah?" he asked. "Baby Jane?"

"We couldn't keep calling her Baby Jane. It didn't feel right." She'd seen the worry in the nurses faces when she'd told them Janiah's new name. By now they all knew she was trying to foster the baby. That she was getting more and more involved when she had such a long way to go to get approved by DCS worried her too. But her heart couldn't stop caring for the baby that had been abandoned. The fact that Lori had been abandoned by her father and understood the pain that she still lived with only made her want to be there for Janiah more.

"Just be careful, Lori. The mother could still come back and claim her. I don't want to see you get hurt."

"She won't. Besides, she wouldn't get custody if she did. At least not right away. She'd have to complete a rehab program to even be considered for custody." She knew that there was always a possibility of someone coming forward to ask for Baby Jane. It would be something that would keep her awake until she could go through the adoption process.

The waitress Zach had been talking to earlier stopped and took Lori's order. Once she was gone, Lori changed the subject. "I wanted to apologize. I didn't have any business getting angry in the car. It wasn't meant to be at you."

"I know," Zach said, looking up from his drink, his dark eyes locking with her. "Thank you for being on my side. And thank you for standing up to Kelley. It's hard for me to call her out when she gets started. I spent years thinking of her as another mother, part of my and Katherine's family. I know you're right. I know I need to speak up. I just keep thinking if I'm patient I can get her to understand that I'm not moving back to Memphis and I'm certainly not moving back in with them like they hope."

He took a drink from his glass then looked back up at her. "I promise myself every time I make this trip that it will be the last one. But somehow, I end up letting her convince me that she's right. That Andres does need the consistency and security that she and Butch can provide him. That my not being able to be a full-time parent isn't what he needs."

"What makes a parent a full-time parent? Just because you have a job, and I'll admit that it's not always going to be easy being a single parent with a job whose hours can change at any time, doesn't mean that you aren't providing full-time care. Single parents everywhere in the world are working jobs and still making sure their children are taken care of."

"Katherine's parents were older when they had her.

Their idea of full-time parenting doesn't seem to have changed over the years. Kelley was a stay-at-home mom."

"And that's just another excuse and guilty move she's using on you. Don't let her do it. We have to meet each objection your in-laws come up with, with a solution that lets them know that you are prepared in every way. It shouldn't be this way, we both know, but if you want to get your son without having to face them in court, it's what we have to do."

She looked up and saw Zach's eyes studying her. "What?"

"You make me believe we can do this. That soon, all this will be settled and Andres will be coming to Nashville."

"So how about we make that happen? How about we invite Kelley and Butch, with Andres of course, to stay with us for a weekend? Let them see that they have no reason to worry about anything. That you have it all handled. Maybe they just need to see where their grandson will be to help them take that last step to letting him go. And they need to see that you are seriously not considering moving back with them. Let them see that you are putting down roots, not just with me, but with plans for Andres. Start interviewing candidates for a nanny or get things set up at a daycare so that when they show up, they see it's a done deal. I think once Andres is there with you and you show them you have everything set to take over as his 'full-time' father, they won't have a choice but to leave him with you. Not unless they really intend on taking this to the courts."

She waited while he considered her idea. It had come

to her when she started thinking about everything she would need to do to prepare to bring Janiah home. Showing that she was serious about fostering and willing to do whatever was necessary could make a good impression with DCS.

"It sounds great, but I don't see them agreeing to it that easily," Zach said. "But what if I invite them to a party? It isn't something I usually celebrate, but I have a birthday at the end of the month. What if we used that excuse to throw a party? They'd have a hard time declining if I explained that my brother would be there and I wanted Andres to spend time with his cousins. It would be hard for them to decline that after all Kelley's talk about the importance of family."

"I think that's a great idea. We'll tell them it's all my idea so they don't get suspicious, since you usually don't celebrate. And it will be another sign to them that you are ready to move on with your life.

"We'll need a few days to plan it. I have a lot to do with getting approved for fostering in between getting ready for work. And planning a party will take more time."

"Let's look at our schedules before we say anything to Kelley and Butch. I'm thinking maybe sending out official invitations might be good," Zach said.

"Sounds good," Lori said, then yawned. "And so does bed right now. I better go up."

"I'll go up with you," Zach said, then he stood and reached out a hand to Lori.

She stared at him, not sure what he meant. Surely, he

didn't think they were going up to her room. She swallowed. The possibility was tempting.

After a moment, he seemed to understand her hesitation. "What I meant to say was that I'll walk you up to your room."

She gave him her hand and he tucked it under his arm as they started back to their rooms. It was an old-fashioned gesture that made Lori's heart tighten for a moment. One that was so charming that she had to remind herself once again that the two of them were friends, just friends, no matter what they might be pretending to others.

But her heart told her that wasn't true. Somewhere she'd crossed the line between thinking of Zach as just a friend. Not because of their pretense, but because of who he was. Who she was when she was with him.

She'd looked for the perfect man for herself for years, but it hadn't been until she'd accepted that the person she was looking for didn't exist that she'd found Zach. He wasn't perfect, but she could now see that he was perfect for her.

Except he wasn't. Not really. Not when he'd made it plain that he'd had the perfect love once before and the pain of losing it had almost destroyed him.

"Thank you, again. You really don't have any reason to be helping me like this," Zach said, when they stopped in front of her room.

He released her hand, but instead of letting it drop, she found herself moving closer and cupping his cheek. For a moment the world shifted, her pounding heart all she could hear. She wanted to tell him what she'd just discovered. Those feelings of friendship that she had for him were growing, into what exactly she didn't know. How could she when the way she felt around him was something she'd never felt before. Friendship? Love? She wasn't sure. But what she did know was that she'd do anything to make sure he got his son and went on to live the life he'd been dreaming of. Whether she would fit into that life, she didn't know.

Unable to help herself, she stood on her tiptoes and pressed a kiss to his cheek. "I'll always be happy to help you, Zach."

She should have stepped back then. She should have walked away and left things alone. But when his hand came up, brushing her hair behind her ear, she stepped forward instead of away; she stayed up on her tiptoes and replaced her lips with her hand, then pressed her mouth to his.

His lips were warm and firm. She felt his body stiffen against hers and she started to back away when his hands came around her waist bringing her closer. Closer, until her body fit into his as he took over the kiss and all thought left her mind as she melted into him.

A door slammed down the hall, breaking the spell that had held them together as Zach lifted his head from hers. It was the look of guilt that she saw in his eyes that told her all she needed to know. She had been right. Zach wasn't ready to move on from the loss of his wife. He might not ever be ready to do that. And she had to accept that right now. No matter what she felt for him, she wouldn't let that come between the two of them and their goal to get his son back.

Turning, she opened her hotel door, then shut it quickly behind her before he could see the tears that had already begun to fall.

CHAPTER NINE

LORI MANAGED TO get through the first part of her Monday while avoiding both Zach and Sky. She knew that she couldn't hide out in the office and exam rooms all day. Sky was liable to come in and start with her questions at any time, but if she timed her visit to the NICU and labor and delivery unit just right, maybe she wouldn't have to see Zach.

The trip home from Memphis had been awkward as they'd talked about plans for the party. It was her doing, she knew. What had she been thinking to kiss Zach like that? Could she have made it any more obvious that her feelings for him were changing?

The door to her office opened, and just like she had expected, Sky walked in. The new bride was glowing, her skin tanned from the time in the islands and her eyes bright with happiness, until she looked at Lori.

"No knock?" Lori asked, forcing a smile.

"And pretend I hadn't seen you just shut your door? You can't keep avoiding me. What's wrong? Who are you hiding from and why do you look so down when the last time we talked you claimed to be happily in love?" Sky asked.

"I am in love," Lori said, her smile feeling even more

fake as she tried to relax her face. "How about you? Were the Bahamas amazing? You look wonderful."

"Yes, the Bahamas were amazing, but don't change the subject," Sky said as she took a seat across from Lori's desk. "I know you too well. There's something more to all this than you're telling me. Just a week or so ago you were whining over that loser, Donald. Then all of a sudden you are engaged and in love with Zach. To be honest, I can believe the engagement easier than I can believe that you're in love."

There was no keeping the shock of Sky's words off her face. "Why would you say that?"

"Because all the time I've known you, you've been looking for someone to marry. A husband. Not a lover."

"That's not true," Lori started, then stopped. Wasn't it? Hadn't Zach implied the same thing at the wedding before he'd asked her to marry him?

For a moment she didn't have words. She couldn't think past the realization that both Sky and Zach were right. She'd never trusted anyone enough to give her heart to them. And look at her now. She could deny it all she liked, but she was so close to falling for Zach even though she knew it would be the biggest mistake she'd ever made.

"I'm in so much trouble."

Lori started from the beginning, telling Sky about the conversation she and Zach had at the wedding, about his in-laws, his son. About how she'd come up with this great idea for playing the fake fiancée so that his in-laws would see that he was serious about settling down in Nashville and starting a new life instead of moving back to live with them in Memphis. Then she told her about the kiss, that soul-searching kiss that had changed everything between them. When she was done, Sky sat back in her seat and groaned.

"I know," Lori said, agreeing whole heartedly with her friend's interpretation of the mess she'd made. "I've made a mess of things, haven't I."

"Are you sure he's not just using you?" Sky asked.

"None of this is his fault, Sky. He's such a great guy. He made a mistake when his wife died and he's been paying for it ever since. It was my idea to help him. We're friends, or at least that was all we were until my foolish lips decided to change things."

When Sky busted out laughing, Lori couldn't help but join her. She was so glad she'd decided to tell her friend the truth even if she knew Sky wouldn't approve. "So, what do I do now?"

"I can't tell you what to do, all I can say is that you need to be careful. You're already in this absurd fake relationship too deep. Are you sure that Zach doesn't have any feelings for you? Besides friendship, I mean. It sounded like that kiss wasn't one-sided. Is it possible that there could be more between the two of you? Because from what I'm hearing, and seeing on your face, you're falling for this guy."

Lori had rewound the moment they'd kissed over and over, savoring every minute. She hadn't imagined the moment Zach had wrapped his arms around her. And he'd kissed her back. If it hadn't been for the slamming door in the hallway, who knows what would have happened. But she also remembered that look of guilt in his eyes. Whether it was from feeling like he was betraying his late wife or whether it was because he didn't return any of Lori's feelings, she didn't know.

"He's made it clear that after losing his wife, he doesn't want another relationship. Not like that. No matter what you think, I know better than to fall for someone who doesn't have feelings for me." Such brave words when she knew she had been so close to taking that last leap when that hotel door had slammed.

"It sounds like he's still hurting, but that could change. He's already made some changes in his life, showing that he's starting to move on," Sky said.

Lori's phone rang and she took it out, expecting to see a call from the hospital, as she was on call. Instead, it was her mother's name that came up. She started to let it go to voicemail, her mother was probably just curious about her and Zach's trip to Memphis, but it was unusual for her mother to call during office hours. "Hi, Mom. What's up?"

Lori listened to her mom's frantic voice, her body going cold and numb, her brain racing in a thousand different directions. "It's okay. I'm okay. I'll be right over."

Lori stood, her hand dropping the phone onto her desk, then looked at Sky. "There's been a fire…at the house…at my house."

Lori stood by her mom, Sky at their side, as the firemen dragged their hoses back to their truck. It was gone. The house she'd called home for all of her life was gone.

"Our pictures…" her mom began as she wiped at her damp cheeks.

"Remember I scanned all of them into the computer last year and stored them online. I can have them printed out at any time." Lori added that to the list of things she needed to do, knowing her mom would feel better with at least something solid she could hold after all they'd lost. "And we have home insurance."

But it would never be the same. No matter if they rebuilt it to exactly match the small two-bedroom home Lori had grown up in, it wouldn't be the same.

"I'm just so glad you weren't home. When the neighbors called, I panicked. I couldn't remember what day it was." Her mother said.

Lori remembered the way her mother's voice had quivered, her tears clouding her words as she'd realized her daughter was safe at work.

She stepped back, letting another fireman get past them on the sidewalk. "We're fine, Mom. That's all that matters."

"I should have had the electrical work checked last year when we had the work done at Legacy House. Our house is even older than that one. I just kept putting it off." Her mom put her arms around her daughter's waist. "I'll find a place for you at Legacy until we decide what to do."

Lori knew that the home for pregnant women was always full and needed more room that it had already. "Don't worry about it, Mom, I can find someplace to stay."

"She can stay with me and Jared," Sky said. Lori hadn't been able to talk her friend out of coming with her after she'd received the call, even though the office had been full with waiting patients.

"I appreciate the offer, but you and Jared are newlyweds. You don't need me around." And the last thing Lori wanted was to be around her two friends who were so much in love that sometimes they forgot that there were others present. Besides, she didn't need to be reminded any more than necessary of what she didn't have.

"She can stay with me," a voice said from behind her.

Turning, she saw Zach and the senior Dr. Warner had come up behind them. As her mother threw herself into Jack Warner's arms, Lori just stood staring at Zach. "What are you doing here?"

"Jack called me and told me what had happened. I called in a favor and got the rest of the day off." Zach looked from her to the burnt-out shell of her home. "I'm so sorry, Lori."

Lori forced herself not to follow her mom's demonstration and throw herself into his arms. But when he put an arm across her shoulder, she couldn't help turning into him and letting all the tears she'd been holding on to for her mother's sake free.

Zach carried the last of the items they'd picked up at the store for Lori into the house. Though Sky had headed back to the office, he and Jack had waited while Lori and her mother had spoken with the fire inspector and then helped the two of them as they went through what was left of their home. It had only taken a few moments for all of them to realize that there wasn't much that could be saved. There had been a box of jewelry that had been partially intact in Maggie's room, but Lori's room had been a total loss, the only thing he'd seen her take was a small metal truck that she pulled out of the back of what had been her closet. Standing in that room had been devastating for both of them. Lori had lost everything she had. And he didn't want to think about what would have happened if the fire had started a few hours later. The thought of Lori lying burnt in the husk of the bed that had been left had his stomach tied into knots. That loss would have been so much worse than the mere objects that had been lost to the fire. Lori would never have made it out of the house if it had started while she was sleeping.

Which just proved, once again, that he couldn't let himself get involved with her in anything other than friendship. Pulling back from her in that hotel hallway had been hard, but he'd had no choice. Lori deserved more than that friendship. She deserved to have a love like he'd shared with Katherine.

And he wasn't willing to take a chance of losing himself to the grief that had almost destroyed him from loving someone so much that you couldn't imagine living without them.

"Thank you," Lori said as she came down the stairs toward him. "I really didn't want to stay with Sky and Jared."

He remembered how she'd complained about always being the third wheel with her friends on the night of Sky and Jared's wedding. "I have plenty of room. I had the guest room furnished last week so you'll have your own space. Besides, wouldn't it look strange if you didn't stay with me after everything that's happened?"

She reached the bottom of the stairs and he saw the pain in her eyes at his words. "So that's the only reason you offered me a place to stay? So that it looks good?"

"No, that isn't it. I just…we're friends. I would do this for you no matter what," he said.

The look of pain in her eyes changed slightly, turning to disappointment. Friends. They were friends, he was sure of that. But after the kiss, something had shifted. For both of them, though he could never tell her that. The fact that he had wanted her, had felt the need a man should feel but one that had been absent in his life, didn't matter. Lori would want more than what he could give her. She deserved more.

"I appreciate it. I'll start looking for an apartment tomorrow. Right now, I'll take those and then I think I'll turn in."

She reached for the packages of generic clothing and toiletries she'd purchased at the local discount store. She gave him a ghost of a smile before turning away and starting up the stairs. His arms felt empty. He wanted to hold her as she cried out her pain as he had earlier that day, but he knew he couldn't. So, he didn't stop her. He let her return to the room she picked from those upstairs. He understood her need to be alone after her loss. And with the click of her door shutting, he realized he too felt a loss. The loss of the easy friendship the two of them had shared before that kiss had changed everything. He'd lost his wife, and for the first couple months of his son's life he'd lost Andres while he grieved for his wife. Now he was losing that special bond he and Lori had made together. Sometimes he wondered, just how much loss could he be expected to survive?

CHAPTER TEN

By the next morning Lori had put everything in perspective and come up with a plan. Yes, she'd lost everything she owned, but it could have been so much worse. Everything she owned could be replaced. Oh, she'd had mementos of her childhood that she would have liked to keep, favorite clothes that would be hard to replace and copies of her favorite romance books that she had collected over the years, but most everything else could be replaced.

She thought about the small metal truck she'd found and had hidden behind her back when her mother had come up to her. It was the last thing her father, Jim, had brought her from one of his trips. She'd hidden it away years ago, not wanting her mother to know that she still thought of those first years when they had been a family. Maybe that was the reminder she needed. Maybe she needed to accept that she wasn't meant to have that white picket fence family that she read about in her books. But was it really too much to ask for?

Sky had offered to help cover some of her appointments for the day and have the others be rescheduled, but Lori had refused. There was no reason for her to stay home and fret. Besides, she had received a text from Jessica, Janiah's case manager, asking to meet with her in the NICU department that morning.

Hoping to get out of the house before Zach was up, Lori dressed in the scrub top and pants she'd bought the night before and made her way down the stairs. She told herself she wasn't leaving early to avoid seeing Zach.

She shook her head and went back to the list she had begun before the sun had risen. She had more than just herself to think of; she had to find someplace safe and affordable for when Janiah was ready to be discharged. She'd filed the necessary application for foster care approval and was scheduled that week to start the classes that were required. It was only a matter of time before DCS requested a home visit. And as of yesterday, she actually could be considered homeless.

Not that it would have come to that. She could have rented a hotel room or stayed with friends, though definitely not Sky and Jared. But then Zach had offered his home to her, so she actually was staying with a friend. It wasn't his fault if she had hoped it had been more than friendship that had him offering her a place to stay. None of her feelings for him were his fault. He'd told her right up front that he didn't want to love anyone again.

Stop it. You can't keep thinking about Zach that way. He's your friend. Your best friend.

That thought cleared her mind. She had a best friend; Sky had been that person for years. The one she knew she could count on. The one that would listen to her problems and always consider her feelings. And didn't that sound just like what Zach was doing now? He'd been the one to point out that she'd been looking for a baby's daddy instead of someone to spend her life with. No one else had seen that, or at least had the nerve to be honest with her about that.

She smelled the bacon as she headed down the stairs. It reminded her of the first night she'd spent in Zach's home. Had it only been a little over a week? It seemed so much longer. Had she really only known Zach such a short time? Yet here she was, fighting feelings for a man that she shouldn't have. Feelings that had come on so fast. Too fast.

She waited at the bottom of the stairs, not knowing what to do. She'd planned to just slip out the door without seeing him. But now she wasn't sure what to do. It seemed so rude to leave without telling him, especially since that scent of bacon frying told her he was up.

"Ready for breakfast?" Zach asked from the kitchen door.

"Sorry, I really need to get to the hospital early so I have some time with Janiah before I go to the office."

"The nurses tell me you've been coming twice a day. It seems that our Baby Jane has taken a special liking to you too. The nurses say she eats better for you than she does for any of them," Zach said before turning back into the kitchen. "But if you have a minute, I'd like to talk to you about something."

Lori watched as Zach padded on bare feet into the kitchen. His movements were so graceful that it reminded her of a big sleek cat that had a mouse in its sights.

"What's up?" she asked as she followed him, then stopped at the door.

A large buffet ran along the wall that separated the kitchen from the dining room. On the corner of the buffet sat two picture frames. One was of Andres when he was younger, around six or seven months. Dressed in a pair of denim overalls, the little boy gave the person behind the camera a toothless grin. Beside it sat the picture of a beautiful woman, her hair and skin fair, her smile almost as wide as her son's. You could almost feel the love that the photographer had for his subjects. Somehow, Lori was sure it was Zach who had taken both pictures.

Lori glanced at the rest of the pictures on the buffet, and was surprised to find a stack of books. Romance books. Unable to help herself, she went over to the stack and picked them up. The first one had a picture of a cowboy, dressed in leathers and a Stetson hat on the front cover. She went through the rest of the books and saw that they all had one thing in common. They were all written around the fake fiancée trope.

She went back to the first one and skimmed the pages till she found a piece of paper marking a spot halfway through the book. He was actually reading it, a romance book. The thought of Zach staying up at night reading a romance book in bed made her smile. She could just picture it.

The smile left her face and she swallowed. Maybe thinking of Zach, stretched out in bed with nothing but a sheet and a book was the last thing she needed to picture right now.

"Coming?" he called from the kitchen, totally unaware of where her lustful mind was at that time.

She took a seat at the island, then waited as he served

up the slices of bacon and a helping of eggs to a plate, then put it in front of her.

Going back to the stove, he fixed himself a plate then took a seat opposite of her. Still, he didn't speak until he'd swallowed a forkful of eggs and washed it down with some of the orange juice he'd poured them. "I know this is a hard time for you. I just wanted to let you know that you can stay here as long as you need to."

"Thank you, but I promise to be out at least by the end of the week," she said. She forked the eggs then shoveled them into her mouth. The thought of the fire turned her stomach to stone and she had to make herself swallow.

"There's no hurry. I have the room. Why don't you give you and your mom time to think about things? Besides, doesn't it just seem like it would be normal for you to move in with your fiancée at a time like this?"

So they were back to appearances for their fake fiancée plan. She didn't like it; it was much easier staying there when she thought of it as something a friend would do, but he was right. It would seem strange if she was in such of a hurry to move out when as they were engaged she should be making plans to move in.

"I have to think of Janiah. What am I supposed to tell DCS when they ask to do a home visit?" She'd worried about that problem until she'd finally passed out last night.

"Bring them here. There's another room besides Andres's. The two share a Jack and Jill bathroom. I think it will be a couple more weeks, at least, before she's ready for discharge, but we can set a room up in there for her."

"I'll have to tell them what happened, but I think

they'll understand as long as they know I can provide a place for her. Jessica knows we're 'engaged,' I had to tell her before one of the nurses told her, but I've made it plain that we haven't set a date. I'm not sure what will happen though if I'm living here. They might want to do some type of background check if I'm still here when Janiah gets discharged."

While it didn't hurt for DCS to know she was involved with the pediatrician that was caring for Janiah, she wasn't about to falsify any documents with listing Zach as part of the foster parenting application.

"I'm not worried. You know I'll be there to help you with Janiah. This—" he motioned between the two of them "—whole fake fiancée thing has complicated things for you. Let me help you.

"Besides, it's nice to have someone to cook for." He stood and took her empty plate to the sink. She was surprised to see that she had eaten everything while talking to him, though minutes ago she'd been barely able to get a bite down.

"So, you'll stay?" His offer was sincere and she really didn't want to get caught up in a lease until she and her mother heard from the insurance company and decided if they wanted to rebuild.

"I'll stay. Thank you." Staying here, sharing a home, would be another step into Zach's life, which seemed even more dangerous than playing at being involved, but it seemed right. She wondered if she should tell him about another one of the romance tropes, forced proximity. Would he run out and buy more books?

"I saw that you picked up some reading material," she

said. She stood and walked over to the sink and began working on the dirty dishes.

She looked over to see the dark tone of Zach's face turn red. "It's not something to be embarrassed about."

"I wanted to make sure I was doing this faking thing correctly," he said, coming over to take a dish from her.

As they finished the washing up, she decided it was better that she not mention anything else about the books. He was only half through the one book and she wasn't sure how he was going to feel about the ending, where the hero and heroine got their happily-ever-after. Or how she was going to feel when she and Zach didn't, no matter how much she was starting to want to.

By Friday, the two of them had gotten into a routine. Though they were both busy, they managed to meet in the kitchen every morning for breakfast where they'd talk about their plans for the day. At night one of them usually picked something up for the two of them to share while they made plans for the party that they'd invited Zach's in-laws to.

It seemed like they were sharing everything in their lives, which was why when she walked into her office and found Zach waiting with Jessica for the meeting the case manager had requested, she was surprised.

"What's up?" Lori asked, as a knot began to form in her stomach. "Is something wrong with Janiah?"

"No. There are no changes since this morning. They increased her morphine over night, but we knew that might happen," Zach said as he stood. "Jessica asked to meet with me here."

His look said he didn't know why he'd been called there any more than she did. If the case manager had needed any information about the baby's care, she could have met with him in the NICU.

Lori walked over to her desk and sat. Was it possible that she had been turned down for fostering Janiah? Was that why Jessica had asked Zach to join them? To help Lori accept the news?

"I appreciate the two of you giving me your time. I have to say, I'm surprised that you still want to foster, Lori, especially with so much going on right now. I heard about the fire," said the case manager.

The fire. Lori hadn't even thought about the nurses in the NICU department talking about the fire in front of Jessica, though she certainly should have. She'd been so busy that she hadn't even thought about talking to Jessica about it. But it made sense that the case manager would need to know if she was responsible for a baby that would need foster care at discharge—she'd have to know that the foster parent still had a home for them.

"I'm sorry, I should have told you. As far as the fire is concerned, I'll have a place to bring Baby Jane home to when she gets discharged. But can I ask you a question? Why did you invite Dr. Morales to this meeting?"

"I was told today that you two were living together and you had told me that the two of you are engaged. I don't know your plans, but I thought he might want to be added to the application process." Jessica looked over where Zach sat beside her. "Was I wrong?"

Lori didn't know what to say. She could see where the information she had to have overheard in the NICU would have made her think that Zach would be more involved with Lori fostering Janiah, but hadn't she made it clear when she'd first spoken to Jessica that she was doing this as a single parent? "At this time, I'm applying by myself, as a single foster parent."

"I'm so sorry. I just assumed if the two of you were planning to get married and now living together..." The woman trailed off, looking confusedly between the two of them.

"Does it make a difference?" Zach asked. "I mean, anyone can see by Lori's application and by the time she has spent with the baby that she's the right person for Baby Jane. She's a midwife with a good reputation. She's caring and generous. You have to know that she'll provide a good, safe home. I've seen her with my son. She's great. Any child would be glad to have her as a foster parent."

His phone rang and he pulled it out. Lori could tell by the questions that he asked that it was the hospital. When he looked up at her, his eyes filled with worry, she knew that it had something to do with Janiah.

"Increase the morphine and start the clonidine, per protocol. I'll be right there," Zach said as he stood and headed for the door. Lori followed him out the door, Jessica behind her.

"What happened?" Lori asked as she caught up with him.

"She had a seizure. Not a grand mal, but still..." he trailed off as they exited the building and headed to the path that led to the hospital.

By the time they got to the NICU, Lori was out of

breath from trying to keep pace with Zach. She and Jessica stood to the side while he examined Janiah, listening to her lungs and heartbeat. The seizure had ended and when Lori checked the monitors, they showed that the baby's vital signs were stable, her respiratory rate within normal limits. Whether this was because of the morphine being increased, the sedation relaxing the baby to sleep or the results of the seizure's effect on the baby's body, Lori didn't know.

"Is she going to be okay?" Jessica asked from beside her. "I know this is common, but it seems it would have happened earlier."

"With her being premature and her mother positive for amphetamines and benzos, it's made her care different than most cases. Zach was aware of that and has had the nurses watching her carefully. The fact that they've had to increase the morphine on a regular basis wasn't a good sign. This is a setback, but I know she's in good hands with Zach and these nurses."

"He seems to be very good at this," Jessica said as they both stood back and watched as Zach gave more instructions to the nurses. "I have to admit, I still don't understand why he isn't applying to be a foster parent with you."

"We've only been—" Lori hesitated, not sure what to say without giving the case manager the wrong idea about the two of them "—together, for a few weeks. Our relationship is so new that we want to take things slow for now. Zach knows I'm committed to fostering Janiah, and I want to look into the possibility of adopting her too. He's supportive of both."

The expression on Jessica's face told her that the case manager still didn't understand everything that was going on between Lori and Zach. But then Lori was just as confused on that matter. Sometimes, when they were alone at night, discussing their day and planning his party, Zach would smile at her with something in his eyes that looked like more than just friendship. And when they parted for the night, there was always this awkward feeling between the two of them, a feeling that if just one of them made a move, the two of them wouldn't be going to bed alone that night. The night before, she'd almost done it, made that move that would change everything between them.

But when she'd gotten to the bottom of the stairs, she'd lost her nerve and instead had headed for her room with only a murmured "Good night" before almost sprinting to her door.

"But you are living with him. You consider his home your home right now?" Jessica asked.

"I do," she said. Coming to Zach's house at night felt just like coming home. Knowing he was waiting for her had her rushing there every night she had off. She knew she shouldn't let herself feel that way. She was only setting herself up for heartache once Zach had his son back with him and she had to move on.

"Okay, then. I think we can put in the application that you have a permanent residence with Dr. Morales and that will cover the living arrangements. There will still have to be a home visit. And because he lives there, we'll have to do a background check on him too. Of course,

I'm not worried about either of those things, but they are necessary."

Lori tried to listen as the case manager made arrangements to meet with Lori for the home visit, but her eyes kept watch over Janiah as she slept.

CHAPTER ELEVEN

FOR THE REST of the day, Lori went about her day seeing patients in the clinic, reminding herself that Janiah was in good hands with Zach and the nurses. She'd made them all promise to call her if there were any changes, so when her phone rang, she almost dropped the phone in her panic before she realized it was the labor and delivery department calling.

Becky English was finally in labor after going a week over her due date. It was the fourth child that Lori would deliver with Becky and Will, two girls and a boy, and today another boy. Becky had told her that being an only child, she'd always dreamed of having multiple children so that they'd have someone to play with and grow up with. Her husband, Will, had been one of three, telling his wife all kinds of horror stories of what three boys could do to each other, but Becky had stood firm. She'd wanted four and now she would have them. From the smile on Will's face, Lori knew that Will was just as excited as his wife to meet their new little one.

"You're almost eight centimeters and the baby's moving down nicely. I know you went fast with your last one, so I don't think it will be much longer. I'm going to step out for few minutes to call the office to let them know I've got a delivery and then I'll be back."

She left the room, as the nurse and Becky's husband, Will, began coaching her through the next contraction and was surprised to find Zach waiting outside the room.

"Did something else happen?" Lori asked, her heart skipping a beat with the panic she felt.

"No, there've been no changes. I think starting the clonidine is helping and the nurses are keeping her from as much stimuli as possible. I just wanted to hear what Jessica said. I'm afraid I shouldn't have let her know that her handling of this, the way she acted like you needed me on your application, made me angry. Did I cause any problems for you?" He leaned against the wall outside Becky's room, his posture telling her that he'd had a tiring day. "Is the engagement going to cause problems for your fostering Janiah?"

She loved how concerned he was for her and also the way he had begun to refer to the little abandoned baby with a real name. "I don't think so. I told her to consider your home as mine, but I think it makes it even more important now that we get Andres away from your in-laws soon so we can stop this pretend relationship."

Zach pushed away from the wall, his body so close to hers now that they almost touched. And there it was again. That look he gave her, was that what people called yearning? The way his eyes locked onto hers like they wanted something from her. But what? She held her breath. Waiting for him to say something, to do something.

And then he looked away, and it was gone. "Let's talk about it tonight at home."

She wanted to stop him, ask him what it was that he'd been thinking, been feeling. But what if she'd imagined it all?

So instead, she nodded her head, then turned and headed to the nurse's station to make her call. Right now, she needed to concentrate on her patient.

An hour later, she was happily handing a little baby boy, kicking his feet and screaming loud enough to be heard down then hall, to his proud parents. "I think he's bigger than the last one. He's certainly louder."

She finished her work and helped the nurses get both mama and baby comfortable. And when Becky and Will asked one of the nurses to get a picture of them with Lori, she smiled and obliged them. But when they showed her the picture, and she took in the look of such love on the two parents' faces, the way Will was smiling down at his wife and new son, it tugged at that empty spot in her chest that always seemed to appear whenever she saw a father and their child together. Had her father looked at her that way when she was born? If so, what had happened that had changed things?

She had memories of her father, them chasing fireflies together on summer nights, playing card games together until it was time for bed, crying after he'd hugged her bye before climbing into his big truck and leaving. Then the memories became farther and farther apart, as her father began missing birthdays and holidays. Until one day he'd driven off and never returned.

At first, she'd cried and blamed herself. Then she'd gotten angry at him, swearing that she never wanted to see him again. Later, with her mother's help she'd come to understand that the anger wasn't good for her so she'd pushed back her memories of him and pretended he didn't exist. Until times like this, when they crept back into her mind and just wouldn't go away.

Zach was headed out of the hospital for the day, when an arm caught his. Turning he saw Dr. Jack Warner standing beside him.

"Zach, I'm glad I caught you," the older man said, his smile looking somewhat embarrassed. "I was hoping you had a moment to talk."

From what Zach had been told, Jack had partially retired months ago and had stopped doing deliveries all together, so it had to be something personal he wanted to discuss and not a patient. As the only thing the two of them had in common was Lori, he looked around for someplace quiet they could talk. "Sure. How about I buy you a cup of coffee?"

Turning around, they headed toward the café while Jack asked him the usual questions about his work and how he liked Nashville. It wasn't until they'd both gotten their drinks and found a table away from everyone else, that Jack finally got around to the reason he wanted to talk to him.

"You know I'm dating Lori's mother," the older man said. "And she's worried about this engagement that it seems you and Lori have rushed into. With the fire, and that stress, I'm worried about her. I've been trying to reassure her that you two know what you're doing, but she asked me to talk to you. I've reminded her that you're grown adults. Smart. Responsible. And I know the two of you aren't planning to wed anytime soon, right?"

Zach nodded his head, not knowing what to say to the man. What did he want? For Zach to announce his undying love for Lori?

Undying love? It sounded so wonderful until you were stuck living with that love all by yourself. When the person you had proclaimed that undying love for was gone. What were you supposed to do with that love then? Hadn't Lori told him that Jack had lost his wife? But here the man was, worried enough about another woman that he was willing to question another colleague just to put that woman's fear at rest. "Everybody tells you that you have to move on after you lose someone you love, but no one tells you how. How did you do it?"

Jack sat back and stared at him, Jack's thick gray eyebrows drawing together in a straight line. Zach felt the heat of that stare as if he was being studied under a microscope and he knew the man was seeing right straight through to that part of him that had been destroyed when he'd watched Katherine take her last breath.

"I don't know that you really ever do move on," Jack said, picking up his drink, his eyes finally leaving Zach. "No. That's not right. Let me say that differently. You do move on, you have to at some point. But moving on with your life, doesn't mean that you forget. You still have your memories. You still have the love you felt for that person. You don't move on without those. You'll carry that with you no matter where you go, because it's part of you."

"But if you take all that with you, are you really moving on? Like you said, you still love that person."

"Just because you lost someone you loved, that doesn't mean you can't love again. The heart is an amazing thing, a remarkable organ that provides us with life. But the heart which we use to love with is bigger than what you see in an X-ray or CT. It can hold more inside it than any cardiac function test can measure. The human heart we refer to when we love someone just gets bigger and bigger, as big as it needs to be. It's not limited. It expands to love our children, each time one is born. It doesn't replace the love you felt for one child with the love of another one. It can love both."

It was Zach's turn to stare at the man. He knew what Jack was trying to tell him. He could still love Katherine while loving someone else. It didn't have to be one or the other. And Zach could see that was how Jack felt about his late wife and Maggie. Jack still loved the wife he'd lost, but he had enough love for Maggie too.

But that was never how Zach had thought. From the moment he'd lost Katherine, he'd believed he'd never love again.

And then he met Lori. Sweet, kind Lori, who had done so much for him, the only woman he'd met since the death of his wife who'd tempted him into wanting more than friendship with a woman. But how did he know if he had enough love for someone else?

He remembered the way Kelley had pushed at him with memories of her daughter, over and over again as if she was trying to compare Katherine to Lori when it was plain to see that they were two different people.

Even the attraction he felt for Lori was different from what he had felt for Katherine. While he and Katherine had slowly moved from friends to lovers, enjoying each step as it came, the need he felt for Lori was different. When they'd been standing in the L and D hall together earlier that day, desire had flared up inside him so fast that it had almost overwhelmed him with the need to touch her, to hold her, to feel the warmth of her body against his own. It was only the fact that they were in a hospital hallway that had kept him from pulling her into his arms and kissing her, a realization that had had him rushing out of the unit as fast as he could. It was only when he got back to NICU that he realized the guilt he'd expected to come, didn't. And that bothered him almost as much as his need for Lori.

He and Jack finished their coffee, the older man letting him absorb everything he said. When Zach stood to leave, Jack finally spoke. "I know you care about Lori. I think you care more than you realize, or at least more than you are ready to admit. But if you can't love her like she deserves, you need to tell her before it's too late. She was abandoned once. I don't want to see that done to her again."

Lori was still thinking about the delivery she'd done and the picture-perfect family Becky and Will had made when she got home that night. Zach had messaged her earlier that he would order out for them so she wasn't surprised to see a pizza delivery car pulling out of the drive when she arrived. She followed the smell to the kitchen and found Zach staring out the window.

"Is everything okay?" she asked.

Zach looked up at her, as if he'd just noticed she'd come into the room. "I'm sorry. What did you ask?"

"You seemed far away right then. I just wanted to ask if everything was okay. Did your in-laws call?" Lori wouldn't put it past them to cancel coming to the party at the last minute.

"No, I called earlier today and talked to Andres. Butch assured me that they were planning to make the party. He actually sounded as if he was looking forward to it."

They didn't talk again until they'd gathered the paper plates and napkins and taken what now seemed like their designated spots around the coffee table in the family room that Zach brought up the subject of the case manager.

"Jessica called me after I saw you in Labor and Delivery," he said. "She wanted an update on Janiah and to let me know that they'd have to do a background check since we are living together."

"I meant to tell you about that tonight. I hope it's not a problem. I think you just have to sign a form agreeing to it."

"It's fine. Not a problem," Zach said, handing her a plate and opening the pizza box.

She took a piece and put it on her plate, not bothering to take a bite.

"What's wrong?" Zach asked. "If it's Janiah, I checked on her a few minutes before you got here. There've been no more seizures."

"I stopped by to see her before I left the hospital." And then she'd stood there for half an hour before she could force herself to leave. "Am I doing the right thing? Pushing to foster Janiah and to adopt her? Or am I being selfish?"

"Why would you ask that? You already love that baby. You've done a lot of work to get qualified for fostering. What happened to make you think that baby wouldn't be lucky to have you as a mother?"

"I'm just worried that maybe she needs more than me. I grew up without a father. Do I want that for her?" Lori felt so confused. Yes, she'd grown up without a father, but she'd still had a good childhood. A happy one for the most part. Maybe it was because she'd had a father for a few years that she had missed that when it was gone.

"I'm going to be single father to Andres. I know he'll miss having a mother, but there's nothing I can do about that. All I can do is love him."

Lori knew he was right. Lori was willing to love Janiah twice as much if necessary. And Zach was going to be a great father. Saying that Janiah would be better with someone else was like agreeing with Kelley that Andres needed both her and Butch to care for him. "You're right. I will love Janiah and give her the best life possible."

"We both know there could be complications with any baby born to a mother who tested positive for drugs. I've ordered a CT. It will tell us if there is anything besides the withdrawal that caused the seizure. Without having any history on the mom, it's hard for us to know what else to look for. There's no sign of infection. We can rule that out. But there's a possibility that there could have been some fetal distress during labor that we couldn't be aware of. If so, there could be some permanent damage to the brain. You need to be prepared for that."

Lori had already considered that possibility. It didn't change a thing about her wanting to adopt Janiah. It scared her, but it didn't change her mind. "I am."

"I knew you would be. It's why I think you will be a great mother for her. She needs someone that's prepared to love her no matter what," Zach said. He took a swallow from his glass of wine.

"And as far as Janiah needing two parents, there's always my invitation to marry you." He smiled, letting her know that he was joking.

She understood that he wasn't serious. He had come a long way in the past weeks from being the man who thought he had to have a wife to raise his son. Not that it had been because of her. Not really. She'd just been the one to point out the mind games his mother-in-law had been playing with him. He'd just needed to get over his guilt of leaving his son's care to his in-laws at the beginning. She knew he had accepted now that though he might have made the wrong decision then, he was doing the right thing now for his son.

But what if he was serious? Would you take his offer now? Could you live with him as his wife, raise children with him, knowing that he didn't love you? That he couldn't love another woman after losing his wife?

She refused to answer the questions that flooded her mind. Better to change the subject than dwell on things she had no answer for. "So, tell me about the nanny that's coming to interview."

They discussed the applicants he'd spoken with over

the phone, and the one he'd chosen to interview in person, then moved on to the arrangements he'd made with the caters for the party.

They finished half the bottle of wine, and cleaned up the leftovers of their dinner before they headed up the stairs to bed. Once more there was that awkward point where the two of them would go to their separate rooms. Once more she saw that longing, that hunger, in Zach's eyes when he told her good night, then hesitated before he turned toward his room.

She stood there watching him leave her, hoping that he'd turn around and reach out a hand toward her. When his door shut, she let out a breath she didn't realize she was holding. It would be another night she'd sleep alone. Another night that the two of them could share, if just one of them had the courage to take that step.

She walked toward his door, lifting her hand to knock, then stopped. What if she had read that longing look in his eyes wrong? What would it do to their friendship, the only thing he'd said he could offer her, if she slept with him? And how would she ever walk away from him if she allowed them to get any closer?

It was already a painful edge she walked between their friendship and the feelings that were growing between them. Painful because she knew if she ever let down her guard and allowed herself to love Zach, all that waited for her would be the heartbreak of knowing he could never feel the same for her.

Slowly, she dropped her hand, then walked away.

CHAPTER TWELVE

"You know, it feels really strange to be blowing up balloons for your own birthday party," Zach said, attaching a string to another yellow balloon before tying it to the other ones he'd been working on. He'd insisted that he'd grown out of the age for wanting balloons, but Lori had reminded him that Andres would love them.

"Stranger than throwing yourself a party?" Lori asked as she worked to tie two balloons together, reaching for one of them as it floated from her hand.

Zach grabbed the string, pulling the balloon down right before it joined its friends that were huddled on the ceiling. "At this rate there will be more up there than on the chairs."

"Less talking, more blowing," Lori teased, a smile cracking open a face that had been way too serious the last few days.

The doorbell rang and they looked at each other. They'd both come home early to finish the decorating and all their supplies had been delivered earlier in the week except for what the caterer was bringing them the next day.

"Maybe it's an early birthday present," Lori said as they went to the door.

But when Zach opened the door, the surprise was much more than a birthday gift. Standing on the porch stood his in-laws with Butch holding Andres, who was fast asleep and draped across his shoulder.

"This is a surprise," Zach said. "I wasn't expecting you till tomorrow."

"We decided it would be best to drive down early," Butch said. The sour look on Kelley's face said she didn't want to be there at all. "You never know what could happen in the morning and we didn't want to miss this party. Where can I take him?"

Zach was so surprised that for a moment he just stood in the doorway.

"His room is up the stairs on the right," Lori said, pulling on Zach's arm so that he stepped out of the way.

As Butch and Kelley came in the room, Zach realized that this was really happening. Andres was here, in the home Zach had made for the two of them. "I'll take him."

Zach reached over and took his sleeping son from Butch, the weight and warmth of the toddler turning his heart into a gooey mess. He was home. Andres was finally at home.

He looked over to where his mother-in-law stood in the doorway as if she was ready to run back to the car. The look she was giving the boy he held in his arms said she would be taking the child with her when she ran.

At that moment, Zach decided he'd had enough. Enough of trying to be gentle with his in-laws. Enough of letting them dictate when and where he'd see his son while they made him feel inadequate. His son would not spend another moment out of his care. If it meant calling a lawyer and fighting in the courts, so be it. He'd just have to live with the fact that Katherine would never have forgiven him for doing such a thing.

"Kelley, it's so nice to see you again. Come in. We're so glad you could come for the party. I can't wait to meet the rest of Zach's family. Can I get the two of you something to drink?" Lori said from beside him.

Zach could still hear the sound of Lori's voice as she coaxed Kelley into the room as he walked up the stairs to the room he'd made for his son. Turning on the light, he looked at the crib that had been sitting empty since he'd bought it. Lori had made it up just the night before so Andres would have a place to nap.

"It's a nice room," Butch said from behind him as Zach laid his son on the mattress that had never been used, and then covered Andres with a blanket that Zach couldn't even remember buying.

"I hope he likes it," Zach said, before turning toward his father-in-law. After Katherine had died, Butch had been a rock for Zach, helping him make the funeral plans and listening to Zach when he'd needed someone. He'd always admired the man, had never dreamed that the man he had come to love would fight him over his grandson.

"He will, I'm sure." Butch moved into the room and shut the door behind him. "I hope you don't mind our showing up early. I had to do some talking to convince Kelley to come. It seemed best to just get her in the car before she could come up with any reasons to cancel."

So, his mother-in-law had been giving Butch a hard time about coming. "She was going to cancel? Why?"

Butch rubbed at his face, then stared up at the ceiling. The man had aged more than years since he'd lost his daughter. "We knew what you were doing the moment we got the invitation. I can't say I'm surprised. I've known this day was coming. Expected it."

Butch looked into Zach's eyes, and he understood the pain he saw there. "I don't want to hurt you or Kelley. Katherine wouldn't want me to do that. But I need my son."

Zach glanced down to where Andres slept, with no worries in the world. He had no idea of the war that had been going on around him for the last months.

"I know. I've tried to tell Kelley for months, since you moved, that it was time to let Andres go, but..." Butch ran his hand over his face again. "Katherine's death did something to her. It left a hole."

"And Andres filled it," Zach said. "I know. I saw it from the beginning. I should have done something then. I never should have let Andres go that first day."

"To be honest, I don't know what we would have done if you hadn't. Taking care of Andres helped both of us. It kept us from spending every moment thinking about Katherine." Butch moved toward Zach, his hand coming to rest on Zach's arm. "I know we should have let the two of you go earlier. I know you need to make your own life. It was selfish of us and I'm sorry for that."

Butch turned to walk away, but Zach stopped him. "So, you're not going to fight me? Because I'm not going to be manipulated into letting him go back to Memphis. He's staying with me."

"I'm not going to fight you. I think Andres will be

happy with you and Lori. I like her. She seems to be a nice woman. I also like the way you look at her. It's the first time I've seen your eyes alive except when you're with Andres. I think Katherine would like Lori too. She'd be happy that you've found someone to love."

Zach didn't know what to say, though some of the guilt he felt for the feelings that he was having for Lori eased just a bit.

"I wish I could speak for Kelley, but that woman has always been stubborn. I'll do what I can." Butch gave him a weak smile. "But it will be up to you to convince her that Andres belongs more with you than with us."

Zach waited until Butch left to walk back over to the crib to watch his son sleep. When the boy began to stir, he patted his back as Andres settled back into sleep. "It's okay, son. You're home now. And your daddy is never going to let go of you again."

Lori looked toward the stairs as Butch came down, disappointed that Zach didn't come down after him. She needed reinforcements.

Keeping Kelley from following her husband up the stairs had almost been more than she could do, but she wanted Zach to have a moment with his son without her taking it over. So she'd taken the woman on a tour through the downstairs with Kelley not saying a word, though every once in a while, Lori would see that mask of disinterest slide away. Even though it was dark, she pointed out the kitchen window to where a fenced-in yard held a play area for Andres. But when she'd seen the paperwork Zach had filled out that morning after one of the nanny interviews he'd done, she'd covered the stack with a cutting board. She wasn't about to start that conversation with Kelley, though she knew from the look on Zach's face as he'd carried his son up the stairs that it would have to happen. There was no way he was letting his son go this time.

"Show me where Andres is sleeping," Kelley said to her husband when he joined them.

"There's no need. Zach's settling him in," Butch told his wife as he walked past the two of them, headed toward the front door. "I'll go get our bags."

Lori tensed. Their bags? They were staying there, with Lori and Zach? Of course they were. Had Lori really thought that Kelley was going to leave Andres here without her?

"Then Lori can show me upstairs where we will be staying," Kelley said, looking at Lori as if the words had been an order.

"Sure. Just give me a moment to get the guest room ready," Lori said, then ran up the stairs as fast as she could, hoping the woman wouldn't follow her.

As she headed down to the guest room, also known as the only other room with a bed besides Zach's room, she stopped at Andres's doorway to find Zach standing over the toddler's crib. Without hesitating, she went to his side and took his arm, hauling him out of the room as she tried not to wake his son. "Did you know they were planning to stay with us?"

"I wasn't expecting them at all tonight, but I'm not surprised they're staying. From what I can tell, it took everything Butch had to get Kelley to agree to come. We had a talk. A good one."

"You can tell me about that later. Right now, we have to figure out what we are going to do before Kelley comes looking for the two of us and finds out that I'm staying in the guest room."

"Why would that be a problem," Zach asked, then moaned. "Because she'd see that the two of us aren't sleeping together which…"

"Which would look really strange for two people engaged and sharing a home," Lori finished for him. "Yeah, because of that. I've got to move my stuff out of the room and into yours. That woman is so high-strung right now, if she sees any evidence that we are not what we say we are, she's going to call us out on it and cause trouble. It's like she's looking for a reason to leave and I have no doubt that she'll try to take Andres with her."

"She's not going to take him. I've already spoken with Butch, but yes, we can talk about that later. What can I do?" Zach asked, his eyes going back to the room where his son slept.

"Just tell them I want to get the room ready and keep them busy for a few minutes," Lori said. Realizing she was still holding on to his arm, she let go. "I'll have to move all my stuff to your room for the night."

As the two of them went in different directions, Lori couldn't ignore the fact that it looked like the two of them might finally be sharing a bed. She knew that it was entirely inappropriate that she was excited about the prospect. If Zach had wanted her in his bed, he would have asked her. Now it would be like it was being forced on him.

She shoved those thoughts aside as she quickly gathered what belongings she had accumulated after the fire, tossing them into pillowcases. She stripped the bed and made it again with sheets she found in the hall linen closet. After she moved her things to Zach's room, not allowing herself more than one look at the big bed in the center, she headed back down the stairs.

The entryway was empty but she could hear voices… and was that laughter coming from the family room?

Going through the kitchen, she found Kelley with a glass of wine, leaning against the island as Butch and Zach worked on the balloons that had been left to blow up. The two men seemed to be having a good time working together, and for a moment Lori thought she saw a slight smile on Kelley's face.

"It looks like I've missed most of the fun," Lori said as she watched the two men begin to put up the decorations. She nodded when Kelley offered her a glass of wine.

"They've always gotten along so well," Kelley said before taking a drink from her own glass. "Katherine was a daddy's girl. She always said that Zach reminded her of her father with his patience and humor. It made her so happy to see the two of them together."

"She was lucky to have them both," Lori said softly. This softer, vulnerable Kelley was a different part of the woman than Lori normally saw. For the first time she fully understood that Katherine's mother was still deeply grieving over the loss of her daughter. Lori could see now that she'd buried a lot of her grief by putting all of her energy into caring for Andres. No wonder the woman was afraid of losing Andres. With her grandson gone, she'd have no choice but to face that grief.

"Does your father like Zach?" Kelley asked.

The question was so unexpected that Lori had to take a drink of her wine before she answered, making sure to keep her voice steady. "My father left when I was young. I don't know where he is or even if he's still alive."

Kelley turned and looked at her then. "Is that why you're so determined for Zach to have Andres here in Nashville?"

"Maybe that's some of it. But more than that, I'm determined for Zach to have his son because he deserves him. He loves his son. He'd do anything for him. You know that. You know that Andres belongs with his father."

"He could have been with Andres at our home. There was no reason for him to change things and move to Nashville."

"You had to know that Zach would want to move out with Andres on his own someday. You couldn't expect him to spend the rest of his life living with his in-laws," Lori said.

"I think it's time for bed for this old man," Butch said as he joined them, Zach right behind him. If he'd overheard anything Lori had said, he didn't show it.

"We'll take you up," Zach told them, before taking one of the bags Butch had.

Lori saw that Kelley had taken what looked like a diaper bag, no doubt packed with Andres's things. "We can stop by Andres's room to drop that off."

Lori took the woman to Andres's room, then hustled her out to the guest room where Butch was waiting for her before she could wake the child. It had been a long day and Lori knew the next one could prove to be just as long. She started downstairs to clean up only to meet Zach coming up. She could see that he'd turned off the lights, giving her no reason to go down.

They climbed the stairs together, then stopped at the spot where they normally would have gone separate ways. The night before she had hesitated at that same spot, waiting for Zach to say something, do something, to explain the reason he looked at her with such longing each night, but never said the words she wanted to hear. Couldn't he see the same longing he had for her in her eyes?

But then how could he when she'd never explained to him that she felt that same desire she could see in his eyes? Maybe this was all meant to be. Maybe it was time to speak up and let him know that she wanted him. That while she was faking an engagement with him, there was nothing fake about the need that she had felt from the first night she'd spent there.

She'd talked herself out of knocking on his door last night because she'd been afraid of getting hurt. Tonight, she wasn't going to let her fear stop her.

"I want you," she said, the words inadequate for the desire she felt to be with him. "I want to sleep with you. I want you to hold me tonight. I want to make love with you."

CHAPTER THIRTEEN

ZACH SUCKED IN a breath. He'd tried to hide his desire for Lori. She deserved so much better than him. When he'd met her, he'd been so messed up, struggling with his cowardly choice of leaving his son in his in-laws' care after his wife's death. But she'd done something no one else had done. She'd listened to him, then told him to get his act together, make a plan and get his son back. She'd had a belief in him that he hadn't had in himself since Katherine's death. And though he was stronger now, he still didn't deserve someone like Lori, someone with so much love. Love that he didn't know if he would ever be brave enough to return.

But what he did know was that he wanted to hold her, to make love to her, to give her this night that they both wanted.

She looked away from him. Embarrassed for telling him that she wanted him? He lifted her chin till their eyes met. "I want that too. I want you in my bed tonight. I want to make love with you."

He kissed her lips, just a caress at first. She tasted so good as his hands shifted into the soft silkiness of her hair. He tilted her head to take the kiss deeper. Her lips were so soft and pliant as they opened under his demanding mouth. As his tongue danced with hers, his body became hard, his muscles straining as he tried to pull himself back from the temptation of stripping them both bare right there in the hallway. It was only the thought of Kelley and Butch that made him stop the kiss before they could go any further.

He rested his head on hers as he tried to catch his breath. When he raised his eyes to hers, he saw undisguised pleasure there. He smiled at her, then took her hand, leading her down the hall to his room.

When he'd shut the door behind him, he led her to the bed. He moved the two pillowcases filled with clothes off the bed. Not waiting to turn down the bed, he sat and pulled her down to his lap.

"Are we really doing this?" Lori asked as she wrapped her arms around his neck.

"From what I've read in those romance books you recommended, this was inevitable." His lips settled in the curve of her neck and worked their way up as she moved to give him more access, her body pressing into his lap. He stopped for a moment, needing to get a stronger hold on his body's response.

"So, you got to the good parts, huh? Which trope? The fake fiancée or the forced proximity?" Lori asked before she let out a moan as his mouth continued its path up her neck and behind her ear.

"Does it matter?" he asked. He shifted her in his lap as he began to unbutton her blouse. "I can promise you one thing. I won't be faking anything tonight."

"No faking anything tonight, I promise," she swore to him.

He shifted again, letting her feel the hard length of him against her. He felt her body tighten in his arms before she shifted her own body, turning in his arms until she was straddling him. The wicked smile she gave him was all the warning he had before she pressed herself against him and crossed her legs around his back.

His lips took hers, and his hands were trembling as he undid the last button on her blouse and almost ripped it off her body. When he went to undo her bra, her hands came up between them, pushing him away.

"Too slow," she said, undoing her bra and throwing it across the room.

Then her hands began unbuttoning his own shirt before they moved down to the button of his jeans. He almost laughed at the way her eyebrows scrunched into a line and she bit down on her bottom lip as she tried to figure out how to undo his zipper while they sat entwined together.

"Let me help," he said. She gasped as he lifted her up and in one quick twist of their bodies had her lying on her back, his body over hers. He undid the legs she'd crossed around him and stood. He shed his jeans as she wiggled out of her pants, the movement as erotic as any he'd ever seen. Then she slowly peeled her underwear off,

"I thought you said I was going too slow," he said, consumed by a hunger he'd never felt at the sight of her laid out bare on his bed.

The wicked smile on her face made him laugh as he moved over her, then rolled her to her side so that they were facing each other. His hand skimmed down her chest, circling her breast, palming her nipples. His hand swept lower until it slid between her legs. He stopped and her body went still. "I might have learned a little more than how to play a fake fiancé from those romance books."

Then his fingers slid between her folds and entered her. The gasp she made quickly turned into a moan as he continued to stroke her. She pulled his head down to her and kissed him with an intensity that almost undid him as he slipped his fingers in and out, each time sliding between her legs before entering her again. Her body arched against him and his mouth swallowed her moans.

He pulled back and just looked at her. With her hair spread across the bed in tangles, her lips bright red from his kisses and those bright green eyes a little wild, it was a sight he would never forget. She was beautiful in every way, inside and out.

And she deserves better than you.

Yes, yes, she did deserve better than him. She deserved a man with a heart that hadn't been broken. She deserved the type of love you only experience once in a lifetime.

He remembered what Jack had said, that you could feel love again, but would it be enough? Could you love the second time around as deeply as you had loved before?

She reached up for him, running her hands up his chest to wrap around his neck, pulling him down to her, making him push away all the guilt that wanted to drown him. Her lips touched his and he covered her with his body, the slide of her skin against his own driving him to madness.

No, he wasn't the man that deserved her, they both knew that. But as he entered her, filled her, and felt her quiver as she broke apart in his arms, he swore that for just tonight, he would let himself believe that he could be that man.

Lori stood beside Zach as he introduced his brother and sister-in-law to her and as he held Andres. The pride in his voice as he introduced his son to his family and friends made Lori's heart melt. When they'd woken that morning, she was surprised that there was no awkwardness between the two of them though neither of them commented on the night before. Zach had told her of his conversation with Butch the previous night, and she knew his attention was fixed on having his son with him because that was the most important thing for both of them right then. They still had to worry about how Kelley was going to take the news and how they were going to handle it if she fought against Butch's decision. But they decided they couldn't let that ruin the party as the rest of the guests had no idea what was going on in the background. And so, they went through the motions of the party.

When Andres, tired from being held by his father, wiggled out of Zach's arms she was surprised when he went to Lori and held up his arms to her. She picked him up and put him on her hips, the weight of him feeling so natural to her. Almost too natural, as she knew she was quickly falling for the toddler just as she had for his father.

The two of them had bonded over bath time that morning after he'd eaten his breakfast. She'd thought it would be a fight when she'd taken the toddler out of his high chair and told Butch and Kelley that she was going to get him ready for the party. But when Kelley had started toward her, Butch had placed an arm in front of her, giving her a look that stopped her. Why Butch was helping her, she didn't know, but she appreciated it. She and Andres had played in the tub till not only was Lori soaked, but the bathroom floor was covered with bubbles. The child's laughter had been so carefree that Lori wondered if he was already feeling at home. But then children accept change so much easier than adults.

She and Zach had already discussed the fact that leaving the only home he knew and not seeing his grandparents every day would be an adjustment for Andres. Zach had decided that asking the nanny he intended to hire to stop by and meet his son might help. Lori just hoped that Kelley didn't run the woman off before he got a chance to give her the job.

No, she wasn't going to let thoughts of what could go wrong ruin this day. Andres was home, and if Butch was to be believed, he'd be staying there with them. No, not with them, with Zach. Her part in this was just temporary and she needed to remember that.

Last night, after they'd made love, there had been no words of love or of a future together. So wouldn't that mean that last night had really just been sex, not making love? But that wasn't what it had felt like to her.

She'd started to tell Zach how she felt afterward. How she'd been falling in love with him since that night at the wedding. But she held back. He'd made it clear that he didn't want to be romantically involved with anyone from the beginning. Telling him that she loved him now would put their friendship at risk. Last night she'd felt like one of her romance novel heroines, except she knew she wasn't going to get a happily-ever-after. They'd had a wonderful night together, but nothing had changed between the two of them. She was there for a purpose, and if things went right today, Zach wouldn't need her after tonight. But was it too much to ask for just a little more time with him before she left? The longer she stayed the harder it was going to be for her to leave. And she had to start making plans for her and Baby Janiah. But still...

A few weeks ago, she would have sworn that all she needed to make her happy was to be a mother. Now she knew that wasn't true. She needed more. She needed a man to love her and one she could love without having to hide her feelings. But it wasn't just any man she wanted. She wanted Zach. She wanted him to be that man. Only, he couldn't be. Not by any fault of his own, it was just the way it was. He'd lost someone he loved and he didn't want to risk loving someone again, if he even could love someone again.

"Can he go outside with us?" One of Zach's nieces, Helene, asked from beside her. Though the girl looked to be barely twelve, Lori had seen how she mothered her little brother and sister.

"I don't see why not," Lori said, looking to where Zach had stood just moments earlier, but found that he'd walked off without her noticing. "Go ahead outside. Just let me check with his dad and then I'll bring him out."

She walked through the house, still carrying Andres while speaking with Zach's family and then Kelley and Butch, but no one seemed to know where Zach had gone. She was about to head up the stairs when he walked in from the front porch holding his phone in his hand. When his eyes met hers, she knew something was wrong. Just moments earlier he'd been laughing and joking, now he looked as if the weight of the world had been handed to him.

Her heart seemed to stutter with the only word she could get out, "Janiah?"

"That was Dr. Davis. She's got weekend call, but I asked her to keep me up-to-date on Baby Girl Doe." The fact that he was using the proper name for Janiah sounded so cold that it sent a chill through Lori's body.

"What happened?" she asked, her arms tightening around the little boy squirming in her arms.

"She's had another seizure, this one lasted longer than the first one. They've titrated the morphine and they're taking her for an MRI now."

"Okay, so this happens sometimes, right? You've had patients in the NICU for a month for withdrawals. It's just going to take some time."

"Dr. Davis and I are concerned about the new seizure. Neither one of us would have expected another one at this point. But the real concern is—" he held out his arms to his son, taking Andres from her, then put his arm around her waist "—she hasn't woken up since the seizure. She's only minimally responsive right now."

Lori's mind raced through all the reasons for Janiah being unresponsive and went straight to the worst-case scenario. "Do you think she has a bleed?"

"It could be that she's just postictal. She could wake up and be fine. We'll just have to wait and see."

But Lori didn't want to wait, she wanted to see Janiah for herself. "I have to go. She shouldn't be alone, not now. I'm sorry, I know it's your birthday, but I need to be with her. She needs to know someone loves her."

"It's okay, I've already told Dr. Davis you would be coming. I'd go too, but…" Zach looked to where his guests were gathered and Lori saw that Kelley was headed toward them.

"What's going on?" Kelley asked, reaching out for her grandson. When her grandson shied away from her, turning into his daddy's shoulder, the woman looked like someone had slapped her.

"Kelley, why don't you take Andres out to play with his cousins, if that's okay with you Zach?" Lori asked. While she thought the woman was overbearing and had definitely been wrong in her treatment of her son-in-law, Kelley loved her grandson. "Helene was asking to take him out there with them."

Turning to Zach she said, "I don't know how long I'll be gone. Can you tell everyone goodbye for me?"

"You're going somewhere? You're going to leave the party?" Kelley called as Lori headed up the stairs.

Lori ignored her. Zach could explain for her. Right now, she needed to get to the hospital because there was a baby, one she had begun to think of as her own, surrounded by doctors and nurses, but still all alone. Someone had to look out for her, and Lori had chosen from the moment that little newborn had clutched her finger to be the one to do it.

Zach shut the door behind Lori. He didn't like the idea of her going to the hospital alone. She needed someone with her if the news they got back from the CT turned out to be bad. She had been so determined to be there for Janiah, but who would be there for Lori? Somehow, he knew in his heart that he should be the one there with Lori. Not as a doctor, but as Lori's friend? Lover? What?

He'd sworn to himself that he would not get involved with another woman, not romantically. But wasn't it about time he accepted the changes Lori had brought into his life? Not Andres, though she'd certainly given him the courage and support for him to get his son, but the other changes in his life. He was happy. For the first time since he'd lost his wife, he was healing. He felt like he might actually be able to love again.

And it scared him. Scared him so bad that this morning when he'd gotten up, he'd acted like nothing had happened between the two of them last night. While all the time he'd been thrilled to see Lori lying next to him. For several minutes, he'd just lain there and let the fact that she was there beside him sink in. He'd expected it to feel awkward, but instead it had felt right. It had felt like a part of him had healed. The pain of losing Katherine would never go away, he knew that. But he remembered what Jack had told him too. There was room in his heart to love again, if he was willing to allow it.

But still there was that fear of going through the pain

of loss again. He wasn't sure he'd be strong enough to survive another loss. He'd failed Andres before, he couldn't risk doing that again.

The doorbell rang and he looked at his watch. Carol, the new nanny, was right on time. Before he even opened the door, a plan started forming in his mind.

After he explained about the party, he took Carol to the most important person she needed to meet. While Andres was shy at first, it didn't take the woman but a few moments to get him to warm up to her. He'd known the moment he'd met her that she would be perfect for dealing with both Andres and Kelley with her Mary Poppins looks and her sweet but firm manner.

"Is there any chance you're free to start this afternoon? I have someone at the hospital I need to go see, but I don't want to leave Andres." He'd only just offered the woman the job but he had to ask. The longer Lori was at the hospital by herself, the worse he felt. He knew her mother was working because she'd been unable to attend the party. If Carol couldn't do it, his other choice would be Kelley and Butch, something that his mother-in-law would be sure to use against him.

"I'm free and happy to work, though I'd like to be walked through the rest of the house if you've got the time. I like to know the layout before I take a job. Little ones can escape into all kinds of places. It's better to know where dangers might lie," Carol said.

"No problem. I appreciate the help. I just need to introduce you to Andres's grandparents first," Zach said as he took her upstairs. When they made it back downstairs, he took her through the kitchen to the family room where most of the guests, including his in-laws, had gathered. Then he took her up to the second most important person she needed to meet.

The introductions were awkward as the two women seemed to be sizing each other up. Butch, the smart one, managed to escape into another room. Zach was left unarmed as Kelley began shooting questions at Carol faster than she could answer them.

"The agency runs a background check and I've checked Carol's references. They've all been glowing. She's more than qualified to care for Andres." Zach turned from Kelley to Carol. "I really appreciate you stepping in and helping me. I'll be back as soon as possible."

"What? You're leaving too?" Kelley asked. "I don't understand. You're supposed to be off. You never did explain why Lori had to go see this Baby Jane. And now you're going too? You have guests."

"Who are all welcome to stay or leave. I've spoken with my brother who will be happy to stay until the guests leave and Carol will be here with Andres, so if you and Butch need to head home I understand."

"I'm not leaving my grandson with a stranger. This is exactly what I've been telling you. You are not prepared to care for a child. I'm going to talk to Butch right now and I can promise you that we will be here when you get back."

He was tired of all this arguing and he was tired of trying to placate his in-laws. He'd not heard a word from Lori or Dr. Davis. He needed to leave. He needed to see the baby and Lori. "Fine. Stay. We'll talk when I get back. Until then, Carol will be staying as Andres's nanny. I expect you to be polite."

Before Kelley could say another word, he walked out the door, leaving his mother-in-law speechless for the first time since he'd met her.

CHAPTER FOURTEEN

LORI SAT AND watched a tech apply electrodes to Janiah's little scalp. She wanted to hold the newborn and reassure her that she wasn't alone, that there was someone there to watch over her, but all Lori could do was watch and wait. And it left her feeling useless.

She'd arrived at the hospital to find that Janiah had had another seizure, this one lasting longer than the other one. She'd spoken to the neurologist that had been consulted, but all she had been able to do was suggest a medication change. When the neurologist had asked what her relationship to the baby was, Lori had been at a loss for words. Not knowing what to say, Lori had been honest and told the woman about the mother's abandonment and her request for fostering the baby. Because Lori had delivered the baby, she knew it did give her access to the baby's medical care, but it did not give her any right as far as making decisions. So, after speaking with the nurse, she called Jessica, the case manager, and notified her of Janiah's health care concerns. After that all she could do was sit and watch as nurses, doctors and techs cared for the child she'd come to think of as her own.

So she just sat and worried about Janiah, about the baby's future and about their future together. And when she wasn't worrying about the baby, she worried about her and Zach. What would happen between the two of them now? Would they remain friends? Lovers?

No, not lovers. She knew that wouldn't work. Not for her. So, friends. Good friends. But would that be enough after what they'd shared, not only last night, but the last three weeks. She'd never been so close to anyone. Never felt so comfortable around someone. Not like the way she felt around Zach.

Someone moved next to her and she looked up and there he was standing beside her. Zach. As if her heart had willed him to come to her. At the sight of those brown eyes of his, her heart sang with a joy it had no right to. Then she realized what his being there could mean. Did the pediatrician and neurosurgeon not want to tell her how serious Janiah's condition was? "They called you? Is it bad news?"

"No, I came for you and Baby Janiah," Zach said, pulling up a chair beside her.

"But what about the party? Kelley? You know she'll use this against you," she said. "Butch might understand that Andres belongs with you, but I don't think Kelley is ready to let go. She still seems to think that you are going to move back to Memphis and live with them as just one big happy family."

"She can't really believe that. And I asked the nanny I hired, Carol, to stay with Andres for a few hours. It will give Kelley a chance to see that single parents with demanding jobs like ours can make sure our children are cared for even if we can't always be there. Besides, it doesn't matter what she thinks anymore. I've tried to be respectful to Kelley and Butch for Katherine and also Andres's sakes, but I've had enough. Butch understands that. Hopefully he can make his wife understand that too before I return tonight."

An alarm went off on one of the monitors and Lori jumped up. Zach's arm came up and around her, and as she lost her balance, he pulled her to his side. "Be careful. It's okay. Her heart rate is just a little high right now. Probably from all the attention she's been getting. I take it they got the MRI?"

"Yes, but I haven't heard anything as far as the results. I thought maybe Dr. Davis had called you and that was why you were here." Lori stepped away from Zach, the warmth of him making her want to curl into his arms, something that she couldn't let herself do. She had to be strong. She wouldn't always have him there to lean on.

"No, I haven't heard anything from them since the first call. I'm sure they'll tell you what they've found as soon as possible."

"Will they?" Lori asked. "I've been here watching everyone working so hard to help her, and all I can do is sit here. And the only reason I've been given that privilege is because I was the midwife that delivered her."

Zach looked at her with surprise. "You've been by this baby's side since that day, making sure she has someone to look out for her when her own mother left her within an hour of her birth. Everyone in this nursery knows that. Yes, they have to be careful because of the privacy laws and yes, they've been able to keep you informed because you are involved as a midwife with her delivery. But does that make a difference? We all know it's more than the job with you and Janiah. And from what the staff says about the way she responds to you, she knows it too."

Lori walked over to where Janiah lay, her head now bandaged with gauze over all the electrodes attached to her tiny head. There was an IV in each arm, one which was attached to a bag of lactated ringers to keep her hydrated, the other Lori had seen them using for the IV morphine and other medications. They'd also placed a tube in the baby's nose that went to her stomach so they could feed her. How did all those mothers who knew nothing about the medical world stand seeing their babies this way? Lori knew the necessity of every one of these tubes, but they still had the ability to scare her. The sight of an innocent baby being surrounded by all of those tubes and beeping monitors was just too much. All she wanted at that moment was to hold Janiah tight and reassure her that she wasn't alone and she was going to be okay.

Zach's hand came to rest on her shoulder, and that was when she realized that he was there for her for the same reason she was there for Janiah. He didn't want her to feel that she was all alone either.

But she would be. Soon, if things went as she hoped with her application for fostering Janiah, she'd be a single mother. Zach would be there as a friend, she hoped, but he would be busy with the life he'd planned. The one he wanted with just him and his son. She wouldn't have him to lean on then. Oh, she'd still have her friends and her mother, but she would still be alone at night when she put Janiah to bed.

After talking to Zach at the wedding she'd realized that she had only been shopping for a baby's daddy, instead of looking for someone to love, because she'd thought having a child in her life was all she had ever really wanted. It wasn't like a child would leave her, abandon her. A man though? How could she ever hope to trust one with her heart when she knew they could just up and leave her at any time? How could she live with that fear?

But now? After living with Zach and playing at being his fiancée, she knew she wanted more. She wanted that forever love, the kind of love that he had been up-front about not ever wanting again. And for the first time, she understood how he felt. Because she didn't want just any love, she wanted Zach's love. She wanted to be able to trust him with her love. She wanted him to love her the same way that she loved him.

And if he wasn't ever able to give her that love? Was it possible that she would become like him? Was it possible that she'd never be able to let go of her love for him and find someone else to love her? Would she always wander around in her crowd of friends, but still be all alone?

The monitors above Janiah's head went off again, the sounds echoing through the nursery as she watched Janiah's body stiffen, and her eyelids begin to blink rapidly. She was having another seizure. Lori moved away as Zach stepped over to the isolette where Janiah continued to seize.

Four hours later, Lori and Zach dragged themselves back to Zach's house. The news from the MRI hadn't been good. While she'd been hoping that it was just the drug withdrawal that was causing Janiah's seizures, it had been determined that it was something worse. The neurologist and doctor had both come to the conclusion after reviewing the results of the MRI that Janiah was suffering from neonatal encephalopathy due to what looked like a small brain injury making her neurologically unstable. While the brain injury appeared so small that it hadn't been seen on the CT, they suspected that it had been present at birth and probably stemmed from a hypoxic injury during labor.

And while Lori didn't want to believe it, she couldn't deny the fact that the baby could have been in fetal distress for hours while her mother had been in labor. There was no fetal tracing to review. The mother had been placed on the monitor just moments before giving birth. How long Janiah could have been in distress causing her to become hypoxic, they had no way of knowing. All they could do now was hope that the damage was mild, something that the neurologist had assured her was possible. It had all been too much to take in at one time. For now, the seizures had stopped and Janiah was stable.

Her plan had been to shower and then take a short nap before returning to the hospital, but when Zach opened the door, she knew that wasn't going to happen anytime soon. Standing at the door was Kelley who must have been watching out the window waiting for their return. Zach had told her that he'd received several texts and a call from his mother-in-law while they were at the hospital, but he'd ignored them once he'd made sure that Andres was okay.

But now there was nothing to do but face the woman, something Lori had neither the time nor the patience for. She started to walk past Kelley until she saw that there was another woman standing behind her. Was this the nanny Zach had hired? If it was, it would be a miracle if she didn't quit after being left all afternoon with Kelley.

"Would you please tell this woman that she can leave? The woman has refused to leave us alone with our grandson." Kelley's face was turning red, telling them all just how angry she was at not getting her way with the nanny.

"Lori this is Carol, Andres's new nanny. Carol, this is Lori," Zach said, introducing the woman as she stepped around Kelley.

"It's nice to meet you," she said before turning to Zach. "I'm so sorry if I misunderstood your instructions."

"There was no misunderstanding. I appreciate you helping me out today. Let me walk you out to your car," Zach said, before looking at Lori. "I'll be right back."

Lori watched the two of them walk out the door, then glanced back at the stairs wishing for a way to escape. She realized Butch had come into the room at some point. The man looked as if he'd had a day almost as bad as hers. Leaving him now to deal with his wife alone didn't seem like the right thing to do.

"Why don't we all go have a glass of wine?" Lori asked. "Then we can talk about everything like rational adults."

Lori knew she'd used the wrong words the moment they'd come out. She was tired and irritable and not in the right frame of mind to deal with the woman.

"Are you saying I'm not rational? Is that why Zach felt the need to ask the nanny to stay with Andres? Because what, I've suddenly become what? Unstable?"

Lori felt a whole new respect for the poor nanny who'd had to deal with this while they'd been at the hospital. "I didn't mean to imply that you were not being rational. I was referring to all of us. We need to sit down and talk about how things are changing."

"I don't see why things need to change at all. There's no reason for my grandson to have a nanny, an outsider, when Butch and I can be with him all the time. Zach can move back to Memphis and things can be like they use to be. We'll be there to make sure that nothing happens to Andres when Zach's not there."

Kelley was becoming frantic now and Lori knew she needed to deescalate the situation, but her patience had been strained all day waiting for doctors and medical results. Besides, hadn't Zach been patient for months? What had that gotten him? Nothing but more of the same. Excuses as to why his son needed to stay with his grandparents. It was more than Lori could take. "Keeping Andres to yourself isn't what he needs. You won't always be able to keep him safe, no matter how hard you try. He needs to experience the world, not be wrapped up in cotton and hidden away."

"That's not..." Kelley began, before Lori interrupted her.

"Yes, it is. That's exactly what you are doing. You've even tried to hide him away from his father. His father who loves him so much that he is willing to do anything to have his son with him."

"I don't care if you are going to marry Zach, you can't talk to me that way. You don't understand."

Lori tried to make herself take a breath and calm down. She understood that Kelley was just panicking because she knew that she had already lost where Andres was concerned. But there was a baby with no one except for her in the NICU right now. While here they were arguing over a little boy who was so lucky to have so many people love him that they were ready to fight for him. Life wasn't fair. Lori had learned that early in life. But this…this was unnecessary and it needed to end now.

"No, it's you that doesn't understand. Zach has done everything you've asked of him for months. Yet it takes me, someone who's only known him for a short time to see how he's being manipulated by you. You've used his lack of judgment when his mind was crowded with grief against him for months. I understand that you were grieving too. And Zach saw that. He gave in to you so many times because he knew you were grieving like him. But then, when you could see that he was ready to raise his son, you wouldn't give him back."

"We…" Kelley started but stopped when Butch put his hand on her shoulder.

"Do you even realize how far Zach was willing to go when you threatened to take him to court? He was willing to do anything, even marry someone he barely knew. This engagement of ours, it's all been to help him get his son back. You were so set on the fact that he couldn't raise Andres alone that he was willing to fake an engagement to me to make you think that he had found someone to love and help him raise his son. But this wasn't even about you thinking he wasn't capable. It was just another excuse you were using to hold on to Andres. To use the boy to fill the hole in your heart that losing your daughter left, wasn't it?"

Kelley had stopped interrupting her and it wasn't until she noticed that Butch was looking past her that she realized Zach had come up behind her.

"You lied to us?" Butch asked. "I trusted you, thought that you were moving ahead with your life, as Katherine would have wanted you to, but you were lying to us the whole time."

It was the disappointment on the man's face that finally cut through the anger that had spurred Lori's rant to Kelley. Now, realizing what she had said, what she had done, Lori knew she'd gone too far. She'd just ruined everything for Zach.

She heard Zach answer as he tried to explain things, but she couldn't stay and listen to Kelley and Butch berating him. If she'd just ignored Kelley and gone upstairs to begin with, this wouldn't have happened. She headed up the stairs not looking back. When she got to the top of the stairs she went to Andres's room, checking to see if the voices that she could still hear had awakened him.

But the child lay still sleeping in his crib. Would he ever know how hard each of those adults had fought for him? Would he realize how lucky he was to have a father that would do anything to be in his life every day? Covering him with a small blanket, she left him to his dreams. Maybe someday, when he was much older, Zach would tell him about Lori and how she'd tried to help him.

She left the baby sleeping soundly and headed to Zach's room. Opening the door, the first thing she saw was the bed they'd shared the night before. Was it only just a few hours ago that Zach had held her in his arms? It seemed as if it was a lifetime ago that they'd lain there together, their bodies joined together so perfectly. She'd wanted one more night in Zach's bed, just one more. She'd promised herself that one more night would be enough. She'd lied. But then hadn't she been lying for weeks now? She truly had to be the worst fake fiancée that there had ever been. Even the ones in her romance books had done a better job than she had.

She'd fallen for a man who had made it more than clear that he didn't want to ever love another woman. She'd slept with the man, knowing it was just going to make things more complicated between them. And then she'd messed up and lost her temper, telling the last people she needed to tell that it had all been a ruse.

All she could do now was leave before she messed things up anymore. Glancing around the room, she grabbed the pillowcases which held the small amount of stuff she owned and went into the bathroom to get the rest. She came out and allowed herself one more look around the room before she shut the door on all the hopes and dreams she'd allowed herself the night before.

She was glad to see that there was no one waiting for her when she started down the stairs. But when she got to the bottom step, she could hear voices coming from the kitchen. Zach's voice, but not the one he usually used around his in-laws, the gentle voice that was patient with the older couple out of love and respect. No, this time his voice was hard as steel. He was fighting back, at last. A part of Lori relaxed. It told her that there was no way his in-laws would be taking Andres from him tonight.

She slipped out the door without looking back, assured from what she'd heard that even though she'd made a mess of things, Zach would get the one thing he wanted in life. His son.

CHAPTER FIFTEEN

IT HAD TAKEN over an hour for Kelley to calm down enough for Butch to get her in the car to make their trip back to Memphis. Zach had offered for the two of them to stay another night, but Butch had insisted it would be easier now that the decision had been made to keep some distance from Andres for a while. Zach had quickly agreed. As soon as their taillights had disappeared, he'd rushed up to Andres's room to make sure it wasn't a dream. Finding his son asleep in his room, the next thing he'd done was to look for Lori so he could tell her the good news. Andres was totally his now.

He'd expected to find her asleep in his bed. When she wasn't there, he'd called the nursery to make sure she'd made it there safely. Once he'd spoken to one of the NICU nurses who confirmed that she was there, he'd relaxed. Only to find moments later that he was actually angry at her. Not for telling Kelley and Butch about the fact that they had been faking a relationship— his mother-in-law was good at getting people to lose their temper and say things they wished they hadn't said. No, that wasn't why he was angry. He was angry that she'd taken all her things with her, leaving him with no doubts of her not returning, without even talking to him. It looked like she had decided that since there was no more reason to pretend to be his fiancée, she could just leave and forget about him. What about last night? What about the weeks they'd shared together? Was he supposed to pretend now that the time they'd spent together had never happened? Was that what she wanted?

Wasn't that what you told her you wanted?

Yes. Yes, that was what he'd told her he wanted. No romantic entanglements. No talk of love or a happily-ever-after. Just friendship. But friendship would never have included the two of them sharing a bed. Nor would it make him feel this ache in his chest.

He saw the romance book lying on his nightstand where he'd been reading it a few nights earlier. It was the first one he'd picked up. He'd made it to the last two chapters of the book. So far, the couple had managed to fool everyone with their fake engagement, but they had begun to have feelings for each other, making things more complicated between the two of them.

Sitting down, he turned to the last page he'd read. Maybe with the help of these two characters, he'd be able to figure out things between the two of them.

Zach saw her the moment he walked into the nursery. He'd known she'd be there. According to the NICU nurses, she'd been there every night for the last three days, coming and going between office hours and then spending hours at a time by Janiah's bedside each night. He'd gotten another doctor to cover for him so that he could get Andres settled.

And he'd thought about Lori.

"How is she this evening?" he asked, though he'd kept up with the baby's condition through the nurses.

Lori looked up at him, her eyes underlined by dark shadows. She was wearing herself out fast. She needed rest. She needed someone to care for her like she cared for Janiah. "She hasn't had a seizure since…since the night of the party, so the neurologist is hopeful. She's begun eating again. I just finished feeding her. The nurses say she eats better for me than for them so I try to help out."

"They told me. They also tell me that you're wearing yourself down. You need to take care of yourself so that when she gets discharged from the hospital, you'll be ready."

"I know," she said, looking back to where the baby lay sleeping. "How's Andres?"

"He's getting used to all the changes. We both are, I guess."

"I'm sorry for what happened with Kelley and Butch. I never meant for that to happen. I just…"

"It worked out for the best. I had a hard talk with them. I don't think that they intended for things to turn out the way they did when they first offered to help out with Andres. I think they really wanted to help me. They seem to realize now that it was time to let go. I think seeing me move on helped them, even if it wasn't all real."

"I'm glad for you and Andres. The two of you belong together," Lori said, her words ringing true.

"Do you have time for a walk? We could go up to the garden," he said. He held a hand out to her and waited. When she took his hand, he let the breath he'd been holding go. He led her to the one set of elevators that would take them to the rooftop garden. At this time of night, he knew they should find it deserted.

"I guess we should talk. I haven't said anything to anyone about ending the engagement. I wanted to talk to you first," Lori said as the elevator doors closed. "And I need to give you this back."

She took the diamond ring he'd bought her off her finger and handed it to him. Unsure what to do with it, he stuck it in his pocket.

He was more nervous than he had ever been. He didn't have the words to explain his feeling like the hero in the romance books he'd read. He just knew that in the last three days not having Lori in his life had been miserable. He'd realized then that it didn't matter how scared he was of loving someone again, of losing someone again. Not having Lori at all would be just as painful.

The doors opened to the garden and they stepped out. There were lights strung across the paths that wandered in and out of the raised flower beds that the hospital volunteers took care of.

He tried to think of something that a romantic hero would say, but nothing came. He decided it was best to admit the truth. "I miss you."

"It was best that I left when I did. After what happened that night... I guess I started to believe in our pretense myself." Lori stopped walking and he stopped beside her. "I've read too many romances. I should know by now that real life doesn't work that way."

Unable to stop himself, he took her hand. "That night was wonderful, but it wasn't enough. You're right, real life isn't like the books. But that night was real, just like all the other nights we've spent together were real. This…how I feel about you…it's real. That's what I want—a real relationship. Not one built on pretense. I want you with me because you want to be with me. I don't care if you're my real girlfriend, or my real fiancée. Because this love I feel for you isn't a pretend love, it's real."

"I don't understand. I thought you said you couldn't ever love someone again." Lori pulled away from him, stepped back. "How do you know that it's real? How do I know you haven't gotten carried away with the pretense like I did?"

"Do you really believe that's what happened? If so, wouldn't it all have ended when you told Kelley the truth? When you ended the pretense?" He stepped up to her. He had to let her know how much he loved her. But how? "I once believed that I would never be able to love another person in my lifetime. Not only because of my fear of having to feel that loss, but because I didn't think I had any more love to give. But I was wrong. You opened up a part of my heart that I didn't know existed. Now all I need is for you to walk in and take it."

He took her face in his hands. "Now tell me the truth. No pretense. No lies. Do you love me, Lori?"

His heart raced as he waited for her answer. What if she really had been caught up in the pretense?

Her hands came up and covered his. Her tired eyes were suddenly bright with tears and her lips seemed to tremble as she said, "Oh, yes, Zach. I really, really do love you."

EPILOGUE

THERE WERE NO pink roses in crystal vases. There was no string quartet. Instead, Lori and Zach had decided that a child-friendly ceremony and reception fit the two of them better as they wouldn't consider getting married without Andres and Janiah at their side. So, it had been decided that the wedding would be held outside. They'd found the perfect venue with a garden path that led to a large courtyard and plenty of room for the kids to run and play.

It had been just over a year since the night they'd attend Sky and Jared's wedding. Sky liked to take credit for the two of them finding each other, while Bree and Knox claimed that they had witnessed the moment they'd fallen in love. All four friends knew that Lori and Zach's first engagement hadn't been real, but they all seemed to want to ignore it. Lori choose to let them.

"It's almost time. Are you ready?" her mother asked.

Lori looked down at the vintage tea-length dress that she'd somehow managed to keep clean while chasing Janiah around the dressing room, trying to get the bow in the toddler's hair. They'd both been laughing and out of breath by the time Lori had caught her. Looking over at her daughter now, she could see the bow was tilted to one side, but she didn't care. The fact that her daughter was healthy and able to run and play was a miracle that she celebrated every day. There were still obstacles ahead of them, her growth rate was behind and there were developmental delays, but Lori knew that together she and Zach would face those as they came.

She held her hand out to Janiah. "Let's go see your daddy."

Then taking her mom's hand, she started down the stone pathway where her friends and family waited.

The first faces she saw when they turned the corner that took them into the courtyard were those of Sky and Jared. And in their arms, was Baby Jack, named after his grandfather who sat beside him. Lori had delivered the baby just a month ago. Handing that baby to her friend had been a dream come true for both of them.

Beside Sky, Bree and Knox sat with their daughter, Ally, who had excitedly informed Lori the night before that she was going to be a big sister in six months. Though Bree had already told her, Lori acted surprised for the little girl's sake.

Lori spotted Kelley and Butch in the next aisle, the two of them waving at their grandson who stood at the front. Lori couldn't say that things had all gone smoothly between Zach and his in-laws, but they were working on it. It didn't hurt that Butch and Kelley had been given unlimited time with Andres. It had become a habit for the two of them to visit every other weekend which Lori thought was just as good for Andres as it was for his grandparents.

They stopped and her mother kissed her cheek before taking Janiah and sitting beside Jack.

As soon as her mother and daughter were settled, Lori allowed herself to look to the front of the courtyard where Zach stood holding their son's hand. In a matching dark suit, the two-and-a-half-year-old was almost as handsome as his father.

Unable to help herself, she waved at her little boy, only realizing her mistake when Andres pulled away from Zach and ran down the aisle to meet her. Laughing, she gave her son a hug before taking his hand in hers. Then she looked up to see that Zach had followed his son down the aisle.

"Ready to do this?" he asked her, his smile wide and his brown eyes filled with love.

Lori looked from Zach to their son, then smiled back at him. "Hold on one moment."

Hurrying back to her mother, Lori took Janiah into her arms and then walked back to where Zach and Andres waited.

"Ready now?" Zach asked, taking his daughter from Lori.

"Yes, now we're all ready."

* * * * *

*If you missed the previous story in the
Nashville Midwives trilogy,
then check out*
The Rebel Doctor's Secret Child

*And if you enjoyed this story,
check out these other great reads from
Deanne Anders*

Unbuttoning the Bachelor Doc
A Surgeon's Christmas Baby
Flight Nurse's Florida Fairy Tale

All available now!

MILLS & BOON®

Coming next month

SECOND CHANCE IN SANTIAGO
Tina Beckett

Vivi tried on a fake smile.

'Hi! I didn't know you were at Valpo Memorial. At least not until I saw you in the operating room.'

That dark gaze stared her down for a minute or two. 'Didn't you?'

Cris's words took her aback and she frowned. 'I'm not sure what you mean by that.'

'Surely my name was on the list of hospital staff when you came here looking for a job.'

He made it sound like she'd been desperate or something.

'Actually, I didn't 'come here looking for a job.' I saw a posting at the hospital where I was *already working* as a scrub nurse and applied. I didn't scour the website looking for familiar names.' She threw in, 'Besides, I might not have even recognized your name if I'd seen it.'

That was a mistake, and he knew it because one side of his mouth curved. 'Oh really? I got a few letters that seemed to indicate otherwise.'

Yes, she had written several long pages of prose that reiterated what she'd said the last time she saw him…that she would love him forever. That she would never ever forget him.

Her face heated. 'I was a child back then.' And she didn't talk about the fact that he hadn't written her back because she didn't want him to know how soul-crushing it had been that he hadn't cared enough to respond.

The way she'd never responded to Estevan's texts? No. That was not the same. She was convinced that he'd never really loved her—or he wouldn't have been able to jump into another relationship so quickly. It seemed she was forever doomed to love men more than they loved her. But not anymore.

'It seems we both were.' His face turned serious. 'And now we're both adults, so I assume we can both work at the same hospital—the same *quirófano*—without it causing a problem, correct?'

Continue reading

SECOND CHANCE IN SANTIAGO
Tina Beckett

Available next month
millsandboon.co.uk

Copyright © 2025 Tina Beckett

COMING SOON!

We really hope you enjoyed reading this book.
If you're looking for more romance
be sure to head to the shops when
new books are available on

Thursday 19th June

To see which titles are coming soon, please visit
millsandboon.co.uk/nextmonth

MILLS & BOON

FOUR BRAND NEW BOOKS FROM
MILLS & BOON MODERN

The same great stories you love, a stylish new look!

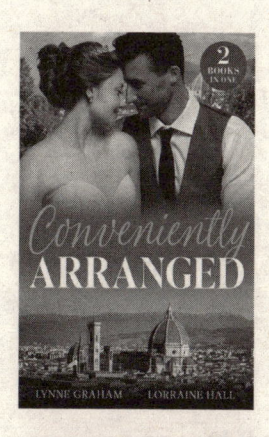

Conveniently ARRANGED
LYNNE GRAHAM · LORRAINE HALL

WANTED: HIS HEIR
MAYA BLAKE · DANI COLLINS

DEFIANT Brides
Tara Pammi · Michelle Smart

THE BILLIONAIRE'S LEGACY
ABBY GREEN · NATALIE ANDERSON

OUT NOW

Eight Modern stories published every month, find them all at:

millsandboon.co.uk

afterglow BOOKS

Afterglow Books is a trend-led, trope-filled list of books with diverse, authentic and relatable characters, a wide array of voices and representations, plus real world trials and tribulations. Featuring all the tropes you could possibly want (think small-town settings, fake relationships, grumpy vs sunshine, enemies to lovers) and all with a generous dose of spice in every story.

♪ @millsandboonuk
◉ @millsandboonuk
afterglowbooks.co.uk

#AfterglowBooks

For all the latest book news, exclusive content and giveaways scan the QR code below to sign up to the Afterglow newsletter:

SCAN ME

afterglow BOOKS

- Sports romance
- Enemies to lovers
- Spicy
- Workplace romance
- Forbidden love
- Opposites attract

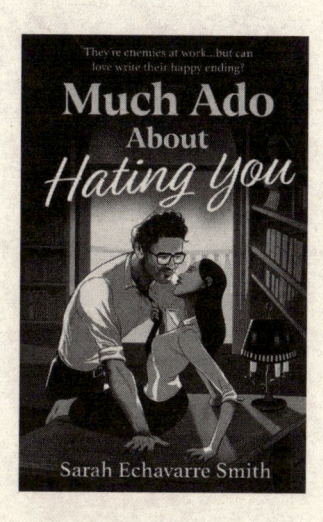

OUT NOW

Two stories published every month. Discover more at:
Afterglowbooks.co.uk

LET'S TALK
Romance

For exclusive extracts, competitions and special offers, find us online:

- **f** MillsandBoon
- **X** @MillsandBoon
- **◎** @MillsandBoonUK
- **♪** @MillsandBoonUK

Get in touch on 01413 063 232

For all the latest titles coming soon, visit
millsandboon.co.uk/nextmonth

OUT NOW!

Opposites Attract: Rancher's Attraction

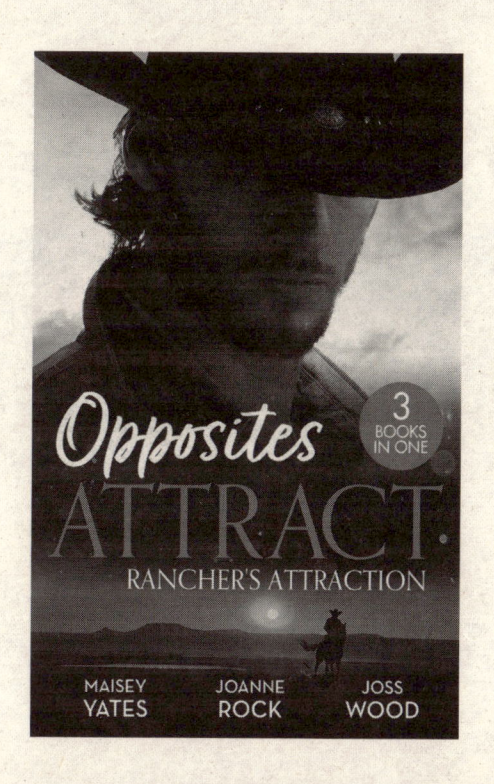

3 BOOKS IN ONE

MAISEY YATES • JOANNE ROCK • JOSS WOOD

Available at
millsandboon.co.uk

MILLS & BOON

OUT NOW!

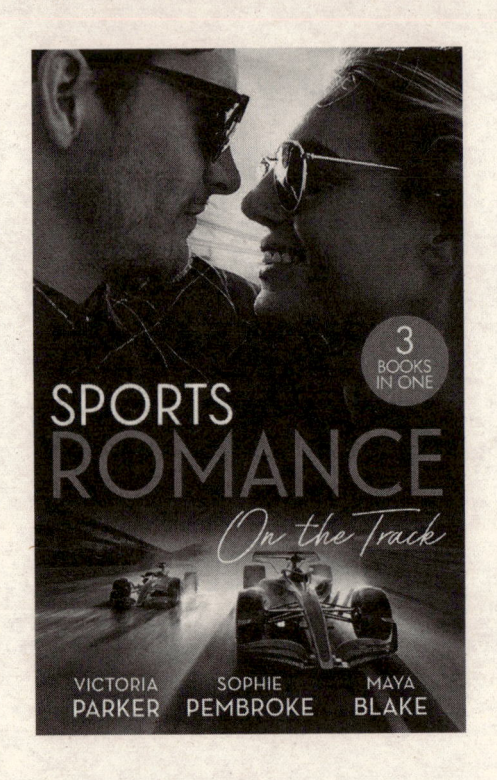

SPORTS ROMANCE
On the Track

3 BOOKS IN ONE

VICTORIA PARKER · SOPHIE PEMBROKE · MAYA BLAKE

Available at
millsandboon.co.uk

MILLS & BOON

OUT NOW!

ROMANCE ON DUTY

UNDERCOVER
Passion

3 BOOKS IN ONE

CINDI MYERS JO LEIGH SARAH M. ANDERSON

Available at
millsandboon.co.uk

MILLS & BOON

OUT NOW!

Princess BRIDES — A ROYAL BABY

3 BOOKS IN ONE

AMY RUTTAN · CATHERINE MANN · JENNIE LUCAS

Available at
millsandboon.co.uk

MILLS & BOON

MILLS & BOON
A ROMANCE FOR EVERY READER

- **FREE** delivery direct to your door
- **EXCLUSIVE** offers every month
- **SAVE** up to 30% on pre-paid subscriptions

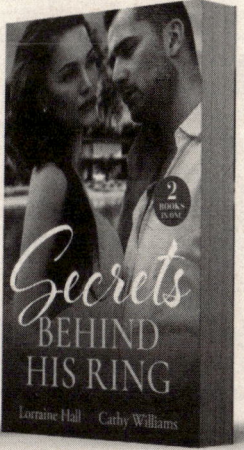

SUBSCRIBE AND SAVE

millsandboon.co.uk/Subscribe

MILLS & BOON

THE HEART OF ROMANCE

A ROMANCE FOR EVERY READER

MODERN — Prepare to be swept off your feet by sophisticated, sexy and seductive heroes, in some of the world's most glamourous and romantic locations, where power and passion collide.

HISTORICAL — Escape with historical heroes from time gone by. Whether your passion is for wicked Regency Rakes, muscled Vikings or rugged Highlanders, awaken the romance of the past.

MEDICAL — Set your pulse racing with dedicated, delectable doctors in the high-pressure world of medicine, where emotions run high and passion, comfort and love are the best medicine.

True Love — Celebrate true love with tender stories of heartfelt romance, from the rush of falling in love to the joy a new baby can bring, and a focus on the emotional heart of a relationship.

HEROES — The excitement of a gripping thriller, with intense romance at its heart. Resourceful, true-to-life women and strong, fearless men face danger and desire - a killer combination!

afterglow BOOKS — From showing up to glowing up, these characters are on the path to leading their best lives and finding romance along the way – with plenty of sizzling spice!

To see which titles are coming soon, please visit

millsandboon.co.uk/nextmonth